PRAISE FOR JAMES SWAIN

"No one in the world does this stuff better than Jim Swain. No one knows it better or writes it better. Satisfaction guaranteed."

—Lee Child

"James Swain is one of my favorites. His books never fail to entertain, teach and surprise. *Take Down* is his best yet, with his knowledge and experience dripping off of every page, and a character like Billy Cunningham to lead the way. Great stuff."

—Michael Connelly

"James Swain is the best at writing fast-paced thrillers about Las Vegas thugs and conmen."

—R. L. Stine

"Nobody knows the dazzling reality of cons and capers in Las Vegas better than James Swain, from the luminous illusions of casinos to the dark side of buried bodies in the desert."

—John Langley, executive producer and creator of *COPS*

"For all the blinking bright lights, this is a dark, decadent world, and Swain is a master at representing its allure, its thrills and its dead-end danger."

—Phil Jason, *Florida Weekly*

SUPER CON

ALSO BY JAMES SWAIN

Billy Cunningham Series

Take Down

Bad Action

Jack Carpenter Series

Midnight Rambler

The Night Stalker

The Night Monster

The Program

Tony Valentine Series

Grift Sense

Funny Money

Sucker Bet

Loaded Dice

Mr. Lucky

Deadman's Poker

Deadman's Bluff

Wild Card

Jackpot

Peter Warlock Series

Dark Magic

Shadow People

SUPER CON

JAMES SWAIN

THOMAS & MERCER

Published by Thomas & Mercer, Seattle

www.apub.com

ISBN-13: 9781542046404
ISBN-10: 1542046408

Cover design by Mike Heath | Magnus Creative

Printed in the United States of America

To Liz

A FINAL REQUEST

Las Vegas was where people came to make bad decisions, the town carefully constructed to propel visitors toward disaster. Every year, forty million tourists made a variety of bad decisions, including sleeping with people they barely knew, getting drunk enough to pass out in public, and gambling away their hard-earned dough on games they had virtually no chance of winning. That was the town's origins, and it wasn't changing anytime soon.

Even the town's wise guys made bad decisions. Billy Cunningham was such a person, and his bad decision was to return to Vegas knowing a Chinese gangster named Broken Tooth wanted him dead. Broken Tooth had already sent a hit man to kill him and might try it again.

Billy had decided to risk it. People who cheated for a living risked getting hurt. It came with the territory. Cheat in a poker game, and you risked getting your thumbs broken. Cheat a casino, and you risked being hauled into a back room and beaten up. And if you double-crossed your partner when fixing the Super Bowl, you ran the risk of having a contract put out on your life.

Caesars was jumping. The entrance resembled a parking lot, and Billy watched the cab's meter run while waiting to be dropped off. Soon he was in the main lobby. While guests waited on line to register, there was a bust going down, courtesy of the gaming board. The busted cheat wore silver bracelets and stared dejectedly at the floor. The gaming agents were so focused on their suspect that they didn't see Billy come in.

He circled around them. The busted cheat's wardrobe screamed Russian. Run-down Nikes, a threadbare sports jacket, and a sheared haircut more befitting a war refugee. The casinos knew about the Russian gangs and had trained their surveillance teams to be on the lookout. Their scam was called whacking. A Russian cheat would stand next to a particular make of slot machine and record the machine's play on a cell phone. The machine had a flawed random number generator chip that spit out predictable sequences every few hours. The Russian left and went to a motel, where the information was sent to a foreign server that calculated when the machine would pay a jackpot. Upon returning, the Russian would play the same machine and eventually win.

A great scam, unless you happened to get caught. Nevada had a law that forbade using an electronic device to beat its games, including cell phones. Cheats who got busted using devices went down hard.

"Coming through," a voice said.

A uniformed bellman pushing a luggage cart bore down on him. His name tag said KENNETH/SAN DIEGO. As Billy moved to let him pass, the bellman stopped and drew a pocket-size Beretta from his pants. He jammed the barrel into Billy's rib cage.

"Start walking toward the elevators," the bellman said.

Billy's eyes darted around the lobby. He counted five gaming agents, only they were too preoccupied with their bust to notice that something bad was going down.

"Let me guess. Your name isn't Kenneth, and you're not from San Diego," he said.

"Hong Kong. Keep walking. I'll shoot you right here if I have to," the bellman said.

"With all this heat?"

"I'll be gone before they know it."

The elevators were at the far end of the lobby. He began walking, praying that an opportunity would present itself to alert the gaming agents. The bellman hung close to his side.

"You don't look Chinese," he said.

"Plastic surgery. It took three operations."

"Your English is good, too. No accent."

"Rosetta Stone."

"I'll double your fee if you let me go."

The gun's barrel was suddenly in his ass. It made him jump a little. They came to the bank of elevators, and the bellman summoned a car. Billy stole a glance at the mirrors that lined the wall. None of the gaming agents had followed them. Was this the end? It sure felt like it.

"How did you know I'd be here?" he asked.

"Broken Tooth said you'd come back to Caesars to talk to the football players, iron out the details. Broken Tooth is smart that way," the bellman said.

"How long you been waiting?"

"Two days."

"And the hotel didn't notice?"

The bellman laughed under his breath. "I took a job. They're shorthanded, so I agreed to work double shifts. It was only a matter of time before you came in, and I spotted you."

"You got lucky, admit it."

"Luck had nothing to do with it."

An elevator car landed and its doors parted. The car was empty and they boarded. He spun around and watched the bellman slip the gun into his pocket, then draw a gilded knife with a pearl handle from a sheath hidden by his vest. The tip of the knife was dripping a substance the color of gold, and he guessed it was some kind of exotic poison. Elevators had surveillance cameras, only no one in the casino ever watched them. The doors began to close.

"Any final requests?" the bellman asked.

"Just don't make me suffer," he said.

ONE

Sunday, two weeks before the Super Bowl

Fremont Street was the armpit of Las Vegas, with more derelicts and hookers than you could shake a policeman's nightstick at. It was also home to a dozen no-frills casinos with two-buck beers and penny slot machines.

Tonight's target was the Golden Gate, the oldest joint in town. Billy's crew was working the scam along with a crew called the Gypsies. Six members of Billy's crew and six members of the Gypsy clan made a dozen cheats ripping off one poor casino. The Golden Gate didn't have a prayer.

Billy had never worked a scam with another crew, but this was a special occasion. In two short weeks during Super Bowl weekend, the combined crews would pull a heist with a potential payday in the millions of dollars. It was called a super con and worth the extra effort.

Super cons were different from regular cons. A regular con could be pulled many times, a super con only once. Once a casino determined how it had been ripped off by a super con, the other joints in town were notified in order to stop it from happening again.

Before the super con went down, the two crews needed to get acquainted. As a test run, Billy had decided they should pull a scam called playing the lights on the Golden Gate, which required plenty of cooperation. If the crews could pull this off, the super con would be easy.

Billy was the captain of his crew. Because the casinos knew him, he wore disguises during jobs. Tonight's getup consisted of a baseball cap, nonprescription glasses called zeros, and a rubber tire beneath his shirt. As another precaution, he entered a casino twenty minutes after his crew. To kill time now, he decided to try out the zip line on Fremont Street. It looked like a pure adrenaline rush, and right up his alley.

"Sure you don't want to join me?" he asked.

Leon, his African American limo driver, shook his head. Billy had recently started giving Leon a cut from each job to ensure Leon's silence if they got busted. Leon was living large and loving it.

"No thanks, boss. I'm afraid of heights."

Billy's cell phone rang. He was hoping the caller was an old flame named Maggie Flynn. He liked to think Mags still cared about him, but maybe he was kidding himself. When it came to love, he was a sucker, just like everyone else. He answered with a cheery "Hello."

The caller was male and spoke with an Asian accent. "Cunningham? My name Wan Kuok-koi. People call me Broken Tooth. You know who I am?"

Some names rang bells. Others set off fire alarms. Broken Tooth was a Chinese gangster who ran a gang of Triads. Prostitution, loan-sharking, and contract killing paid the bills, but the big profits came from gambling. Billy wondered what had brought him to this side of the pond. "Sure do. I'm busy right now. Let's talk some other time."

"We talk now," Broken Tooth insisted. "I got a job for you, make us both rich."

"What kind of job?"

"No discuss over phone. We meet up, and I explain the deal."

"Sounds like a plan. I'll call you back in the morning."

"No good. We meet tonight."

There was desperation in Broken Tooth's voice, and Billy guessed the guy was broke. Normally, he had a soft spot for hustlers down on their luck, only this joker was out of line. "Listen, pal. I'm working right now. We'll get together tomorrow, and I'll buy you lunch."

Broken Tooth cursed him. Billy had heard enough and said, "Lose my number," and hung up. To the tattooed attendant running the zip line he said, "Let's get this show on the road."

"Which did you pay for, the zip or the zoom?" the attendant asked.

"The zoom. I heard that was the way to go."

"Only if you want to be a superhero. Put on this uniform."

He climbed into the flight uniform and zipped up the front. "This feels tight."

"It's supposed to feel tight," the attendant said. "If it were loose, you'd fall out and plunge to your death. Lie down on the table so I can strap you in."

He lay on his stomach on the table in the room's center. The attendant attached hooks on the back of the uniform to a thick metal cable that ran the length of Fremont Street, which let riders exceed forty miles per hour while dangling in the air like Peter Pan.

"Has anyone ever fallen?" he asked.

"Not recently," the attendant said.

"You sure about this, boss?" Leon asked.

"Damn straight," he said. "See you back at the limo."

The attendant flipped a switch. The wall in front of the table lowered, and a blast of cold air invaded the room. He felt like he was about to be shot out of a cannon, and he took a deep breath. The attendant gave him a gentle push, and he slid off the table and flew headfirst down Fremont while dangling from the cable. His heart was racing, and down below he spied the break-dancers and half-naked women hustling tourists for tips. It was as sleazy as a carnival sideshow, and he wouldn't have traded it for any city in the world.

At the ride's end was a landing platform. A female attendant unstrapped him, and he stepped out of his uniform, his skin tingling from the adrenaline rush. If he ever hooked up with Mags again, he'd make sure to bring her here.

Taking the elevator to the street, he encountered his first problem. The Shriners were in town for a convention, the sidewalks teeming with drunks wearing maroon fezzes. Instead of blending in, he was going to stand out like a sore thumb in his disguise.

He ducked into a shop called Hats R Us. When he emerged, he was wearing a fez with a tassel and looked like the rest of the gang. Except he needed a drink. Inside a dive called Mermaids, he purchased a strawberry daiquiri. Fremont Street had the market cornered on bad food, and the bartender tried to talk him into an order of deep-fried Twinkies, but he took a pass.

- - -

Drink in hand, he entered the Golden Gate. It was a low-ceilinged joint and very loud. He found Victor Boswell, the leader of the Gypsy clan, in the back playing a slot machine, a carved walking stick propped against his chair. He took the chair beside the older man.

"I won a hundred-dollar jackpot earlier," Victor said with a laugh.

"Dinner's on you," he said.

"That won't pay for appetizers. Whatever happened to the endless buffets the casinos used to serve? I used to take my family to them all the time. Saved me a fortune."

"Gone but not forgotten."

"I've been watching your crew. You've schooled them well. The big guy's got it down pat. What's his deal?"

"Travis dealt blackjack at Palace Station and was cheating on the side. He was about to get promoted to pit boss when I recruited him."

"You've got to be sharp to be a pit boss."

"Travis has eyes in the back of his head. He's also good under fire."

"I like him." Victor fished some coins out of his bucket and fed them into the machine. "The girls are also good. So's the fat guy. The two punks, I'm not so sure about."

Victor was talking about Cory and Morris, the screwup kings. Cory and Morris were reformed potheads, or so they'd led Billy to believe.

"What did they do?" Billy asked.

"Nothing. They know how to move."

"Then what's bothering you?"

"Their appearance."

Cory and Morris had to be two of the most innocent-looking cheats in town; it was one of the reasons Billy had recruited them into his crew. "What's wrong with their appearance?"

"They barely look legal," Victor explained. "Caesars got in trouble for letting underage kids play in their poker room, so the casinos are carding anyone who doesn't look old enough. I should know; it happened to my daughter Kat."

Cheats had to look unspectacular when doing business inside a casino. A cheat needed to blend in and avoid scrutiny. To be remembered often spelled disaster down the road.

"I'll give them a makeover," Billy said.

His cell phone vibrated. Travis had texted him.

We have a problem

"Something's up. Let me go check on the troops."

"Look at that, I hit another jackpot," Victor said.

TWO

Billy headed over to the blackjack pit to see what the trouble was. The Golden Gate's blackjack tables had maximum bets of a hundred dollars, which was puny for Vegas. Fremont Street attracted a blue-collar crowd, and it was all the traffic would bear.

Travis stood inside the pit, clutching a bottle of Bud. Travis's job was to watch the action and signal the crew if security swooped in. Billy edged up beside the big man.

"You rang?" he said under his breath.

"False alarm," Travis said. "I thought a security guy was watching us, but he split. What's with the fez? You look like an Arab."

"There's a Shriner's convention in town. Everyone getting along?"

"So far, so good. The Boswells are real pros."

Billy shifted his attention to the five blackjack tables closest to the entrance. At each table a member of his crew sat in the last seat, to the dealer's right, in the position called third base. A member of the Gypsies sat to the dealer's left, at a position called first base. The Boswells were betting a hundred dollars a hand, and they were winning big.

That was because Billy's crew was cheating. Each member had a small mirror concealed in their hand called a shiner. By holding the shiner against the table at an angle and slightly lifting that hand, his crew could secretly glimpse the cards as they came out of the dealing shoe. This let his crew know the value of the dealer's hand before the dealer did.

His crew signaled this information to the Boswell at their respective tables. The Boswell would play accordingly and rip off the joint. The advantage of having two cheats working a game was that the Boswells could play loose and draw no heat.

Most scams had flaws, and playing the lights was no exception. If a shiner caught the light the wrong way, a reflection would hit the ceiling. These reflections resembled dancing fireflies and were easily spotted by pit bosses.

It was Travis's job to watch the ceiling. If a dancing firefly appeared, Travis would drop his beer bottle and curse. This was the signal for everyone to clear out.

"You mind covering for me? I need to piss," Travis whispered.

"Go ahead."

Travis left. Moments later, a security goon wearing a polyester suit and a cheap tie appeared at Cory's table. Billy stiffened, believing Cory had exposed the shiner, and the goon had been sent to bust Cory. The goon circled the table, bypassing Cory, and went straight to the Boswell at first base, which happened to be Nico, Victor's favorite son, and demanded to see Nico's ID. Nico had on his best choirboy face and handed over his driver's license. Casinos didn't interrupt a player unless there was good reason, and Billy got ready to run.

Travis edged up beside him. "The older I get, the better that feels."

"Pull everyone off the game. Nico got made," he whispered.

"What did he do?"

"The hell I know. Do it right now."

He headed for the front doors. He planned to hit the sidewalks on Fremont and find the nearest bar, where he'd make a hasty trip to the men's room and lose his disguise. Then he'd meet up with Victor and decide how to deal with Nico's fuckup.

"Wait—the goon's backing off," Travis said.

He stopped and turned around. The goon had returned the ID and was patting Nico on the shoulder like it was a big misunderstanding. The storm had passed, but his radar wasn't coming down. Something was wrong with this picture, and he tried to determine what it was.

Finally, it hit him. The goon was working without backup. That never happened.

Every casino had procedures when dealing with problems. If a player needed to be checked out, two goons were sent. While one goon talked with the player, the second goon acted as backup. If the player tried to run, the second goon would knock him to the floor and sit on him.

There was no backup with Nico. Just the goon in the polyester suit, asking for ID. That told Billy that surveillance had used the opportunity to take high-definition photos of Nico's face with a pan-tilt-zoom camera. These photos would be run against a database of known cheats in the hopes of making a match. Nico was in surveillance's crosshairs.

But would they make a match? The Boswells were masters of evading the law, and he wanted to believe that there wasn't an incriminating photo of Nico on any computer. But as he'd learned long ago, you could never be too careful when it came to stealing.

"Give the signal anyway," he said.

"You sure?" Travis groaned.

"Damn straight I'm sure. You got a problem with that?"

"We haven't made any money. I'm a little short this month."

"Do it anyway."

As Billy headed out the door, a beer bottle shattered on the floor.

"Aw, shit," Travis cursed loudly.

THREE

The Beauty Bar Saloon on Fremont didn't know what it wanted to be. A claustrophobic space with crummy lighting, it had a bar in one corner and a nail salon in another, while against the far wall sat a makeshift stage that served as a showcase for local bands.

Despite its identity crisis, the Beauty Bar was one of Billy's favorite spots to retreat to after pulling a heist. The clientele was an eclectic mix, with lots of tattoos and piercings. If any undercover cops or gaming agents came in, they'd get made right away.

The Beauty Bar also had an outdoor seating area where name acts were often booked. It wasn't being used tonight, and Billy bribed the manager for the privilege of sitting beneath the stars with Victor. They sat at a picnic table, far away from the surveillance cameras on the side of the building. The young hustler drank a beer, the older man a bourbon and water.

"Why did you call off the play? Nico didn't get made," Victor said.

"It didn't smell right. The casino sent one security goon to check Nico out. Normally, they send two," he explained.

"Maybe they were shorthanded. The casino was packed."

"That could be. But my gut told me surveillance wanted to get a closer look at Nico so they could run his picture against a cheater database."

Victor's face turned to stone. "I talked to Nico. The goon came over because Nico looked like a guy who had given them trouble last night. When the goon realized it was a case of mistaken identity, he apologized and walked away. It was nothing."

"You're saying I shouldn't have called off the play."

"I wouldn't have."

Billy didn't like to be challenged and put his beer on the table. "Nico read the situation wrong. The goon had already made him before he came over."

"What are you talking about? Nico didn't screw up."

"I never said he screwed up. But the goon knew Nico wasn't clean. A tech up in surveillance sent him to talk to Nico so the tech could take a clean shot of Nico's face."

"You're sure about this?"

"I'm positive, Victor."

Victor stared into his drink. Victor had been thieving well before Billy was a gleam in his daddy's eye, and he deserved respect. Billy would give him that respect, but he still had to explain the situation, even if it meant bruising Victor's feelings.

"Can I tell you how I figured it out?" Billy asked.

The older man lifted his gaze. "Go ahead."

"The Golden Gate's a dump. Most people playing blackjack are sweating out their Social Security checks. Nico was betting a hundred a hand and deserved preferential treatment. When the goon told Nico it was a case of mistaken identity, he should have given Nico a free meal coupon or sent over a cocktail waitress to refresh his drink. The goon didn't do that because he'd been told Nico wasn't clean."

Victor thought about this. A knowing look spread across his lined face.

"I missed that. Are we screwed?"

"Hard to say. They didn't bust your son, which in my book is a happy ending."

"Should I pull Nico off the job, send him back home?"

"We need Nico. Let's put him in a disguise instead. We'll dye his hair, stick glasses on him, and paint a mole on his puss. We'll set him up with a fake ID that matches his new look. He'll fly under the radar, no problem."

"I like it," Victor said. "I've made it a point to move around a lot. We hit a casino on an Indian reservation, we don't go back for a few years. There are enough joints for us to do that. You're strictly working Vegas, aren't you?"

He nodded. Most hustlers spent a chunk of their lives staring at the double white line in the highway while driving between jobs. That had never sounded appealing to him, so he'd planted his stakes in the neon city and seldom strayed.

"You ever rip off the same joint twice?" Victor asked.

"There are joints in town I've ripped off a dozen times. They just don't know it."

"Most guys wouldn't have the balls."

"It's an acquired skill."

Victor raised his eyebrows, wanting to hear more.

"Back in Providence, I dealt a rigged blackjack game in an illegal casino. One Saturday night, two hoods came in with their girlfriends and sat at my table. The hoods were part of a local crime family and not guys to screw with. The game had six decks. All the high cards had their backs roughed with sandpaper, which I could feel by touching them. The dealing shoe had a special lip, which let me invisibly hold back the top card. Even though the cards were shuffled, I could control the hands by holding back high-value cards from the players when I wanted."

"And since the players can't touch the cards in a multideck game, the scam flew by them," Victor said.

"Correct. Lou Profaci, the owner, comes to my table and tugs on his ear, which means, 'Let them win.' Now, this makes no sense to me. But Lou's the boss, so I let the hoods win.

"I go on break. Lou catches up with me in the back room. I tell him the hoods are up eight grand, isn't he afraid of them leaving with the house's money? Lou pulls back the curtain to the window. It's snowing outside. Lou says, 'Those ugly mopes ain't going anywhere. Go back there and take their money.' I'm getting nervous, so I say, 'You think they won't notice?' And Lou says, 'Let their girlfriends win.'

"It was pure genius. The girls are betting ten bucks a hand, the hoods two hundred a hand. I start dealing so the girls win and the boys lose. An hour later, the hoods are down twenty grand while the girls are up three. The girls are having a great time, and no one's complaining."

"The hoods didn't catch on?"

"Naw. Dumb mutts even tipped me. It was a great lesson. Anything's possible if you play it right."

"Okay, you've convinced me. Nico gets a makeover and stays. I'll let you and your team do the honors."

They picked up their glasses and headed for the entrance into the bar. Billy got a text from Leon, telling him that he needed to come outside. Billy guessed that Leon had parked his limo illegally and was about to get towed. It wasn't the first time it had happened.

Victor stopped a few steps from the door and faced Billy. "I'm sorry I doubted you. You know this town better than I do. I hope it won't affect our doing business together."

"It hasn't so far," Billy said.

FOUR

Billy's crew was inside the Beauty Bar, the ladies getting pedicures and drinking martinis, the guys chugging beer and watching sports on the assorted TVs. Travis had departed, and Billy guessed the big man had Ubered it home. He hadn't appreciated Travis's comment about needing money. It was bush league, and it hinted at bigger problems.

"Leon needs us," he told his crew. "Let's go."

The sideshow that was Fremont Street was in full swing, and they sifted through the human carnival and made their way to the elevated parking garage where the limo was parked. Billy climbed to the first landing and waited until his crew had joined him.

"What do you think of the Boswells?" he asked.

"They're smooth. I like them," Pepper said.

"The girls rock," Misty added. "The one named Kat told me she's been thieving since she was six years old, if you can believe that."

"The guys are good, too. I can work with them," Cory said.

"They have my vote," Morris said.

Gabe was the last to reach the landing and spent a moment catching his breath. "Have they told you how this super con works? Or is that still a secret?"

"Victor hasn't tipped his mitt yet," Billy said.

"Does his family know?" Gabe asked.

"Victor hasn't revealed it to them, either. He wants everyone kept in the dark. I can't say that I blame him. You know what they say, loose lips sink ships."

Most cheats would never agree to a scam whose secret was unknown to them. Had Billy and his crew not traveled to the Boswells' home base of Sacramento and been given a live demo of Victor's super con, they probably would have turned down the job. But Victor had baffled them so thoroughly with his ability to win at blackjack that they'd signed on.

"Victor liked the way you guys worked as well," Billy said.

He continued up the stairs. At the second-floor landing, he opened the door and stepped outside. The black stretch limo was parked on the far side of the garage with the windows down, only its driver was nowhere to be seen.

"Where's Leon?" Pepper asked.

"Beats me. Hey Leon, where you hiding?" Billy called out.

No answer. It wasn't like Leon to go AWOL during a job. Billy didn't like it and took out his cell phone and called his driver. Seconds later, he heard a muted ringing.

"Where's that coming from?" he asked.

His crew surrounded the limo. Gabe pointed at the trunk.

"It's coming from there," Gabe said.

Billy put his ear to the trunk. The sound of a ringing cell phone was indeed coming from the trunk's interior. He ended the call, and the ringing abruptly stopped.

"Hey Leon, are you in there? Make some noise if you can hear me, man," he said.

A muffled plea for help escaped from the trunk.

"You hurt?" he asked.

The answer was yes. He guessed a street gang had mugged Leon. Vegas gangs were not content to rob their victims, but also preferred to beat them to scare the victim from filing a police report. A hospital visit was in order for Leon. Billy saw no reason for all of them to go.

"Pepper and Misty, I want you to cab it home," he said. "Gabe, you go with them. Cory and Morris, you stay here with me."

Pepper looked upset. "Will you call us later? I want to know if Leon's okay."

"You have my word. Now get moving."

As Gabe and the girls headed for the stairwell, three Asians jumped out of a car and blocked their path. The smallest, who appeared in charge, wore a linen shirt adorned with Hawaiian ukuleles and had goose bumps clustered under his eyes like those on the belly of a toad. In his hand was a Batman lunch box. His henchmen were built like sumo wrestlers and wore navy sports jackets. Colorful tattoos poked out of their shirt collars, suggesting a greater array of body art hiding beneath. They drew guns. Pepper, Misty, and Gabe retreated back to the limo.

"Who are those guys?" Cory asked.

"Beats me." Billy held up his hands to show he wasn't armed. "Take our money. Just don't hurt us."

The diminutive one scowled. "You Cunningham?"

"That's me. Who are you?"

"Broken Tooth."

"Your tooth doesn't look broken to me."

The Asian stuck his hand into his mouth and extracted the crown covering his upper front incisor, revealing the sharpened stump of a real tooth. "We need to talk. Get in limo with your friends, and one of my men will drive to your house."

Billy lived in a penthouse condo in Turnberry Towers. His neighbors and the condo staff believed he sold high-end real estate for a living and had no idea of his criminal activity. If he brought Broken Tooth and his henchmen to his place, his cover would be blown.

"Can we use your place?" he asked the girls.

"I guess," Pepper said.

"The fridge's bare. We can't offer them anything," Misty said.

"I'm sure they'll understand." To Broken Tooth, he said, "Let's use my friends' place instead. It's inside the Las Vegas Country Club."

Broken Tooth scowled. "You trying to set me up?"

"Not at all. My place is small, that's all."

"You pull shit, I hurt your friends, make you watch."

"I won't pull any shit. Why did your men put my driver in the trunk?"

Broken Tooth stuck the crown back in. The facial recognition software used by the Vegas cops to spot criminals was second to none, and Billy guessed Broken Tooth had gotten the crown made so he wouldn't be recognized during his visit.

"Your driver has a big mouth. My men shut it," Broken Tooth said.

"His name's Leon. There was no reason to hurt him."

"This isn't starting out right. You don't question me, understand?"

"You want to do business, don't hurt my people. That's the deal. Take it or leave it."

"You don't call the shots. I call the shots. Get in the car, or my men will blow your brains out."

The henchmen took aim at Billy's head. Pepper let out a squeal.

"Do what he says, Billy."

Billy knew a bluff when he heard one. Broken Tooth hadn't come here to kill him, and he crossed his arms and stood his ground. Broken Tooth caved and had his henchmen lower their guns. The trunk was unlocked, and Leon climbed out, his face a bloody mess.

"You okay?" Billy asked him.

"I'll live," Leon said.

- - -

The limo raced down the exit ramp. Broken Tooth followed in a rental, tires squealing.

The henchman in the backseat was not friendly. His neck was wider than his head, and he wore a permanent frown. Billy tried to small talk him.

"You got a name?" Billy asked.

"Ah," the henchman replied.

"How about your partner?"

"His name Ah, too."

"Is that short for something?"

"Not short for anything. It means little one."

The little ones. That's just great, Billy thought.

Soon they were stuck in traffic, the harsh streetlights bouncing off the limo's tinted glass. Billy leaned back in his seat and stared at the swirling mass of humanity flowing past. Broken Tooth was a wild card; the rules he played by were different from the code that he and his crew adhered to, and he felt certain that a business relationship would end badly. Pepper dropped her hand on his knee and gave it a squeeze.

"These guys scare me," she whispered.

"They're really a lot of fun, when you get to know them," he said.

"Is that supposed to be a joke?"

"Sorry."

"Tell me you have a plan, just to make me feel better," she said.

Getting out of tight jams was his specialty. He'd had guns pointed at him before and managed to walk away intact. But this situation was different. His crew was being threatened, and he needed to protect them as well.

"Don't worry. I'll think of something," he said.

FIVE

Misty and Pepper shared a fancy three-bedroom house on a cul-de-sac in the Las Vegas Country Club with a couple of mangy mutts rescued from the Humane Society. The dogs were supposed to be protection in case of a robbery, but after taking one look at the little ones, they retreated to a distant bedroom with their tails between their legs and did not reappear.

Broken Tooth had a look around before settling on the screened lanai as the desired spot to have their chat. Broken Tooth had a mean streak a mile long, no doubt compensating for the fact that his right arm was badly mangled and the two middle fingers did not extend fully. Billy had read that the average life span for a gang boss in China was fifty, which meant that Broken Tooth had a few more years of stealing left before he was sent to meet his maker.

Once everyone was settled in, Broken Tooth found the controls for the swimming pool and made colored lights illuminate the chlorinated water while soft rock played over the speakers hidden in the fake rock sculptures. The Chinese gangster still had his lunch box, which he held protectively by his side with his good hand.

"Tell me your names," he said to the girls.

"Pepper."

"I'm Misty."

"Take off your clothes and get in the pool."

The girls looked to Billy for help.

"Is this necessary?" Billy asked.

"Very necessary. Now tell them to get in the water. Deep end," Broken Tooth said.

"You'd better do as he says," Billy said.

Pepper and Misty got naked and climbed down the ladder into the pool. They swam into the deep end and remained there, treading water. They both sunbathed in the nude every day and sported zero tan lines. Broken Tooth smiled approvingly.

Cory, Morris, Gabe, and Leon stood by helplessly. The little ones were eyeing them like hawks, prepared to draw their guns if one of them made a false move. Billy patted the air, and the four men lowered themselves into the plastic chairs beside the pool.

"Much better," Broken Tooth said. "I hear you're one of the sharpest guys in Las Vegas. That you are able to rip off the casinos, and they can't catch you."

"I've never ripped off a casino in my life," Billy said.

"That's not what Tommy Wang says. Tommy says you the slickest crook he's ever met."

"Tommy who?"

"You going to play stupid with me? Too late for that. Tommy told me all about you, said you helped him rip off a casino at roulette so he could pay me back the money he owed me. Tommy didn't know how you rigged game, said you were real smart."

"So he's just guessing."

"I don't think so. You know what Tommy does for a living? He's an accountant with a big manufacturing company, manages lots of money. Tommy wrote down all the times he won and then figured out what the odds were. Take a stab."

One of the ways to catch a cheat was to calculate the cheat's winnings against the game's percentages. Billy knew he was trapped and did not reply.

"Four-and-a-half-billion-to-one," Broken Tooth said.

"So he got lucky. It happens sometimes," he said.

"You trying to be funny?"

Broken Tooth made a chopping motion with his hand. The little ones drew their guns and took aim at Pepper and Misty. They didn't seem to care if half the neighborhood heard the shots.

"Stop! I'll do whatever you want, just don't hurt them," he said.

Broken Tooth shot him a murderous look. A long moment passed.

"Are you going to play straight with me?"

Billy nodded. "Yes, sir," he added for emphasis.

"No more games?"

"No more games. You need help, I'm your man. Just don't hurt my crew."

"I'll be nice this time. But it's the last time. You mess with me again, and I'll tell my men to kill your friends."

"You have my word; it won't happen again."

Broken Tooth told the little ones to stand down. Then he went to the screen door that led to the backyard and motioned for Billy to follow. Billy did as told and glanced over his shoulder before going outside. Pepper and Misty had swum over to the edge of the pool and were holding on for dear life. Their breathing was loud and frantic.

- - -

The full moon cast a long shadow across the neatly trimmed grass. Broken Tooth placed the lunch box on the ground, then took a pack of squares from his shirt pocket, banged one out, and lit up. He tossed Billy the pack. It was a Chinese brand called Double Happiness. Billy had quit smoking years ago but lit up to be sociable. No sooner had the smoke reached his lungs than he started violently hacking. It had to be the vilest thing he'd ever put in his body.

"You don't like?" Broken Tooth asked.

Billy spit in the grass. “Must be an acquired taste.”

“I know what you’re thinking. What’s this fucking guy doing in Las Vegas? Why isn’t he in China, where he belongs?” Broken Tooth laughed under his breath and sent ribbons of purple smoke through his nostrils. “I’ll tell you why. There’s only so much money you can make selling drugs or killing people. Big money comes from gambling. Problem is, all the casinos on the island of Macau are controlled by government, so there’s no room for me. That leaves fixing sporting events. That’s where I make my money.”

“Fixing sporting events takes a lot of nerve.”

“Shut up. I’m not finished.”

“Sorry.”

“Betting on sports is different in Asia. Everyone and their sister does it. People have bank accounts online and bet on gambling sites. Everything’s legal. You know how many sites there are where you can make a bet?”

“I don’t have a clue.”

“You’re a smart guy. Guess.”

When it came to online sports betting, the good old US of A was well behind the global curve, with legalized betting on a computer years away from being put into law. Because of this, Billy hadn’t paid much attention to it. The day it became legal, he’d figure out a way to rip it off.

“A hundred?” he guessed.

“Try seven hundred,” Broken Tooth said. “You starting to get the picture?”

It was a big number, and Billy nodded. Seven hundred gambling sites translated into seven hundred deep-pocketed suckers who could be fleeced. “With that many, you can take down a site for a huge score and then go to the next, with no one being the wiser,” he said.

“That’s right. Easiest fucking thing I’ve ever done. We clear a million bucks a week! I used the money to build a beautiful beach resort in Sanya near Hong Kong. Everything going great, then the money dried up. Now work is stopped, and my builder's yelling to get paid. I'm in deep shit."

"What happened?"

Broken Tooth had worked himself into a lather. He lit up a fresh cigarette to calm down. Several puffs later, he spoke. "FIFA," he said.

"You mean the guys running international soccer ruined your deal."

"Yeah. Greedy assholes killed the duck that laid golden egg."

"You mean the goose."

"Shut up."

"Sorry. Were you paying them off?"

"Fuck, no. You don't bet on sports; you don't understand. Three biggest sports in the world for gambling are soccer, horse racing, and tennis. That's where all the money is if you're going to fix an event. Everything else chickenshit. You with me so far?"

"I'm with you."

"Used to be lots of fixed tennis matches, mostly small tournaments. People governing the sport wised up, started monitoring gambling sites. If they saw a big swing in odds on a match, they alerted the tournament, and the officials would put heat on the players. That put an end to it. That left horse racing and soccer. You ever fix a horse race?"

"Once."

"No like?"

"Not my cup of tea. Too many things can go wrong."

"You're telling me. Horse breaks leg, you lose a whole bunch of dough. Too risky. That leaves soccer. Hundreds of soccer matches played all over the world every week. Lots of teams in smaller leagues, players don't get paid on time, they hate owners."

"They have a grudge."

"Right. It's easy to fix those matches and get the favorite team to lose. We would place bets on a few hundred sites and spread the pain around. No one loses too much, while we win big."

"How did FIFA screw this up for you?"

"Assholes running FIFA live like kings. Stay in fancy hotels, eat gourmet meals, pull down big salaries. Should be enough, only they were greedy and started taking bribes from countries wanting to hold international events. They get caught, and shit hits the fan."

"You mean the police are scrutinizing soccer now."

"Interpol, FBI, Scotland Yard, they're all involved. Too many cops."

"So you stopped fixing matches, and the money dried up."

"There you go. Things started to look real bad. I've been a gangster since I was fifteen, didn't know what else to do. I came to Las Vegas to get away from things. Then last week while I was watching the playoffs on TV I had an idea. I'll fix the biggest sporting event in world and make enough money to finish my resort. That's where you come in, Cunningham. You're going to help me get this done."

The words were slow to sink in. There was only one major sporting event on the horizon, and it would generate more than a billion dollars in wagers, from office pools to illegal bookmakers. The Super Bowl was right around the corner, and this crazy little bastard wanted to fix it.

"It will never work," he said.

"Why not? Because no one's had the balls to do it before? That's the best kind of sporting event to fix. No one sees it coming."

"How do you plan to pull this off?"

"Easy. We spot fix."

"You've lost me."

"Super Bowl has a hundred different proposition bets gamblers can bet on," Broken Tooth explained. "No other sporting event has this. Which team wins the coin toss, which team scores first, that sort of thing. We spot fix four prop bets, make a killing."

"But you need the players to do this."

"I've got inside information on dirty players with the Rebels. You're going to approach them, talk them into spot fixing. I make the bets; we split the winnings. I'll make you rich."

The conference championships had taken place earlier that day, and the Las Vegas Rebels and the Louisville Volunteers had won their games with gritty, come-from-behind victories and were now headed to the Super Bowl in Phoenix in two weeks. Broken Tooth had watched the games and, believing that certain Rebel players could be compromised, had come up with a plan.

"Which prop bets do you have in mind?" Billy asked.

"First injury, first penalty, most penalties, and who wins the coin toss."

"How do you plan to rig the coin toss?"

"That's your job. If you can rig a roulette wheel, you can rig a coin toss."

"Can I think about this?"

"No. I want your answer now."

It was not uncommon for other hustlers to approach Billy with jobs. If Billy said no, the other hustler went away. But this situation was different. If he said no, Broken Tooth might kill him out of spite. He glanced into the lanai. Pepper and Misty sat on the pool edge wrapped in towels. They were chatting up the little ones, trying to make nice. There was no doubt in his mind that his crew would meet untimely ends as well. He had read enough about the Triad mentality to know that they believed a bullet in the head solved most of life's problems.

Seen in that light, he didn't have much choice but to say yes. But that didn't make him a believer. Fixing a lowly soccer match in some jerkwater country where the local cops spent the day sleeping at their desks was one thing; fixing the biggest sporting event in the world was another, and the odds were slim that he could pull it off. But he could go along to buy himself time so he could figure a way out of this jam.

"Time up. You in or not?"

The orange tip of Broken Tooth's foul cigarette glowed in the dark. If he answered too quickly, Broken Tooth would know he was being played. He let a moment pass.

"I'm in," Billy said.

SIX

Going onto the lanai, Broken Tooth chopped the air like he was breaking a board. The little ones rose from their chairs and followed their boss through the slider into the house. Billy had noticed that Broken Tooth avoided using verbal commands with his men, preferring to signal what he wanted done with his hands or facial expressions. That was smart, since no one would ever be able to say that they heard Broken Tooth order his men to commit an illegal act.

Billy's crew visibly relaxed and turned their attention to him.

"What does the crazy bastard want?" Gabe asked.

"Guess," Billy said, heading for the slider.

"Don't tell me he wants to work with us."

"That's right. Our reputations precede us."

"Jesus Christ, what did you tell him?"

"I said yes. I didn't have much of a choice."

He followed Broken Tooth through the house and out the front door to the driveway with his crew a few steps behind him. Broken Tooth retrieved from his rental an eight-by-ten manila envelope, which he slapped into Billy's chest.

"What's this?" Billy asked.

"Information on the Rebel players who will fix the game," Broken Tooth said.

"How can you be so sure these guys will do this?"

"Because they did it before, and you're going to convince them to do it again."

"That's a tall order, don't you think?"

"I'll give you an incentive."

Broken Tooth twirled his finger and pointed. The little ones grabbed Leon and dragged him across the front lawn. The rental's trunk was popped open and Leon thrown inside.

"What the hell are you doing?" Billy said.

"Insurance policy," Broken Tooth said. "I'll keep your driver until this is over. That way, you won't try to double-cross me."

"You don't trust me."

"I don't trust anyone."

"Wait a minute. I want to talk to him." Billy crossed the lawn and stuck his head into the trunk, making eye contact with Leon. "I'm really sorry about this."

Leon's head rested on the spare tire. He gave Billy a knowing wink. Leon was trying to play it cool, but the fear in his eyes was unmistakable.

"Keep the faith, man. I'm going to get you out of this," Billy said.

"I'm going to hold you to that," his driver said.

The trunk was slammed shut. Leon was single and didn't have any immediate family. If he went missing for a few days, no one was going to file a missing person's report with the police. The only person who really cared about Leon was Billy, and he cared about Leon a lot.

"Take care of my driver, okay?"

"We'll treat him like a baby," Broken Tooth said. "Won't we?"

The little ones shared a mean laugh. They came across as the type of bastards who'd take pleasure in making Leon's life miserable while he was in captivity. They climbed into the rental with Broken Tooth at the wheel. The engine roared to life, and the driver's window came down. "I'll call you every day for a status report. Don't disappoint me, Cunningham."

"Do you really think we can fix the Super Bowl?" Billy asked.

"You make it sound like a big deal."

"It is a big deal."

"Super Bowl will be easy for a smart guy like you. Remember, I don't like being disappointed. Call you tomorrow."

"Got it."

Broken Tooth drove around the cul-de-sac several times. Each time he passed Pepper and Misty's house, he stuck his head out the window and glared menacingly at Billy and his crew like they were his worst enemies. The little bastard had written the book on intimidation. The game got tired, and the rental finally drove away. Billy started to go inside when he had a thought that left a taste in his mouth as foul as one of Broken Tooth's cigarettes.

"Who gave you my phone number?" he said angrily.

- - -

"Let's take this inside," Billy said.

His crew followed him into the foyer. He shut the door and turned around to face them. His crew didn't scare easily, but this was one of those special times. "Okay, class, today's assignment is to figure out how we're going to fix the coin toss at the Super Bowl so I can get some players on the Rebels' defense to fix a handful of plays. Any ideas?"

"I don't know about this, Billy," Cory said. "Plenty of gamblers have tried to fix the Super Bowl, and they all got caught red-handed and went to jail. There's too much security surrounding the game for it to be compromised."

"Well, I guess there's a first time for everything," he said.

"What's in the envelope?" Gabe asked.

"Information on the Rebel players who Broken Tooth says are dirty."

Gabe's passion was betting on sports, and he let out a whistle. "There are dirty players on the Rebels team? Jesus, Billy, if you can get to them, then this just might work."

"You think so?"

"Sure. A fix is nothing more than a conversation. If there are players who have done this before, then you're halfway home."

"Then let's start working on this right now. Broken Tooth seems to think that if we can rig the coin toss, the rest will be a walk in the park. Gabe, is that possible?"

"I don't see why not," Gabe said. "I've rigged slot machines to pay off jackpots. Gaffing a coin to fall a certain way shouldn't be any harder. What about the referee who tosses the coin at the start of the game? He'll have to be involved."

"That will be Cory and Morris's job," he said. "Find out who the ref is and see if he can be bribed into helping us. You need to get on this right now. I'm supposed to give Broken Tooth an update tomorrow. If he doesn't think we can pull this off, Leon's a dead man."

Gabe nodded. Cory and Morris did as well. Leon's life was on the line, and they needed to come up with a plan that would sound good enough to keep things moving forward.

"Now I need to ask all of you a question," he said. "How did this fucking guy find us? He knew we were on Fremont Street and where the limo was parked. And he has my cell number. He didn't find that information on the Internet. Someone gave it to him."

He studied his crew's faces before speaking again. "Who did it?"

"I didn't tell anybody where we were tonight," Pepper said.

"Me neither," Misty said.

"Same here," Gabe said.

"Neither did I," Morris said.

All eyes fell on Cory. Cory was dating Gabe's oldest daughter, and they were hot and heavy in love. It was a sore point, and Billy wanted the relationship to end.

"How about you, Don Juan? Did you tell Alexis where you were going tonight?"

"I told her Morris and I were going to see a movie," Cory said.

"That's all? No mention of Fremont Street?"

"No sir."

The foyer grew silent. Billy could remember every casino scam he'd ever pulled right down to the threads he'd been wearing, and he played back the night's events that had led up to their confrontation with Broken Tooth in the covered parking garage. The Chinese gangster had known exactly where to find them, which meant they'd been set up.

He kicked the front door with all his might. It sent a searing pain through his big toe, and white-hot flashbulbs exploded in front of his eyes. He hobbled on one foot, not knowing which hurt more, his toe or the betrayal. A stream of profanity escaped his lips.

His crew had figured it out as well. No one spoke for fear of further angering him. He didn't get like this very often, but when he did, his crew knew to stay out of his way.

"Do you still have your gun?" he asked Pepper when the pain had subsided.

"What do you want a gun for, Billy?"

"Just answer the question."

"Yeah, it's in my night table."

"Go get it. And make sure it's loaded."

Pepper went and got her gun. It was a Springfield XD 9mm, just small enough for Billy to slip into his pants pocket. He looked at the others before going out the front door. They understood the gravity of what had happened and knew that he had no other choice.

Except Pepper. She wasn't catching on, or if she was, she wasn't able to process it, and she followed him outside. The darkness made the conversation easy.

"Where are you going?" Pepper said.

"To have a talk with Travis."

"Why do you need my gun?"

"Because Travis fucked us tonight. That's why he left the Golden Gate early."

Pepper brought her hand to her mouth. "Why would he do that? We're his friends."

"He made a crack to me earlier about needing money. He must be broke."

"That's crazy. We would have lent it to him."

"What's done is done. I'll catch up with you later."

The limo was parked in the driveway. Billy got in and started the engine. The headlights found Pepper on the lawn looking like she might be sick. She'd had a fling with Travis a while back and was still soft on him. He lowered the driver's window and stuck out his head.

"Go inside and fix yourself a drink," he said.

SEVEN

Travis, his wife, Karen, and his two stepsons lived in a gated community in the southern foothills of nearby Henderson. A thousand-plus homes meandered along the top of the McCullough mountain range that overlooked the neon city. There was a guardhouse with security cameras that weren't for show. When Billy was a few miles away, he called Travis. It was past midnight, and the big man's cell phone rang several times before he answered.

"Hey Billy, what's up?"

"Sorry for the late call, but we need to talk. There was a problem tonight after you left."

"Don't tell me—"

"Not over the phone. Meet me at Remedy's and I'll give you the gory details."

"Let me throw on some clothes. I'll be there in twenty."

"I'll be at the bar. You still drinking that queer beer?"

"It's called Mich Ultra. I'm trying to shed some pounds."

"I'll be sure to order you one."

Remedy's Tavern was located at the base of Seven Hills on the St. Rose Parkway. A popular watering hole was a license to steal money in a town that never slept, and the place was always jumping. He parked behind the building beneath a yellow security light, took Pepper's handgun off the passenger seat, and got out. From the bar came loud music and peals of laughter. Standing directly beneath the security light, he fired a single shot. The bulb exploded, and the area behind the tavern was thrown into darkness. He waited to see if anyone came out of the bar to check out the noise. When no one did, he got back in the limo.

His mirror had a clean view of the street, allowing him to see cars come and go. The envelope Broken Tooth had given him lay on the passenger seat, and he dumped out the contents and had a look. There were photographs of several football players with the Las Vegas Rebels, along with a handful of newspaper articles about the team. The Rebels were a true Cinderella team: to a group of aging, established stars snagged in the league's expansion draft, management had added several talented players from the college draft and free agents who overperformed. The chemistry had worked, and they were now headed to the Super Bowl.

He tried to read the articles but had to stop. He was so damn angry with Travis that he couldn't concentrate, and he slid the articles back into the envelope for another time. He had first discovered Travis switching dice at a joint called Palace Station. The big man's technique was caveman crude, yet he still managed to get the money. Travis knew when to move, and that was more important than perfect sleight of hand. A familiar white Suburban pulled in. The parking spots in front were taken, and the Suburban drove around back and parked two spots away.

He got out holding the gun at his side. The smell of gunpowder hung in the air, and he wondered if Travis would notice and take off running. Travis also got out and spotted him.

"Hey, Billy, is that you? I thought we were meeting inside."

"Change in plans." Billy started walking toward the Suburban. He raised his arm and took aim. At this short distance, it would be impossible to miss. Travis's legs buckled.

"Why are you aiming that thing at me? What did I do?"

"You set us up tonight, you fucking piece of shit."

"Come on, Billy. You know me better than that."

"You're denying it? Then why the crack about needing money? Like I haven't paid you a king's ransom? New house, new cars, and this is how you repay me."

"I didn't set you up. For the love of Christ, I'd put my life on the line for you, man."

"Are you saying you're not in trouble?"

"I am in trouble, but that doesn't mean I set you up. The two things don't go together."

"Is that a fact."

"On my father's grave, I'm telling you the truth."

Travis wasn't backing down. Either he was being straight or plotting his final stand. Until now, Travis had been loyal, and Billy decided to give him a chance to explain himself.

"Get in the driver's side of the limo and strap yourself in. Then put your hands on the wheel and leave them there."

Travis did as told. Billy went around to the passenger side and also got in. He flipped the key in the ignition, causing the dashboard to light up and cast shadows onto their faces. He rested the gun in his lap with its barrel pointed at the big man's stomach.

"Explain yourself," he said.

"My wife has a baby sister named Jackie," Travis said, his voice trembling. "Jackie's lowlife husband bolted and left her with three kids to raise, so Jackie started embezzling money from the credit union where she works as a bookkeeper."

"How much did she steal?"

"Four hundred big ones."

"That's a lot of money. You sure she isn't snorting blow?"

"One of her kids is special needs. It eats up a lot of cash. The credit union was getting audited, and Jackie called my wife screaming she was going to jail, so in a moment of weakness, I wired her the money. It cleaned me out."

"Is that why you sold us out tonight?" Billy asked.

Travis jerked his head. "What are you talking about?"

"A Chinese gangster named Broken Tooth paid us a visit. He knew where to find us, and he has my cell phone number. You gave him that information."

"It could have been one of the others."

"Fat chance. They were with me."

"So?"

"Broken Tooth's men threatened to shoot us if we didn't play ball. They also kidnapped Leon and are holding him for safekeeping." He was tired of talking and shoved the gun's barrel into the soft part of Travis's belly. The worst way to die was by gut shot. As endings went, it was excruciatingly painful and made the victim needlessly suffer.

"They had guns?"

"That's right. You sound surprised."

Travis rested his forehead against the steering wheel and shut his eyes.

"Spit it out," he said.

"Broken Tooth called me last week right after the Rebels won their divisional game, and he asked me to meet him. I asked him how he got my number, and he said Tommy Wang took our cell numbers off Pepper's cell phone and gave them to him."

"So you didn't give him my number."

Travis lifted his head and opened his eyes. "No sir."

"Good. Keep talking."

"We met and had drinks. Broken Tooth acted cool, and he was sharp. He said that members of the Rebels' defense were dirty, and that if they went to the Super Bowl, he was sure they could be bribed into fixing the game. You told me that other hustlers approach you with scams all the time. I didn't see this being any different."

"How much did he pay you to tell him where to find us?"

"Ten grand. I needed it to cover my bills."

"You could have called me."

"Karen said the same thing—call Billy, he'll bail you out. I was afraid you'd think I was a liability and can me."

"Like this was a better move?"

"I'm sorry, Billy, I really am. Broken Tooth wants you to approach the Rebels players and fix the game. If anyone in this town could pull it off, it's you."

"You think I could fix the Super Bowl and get away with it?"

"Yeah. And make a killing in the process."

Travis wasn't being straight with him. Travis might be flat broke, but the rest of the crew wasn't, and one of the others would have lent him the money. Something else was going on here, and Billy wondered if the big man was holding a grudge and his meeting with Broken Tooth was payback. Billy didn't know what the grudge was about and imagined he'd said something out of line and bruised Travis's ego. Over time, it had festered and led to this act of betrayal.

It was enough of a reason to shoot Travis and dump his body out in the desert for the vultures to pick apart. But he wasn't going to do that. Travis was the first person he'd ever recruited for his crew, and they had a long, profitable history together. He wanted to believe that they were friends, and this was nothing more than a dumb mistake.

As a kid, Billy had found a stray dog that he'd brought home with him. He'd loved the dog and let it sleep at the foot of his bed. One day, out of the blue, the mutt had chomped on his hand. His old man had tried to take the dog to the pound, but Billy had thrown a tantrum, and his father had caved and let the dog stay. Billy had worked with the dog, and it had never bit him again. Travis was like that dog. With training, the big man could be brought around.

But not tonight. Business came first, and he wanted to hear more about these dirty football players. If they'd fixed games before, then there was a possibility they could be talked into fixing the Super Bowl. He withdrew the gun and opened the passenger door.

"I'm sorry, Billy. I'll make it up to you," Travis said.

"You can start by buying me a drink," he said.

EIGHT

The party inside Remedy's was going strong. The place had no real personality, just a collection of pool tables and a lounge with a phony gas-lit fireplace, but that didn't stop people from having a good time. Billy grabbed a corner table and flagged a waitress. Soon they were drinking Captain Morgan and Coke and acting like nothing had happened between them.

"How much did Broken Tooth tell you about these players?" Travis asked.

"Not much," he replied. "He gave me an envelope with photographs of guys who play for the Rebels along with newspaper articles about them. Judging by the photos, they look like a bunch of rich jocks. I can't see them fixing the big game."

"But you don't know their history."

"They're already rich. What's their motivation?"

"These guys are hustlers. It's what they do. Do you follow the NFL?"

"Not since I left New England."

"Patriots fan?"

"My old man was a diehard. I lost interest when I moved out here."

"Did you ever consider fixing a football game?" Travis asked.

"Plenty of times. Football has more money bet on it than any other sport in the country. If a hustler can fix a game, he can pocket millions without drawing heat because there are legitimate gamblers doing it every week."

"Why didn't you?"

"Because I don't like cops breathing down my neck. The NFL has a special division called league security that's always watching the players. We're talking ex-FBI and ex–Secret Service agents here. These guys are paid to stop guys like us from shitting in the punch bowl."

Their waitress hovered nearby. Billy raised two fingers, indicating it was time for another round. Travis stared into the fake fireplace, working on his next lines. Billy sensed that he was trying to make things right and wasn't taking their friendship for granted.

Their drinks came. Travis knocked his back to get up his courage. Then he spoke.

"The Rebels played an exhibition game against the Dolphins in Shanghai last August. It was a meaningless game, but there was still a betting line. With two minutes left on the clock, the Dolphins scored two touchdowns. The Dolphins still lost, but they beat the point spread. The bookies got clobbered."

"The game was fixed?"

"Yup. Broken Tooth told me that a group of gamblers persuaded members of the Rebels' defense to massage the score, which they did by easing up on the Dolphins' receivers and not pressuring the quarterback."

It was an interesting angle. NFL quarterbacks could throw a ball into a receiver's hands with near 100 percent accuracy. He'd seen Tom Brady do this enough times to know it was true. The only thing that could stop a quarterback was the defense knocking his receivers off their routes and pressuring him into hurrying his passes.

"And Broken Tooth wants me to approach these same players on the Rebels' defense to fix the Super Bowl," he said.

"That's right. They've done it before, and they'll do it again."

Billy leaned forward in his chair. "Fixing a game in the preseason isn't the same as fixing the Super Bowl. The Rebels fought to get here. These guys on defense won't do it again."

"Broken Tooth said that the leader of the Rebels' defense is as crooked as a dog's hind leg. Broken Tooth said this guy has been pulling shit since college and getting away with it."

"What kind of shit?"

"Shaving points on games."

Conspiring with an athlete with a history of fixing games was the bread and butter of many professional gamblers. But he still wasn't sold on the idea. The Super Bowl was played on the world's biggest stage, and anything suspicious would be analyzed to death and eventually figured out. Everything would hinge on how well the dirty players pulled off the fix. If they made it look obvious, everyone involved would go to jail.

"Does this player have a name?" he asked.

"Clovis McClain. Everyone calls him Night Train."

"That's the underwear guy."

"That's right. Night Train has more endorsements than any player in the NFL. Cars, watches, his own clothing line, he even has a Saturday morning cartoon show. He's a regular money machine."

"This isn't adding up. If word got out that Night Train was dishonest, it would ruin his career."

"It hasn't ruined him so far. This guy's a hustler. I went online and read up on him. An article said his coaches in college warned the new players not to gamble with Night Train during team trips. A coach called him a card shark."

Cheaters were not born, they were made. If Night Train had been cheating in college, it meant that he'd learned the ropes growing up, possibly from his father or an older brother, and been turned out when he was old enough to fend for himself. Stealing was in his blood, and

Night Train was going to keep on doing it until he got caught. The fix was sounding a lot better than a few minutes ago, and Billy's interest was piqued.

"What's our take?" he asked.

"You're going to do it?" Travis grew excited.

"I just might. But first I want to know what our take is."

"We get territorial exclusivity."

"Meaning what?"

"The Las Vegas sports books are ours to fleece. Broken Tooth gets everything else."

"A hundred million bucks was bet on the Super Bowl in Las Vegas last year. That's ours to work?"

"That's right, Billy. I was thinking we'd steal ten million, just to be on the safe side. It will be like taking candy from a baby."

"Who pays Night Train and the other players?"

"That comes out of Broken Tooth's pocket."

The appeal of fixing a sporting event was its simplicity. The athlete did all the work, while the gambler made most of the money. But there was a downside. If the police found out, the cheat's life would become a living hell, and the cheat would be forced to hire a battery of lawyers to defend himself. This was especially true for baseball and football, which were considered national pastimes and often led to Congressional hearings when games were fixed.

Up at the bar, a pretty lady angrily slapped a video poker machine and said, "How come I never win this stupid damn game?" Her complaint triggered an old memory. Billy had been in a bar when a gang of gaming agents had burst in and placed yellow police crime-scene tape across the screens of the video poker machines. Later, he'd learned that the manufacturer had rigged the game so jackpots never paid out. The deception had been going on for years, yet the gaming board hadn't caught on because it was happening right under their noses.

Broken Tooth was counting on the same thing. It was crazy enough to work.

"I like it. Count me in," he said.

Travis nearly hugged him. "You won't regret this, Billy."

"I sure hope not. How do I connect with this guy?"

"Night Train has a suite at the Octavius Tower at Caesars where he stays after practice. That's where he and his defensive teammates are right now. Secretly, of course."

"Those villas run forty grand a night. Sounds like my kind of guy."

Travis ordered another round. Soon they were holding fresh drinks in their hands.

"I'm sorry, Billy," Travis said. "I should have called you first."

"Don't do it again," he said.

"I won't. Here's to getting rich together."

There was no greater sin than hurting the people you ran with. Travis had screwed up and needed to make amends. There was no better way to accomplish that than by making everyone rich. It would erase any doubts about the big man and his motives.

"I'll drink to that," Billy said.

NINE

Monday, thirteen days before the Super Bowl

The next morning, Billy hit the ground running.

Over coffee, he read the articles Broken Tooth had given him. Night Train was no stranger to trouble, especially when it came to gambling. The NFL prohibited players from hanging out with gamblers and bookies, yet Night Train had been caught in nightclubs, on golf courses, and inside casinos with an assortment of sordid underworld characters.

Nowhere did the articles mention what penalties the NFL had leveled on him for these transgressions. The NFL had a reputation to uphold, and Night Train's associating with hoodlums had tarnished it. Yet it didn't appear that anything had been done.

He noticed another strange thing. The articles had been written by bloggers and had come from news sites. Using his Droid, he got on the Internet and typed *Night Train Gambling* into Google. Links to several dozen articles appeared, all written by bloggers. There was not a single article from a newspaper or magazine about Night Train's gambling.

He refreshed his cup and went onto the balcony. He lived on the thirty-second floor of a luxury condo with a breathtaking view of the

Strip. Not bad for a kid who'd arrived on a Greyhound bus with two hundred bucks in his pocket.

He gripped the railing and stared at the distant Spring Mountains. Night Train hung out with bookies. That meant he had inside information on games that he was betting on. Night Train was breaking the law and putting the sport that employed him in jeopardy. Yet the guy hadn't been punished. Either he had photos of the league's commissioner in bed with a farm animal, or something else was in play here.

He went inside. On the desk in his study was an old-fashioned Rolodex that contained the names and phone numbers of more than fifty concierges employed by the town's casinos. He personally knew all of them, some on a first-name basis. And he knew what made them tick.

He placed a call to Tito Gonzalez at Caesars Palace. Tito was a thirty-six-year-old divorced father of two pulling down forty-five grand a year and driving a ten-year-old Buick LeSabre. Every casino worker had a dream that motivated them to put up with the daily grind of their thankless jobs. For Tito, it was to one day play poker professionally. To accomplish that, Tito needed a stake, and as he'd demonstrated on many prior occasions, Tito was more than willing to compromise his customers' privacy to raise the money.

"Hey, Billy, long time no hear from. How you been?" Tito greeted him.

"I'm doing great. You still playing poker?"

"You bet. I placed sixth in a WPT satellite event last week."

"I've got a business proposition for you."

"I'm at my stand. Let me call you back."

The line went dead. In his mind's eye, Billy saw Tito walking outside Caesars and finding a secluded spot from which to call him back. Billy's cell phone rang a minute later.

"Lay it on me," Tito said.

"Night Train McClain is staying in one of your pool villas," he said. "Rumor has it he likes to play poker. I'd like to make his acquaintance. Can you arrange that?"

"Who told you Night Train had a villa here?"

"A little bird. I'll make it worth your while."

"Night Train's off-limits. Listen, I've got to run."

"Why is he off-limits?"

"I can't tell you that. Nice talking to you."

Billy believed that the negotiation began with the word *no* and was not about to throw in the towel. "How much did you make for coming in sixth in your poker tournament?"

"Seven thousand three hundred and fifty bucks."

"I'll match it."

"Sorry, Billy, but that's not enough. I could get in serious hot water."

"I thought you wanted to quit your job and play cards for a living."

"I'm not there yet."

"I'll give you ten grand for your trouble. Does that float your boat?"

"Still not going to cut it. I've got to get back to work."

"No, you don't. What you need to do is chase your dreams, Tito. You check your bank account every day, and every night you dream of telling your boss to go fuck himself. What's the figure? You have to be getting close."

"I am close. Fifteen thousand eight hundred and forty-six bucks, and I'm out of here."

"Done."

"Don't screw with me, Billy. I'm not in the mood."

"Have I ever messed with you before? Have I?"

"There's always a first time. There's no way in hell you'll pay me that much to set up a meeting with Night Train. You're blowing smoke up my ass, and I don't like it."

Billy pulled Tito's card out of the Rolodex. "You still have an account with PayPal? The last time we did business, I wired you the money."

The line went still, and for a moment Billy thought Tito had run on him.

"I've still got my PayPal account," Tito said.

"I'm wiring you the money. Check in a few minutes, then call me back."

"I'll do that," Tito said, unconvinced.

- - -

Tito was singing a different tune when he rang Billy back. "I can't believe you just did that," the concierge said, unable to hide his excitement.

"Neither can I. You haven't done anything yet," Billy said.

"On the contrary, I made a call and spoke to the great one himself. I set up Night Train and his posse with some lovely ladies last night, so he owes me. There's a card game in his villa this afternoon and a seat with your name on it. Be prepared to lose your money."

"The game's rigged?"

"You bet. A cleaning lady overheard Night Train talking to his pals about fleecing a guy they'd invited over to play and reported it."

Cheating at poker was difficult when only one person was doing the stealing. Team play was a lot easier. A guest would be invited to the game, and the players would orchestrate a scam and take every last cent the guest had. To be forewarned was to be forearmed, and Billy had all the information he needed to play in Night Train's game. But he was still curious as to why Caesars was letting cheating take place.

"Why do you let that go on? Aren't you afraid of people finding out?" Billy asked.

"Night Train is bulletproof," Tito replied. "That fucking guy can do just about anything he wants short of murdering someone, and management's going to look the other way."

"Why?"

"In my job, you don't ask questions like that. It only leads to finding out stuff you shouldn't know. I told him you were a hotshot real-estate salesman. That's the cover you're using these days, isn't it?"

"You've got a good memory."

"Bring plenty of cash. A word of warning. Don't ask Night Train if you can get a selfie with him. He'll get ugly with you."

"Doesn't like to get his picture taken?"

"No sir. The NFL prohibits the Rebels from hanging out at the casinos during the season. If word leaked out Night Train was gambling and whoring at Caesars when he was supposed to be preparing for the Super Bowl, all hell would break loose with the NFL's head office."

"He's not preparing for the Super Bowl?"

"I didn't say that. He's at a team meeting right now. He'll be back in the afternoon. Poker game starts at three."

"Does his team know he's at Caesars?"

"I'm sure they do."

"And they let that kind of crap go on?"

Tito guffawed into the phone. Billy didn't like being laughed at and bristled.

"What's so damn funny?"

"I thought you were a sharp guy."

Billy nearly said *Sharper than you* but bit his tongue. "What's that supposed to mean?" he said instead.

"It means that you don't understand what you're getting yourself into, my friend," Tito said. "The NFL isn't about football, and it never was."

"Then what's it about?"

"Show biz."

"Is that supposed to be a joke?"

"It's whatever you want it to be. Get here early so an employee can escort you to the villa."

Billy didn't like ending the conversation being left in the dark. "You going to explain yourself, or do I have to beg?"

Tito laughed again, and the line went dead.

Billy's next call was to Victor Boswell. He had decided not to tell Victor about the unpleasantness with Broken Tooth for fear that Victor would call off the super con.

"Hello, Billy, how are we doing today?" Victor asked.

"Couldn't be better," the young hustler said. "My crew is itching to know the secret of your super con. Are you ready to tell me?"

"Not yet."

"Afraid I might go and pull it myself?"

"I know you wouldn't do that. But I can't say that about your crew."

"They wouldn't do that, either. They just want to know what they're getting involved with. They might back out if your super con uses electronic equipment. The casinos have developed new ways to detect that stuff."

"There's no electronics involved," Victor assured him. "Want to come over? I'll give you another demonstration, then we can hammer out the details of how this is going to work."

Any time spent with Victor was always an education in the fine art of cons and grifts. Billy said yes, and Victor gave him the address of the rented house on the north side of town where his family was staying.

"I'll be there in thirty," Billy said.

"Hundred bucks says you can't figure out what I'm doing," Victor said.

"You're on."

TEN

Billy pulled into the driveway of the Boswells' rental house and killed the engine. Many crews that traveled for jobs had switched from staying in hotels to renting houses. Owners of rentals rarely keep records, and for a thief, that was always a good thing. The Boswells' rental was a testament to suburbia, with a basketball hoop over the garage door and an artificially green lawn. He texted Victor to say he'd arrived.

He got out of his car and had a look around. Like a bad penny, gaming agents had a habit of turning up, usually in the form of a stakeout. The car parked across the street was empty, as well as the SUV down the block. He decided it was safe and crossed the lawn.

Victor greeted him at the front door. His host wore a starched white shirt and black dress slacks, and he had a cigarette tucked behind his ear. Victor was getting on in years, but instead of trying to hide his age, he owned it and was the epitome of class. Leaning on his cane, he escorted Billy to a gaming room in the rear of the house with a felt blackjack table in its center.

"Want some coffee? I just made a fresh pot," Victor said.

"I'm good. Did the blackjack table come with the house?"

"I bought it from the Gambler's General Store. Wanted to be ready for the big day."

"Are you practicing the super con on your family?"

"Every day. They still can't figure out how it works."

"You like keeping them in the dark, don't you?"

"Come to mention it, I do. This might be the best play I've ever come up with. Ready to take another shot at the champ?"

"You bet I am."

Billy walked behind the table and took the dealer's position. Victor took the chair across from him and stuck the unlit cigarette in his mouth. Victor had smoked since he was a kid but had quit after one of his children had pointed out that his lips trembled whenever he got nervous, sending a smoke signal to observant pit bosses.

The game was handheld, single deck. Billy shuffled the cards and had Victor cut them with a plastic cut card. He placed the deck into his hand in preparation to deal.

"Place your bets," Billy said.

Victor had three denominations of play chips stacked in front of him. Thousand-dollar chips, five-thousand-dollar chips, and ten-thousand-dollar chips. He slid three ten-thousand-dollar chips into the betting circle.

"That's a big bet to start with," Billy said.

"I'm feeling lucky," Victor said.

Billy's cheeks burned. Victor wouldn't make a bet that large unless he knew what the outcome was going to be. Yet he had done absolutely nothing to compromise the game.

Billy dealt the hand. Victor got a blackjack, which paid three-to-two.

"Would you look at that," Victor said with a grin.

"What the hell are you doing?"

"Deal another round. You'll catch on eventually."

"What are you saying—that it's right in front of my nose?"

"You know what I'm doing, you just don't recognize it."

Billy dealt another hand, which Victor won with a huge bet. Then Billy dealt three more rounds. Victor won the first but lost the next two.

On the hands that Victor lost, smaller bets were placed, indicating that he knew which cards were going to be dealt to him.

"What happens if a pit boss smells a rat and stops the game?" Billy asked.

"He won't find anything," Victor said.

"Can I look anyway?"

"Be my guest."

Billy gave the deck a thorough examination. Because players were allowed to touch their cards in single-deck games, cheats had resorted to marking the backs of the cards with secret substances, allowing the cheat to learn the values of the cards as they were dealt. By knowing the dealer's cards, the cheat had a huge edge over the house and cleaned up.

The deck was normal. Victor said, "I bought the cards with the table."

"You like rubbing it in, don't you?"

"Just being honest with you."

"What if the pit boss pulled you into a back room and patted you down?"

"You think I've got a camera up my sleeve?"

"I wouldn't put it past you."

Victor cuffed his shirtsleeves. Cheats often strapped cameras to their wrists to spot the dealer's hole card. The information was transmitted to the cheat's partner, who sat in a cocktail lounge, looking at a live feed on a laptop. The partner signaled the information to the cheat using a device called a thumper, which was strapped to the cheat's leg.

Victor's sleeves were clean.

"I can do this in my birthday suit, in case you were wondering," the older man said.

Billy was starting to feel stupid. After taking the cards out of the discard tray, he added them to the deck and reshuffled.

"Let's try it now," he said.

"Trying to mess me up? I like your spunk," Victor said.

The next round was Victor's as well. Victor had won $30,000 of the house's money in the amount of time it took to drink a beer. Billy noticed something he hadn't seen before. The corners of Victor's eyes narrowed as the cards were dealt. That was a tell, and Billy picked up a card and examined its back.

"You're using luminous readers. The cards are marked with luminous paint, which you're reading with a special pair of contact lenses. That's your scam."

"That's as old as the hills, Billy. No one uses luminous readers anymore."

"Which is why you resurrected it. Marking cards with luminous paint is so old that pit bosses in Vegas have stopped looking for it."

"But a pit boss *can* look for it," Victor reminded him. "And if the pit boss finds the marks, I'm screwed."

"If you're not using luminous readers, why did you squint?"

"Allergies. Check the tray if you don't believe me."

Every blackjack game had a discard tray that the dealer placed cards into after the hand was over. The trays were made of translucent red plastic, which acted like a filter and let the pit boss look through the rear wall of the tray and spot luminous paint on the backs of cards.

Billy placed a card into the tray and stared through the rear wall. No secret markings popped up. He did this with more than a dozen cards. They were all clean.

Billy took a C-note and gave it to Victor. "You win. I have no clue what you're doing."

"That's high praise coming from you," Victor said.

They heard the front door slam. "That must be one of my kids," Victor said.

"Hey, Dad," a female called from the front of the house.

"Kat? I thought you went to the Tropicana to practice your strong-arming," Victor said.

"That was the plan," she called back. "I got made and had to leave."

"You got made? What happened?"

"I need a drink. Can I get you something?"

"I'm good."

A moment later, Kat Boswell came into the room holding a can of diet soda. She was barely legal and wore blue and purple streaks in her hair to make herself look older. She said hello to Billy before sitting down beside her father at the blackjack table.

"Who made you?" Victor asked.

"Casino security," she said. "I was working a blackjack game with a green dealer. He dealt me a twenty-two and I pounded the table and said, 'Yeah, twenty-one!' and the dope paid me off. It happened so fast, I didn't think anyone noticed."

"Do you think you were being watched?"

"It sure felt that way."

Strong-arm cheating encompassed the rankest scams imaginable, including lying about your hand and betting late. Cheats practiced these scams to build up their nerve.

"Tell me exactly what happened," Victor said.

Kat took a swallow of soda before putting the can in a cup on the table. "A security goon came to the table and said that I looked like a woman who'd given them trouble last night. He wanted to see some ID, so I gave him my driver's license."

Victor's eyes flashed. Security at the Golden Gate had used the same line on Nico. "Was the goon by himself, or did he have backup?" Victor asked.

"He was working solo. He spent a minute reading my license. Then he handed it back to me and said it was a case of mistaken identity."

Now Victor looked worried. Nico Boswell had been given the same bullshit line.

"Did he offer to give you a free drink or comp you a meal?" Victor asked.

"Nope. Fucker didn't offer me anything," Kat replied.

"This isn't good, Kat."

"It gets worse. I decided to leave. On my way out, I glanced over my shoulder, and the goon was tailing me. I went to the valet and got my car—"

"How many times have I told you, never use the valet," Victor scolded her. "You don't know where they take your car or what they do to it."

"I'm sorry, Pop. I wasn't thinking."

Victor loved his children more than anything in the world, and he placed his hand on his daughter's arm and gave it a fatherly pat. "Never again."

"I promise, never again."

"Good. Continue your story."

"As I pulled onto the Strip, I saw a line of yellow cabs at the curb, waiting for fares. One of the cabs started to follow me. At the next intersection, I did a U-turn and lost the asshole."

"You lost him."

"That's right."

Victor swallowed hard. He was thinking the same thing Billy was thinking. Kat may have lost the tail, but she hadn't lost the people who were following her. The sixty-four-thousand-dollar question was, did Kat realize that?

"Did you drive straight back here?" Victor asked hesitantly.

"Come on, Pop, I'm not that dumb. I pulled into a strip mall and inspected the car. First I checked the roof to see if there was a silver disc attached. You told me that the cops put them there so police helicopters can follow vehicles in traffic. Well, there wasn't, so then I climbed underneath, and lo and behold, guess what. I found a GPS tag in a plastic case held to the bottom of the car with a magnet. I opened it up, and it had a miniature transmitter and two AA batteries. They must have put it on while I was inside the casino."

"It wasn't hard-wired to an electrical wire in the car," Victor said.

"No. It was a short-term surveillance."

"Did you destroy it?"

"I was going to chuck it into the trash, but then I had an idea. There was a Papa John's in the strip mall, so I climbed underneath one of the delivery cars and reattached the transmitter. A delivery boy came out with some pizzas and took off."

Kat's ingenuity made Billy smile. The GPS would send an uninterrupted signal, allowing its holder to track the location of the rental on a laptop map. Whoever had attached the tag would spend the rest of the day chasing a pizza delivery boy and not knowing it.

"Then you drove home," Victor said.

Kat had a gypsy's skeptical eyes. She gave her father a look that would have turned most men to stone. "Of course not! I went to McCarran and dumped the rental. Then I took a stroll through the main terminal to make sure I wasn't being tailed."

"For how long?" Victor asked.

"Thirty minutes. You're going to see some charges on my credit card."

Victor rolled his eyes. "You went shopping?"

"I had to do something to kill the time."

"How much did you spend?"

"Enough to jump-start the economy. The good news is, no one followed me. I rented a car from another company and drove here."

Kat's tale was over. Victor gave her a hug and told her she'd done good. Her father's words brought a smile to her face, and she bid Billy good-bye before leaving the room.

"Jesus Christ, this isn't good," Victor said.

Billy felt the same way. Two different casinos had made Kat and Nico. It could have been a coincidence, only Billy didn't believe in those. More than likely, the gaming board had Kat and Nico on their radar and had distributed their photographs to the casinos.

"This smells like the gaming board," Billy said. "Did Kat and Nico get caught together in a casino recently?"

"Not that I know of," Victor said.

"Would they tell you if they'd screwed up?

"Absolutely. My children are trustworthy." Victor paused. "Do you still want to go through with this? I won't be pissed if you pull out."

"Are you pulling out?" Billy asked.

"I can't. The super con has a shelf life. If I don't pull it off soon, it will never happen."

A shelf life. Now Billy was really confused. If he didn't hang around, he'd never find out Victor's secret, and that would bother him, along with not cashing in.

"I'm not going anywhere. We'll give Kat a makeover along with Nico," Billy said.

"Works for me," Victor said. "Now, let's iron out the details."

ELEVEN

Billy and Victor spent the next hour working out the super con. Their plan called for five teams to descend upon five different Strip casinos next Saturday evening with the purpose of scamming a high-stakes blackjack game. If successful, each team would steal two million bucks of their respective casino's money.

Ten million bucks in a single night. In the old days, stealing that much would set off alarms. But times had changed, and it was not uncommon for high rollers to win millions of dollars during a single outing. The unlucky casino had no choice but to accept the loss.

The five teams would be evenly split. One member of Billy's crew paired up with a Boswell. Billy, Travis, and Victor would act as monitors to deal with emergencies and make sure no one screwed up.

The five casinos they planned to hit were the Mirage, Aria, Mandalay Bay, Luxor, and the MGM Grand. Because of his limited mobility, Victor would cover a single casino, the Mirage, while Billy would cover Mandalay Bay and Luxor, leaving Travis the MGM Grand and Aria.

"Hungry?" Victor asked when they were done.

"Thanks, but there's a poker game at Caesars that I've got a seat in."

"What scam are you pulling?"

"The gift shop play."

"That usually gets the money. Good luck."

- - -

Whenever time permitted, Billy took the Strip. The casinos lined it like fortresses filled with gold and treasures, and the sight of them never failed to get his heart racing. Like a kid in a candy store, he just couldn't get enough of them.

He got a call from Gabe on his cell phone. He'd tasked his crew with figuring out how to fix the Super Bowl and guessed they'd stayed up all night devising a plan.

"Good morning," he answered. "Or should I say good afternoon. How's it going?"

"It's going great. I'm here with Cory and Morris and the girls," Gabe said on a speakerphone. "I've created a gaffed coin that will let us rig the coin toss at the Super Bowl."

"And not get caught," Cory chimed in.

"You're going to love this," Morris added. "It's spotless."

"They tried it out on Misty and me. It really works," Pepper said.

"The scam uses a transmitter hidden inside a cell phone that works up to a hundred yards away," Gabe said. "If we have one of our crew sitting in the front row near the fifty-yard line, it will work. All we have to do is get the head referee to play along, and we're home free."

"How do you plan to do that?" Billy asked.

"Morris and I are having breakfast with the head referee in Phoenix tomorrow morning," Cory said. "He seems amenable to talking with us."

"Think he can be bought off?" Billy asked.

"Yes. Word is, he has gambling debts, so we're taking lots of cash with us."

Billy smiled into the phone. His crew had done their job; now it was his turn to get Night Train and his teammates on board. The turn for Caesars was up ahead, and he flipped on his indicator. "I'm going to meet the football players. Wish me luck."

"Good luck," his crew chorused.

- - -

He pulled into the valet area and popped the trunk before getting out. He kept a strongbox next to the spare tire filled with money, and he removed two ten-thousand-dollar stacks of hundreds and slipped them into the pockets of his sports jacket.

Entering Caesars was always a thrill. The joint was a testimonial to excess, the design overblown and over the top. In a winding, centralized hallway was a life-size replica of Michelangelo's *David.* A shop called Emperor's Essentials sold booze and overpriced branded accessories, the manager a young woman with a gorgeous smile. Her name tag said ELLE/DALLAS. "See something you like?" she asked playfully.

"Just window shopping," he said.

"There's no charge for looking. What's your name?"

"Billy. You're new here, aren't you?"

She feigned surprise. "I am. How did you know?"

Caesars was a favorite target for Billy's scams. Management gave dealers a loose rein and left them more susceptible to being compromised by cheats. As a result, he knew the joint like the back of his hand, including the stores and restaurants.

"I come here a lot. How long have you worked here?" he asked.

"I just started part-time. I'm enrolled at UNLV's hospitality management program."

"I hear that's a good school. Do you sell playing cards?"

"It's one of our biggest items. How many decks do you need?"

"Four."

Elle opened a glittering display case containing decks of Caesars playing cards. These cards had their corners rounded to prevent cheats from reintroducing them into games.

"Sorry, but I need regular cards," he said.

Elle closed the case. From a drawer, she removed four decks of Bicycle playing cards, two red, two blue, and placed them on the counter. The Bicycle cards weren't big movers, which was why they lived in the drawer.

"Do you have any glue?" he asked.

"All we carry is Super Glue," she said.

"That will work."

Elle rang up the sale. Each deck cost $9.99, while the glue ran eight bucks. Out in the real world, the same items cost a third. Shopping in Vegas had once been a bargain; now it was like getting your pocket picked. She handed him his change along with his purchase in a plastic bag.

"Don't be a stranger."

"I won't," he said.

- - -

The men's room had more tile than a quarry. He locked himself in a stall and placed the plastic bag at his feet. Taking out his Swiss Army knife, he flicked open the blade. There were a variety of different Swiss Army knives on the market. His was called Swisslite and was the smallest model the company sold with just a single blade.

From the bag, he removed a blue deck of Bicycles and held it up to eye level. With the precision of a surgeon, he made a perfect cut in the plastic at the bottom of the box. Done, he slid the box out of the plastic and placed the plastic in the bag for safekeeping.

Using the blade, he worked away the stamp that sealed the box's flap. Bicycles had a stamp that guaranteed they'd been manufactured with the highest standards. Most players wouldn't play with a deck without a stamp, fearful the cards had been tampered with.

Taking the deck from the case, he removed the jacks, queens, kings, and aces. He was going to turn them into what hustlers called "touch cards" so he could secretly know their value when they came off the top of the deck.

The rest of the cards were put in the bag along with the box. The jacks, queens, kings, and aces went into his lap. He opened the nail file on his knife and scuffed up the short end of each card. Jacks got one scuff, queens got two, kings three. For the aces, he ran the file down the entire end.

Done, he retrieved the cards from the bag and returned the touch cards to their spots in the order. The reassembled deck went into the box and was resealed. Then the box was slid into its plastic case, and the Super Glue made the casing whole again.

He repeated the procedure with the other three decks. By the time he was finished, it was two forty. He left the restroom with the bag and headed back to Emperor's Essentials.

- - -

Elle acted happy to see him. "Back so soon?"

He placed the bag on the counter and removed the four doctored decks. "I'm sorry, but my friends have decided that they want to play with casino cards. Can I exchange these?"

"I don't see why not. Same number?"

"Please."

She took the four doctored decks out of the bag and returned them to the drawer. He hid a smile. A legendary hustler named Titanic Thompson had invented this hustle a century ago, and it hadn't gotten old. Four decks of casino cards were removed from the cabinet and placed in the bag. She rang up the exchange.

"Anything else I can help you with?" she asked.

The exchange couldn't have gone better. Only it wasn't time to walk. He needed to create a moment that would distract Elle from what had just happened.

"May I call you sometime?" he asked.

"Depends what you have in mind."

If the number of women he'd dated was any indication, he was a good judge of the female disposition. Elle impressed him as being a wild child and willing to take a dare.

"Rooftop rides on the Stratosphere."

"Been there, done that."

"Zip line down the Fremont Street Experience."

"You talking about SlotZilla? I was there the day it opened."

She was a toughie. He put his hands on the counter and leaned in. "How about if I take you swimming with the sharks at the Shark Reef Aquarium at Mandalay Bay? Just you, me, and thirty whitetip reef sharks. It's the most fun you can have with your clothes on."

"But that's just for special guests of the hotel."

"I've got juice. What do you say?"

"You're on, hotshot."

Elle recited her number, and Billy entered it into his cell phone's directory, then read it back to her. She nodded enthusiastically. He'd taken her thoughts to another place, the exchange of the cards fading into the recesses of her memory.

"I'll call you in a few days," he said.

She was all smiles as he left the store.

TWELVE

Billy went to the front desk and identified himself to a receptionist as a friend of Night Train. Soon he was walking down a marble hallway with a female manager who'd been taught to smile whenever in the company of wealthy guests and their friends.

"Are you with the NFL?" his escort asked.

"Do I look like a football player?" he replied.

"I meant with the commissioner's office."

"No, I'm just a friend."

They entered the lobby of the Octavius Tower and stepped onto a waiting elevator. His escort had just shared an interesting piece of information. The NFL commissioner's office knew that Night Train was hanging out at Caesars right before the Super Bowl. Athletes prepared for major sporting events by practicing, getting plenty of sleep, and eating well-balanced meals. None of those things were going to happen while staying in a Vegas casino.

They got off on the second floor, their final destination a polished wood door. His escort knocked, and the door opened to reveal a giant Samoan wearing workout shorts and a sleeveless T-shirt. For reasons unexplained, the Polynesian island of Samoa had produced more professional football players than any other foreign country. Billy had to think the place was dull as sin, and the young men were desperate to get off.

"Hello, Sammy," the escort said pleasantly. "This is Mr. William Cunningham. I believe you're expecting him."

Sammy gazed at Billy. "You the real-estate guy?"

"That's me," he said.

"You bring lots of cash? We don't take credit cards."

Either Sammy was dumber than Miss South Carolina, or it was just an act. Billy produced the stacks of money from his sports jacket.

"Well, come on in," Sammy said.

The escort departed, and Billy entered the villa. Vegas casinos boasted some of the most extravagant accommodations on the planet, and the villa had the feel of a collector's well-kept home, with museum-quality Greek urns and life-size statues filling the foyer.

"Is this stuff real?" Billy asked.

"Beats me," Sammy said. "Watch your step. We were throwing a football around earlier, and one of the urns bit the dust."

Sammy escorted Billy through the villa to a spacious covered patio overlooking the hotel pool. Sammy walked with a pronounced limp and looked to be in pain.

"You okay?" Billy asked.

"I always limp after a game," Sammy explained. "It will ease up in a few days."

The patio was the villa's showpiece and was drenched in expensive furnishings. In its center sat an antique poker table with four giant football players sitting around it. Sammy made the introductions. "This is Cunningham, the real-estate guy."

Night Train was the first to say hello. He was Hollywood handsome and wore a white silk shirt unbuttoned to his navel and tasteful jewelry. He flashed his well-known smile and pointed at the empty chair at the table. "Have a seat. Guys, introduce yourselves to our guest."

The others took turns identifying themselves. The lone white guy was named Assassin and had a shaved skull and tree-trunk arms. The Hispanic with the cauliflower ear was named Clete, and the black guy with the stoner smile was Choo-Choo. It was like entering the land of the giants, and Billy shook their hands before taking the empty seat. Placing his money on the table, he said, "Who's the banker?"

"I am. How much you got there?" Night Train asked.

"Twenty thousand big ones."

"That works." Night Train turned the money into chips and slid the stacks to his guest. Two brand-new decks of Bicycle playing cards still in their boxes sat on the table. One deck was red, the other deck blue. Night Train also slid the decks to Billy.

"You can do the honors," Night Train said.

Billy removed the decks from the boxes. The jokers and advertising cards were discarded and the cards shuffled. Billy made sure the shuffles were sloppy and uncoordinated. He had hustled other cheats before and knew the importance of presenting himself as a rube to his victims.

"First ace deals." Billy dealt cards faceup around the table using the red deck. The ace of hearts fell to Night Train. "Your deal."

He slid the blue deck to Night Train. Night Train presented the deck to Sammy to be cut. Sammy cut the cards and passed them back to Night Train. So far, the game appeared clean, although Billy knew it wouldn't stay that way for very long.

"I don't want to play any of that bullshit Texas Hold'em," Night Train said. "Game's seven-card stud with a five-hundred-dollar ante. You cool with that, Mr. Real-Estate Man?"

"I'm game," Billy said.

Everyone threw $500 into the pot. Night Train dealt each player two facedown cards and one faceup card. By the time the game was over, each player would have seven cards from which they'd make their best hand using five cards. Billy glimpsed his facedown cards. He'd drawn two clubs. His faceup card was also a club. The odds of his pulling a flush were strong. Flushes usually won in seven-card stud.

"Raise," he said when the bet came his way.

Sammy and Assassin dropped out. On the next round, Billy drew another club. He again raised when the bet came his way. Choo-Choo and Clete bowed out.

"Looks like it's just you and me," Night Train said.

Billy was dealt another club and made his flush. When it came time for the reveal, there was more than ten thousand in the pot. Night Train's face crumbled upon seeing Billy's hand.

"I didn't think you had it," his host said.

"Beginner's luck," he said.

"Way to go," Sammy said.

"I think he's a ringer," Clete half joked.

He raked in the chips. This was starting out well, but it wouldn't end that way. There was a science to cheating at cards that relied upon letting a victim win early to bring down their guard. When the victim was properly fattened, the cheats would go for the kill.

"How about a cold drink?" Night Train asked.

"I could use a brew," Billy said. "I think congratulations are in order. You guys played a hell of a game yesterday."

"Thanks. We played so good that our coaches gave us the afternoon off. Choo-Choo, how about a cold beer for our guest."

Choo-Choo took a glistening Corona from a cooler and popped the cap with his teeth.

"That's impressive," Billy said.

The deal rotated to Clete. Clete announced the game was five-card draw and sailed the cards around the table. Billy watched intently but saw no sleight of hand. There were only so many ways to cheat at poker. Peeking the victim's cards through a wall was a common method, marking the backs another. Playing on a patio ruled out peeking, and Billy had done a riffle test while shuffling and had not spotted any marks. So how was Night Train going to fleece him?

Ten minutes later, he found out.

The deal was back to Night Train. Sammy gave the red deck a cut, and Night Train slid the deck off the table and squared it. For a fleeting instant, the red deck was out of sight. Then Night Train started to deal. The hair stood up on the back of Billy's neck.

"Seven-card stud with a thousand-dollar ante," Night Train announced. "Let's see if I can win some of my money back."

Despite the move's invisibility, Billy knew what had occurred. Night Train had switched a stacked deck in his lap with the red deck on the table. Long hours of practice had gone into the move, most likely in front of a mirror. Hustlers called this a cooler because it was thought that the switched deck was cooler to the touch.

Billy threw a thousand bucks into the pot and checked his hand. His faceup card was a jack and his two facedown cards were also jacks. Three jacks was a powerful starting hand, and he guessed the deck was stacked for him to get a full house, while another player would get four of a kind or a straight flush and clean him out.

Assassin started the betting, Clete raised, and Night Train raised him. By the time the bet came to Billy, it was up to four thousand bucks.

"Call," he said.

As his chips hit the pot, his elbow deliberately brushed his Corona. The bottle fell over and splashed beer on the player's hands as well as the blue deck sitting to the side, ruining everything. Night Train's eyes flared. Billy played stupid and apologized up a storm.

"I am so damn clumsy it isn't funny. I'm sorry, guys."

Nobody spoke. Without cards, there was no game. That was fine, except Billy had $15,000 of the football players' money, most of which he'd won off Night Train. If they ended the game now, he'd leave with that money. Night Train was having none of that, and he placed a call to the concierge on his cell phone.

"I need two brand-new decks of cards brought to my villa. One red, one blue. Hurry up."

Billy engaged in small talk while they waited for the cards. Night Train was quietly fuming and not happy with this change of events. He had been cheating other athletes since college and probably had never been cheated himself. That was about to change. There was a paddle for everyone's ass, and the famous football player was about to get royally spanked.

THIRTEEN

A uniformed bellboy delivered two brand-new decks to the villa. The cards were in a plastic bag from the Emperor's Emporium along with a receipt. Billy smiled to himself, feeling confident that at least one of the decks in the bag had his secret scuff marks on it.

Night Train paid the bellboy for the decks and generously tipped him.

"Can I get your autograph?" the bellboy asked.

Night Train scribbled his name on a napkin using the bellboy's pen. Night Train was a different person around the bellboy, with a broad smile creasing his face and a friendly demeanor. He went back to being a prick when the bellboy was gone.

"Let's get this game going," Night Train said.

The new decks were removed from their boxes and shuffled. Billy assisted in this ritual and felt his secret scuff marks on the edges of both decks.

"My deal. Let's change things up and play Texas Hold'em," Night Train said. "Thousand-dollar ante, boys, no blinds."

Earlier, Night Train had called Texas Hold'em a bullshit game. The fact that he'd chosen to play it now was an indication that he had a method of cheating specific to Texas Hold'em that he planned to use.

Employing specific scams for different games was done to confuse victims and was common among hustlers who cheated at poker.

Night Train dealt the round. Billy got crummy cards but played them anyway. Night Train began toying with his chips. As if on cue, the others dropped out. Night Train kept raising and Billy kept calling. Night Train triumphantly revealed a pair of kings. Billy threw his cards into the muck without showing them.

"Good hand," Billy said.

"What did you have?" Night Train asked.

"Rags."

"Hah. I knew you were bluffing."

The scam was called playing top hand. By toying with his chips, Night Train was telling the others his cards were strong. The others folded, letting Night Train play heads up against Billy. Over the course of the night, the player in the game with the best hand would go up against Billy and would drain Billy's bankroll until he was flat broke.

The deal came to Billy. It was payback time.

"Texas Hold'em, thousand-dollar ante, no blinds."

The football players tossed their chips into the pot, and Billy dealt the cards while feeling the edges. Of all poker scams, using touch cards was one of the strongest. The cheat didn't have to stare at the cards while reading the marks but let his fingers do the work.

In Texas Hold'em, each player got two cards. By feeling the cards, Billy knew that his opponents had weak hands, except for Night Train, who'd been dealt an ace and king, known as Big Slick. Night Train again toyed with his chips and the others dropped out.

"Five thousand," Night Train said.

Billy peeked at his two cards. He had a pair of sevens. He decided to call Night Train's bet and threw chips into the pot. Picking up the deck, he burned the top card and dealt three community cards, called the flop. Ace, seven, king. Night Train had two pair, while he had three of a kind. He couldn't have scripted it better and put on his best poker face.

"Ten thousand," Night Train said.

"Call," he said.

He threw more chips into the pot, picked up the deck, burned the top card, and dealt another community card, called the turn. It was a deuce. Nothing had changed.

"How much you got left?" Night Train asked.

He counted his remaining chips. "Twenty thousand, two hundred."

"Twenty thousand, two hundred it is."

He hesitated. Night Train had to believe his hand was best. He didn't want to act too quickly and tip off his winning cards.

"What do you have, an ace in the hole?" he asked.

"Call me and find out," Night Train said.

He made the call. He burned the top card and dealt the final community card, called the river. It was a four, another meaningless card. He'd won the hand.

"What have you got?" Night Train asked.

"Hold on. We're not finished betting," he said.

Night Train's eyebrows arched suspiciously. "You're out of chips. We don't take checks or IOUs in this game, Mr. Real-Estate Man."

The others laughed. Billy made a show of removing his wristwatch and tossing it into the pot. "That little baby is a Rolex Presidential eighteen-karat-gold watch with a retail value of twenty-five thousand bucks. Check it out if you don't believe me."

Night Train examined the watch, then passed it around the table. Assassin seemed to know a thing or two about jewelry and said, "It's the real deal."

Night Train tapped his fingertips on the table. Billy had tried to bluff him earlier and lost. This felt no different, and he flipped over his cards. "I call. Aces and kings."

He showed his cards. "Three sevens. I win."

Night Train stared in disbelief at the cards. Billy raked in the pot and counted his chips. He'd won $60,000 of the football players' money.

"Sixty grand. Pay up."

Night Train slowly shook his head.

"What's that supposed to mean?" he asked.

"It means I don't have the money. I'll have to owe you."

"You said this game didn't take IOUs."

"Look, man, I'm good for it. I'll have the money wired from my bank. You'll have it tomorrow."

"Fair enough. You got a pen and something to write on?"

"Choo-Choo, help our friend out here," Night Train said.

Choo-Choo fetched a ballpoint and a notepad from inside. Billy used them to write up an IOU for sixty large, which included the date, names of participants, and where the game had taken place. Up until now, they'd been playing a friendly game of poker; that was about to change in a negative way, and he stood up from his chair in case he needed to take off running, then slid the IOU and pen across the table to Night Train's spot.

"Here you go," he said.

Night Train lowered his head to read the IOU. As he did, Billy took out his cell phone. It was a Droid, and it had a unique feature not available on other cell phones. If the user forcefully snapped his wrist, the Droid's photo app came to life. Lowering the cell phone to his side, he snapped his wrist below the table, then raised the phone to chest height and snapped a photograph of Night Train putting his John Hancock on the bottom of the IOU. The Droid's flash was like a bomb going off, and Night Train leaped out of his chair. "What the hell are you doing?"

"Memorializing our agreement," he said.

"No photographs."

"Then how's anyone going to know that IOU came from you?"

"Don't you trust me?"

"Not really."

Night Train came around the table. The look on his face betrayed real apprehension. "Listen, man, I'm going to be straight with you.

We're not supposed to be at Caesars right now. If that photograph ever got out, the media would destroy us and we'd all get hurt. You don't want that to happen, do you? So just make it go away."

"All right. But I want some collateral with this IOU," he said.

"If I give you my father's watch, will you erase that picture?"

"Let me see the watch first."

Night Train retreated into the villa and returned holding an old wristwatch with a cracked leather band and a faded inscription on its back.

Presented to Frank McClain

For thirty-five years of service

1975 to 2010

By

Thomas H. Wilson Co.

"My daddy gave this watch to me before he died," Night Train said. "It's worth more to me than all the tea in China. Is that good enough for you?"

"That works." Billy slipped the timepiece into his pocket. Holding the Droid so Night Train could see the screen, he deleted the incriminating photo. Night Train visibly relaxed.

"Happy now?" he asked.

"Yeah," Night Train said.

Night Train and his pals were veteran cheats and had probably never lost this much before, and he wondered how long it would take before it kicked in that they'd been swindled. He wrote down his cell phone number on the notepad and left it on the table.

"That's my number. Call me when you have the sixty grand," he said.

Then he got the hell out of there.

FOURTEEN

Billy was flying high as he left Caesars. There was an art to swindling another cheat that required a delicate level of finesse. The fact that Night Train hadn't threatened to throw him off the balcony told Billy that he'd handled things just right.

Traffic barely moved. A show was being filmed at the LINQ Hotel and Casino, closing a lane to accommodate the production trucks. Vegas should have been a natural location for TV shows and movies, but most production companies avoided the town. The amount of red tape required to film was a nightmare and required sign-off from the dreaded gaming board.

It gave him an idea. If the production at LINQ continued, maybe he could rip the joint off. Films and movies required plenty of people and equipment, all of it a distraction to the casino's surveillance department. Using his cell phone, he got on the Internet and typed *Las Vegas film production* into Google. He got a hit and followed the link to a story in the local paper. A company called Bad Dog Productions was filming a pilot called *Night and Day* at the LINQ starring an actress named Maggie Flynn. How ironic was that? Mags had left Vegas for the bright lights of Hollywood and, like an escaped convict, had gotten caught and sent right back. LINQ's entrance was a block away, and he decided to pay her a visit.

- - -

LINQ was a no-frills joint, the lobby without furniture. A receptionist smiled as Billy approached, happy to have another person to talk to. "Good afternoon and welcome to LINQ."

"Hi. I need to use a house phone," he said.

"House phones are across from the elevators. Are you looking for someone?"

"Maggie Flynn. She's an old friend."

"Ms. Flynn the actress? I spoke with her a few moments ago. Would you like me to ring her room and announce your arrival?"

Maggie had done a number on him before breaking things off, and he decided to repay the favor. "That would be great. Tell her Rand Waters is here to see her."

"Rand Waters the TV producer? I totally love your shows. *Sweet and Sassy*'s my fave."

"Thank you. Those are words I never get tired of hearing."

The receptionist made the call. "Ms. Flynn said to come right up. Room 2081."

"Thanks. You've been very helpful."

He rode alone to the twentieth floor and walked down a hallway littered with room-service trays. When he rapped on the door to Mags's room, a voice from within said, "It's open," and he entered. The suite was on the low end of the Vegas experience and reminded him of an old Billy Joel song. "In hell there's a big hotel where the bar just closed and the windows never opened, no phone, so you can't call home, and the TV works but the clicker is broken." An open script lay on the coffee table. Next to it, a bottle of Chivas and a vial of sleeping pills.

"You could have put me up some place decent, you know," Mags called from the next room. "There's no hot water half the fucking time, and the carpet smells like bad weed."

He picked up the script and started reading. The plot of *Night and Day* revolved around a female gaming agent who solved crimes during the day and ripped off the casinos at night, hence the clever title. For a kicker, the money she stole went to charity.

"For the love of Christ, how did you get in here?"

Mags stood before him wrapped in a bath towel and wearing no makeup. Her eyes looked tired, and she'd lost weight since he'd last seen her.

"I lied to the girl downstairs," he said. "How you been?"

"I should call security and have you tossed."

"I just wanted to say hi and congratulate you. You've got your own TV show."

"Thanks. It's just a pilot."

She let her towel drop to the floor, revealing heavenly skin. There was nothing like Irish hot, and the sight of her took his breath away. From the closet, she grabbed a fluffy white bathrobe supplied by the hotel and slipped it on. "Fix me a scotch, will you?"

"I thought you quit drinking."

"What are you, my sponsor? Straight up, two ice cubes. Make it strong."

He took the Chivas to the minibar and fixed the drinks. Through a picture window, he spied a Ferris wheel behind the hotel that did not have a single rider. Vegas was about action, and this place didn't have any. It was beyond depressing.

Mags parked herself on a couch. He served her drink and pulled up a chair.

"You're staying?" she asked.

"Want to throw me out? Just for old time's sake?"

"No, Billy. You know I still care about you."

He sat down and they clinked glasses. "So what's with the pills? And why are you so thin? You don't look good."

"I take the pills because I can't sleep. I'm on a diet because the cameras add ten pounds to my face and make me look fat. Any more questions?"

"Are you happy?"

"I'm having the time of my fucking life."

"Did your daughter make it out to see you?"

Her face softened. She'd gotten knocked up as a teenager and hadn't raised her kid. Now that her daughter was an adult, she was trying to make amends. "Amber's flying out tomorrow so we can spend a few days together. I can't wait."

"That's great. She's going to see you in a whole new light."

She stared at the floor and started to cry. It happened so fast that Billy didn't know what to do. He pulled his chair closer and tried to console her.

"You look really ugly when you cry," he said.

She laughed through her tears. They'd met on the mean streets of Providence another lifetime ago, and she'd introduced him to the rackets while also breaking his heart. The waterworks ended, and she emptied her glass and made him fix her another.

"Thanks for asking about Amber. So, did you ever rip this place off?"

"Once."

"You told me that you ripped off every casino in Vegas multiple times. Liar."

He brought the new drink and took his spot on the couch. "There was a reason."

"Hmmm . . . you mix these good and strong. I'm listening."

"We were past-posting at roulette and won thirty grand. When the guy in my crew went to cash out, the cashier didn't have enough to pay him off. The cashier asked my guy to come back the next day to get our dough. Needless to say, we never came back."

"Why not?"

"We ripped off the joint during the graveyard shift, so the burden fell on the manager of the day shift to pay us out," he explained. "Believe me, that guy isn't going to pay us without studying the surveillance tapes. If he sees anything wrong, the gaming board gets called."

"That's a cool story. Can I share it with my writers? It would make a good episode."

"Be my guest."

"What past-posting move did you use?"

"The Savannah."

"I'll call you if I need any pointers. You'd like that, wouldn't you?"

Since their relationship had ended, Mags had taken pleasure in torturing him whenever they got together. It was messed up, yet he kept coming back for more.

"I need to beat it. You take care of yourself."

She grabbed his wrist. "You didn't come here for a social visit. There's something on your mind. Spit it out, lover boy."

"I'm working a super con with a family of cheats called the Gypsies. The gaming board has fingered two of the kids, and the father's getting nervous. We might have to bring in reinforcements. That's where you come in. I'll make it worth your while. What do you say?"

"In case you hadn't noticed, I'm not in the rackets anymore. I'm an actress."

"Hollywood's a filthy business. Even when you win, you lose."

"Fuck you."

"I'm talking about one night's work. If your pilot fails, you have a security net. Or you can give the money to your kid and make her dreams come true. It's a sweet deal."

"I should have called security when I first laid eyes on you."

"But you didn't. You knew I had something, and you were dying to hear what it was. You haven't changed, Mags, and you never will. You're a born thief."

"Get out." A phone rang in the next room. "That's probably Rand. He always calls before he shows up, unlike some people I know. Don't let the door hit you on the way out."

He started to leave. He'd planted the seed and needed to make it grow. Turning around, he said, "Sleep on it. I'll call you tomorrow. Your number hasn't changed, has it?"

Her glass missed his head by inches.

- - -

Downstairs in the lobby, he caught his first glimpse of the man who'd promised to make Mags a star. Rand Waters was an aging lounge lizard with fluffy orange hair and a cell phone glued to his ear. His jeans were the five-hundred-dollar variety, his black T-shirt Dolce & Gabbana. He breezed past Billy as if the young hustler didn't exist.

Billy felt the overwhelming urge to coldcock Waters and put him on the floor. Mags was being run ragged, and this prick would go right on doing it until another pretty face happened along.

Waters got on an elevator, and Billy started to follow. His cell phone vibrated, and he pulled it out. He'd gotten a text embedded with a video, which began to play on its own. Leon sat bound to a chair, his face a bloody pulp. One of the little ones entered the picture and slit his driver's throat, creating a bloody apron. Broken Tooth appeared, puffing a cigarette.

"Call me when you get this," the Chinese gangster said.

The elevator door closed in his face. His hands trembled as he made the call.

"Why did you do that?" he said, nearly shouting.

"Because I felt like it," Broken Tooth said.

"That's it? No other reason."

"I don't need a reason to kill people."

"The deal's off. I'm not working with you."

"I know where your pretty friends live. Want them to die, too? I don't think so. Meet me in a half hour at Big Wong. I want to hear how your meeting with the football players went."

The line went dead. It was all Billy could do not to throw the phone to the ground.

FIFTEEN

He drove to Spring Valley and crawled down the three-mile stretch of strip centers known as Chinatown until he found Big Wong. The lunch crowd was long gone and there was plenty of parking. Easing his vehicle into a space, he got on his cell phone and called Gabe.

"Hey, Billy, how did it go with the football players?" Gabe answered.

"I'll tell you later. I need you to explain how the rigged coin toss works," he said.

"You don't sound so hot. Is everything okay?"

He was still seeing red over Leon's senseless murder and had decided to delay telling his crew the bad news. "Everything's fine. Now lay it on me."

"You want me to explain over the phone?"

He'd taught his crew to avoid discussing jobs over the phone whenever possible. But there was the matter of keeping Pepper and Misty alive, so he decided to do it anyway.

"Yes, over the phone."

"Okay, here it is. The coin used for the coin toss in the Super Bowl is a ceremonial coin and is extra thick. That allowed me to fit a mercury slug in its center without it being noticeable. The mercury can be moved with a transmitter hidden in a cell phone. If I want the coin to land heads, I move the slug to the tails side; if I want the coin to land tails, I move the slug to the heads side. It works like a charm."

"Explain the deal again with the head referee."

"The head referee's name's Gordon Barnett, and he's in Phoenix preparing for the game with the other refs. Cory found out that Barnett has gambling debts, so Cory plans to bribe him fifty grand in return for Barnett using the gimmicked coin for the coin toss."

The whole thing sounded risky. Gimmicked coin, a crooked ref, and hoping the dirty players did their jobs right. He'd have to do a strong sell on Broken Tooth to make it fly.

"I need to run. I'll call you later," he said.

- - -

Broken Tooth sat at a corner table eating greasy spareribs. Seeing Billy approach, he chopped the air with his hand. His bodyguard put down his utensils and stood up.

"I thought we had a deal," Billy said. "I help you fix the game, and you spare my driver."

"Sit down," Broken Tooth said.

"I asked you a question. You come into my town and start whacking my people, and you think you're going to get away with it? Fat fucking chance, pal."

"Your driver is still alive."

He rocked back on his heels. "Then who's in the video?"

"Some other guy. Go back through kitchen, say hi to your driver."

"You'd better not be screwing with me."

Broken Tooth licked the grease off his fingers and grinned. The little bastard was toying with him, and he walked to the back of the restaurant and entered the steamy kitchen. The kitchen's back door was ajar, leading him outside to where Broken Tooth's rental was parked. Leon sat in front with the other henchman, looking very much alive.

An invisible weight lifted from his shoulders. "You okay?" he asked through the glass. The passenger window lowered. "Fuckers made me watch," his driver said.

He went back inside and took a seat at Broken Tooth's table.

"You hungry? Spareribs are real tasty," Broken Tooth said.

"No thanks. Who's the guy in the video?"

"Some dumb junkie. Your driver's diabetic, so I sent my men to his apartment to get his insulin. Junkie tried to rob them in the parking lot. Bad idea. My men brought him back to our place and slit his throat."

"And you made my driver watch."

"Why not?"

In kidnap situations, the kidnappers were less likely to snuff their victim the longer they were around him. This wasn't the case with Broken Tooth, who would kill Leon as easily as stepping on a bug. "You like screwing with people, don't you?" he said.

"Just want to remind you who's boss," Broken Tooth said.

"You're the boss."

"That's right." Broken Tooth picked up a piece of romaine lettuce off his plate, which he kneaded between his fingertips until soft. The Batman lunch box was retrieved from the floor and a panel unsnapped. Broken Tooth fed the lettuce to the animal residing inside.

"What's in there, a pet rat?" he asked.

"You think I carry a rat around with me? Fuck you."

"Sorry, man, I'm just curious."

"What I have is a fighting champion." Broken Tooth removed a small wooden cage from the lunch box, which contained a giant green cricket. The insect made a loud hissing noise by vibrating its wings. "His name is the General. I purchased him at an auction in Shanghai for twenty thousand dollars. He is the best fighting cricket in the world."

"Where do they hold cricket fights?"

"Everywhere people like to gamble. They are an obsession in Asia."

Vegas had a large Asian population, and Billy guessed cricket fights were held in private homes with plenty of betting. The General was Broken Tooth's alibi in case the police decided to pick him up and question him. The guy was no dummy; that was for sure. Broken Tooth returned the cage to the lunch box and closed it. "Did you go see Night Train?"

"We were introduced this afternoon. The concierge at Caesars got me invited to a poker game in Night Train's villa. I won sixty grand of his money."

"You cheated him?"

"Let's just say we cheated each other and I came out on top. He didn't have the money to pay me, so we're going to hook up tomorrow so he can settle his debt. That's when I plan to persuade him to fix the game next Sunday."

"Why did you wait? Why not now?"

"Night Train is still a little dazed. When he wakes up tomorrow morning, he's going to realize what happened. It will make him look at me differently and realize that he's not dealing with some schmuck off the street."

"He'll figure this out in his sleep?"

Billy nodded. An important part of poker cheating was cooling out the sucker. After the sucker lost, the cheat needed to convince the sucker that he'd played smart and was simply the victim of bad luck. If this wasn't done, the sucker would go to bed thinking about it and arise the next day realizing he'd been fleeced. He deliberately hadn't cooled out Night Train and felt certain the famous football player would figure out a swindle had taken place.

"You're a smart guy. Always thinking ahead," Broken Tooth said. "So how are you going to fix coin toss at Super Bowl?"

Billy put his elbows on the table. He had no idea if the scam that Gabe had devised would really work, for the simple reason that he'd never tried it before. But he couldn't let his doubt become apparent.

He needed to sell Broken Tooth on his plan and he needed to do it in a big way. "One of my crew used to be a jeweler. He can gaff any piece of equipment you give him and make it look real. He created a special coin that matches the ceremonial coin used for the Super Bowl, only his coin is electronic and can be made to land either heads or tails using a transmitter hidden in a cell phone."

"What about the ref? Have you got him in your back pocket?"

"The head ref for the Super Bowl has gambling debts. My guys are going to bribe him tomorrow over breakfast. All the ref has to do is use our coin for the coin toss, and we're set. The rest will be up to Night Train and his boys."

Broken Tooth nodded approvingly. "How much will the ref set you back?"

"Fifty grand. It's steep, but I don't see that we have any other choice."

"Maybe you can kill ref later and get your money back."

"You know, I never thought of that."

Broken Tooth seemed to be sold on the play and picked at his spare-ribs. If Billy had been talking to a local hoodlum, an offer of a drink or food would have been made as a sign of respect. Broken Tooth had made no such offer to his guest. The significance wasn't lost on Billy. This man was not his friend and never would be.

"What should Night Train's take be? That's the first thing he's going to ask me tomorrow when I go to see him," Billy said.

"Offer him a payout of half a million dollars for each prop bet," Broken Tooth said. "He will try to negotiate you up. Settle at one million for each bet."

"Including the coin toss?"

"Yes."

The scam was now complete. Night Train and his teammates would get a four-million-dollar payday for throwing a handful of inconsequential plays in the Super Bowl. Night Train had larceny in his heart and so did his buddies. They would say yes in a heartbeat.

"How's the payoff work?" Billy asked.

"I will wire the money to Night Train's bank account a day before the game," Broken Tooth said. "Night Train has taken bribes before, so it's safe to assume he has an offshore account. You will need to get his banking information from him."

"Got it. Last question. When will you let Leon go?"

"After the big game is over."

"Is that a promise?"

"You bet."

It was as good an arrangement as Billy could hope for. Rising from his chair, he started to walk out of the restaurant. Moments later, he was back at the table.

"I just had a thought. What if Night Train takes the money and screws us?"

"Night Train is not going to do that. Super Bowl is his last game. He's going to retire. Same for his teammates. They're all getting old and don't care anymore."

"Is that why he's hanging out at Caesars after practice?"

"You got it."

Smart cheats did their homework before doing a job. Broken Tooth got an A-plus for this one, and he found his opinion of the Chinese gangster changing. Broken Tooth knew the angles and understood the risks. So long as he didn't hurt Leon, Billy could work with him, and he left the restaurant believing that he was about to be a part of the first cheating team to successfully fix the biggest sporting event in the world.

SIXTEEN

Most cheats in Vegas lived in sleepy neighborhoods with neatly trimmed front lawns. Their children attended public schools and their wives belonged to the PTA and were den mothers with the Cub Scouts. They tried to blend in, and for the most part they succeeded.

Billy was having none of that. You could either have a long, boring life or a short, exciting one, and he'd opted for life in the fast lane. His penthouse in Turnberry Towers was a perfect example. It was twenty-six hundred square feet of pure opulence, filled with the finest furnishings money could buy. His wardrobe was nothing to sneeze at, either, with enough threads and tailored jackets to stock a haberdashery. Throw in all the expensive watches, cigarette lighters, and jewelry he'd accumulated over the years, and you had a real statement.

Most cheats would never flaunt their wealth, fearful that the gaming board would one day bust them and confiscate everything they owned. Billy saw things differently. The gaming board could nip at his heels all they wanted; it wasn't going to change the way he lived.

He pulled into Turnberry, and a uniformed valet opened his door. He made it a point to tip the staff generously and give them gifts at the holidays. As a result, they watched his back.

"Good evening, Mr. Cunningham. Will you be going out later? I can park the car nearby, if you'd like," the valet said.

"I'm staying in tonight," he said.

"Certainly. By the way, two gentlemen are in the lobby to see you."

Billy had experienced enough surprises in the past few days to last a lifetime.

"Describe them," he said.

"They're both young with curly hair," the valet replied. "They said they needed to speak with you. I thought it was best you know."

It was Cory and Morris. They aspired to run their own crew one day and often met with Billy to discuss scams they were cooking up. An unannounced visit meant something was up.

"Thanks for the heads-up. Do you follow football?"

"Of course, Mr. Cunningham. Doesn't everybody?"

"Who are you betting on for the Super Bowl?"

"The Rebels."

"What's the point spread?"

"Last time I checked, the game was even money."

Inside the lobby, he found Cory and Morris sitting on a couch beneath a piece of wall art that doubled as a waterfall. Both were buried in their cell phones and didn't see him enter. He took their heads and gently knocked them together. "Wake up, knuckleheads," he said.

"Hey, Billy!" they both said in surprise.

"It's a beautiful day. Why aren't you outside stealing?"

"We need to talk to you about Travis," Cory said.

"What about him?"

"Travis called us earlier," Cory said. "He's putting together his own crew and wants us to join him."

Billy's jaw tightened. "You can't be serious."

"It gets worse. I asked Travis what our roles would be and how much he planned to pay us. He promised to give us a bigger share than you're giving us. Then he dropped the bomb and told me that Broken Tooth is backing him, if you can believe that."

"Travis is in business with Broken Tooth?" Billy said.

"That's what he said."

"How did you leave it?"

"I told him that we needed to think about it. Travis asked me not to tell you, and I promised him that I wouldn't. Then we drove over here."

Billy's head was spinning. He'd spared Travis last night, and this was how the big man repaid him. He needed to put a lid on this right now.

"Let's take this upstairs," he said.

- - -

Despite what people thought, there was honor among thieves, along with a list of rules that people who made their living stealing were expected to live by. It was called the *Vory v. Zakone*, or Thieves' Code, and had been established in Russia centuries ago. Billy had been taught the code from his mentor, Lou Profaci, and in turn had drummed it into the heads of every person who'd run with him.

They sat at the dining room table. Billy spent a moment sketching a cartoon on a pad of paper. Done, he turned the pad around and slid it across the table so Cory and Morris could see it.

"It looks like a bag of money," Morris said.

"That's exactly what it is," he said. "In Russia, thieves wear tattoos to signify their loyalty to their profession. A tattoo with a bag of money means the thief is committed to stealing and wouldn't resort to killing to make his living or put another thief in harm's way. If a thief broke this rule, the other thieves would kill him, no questions asked. Make sense?"

Cory and Morris had been raised in a foster home and often reacted identically when a question was posed to them. It was unnerving until you got used to it. They both swallowed hard.

"Yeah, it makes sense," Cory said.

"I get it," Morris said.

"Travis broke that rule," he said. "Broken Tooth approached Travis wanting to fix the Super Bowl. Problem is, Broken Tooth needs me to do the fixing. Broken Tooth knew I'd never partner up with him, so he went through a back door with Travis's help."

Cory's face turned sour. "Why would Travis do that?"

"That's a good question. Travis said he needed the money, but that's bullshit. I would have given him the money. He knows that, and hopefully so do the rest of you."

"You'd be the first person I'd come to if I got in a jam," Cory said.

"Me, too," Morris added.

"Now you're telling me that Travis wants to run his own crew, and he's got Broken Tooth's backing. That doesn't make sense, either. If Travis wanted to leave, I wouldn't have stopped him. There's something else at play here. All I can guess is, I said something out of line, and Travis has been walking around holding a grudge, waiting to pay me back."

"That's way fucked up," Cory said.

"Travis is a traitor," Morris said. "Why didn't you shoot him when you had the chance? The stupid prick got Leon kidnapped."

Billy didn't like to be challenged. Not that long ago, he'd cut Cory and Morris loose, then changed his mind and brought them back into the fold. "I gave Travis a second chance just like I gave you guys a second chance. I'm not apologizing for it. Understood?"

They both nodded simultaneously.

"That doesn't mean that Travis isn't going to get what's coming to him," he went on. "It just won't happen right away. This Super Bowl fix is huge, and I want to see it through."

"But you are going to pay him back," Cory said.

"Damn straight I am. But not right away. Revenge is a plate best served cold."

They both nodded and smiled.

"I need to ask you a question," he said. "Broken Tooth is going to give us the Vegas sports books to fleece, while he takes everything else. Travis said we could make ten million bucks on the four proposition bets. Does that number sound right to you?"

"Travis is lowballing you," Cory said. "He's probably planning to make more and share the money with Broken Tooth, the dirty prick."

"Give me a real number."

"Fifteen million, easy," Cory said.

"And not draw heat?"

"There's so much money bet on the Super Bowl that no one will know."

The Super Bowl fix was sounding better all the time. He fetched three bottles of beer from the fridge, and they went onto the balcony to toast their new venture. The sunlight was starting to fade, soon to be replaced by five million watts of neon burning up the desert night.

"Look, Billy, this all sounds fine and dandy, but what about Leon?" Cory asked, never one to mince words. "Is he going to come out of this with his skin?"

"We dig Leon," Morris added. "He's part of the family."

"Broken Tooth promised to release Leon after the Super Bowl," he said.

"Do you believe him?" Cory asked.

He hesitated. He wanted to think the Chinese gangster's word was worth something, but he now knew that wasn't the case. If Broken Tooth were backing Travis, the Chinese gangster would probably have his henchmen murder Leon just to tie up loose ends.

"No, I don't," he said truthfully.

"Can we save him?" Morris asked.

Vegas was a town that rarely gave you a second chance. If Leon's number was up, it was up. But that didn't mean that Billy wasn't going to try.

"First, we have to find him," he said. "I met Broken Tooth at a restaurant called Big Wong in Chinatown. Big Wong serves authentic Chinese cuisine, and so do a number of other restaurants in town. That's probably what Broken Tooth and his men are eating while they're staying here. The more authentic, the better."

"You want us to check these places out?" Cory said.

"Correct. I'm guessing Broken Tooth is ordering a lot of takeout. Go around lunchtime and see if they come into one of these joints. If you spot them, get in your car and follow them. Hopefully they'll take you to where Leon is being held."

"What then?" Morris asked.

He hadn't gotten that far. He might get a gun and take Broken Tooth out himself and free his driver. Or he'd hire some guys to do it. It didn't really matter. Once he knew where Leon was being held captive, he'd take the necessary steps to save his driver's life.

"I'll think of something," he said.

SEVENTEEN

Tuesday, early morning, twelve days before the Super Bowl

There was nothing glamorous about shooting a TV show. Early mornings, late nights, endless takes. Mags was working on the day's scene when there was a knock on her trailer door.

"Can it wait? I'm memorizing my lines," she said.

"We need to chat for a minute. It's important," Rand said.

"Well, then come on in."

Rand made his entrance. As was befitting a Hollywood producer, he wore designer jeans and a gold T-shirt that appeared glued to his body, along with a pair of sunglasses perched on the tip of his nose. Mags took the shooting script off her lap and tossed it to the floor.

"Whoever wrote this doesn't know jack," she said.

"It's a she, and she's one of the best scriptwriters in the biz," Rand said.

"Well, she doesn't know shit about casinos, and you can tell her I said so."

Today's scene had Mags walking through a casino and catching a player slipping a metal slug into a slot machine. The scene was intended to display Mags's innate ability to spot cons and grifts and was integral to her character as a gaming agent. The problem was, any dummy could spot a slug from a mile away. The scene sucked.

"We have guests," Rand said. "The gaming board decided to pay us a visit. They caught wind that our show features a gaming agent and aren't happy about it."

Her stomach did a flip-flop. She had a history with the gaming board, and it wasn't a pretty one. For eighteen months, she'd acted as a snitch while being under the thumb of an agent named Frank Grimes. To keep Grimes under control, she'd had an affair with him, a decision she'd come to regret. "I thought you cleared the show with the gaming board," she said.

"I thought I had. It seems they just got around to reading the script. Be your usual charming self, and everything will go fine."

"When did you send it to them? Yesterday?"

Rand flashed a phony smile. Mags guessed Rand had delayed showing the gaming board the script because her character moonlighted as a cheat. TV shows were a boon to the local economy, and her producer was banking on the gaming board giving them a pass.

"Have you ever dealt with the gaming board before?" she asked.

"No. What are they like?"

"You're in for a real treat."

- - -

"They're waiting for us inside one of the hotel's restaurants," Rand said as they entered LINQ. "Please be on your best behavior with these folks. I don't want them shutting us down."

"How much of the script have they read?" Mags asked.

"All of it. They even e-mailed me some suggestions. I told them their ideas were great and that I wanted to use them and give them writing credits."

"Aren't we clever."

"I think we're going to be okay. If not, I'll offer to send the show's carpenters over to their houses to do some repairs. That should do the trick."

"Won't the studio object?"

"It's built into the budget. When you shoot on location, you have to bribe the cops or local politicians to cut through red tape and get things done. The best bribe is free repairs. They're impossible to trace."

Guy Fieri's Vegas Kitchen & Bar had more words in its title than entrees on the menu. It was a brightly lit room with as much charm as an army mess hall. Rand escorted her to a corner table where a pair of gaming agents awaited them. One had a shiny butter stain adorning his necktie. It was her old pal Frank.

Introductions were made. The second agent was a stocky Latina named Valles who ran the gaming board's PR department. Clutched in her hand was a copy of the shooting script with no less than fifty yellow Post-it tabs on pages where the desired changes were to be made. A waitress took drink orders. Coffee all around.

Rand picked up the script from the table and casually thumbed through it. "Is this it? I thought there'd be more," he said sarcastically.

"We tried to keep things within reason," Valles replied. "The gaming board plays a prominent role in your series. We'd prefer our agents be showcased in a positive light."

"The main character in the series cheats the casinos. Is that a problem?"

"We think it is."

Valles and Rand locked stares the way bulls lock horns. This was not going to be fun. To Mags's surprise, it was Grimes who seized the moment. "Why don't Miss Flynn and I move to another table so you two can talk this through? It might make things easier."

"That's a terrific idea, Frank," Valles said. "Nice meeting you, Miss Flynn."

"Same here," Mags said.

- - -

Grimes and Mags took a table away from the brewing battle. The waitress was on the ball and brought their coffees. Grimes lifted his steaming mug in a toast.

"Congratulations. Here's to making it," he said.

"Are you trying to be funny?" Mags asked.

"Not at all. Remember the first time we slept together? I took you to a suite at the Wynn and we ordered room service and screwed like rabbits. When we were done, you told me you were going to make it big one day, and now you have. Not many people do that, Maggie."

Mags vividly remembered their first sexual encounter but not for the same reasons. It was the first time she'd seen Frank naked. His body was covered in curly black hair and looked like something that had washed up dead on the beach after a low tide. She'd made him turn off the lights and had shut her eyes and imagined she was screwing a young Harrison Ford.

"Thanks," she said. "So how are things with you? Still pounding the pavement?"

"My boss put in his papers for retirement. I've applied for his job. Unfortunately, a lot of other agents in the department are vying for his desk. All I can do is hope."

"That asshole Tricaricco is finally leaving? It's about time."

"Bill isn't that bad, once you get to know him."

"He wasn't very nice to me. Look, I hope you get the job. You've earned it."

"Do you really mean that?"

"Yeah, Frank, I do. Good luck."

They clinked mugs. Mags believed in keeping your friends close and your enemies closer. Frank was her enemy and always would be, even if she was no longer scamming the casinos. Frank put down his mug and cleared his throat. "I've been meaning to call you. I need your help on a case I'm working. If I can break it, I should get the promotion."

"Help you how?"

"I'm trying to nail some cheaters. You don't have to give me names or anything. Just point me in the right direction."

Mags suppressed the urge to laugh in his face. If anything, she would send Frankie boy in the wrong direction, to hell with his new job.

"What's the case?" she asked.

"Six months ago, a Money Vault progressive slot machine at Galaxy Casino paid off a huge jackpot. The winner was a retired school principal from Sacramento named Linda Olson. The Money Vault slots pays off once every five years, and the gaming board always does a background check of the winners. This lady didn't pass the smell test."

"How so?"

"We studied the surveillance tapes that showed Olson playing the Money Vault. She kept dropping the coins while inserting them in the machine. She also kept looking over her shoulder, as if she was afraid of being watched."

"Maybe she drank too much coffee," Mags said.

"There was more. Her criminal record was clean, but the report from the Driver and Vehicle Identification Database wasn't. Olson had a dozen tickets for speeding. The most recent ticket had come the morning she won the jackpot. She'd gotten pulled over for doing ninety driving to the casino. It made us think that the Money Vault machine was rigged, and she was just dying to get there so she could win it."

"A claimer," Mags said. Claimers were individuals with squeaky-clean backgrounds who worked with cheats to claim jackpots of rigged slot machines. Their take was 5 percent.

"Correct. While Olson waited to be paid off, she went to a restaurant inside Galaxy and had lunch with three people who we think rigged the machine. We pulled photos of them off a surveillance camera inside the restaurant."

Grimes showed her the photos. Three of the people had swarthy complexions and looked related. The fourth was an attractive woman with snow-white hair.

"Is Snow Cone the claimer?" Mags asked.

"That's Olson. I was wondering if you'd ever seen the other three."

The faces weren't the least bit familiar, and Mags shook her head. "Never seen them before. Why do you think they're dirty?"

"Their faces have shown up at several Native American reservation casinos when large sums of money were lost. My boss met with the head of tribal gaming last year, and they decided it was time to start sharing information. The Indians have gotten taken for some major scores."

Native American casinos were considered soft targets among cheats. The dealers were rubes, and the heads of surveillance often got their jobs because of blood ties.

"We think they're part of a family called the Gypsies," Grimes said. "They've been scamming the casinos for years but never caught. If I can bust the Gypsies, it will be a major feather in my cap. They're in Vegas right now."

"You've spotted them?"

"Two of them. They run in a pack, so we're sure the rest are also here."

Mags tried to hide her discomfort. The scam Billy had asked her to be a part of involved the Gypsies. If they got taken down, Billy would certainly go down as well. She didn't want Billy in her life, but that didn't mean she wanted him to get hurt, either.

Grimes jabbed the surveillance photo with his finger. "We made the short one down on Fremont Street at the Golden Gate Casino. The girl to his right was made at the Tropicana yesterday morning. We don't know who the third one is yet, but he should be easy to spot."

The third member of the Gypsies in the surveillance photo had an enormous Adam's apple and would be easy to make in a crowded casino.

"We've distributed his photo all over town," Grimes said. "The moment our friend with the bulging Adam's apple enters a casino, the casino will call us, and we'll come running."

"You're going to bust him?"

"Not right away. We'll take photos and use our facial recognition software to see if he turns up on any other surveillance videos. We're in the process of building a case against the family. When we take it to the grand jury, we want the charges to stick."

The gaming board busted hundreds of cheats every year, with the majority of cases being pleaded out and never going to trial. But this case was different. Grimes had a grand jury in his back pocket, which meant he'd already presented his evidence to the DA's office and gotten their blessing to proceed and build a rock-solid case. Every so often, the DA made an example out of a cheat and put him away in prison for a long stretch. This sounded like one of those special cases, and Mags could not help feeling sorry for the Gypsies.

Rand and Valles appeared at their table. Their arm-wrestling match was over, and they both looked satisfied with the outcome. Mags rose from her chair.

"Good luck with your show," Grimes said.

"Thanks, Frank," she said.

- - -

Mags and her producer walked back to the trailer. Rand didn't have the doctored shooting script in his hand, and Mags quizzed him with a glance.

"Special Agent Valles has a nephew in LA who wants to get into directing," Rand said. "Kid's waiting tables till his big break comes along. I offered to help him, provided the gaming board stays out of our hair."

"Help him how?"

"I'm going to arrange for him to get a directing fellowship at the American Film Institute. If the kid isn't a total douchebag, it should lead to his getting work."

"Can you do that?"

"I sit on AFI's board. I can pull a few strings and get him in."

"Does this kid have any talent?"

Rand burst out laughing. "We'll find out!"

Mags could feel the apprehension that always came before she shot a scene. She didn't have her lines down yet, and the fear of messing up in front of the camera was never far from her thoughts. She pecked Rand on the cheek and headed up the short flight of steps into her trailer.

"We're going to break early today. I'll see you this afternoon at four," Rand said.

"What's the special occasion?"

"Special Agent Valles has agreed to give us a tour of LINQ's surveillance room and show us how they catch cheats. It should give you real insight for your character."

Surveillance rooms were off-limits to everyone except for the handful of casino employees, and Mags had to believe that no hustler in town had ever been inside one.

"How the hell did you arrange that?" she asked.

"What can I say? I strike a hard bargain," he said with a wink.

EIGHTEEN

Billy slept in and awoke at ten. Crawling out of bed, he spied his Droid wiggling like a snake on the night table. Caller ID said "Unknown." He answered it anyway.

"Hello."

"Cunningham? This is Night Train. I got your sixty K. You still got my daddy's watch?"

"Sorry, I lost it in a card game."

"That's not funny," his caller said.

"Just kidding. I haven't let it out of my sight."

"You like messing with people, don't you?"

"Sometimes. When do you want to meet up?"

"Tuesdays are off days for the players. I'm going to rehab and then to get a massage. How about two o'clock at my digs. That work for you?"

Night Train sounded anxious to get his father's watch back. Or maybe he'd figured out Billy's touch card scam and wanted to confront him. There was an urgency in his voice, and Billy realized he had Night Train right where he wanted him.

"That works for me. Do me a favor and tell the front desk I'm coming. It will speed things up when I come back to your villa."

"I can do that. See you at two."

"I'll be there."

- - -

Breakfast was burned toast and coffee. Billy scrolled through e-mails on his cell phone while he ate. Most were from hustlers in town wishing to get together to talk business. Every hustler had a scam that they were working on to beat the joints. Many of these scams were designed to slowly bleed the casino, while others were heists and involved a conspiracy that often included dealers and pit bosses. None of the e-mails actually said this, but they used carefully crafted language that cloaked their author's true meaning. Back in the days of the Mississippi riverboat gamblers, hustlers had developed a secret language that allowed them to openly talk about fleecing people without exposing themselves, and the e-mails were peppered with expressions like "rabbit hunting," "been around the block," and "playing both sides of the table."

He drained his mug. It was a great time to be a hustler, with new casinos opening up every month and his friends cooking up schemes that would net them huge paydays down the road. To each one of them, he sent back the same reply.

"I'm doing business right now. I'll touch base when I come up for air."

Time to get cleaned up. Standing beneath the shower's hot spray, he thought about Travis. They'd talked on the phone every day, and he realized he was going to miss those conversations. Travis understood casino people, most of whom were bitter souls who harbored grudges against their employers and were easily distracted while a scam was taking place.

But those talks were a thing of the past. By betraying Billy, Travis had set himself on the path to ruin. Travis was going to pay for his sins.

Billy had thought long and hard on how to accomplish this and had decided the best way would be to bide his time and wait. Travis would blow the money he'd made from the Super Bowl scam just like he'd blown the money he'd made running with Billy, and then he'd look for another crew to run with. Once Travis was with another crew, Billy would contact the crew's captain and explain what Travis had done to him and how Travis was a liability. This would put Travis in a bad light, and his days would be numbered. Travis might last another year or two, but in the end he'd get a bullet pumped into his head or antifreeze injected in his veins. That was how it worked in the grifter's world. Rats got drowned.

He was getting dressed when Night Train called him again.

"Change in plans. Come by my suite at two thirty."

He didn't like it when people changed times for meetings. If you set a time, you had to stick to it. Otherwise, the other party might get suspicious.

"Something wrong?" he asked.

"Who said anything was wrong?" Night Train said.

"I did. You still want your old man's watch back?"

"What kind of question is that? Of course I want it back. Look, I've got some people flying into town to meet me. We'll be done by two thirty. Then we can hook up."

"Like a date?"

"Don't fuck with me, man."

"Change the time again, and I'll throw your precious watch out the window."

"Do that, and I'll hunt you down."

"I bet you will."

He ended the call and continued dressing. The words were slow to sink in. When they did, he sat on the edge of his bed and stared into space. *People flying into town to meet me.* Wasn't Night Train's stay at

Caesars a secret? Night Train had made it sound that way when Billy had tried to snap a photo of him signing the IOU. It didn't smell right.

It was time to play detective. Opening his dresser, he rummaged through his collection of binoculars that he'd used to scam suckers at poolside card games. He decided on a pair of Canon Image Stabilization binoculars. They were the latest in innovation and offered active image stabilization for superb clarity.

Calling downstairs, he told the valet to bring up his car.

- - -

A half hour later, he pulled into Caesars and went inside. The pool was one of the hotel's star attractions and featured eight different swimming areas. He bribed a pool attendant into letting him rent a private cabana even though he didn't possess a room key.

Kicking off his shoes, he parked himself on a chaise longue. In his lap was a copy of *USA Today* he'd bought at the gift shop; beneath it was the binoculars. When he felt certain none of the other guests were watching, he lifted the binoculars and searched for Night Train's villa on the other side of the pool. He spotted the crooked football player sitting on the balcony with Sammy and Choo-Choo. The three men were engaged in a heated discussion, with Night Train doing most of the talking. It wasn't going well, and Choo-Choo disgustedly tossed a bowl of pretzels in the air.

"Cocktails?" a female voice called out.

He returned the binoculars to their hiding place. Caesars's waitresses wore skimpy outfits and ponytail hairpieces like go-go dancers. Her name tag said GINGER/SAN FRANCISCO.

"Can I interest you in a signature cocktail or an appetizer?" Ginger asked.

"I could use a drink," he said.

She recited the house specialty cocktails. He picked a drink called the Rattlesnake because he liked the name, and a bowl of salted peanuts.

"You a reporter?" she asked.

His face reddened and he mumbled, "No."

"What's with the binoculars if you're not a reporter?"

"I'm a private detective," he lied.

"My boss said if we see anything suspicious by the pool area to report it immediately."

"You going to report me?"

"That all depends on you."

Money talked in the desert, and he stuffed a crisp C-note into the tip glass on her tray.

"Keep going," she said.

"You strike a hard bargain," he said.

"You ain't seen nothing, buster."

He stuffed another hundred into the glass, and she nodded approvingly.

"I'll be right back with your drink," she said.

- - -

The pool billed itself as being European, which meant that women went topless. While he waited for his drink, a buxom lady wearing nothing but bikini bottoms rose and strolled the pool's perimeter, the sight spectacular enough to snap every male head and a few female heads as well. An elephant with a screaming monkey on its back could have rushed past, and no one would have cared. He whipped out the binoculars and resumed spying on Night Train's villa.

Night Train had company. A distinguished-looking male wearing a navy suit and a red necktie sat at the table with the football players. He had corporate written all over him and was doing the talking. If Night Train's expression was any indication, the guest was laying some heavy news on them. The guest kept fingering his tie clasp while he spoke, and Billy focused on it with his binoculars. It was made of gold and displayed the NFL logo.

He shifted the binoculars to Choo-Choo and Sammy. Their lips were tightly shut. Like Night Train, they didn't like what the suit was saying, but instead of talking back, they were being good soldiers and keeping their mouths shut.

He had seen enough and put the binoculars away. The suit was from the NFL, no doubt about that, and probably had been sent to talk with Night Train and his pals about their wayward behavior. The last thing the NFL wanted was news to leak out that a group of star players was partying at Caesars right before the Super Bowl.

Ginger appeared with his order. "That will be thirty dollars, please."

He paid her and added more money to her tip glass. "Thanks for not reporting me. Does Caesars always toss suspicious-acting people they find hanging around?"

"Heck no. We get people snooping around the property all the time," she said. "Just last Saturday I caught a reporter from *TMZ* secretly videotaping a famous actress kissing a guy inside the casino. I alerted management, and they didn't do a thing."

"So why this week? What's going on that warrants tossing people?"

"I can't tell you that."

"But you know."

"Of course. There are no secrets in this place. You're not really a detective, are you?"

"You're right, I'm not. What tipped you off?"

"You're way too cute."

"There's a suit from the NFL visiting the hotel right now. Who is he?"

"Sorry, but that's going to cost you."

Another hundred found its way into her tip glass.

"His last name is Butz, first name Chester."

"Chester Butz, the NFL commissioner?"

"That's what I'm told."

Chester Butz ran the NFL with an iron fist and did not take crap from the players. Billy was having a hard time believing the suit in Night Train's suite was the same person. Using his cell phone, he typed Butz's name into Google and did an image search. A montage of head shots appeared. Each matched the face of the guy talking to Night Train and his teammates.

"Believe me now?" Ginger asked.

"What's Butz doing here?"

"That's for me to know and you to find out."

In Vegas, it was about being in the know, and it irritated Billy that Ginger knew the score while he was in the dark. She gave him a flirtatious wink.

"See you around," she said.

NINETEEN

It was time to go see Night Train. Billy left the cabana and went to the front desk, where the manager on duty had already been alerted of his pending arrival. The manager said, "Mr. McClain said you'd be coming. Do you know the way?"

"Yes, I've been here before," he said.

While Billy took the long walk back to the villas, he tried to figure out why the head of the NFL had flown to Vegas to meet with Night Train and his teammates. There had been no agents or lawyers in attendance, which would have suggested that it was a friendly gathering, only the looks on the football players' faces had suggested the meeting was anything but that.

Choo-Choo greeted him at the door. "I'm not playing cards with you anymore. Night Train's on the patio waiting for you."

He made his way back to the patio. Night Train sat at the head of the table with a shopping bag before him. He guessed the bag contained his winnings and took a chair.

"Want something to drink?" Night Train asked.

"I'm good," he said.

Night Train slid the loot toward him. He opened the bag and had a look inside. Money made the world go round, and there was enough inside the bag to make it go around several times. From his pocket he removed Night Train's father's watch and placed it on the table.

"Here you go."

"Don't you want to count your money?"

"I just did."

"You're a hustler, aren't you?"

"Whatever gave you that idea?"

Night Train picked up the watch and gazed at the inscription on the back. It was a cheap watch, but that didn't diminish its value. Night Train's old man had toiled for years to earn that watch, and his son kept it to be reminded of the sacrifices his father had made.

"I've been beaten at cards before, but never so quickly," Night Train said. "You cheated us."

"Takes one to know one," he said.

"What's that supposed to mean?"

"You rang in a cooler on me, and I spotted it and spilled my drink on the cards."

"I don't know what you're talking about."

Night Train's cell phone rang. The famous football player cursed and dug through his pockets. Out came a fancy alligator-skin wallet, which was dropped onto the table, followed by the cell phone, which Night Train answered. He frowned and rose from the table.

"I'll be right back."

Night Train went into the villa and shut the door, leaving Billy to wait. Night Train's denial didn't shock him; the first rule of getting caught cheating was to deny it and make the accuser prove the allegation. Most people didn't have the courage and would back down.

Ringing in a cooler during a card game required skill and timing, plus stacking the deck to be switched into the game. If one card was out of order in the stack, the scam wouldn't work, and the victim might end up winning the money. Hustlers who used coolers relied on formulas to set up the cards. These formulas were written down and kept hidden in the hustler's wallet. During the game, the hustler would take a bathroom break and use the time away from the table to set up the deck to be switched in. The formula would calculate the game that was being played, along with the number of players, thus ensuring that the hustler got the money.

Every hustler who employed coolers used formulas to stack the deck, and Billy had to believe that Night Train did as well. The formula was written on a piece of paper in the event there was trouble during the game and the hustler had to get rid of the evidence. This was done by crunching the formula into a ball and swallowing it.

He glanced through the glass door into the villa. Night Train was still talking on his cell phone. Reaching across the table, he picked up Night Train's wallet and did a quick search. Every fancy men's wallet had a secret compartment that was nothing more than a clever fold of leather; Night Train's wallet was no different, and he extracted a slip of paper and unfolded it. As he'd expected, it contained Night Train's winning formula for seven-card stud, the same game in which Night Train had switched decks and tried to cheat him.

7-Card Stud/ #6612					
5D	JD	AC	JC	AH	KH
10S	JH	QH	10D	6C	KC
2C	JS	2H	4C	7C	KS
7D	10H	4S	QC	6H	7H
5H	10C	AS	9D	2D	3H
AD	4H	6D	2S	5C	5S
9H	QS	7S	3C	8H	KD

Night Train was finishing his call. Billy placed the formula beneath the wallet so it was hidden from view. Night Train returned to the patio and took his seat at the table.

"Where were we?" the famous football player said.

"You were denying that you used a cooler on me yesterday."

"I never cheated anybody in my life, and that's the God's honest truth."

The best way to catch a cheat was to paint him into a corner with his own lies. Billy reached across the table and dramatically lifted the fancy wallet off the formula.

"What are you carrying this formula in your wallet for? Shits and giggles?"

Night Train was not going down without a fight. "Give me a break, man. That's a game the team plays during trips. I wrote it down because it's complicated, that's all."

"Nice try. Actually, it's the stack you used in our game. There's a code written across the top for easy reference: 6612. The first number tells you how many hands the deck is stacked for. In this case, it's a six, which is how many players we had.

"The second number in the code tells you which hand will be the winner. That number is six, the last hand, which happened to be yours.

"The third number in the code tells you the strength of the winning hand. One is a four of a kind, two is a full house, three is a flush, four is a straight, and five is three of a kind. The third number in the formula is a one, meaning the winning hand will be a four of a kind.

"The last number tells you which player will get fleeced. In this case the number is two, the second player to the dealer's left, my seat. I was supposed to get a full house and bet all my money thinking it was a winner. Only things didn't work out the way you planned."

Night Train stared at the formula before meeting Billy's gaze.

"You're good."

"Glad you think so."

"How long you been in the rackets?"

"Since I was fifteen. You?"

"Twelve. My father ran crooked card games in our basement and taught me the ropes. So how the hell did you cheat us, anyway?"

"I bought a few decks from the hotel gift shop and doctored the edges with a nail file. Then I convinced the girl working the counter to take the doctored decks back."

"So when I had the concierge bring up a couple of decks, he brought decks from the gift shop. That's sweet. I didn't suspect a thing."

"No, you didn't."

Night Train took the news in stride; he'd been beaten at his own game and wasn't afraid to admit it. Billy pushed the paper bag across the table to his host, who acted surprised.

"I don't want your money," he said. "But I do want to talk to you and your teammates. I have a business proposition for you."

Night Train scratched his chin. "And what would that be?"

"I want you to fix the Super Bowl."

"You're crazy. The league constantly watches for fixes. We'd all go down."

"No, we won't. I want to fix some prop bets. The game's outcome won't be affected."

"Hey man, don't think the players haven't discussed fixing prop bets. Problem is, you don't know who's going to get the ball first."

"I have that covered. The coin toss will be rigged."

"Meaning you've got the head referee in your back pocket. Well, that's an interesting angle. Our kicker always boots the opening kickoff out of the end zone, which takes special teams out of the picture. The defense could then commit the game's first penalty from scrimmage and suffer the first injury, and no one would be the wiser. I like it. For the sake of argument, let's say I get my boys to agree to your fix. What's our take?"

The deal that Billy had struck with Broken Tooth was that Night Train and his pals would receive four million to fix the game. But Billy had decided he didn't like those terms. Broken Tooth couldn't be trusted to hold up his end of the bargain, leaving Billy with little choice but to cut Broken Tooth out and offer Night Train a more lucrative arrangement.

"Half," the young hustler said.

"Half of what?"

"Of every bet we place with the Vegas sports books. Since I don't know what the line on the prop bets is, I can only guess."

"Try me."

"Seven and a half million."

"You're going to give us half of seven and a half million bucks?"

"No, your take will be seven and a half million, give or take a few hundred grand. You'll get a full accounting of every bet and every payoff. After the money is collected, your share will be wired to an offshore bank account, which I assume you have. Sound good to you?"

"I'd like to see some good faith money first. It will help me sell this to my boys."

"How much do you need?"

"A hundred grand apiece up front."

"Five hundred thousand bucks. I can do that."

Night Train flashed a smile. Billy had said all the right things. The famous football player rose from the table and escorted his guest through the villa to the front door.

"Do we have a deal?" Billy asked.

"I'm sold, but my boys will need convincing," Night Train said. "They usually do what I say, but I still need to say it. Clete and Assassin are playing golf and won't be back until later. Let me huddle up and discuss. When do you need an answer?"

"Tonight. Sooner if possible."

"I'll call you once I have things nailed down."

They shook hands. It was how business deals were done between hustlers—no contracts or fancy lawyers in pinstripes, just a pumping of the flesh.

"One more thing," Night Train said. "I want you to teach me how you doctored the cards. I'd like to use that."

"You got it," Billy said.

- - -

He took the Strip home. It was late, and the sun had started to descend. As it did, partiers appeared on the Strip's wide sidewalks like predators beginning their daily hunt. Rain or shine, the ritual was always the same; with daylight's passing, the real adventure began.

Traffic crawled. Casino billboards ran continuous loops of the acts playing in their showrooms. Singers came and went, but it was the magic acts and impersonators who hung around the longest, their illusions more in keeping with the false dreams of wealth that the casinos pushed upon their customers. "Caller Unknown" lit up his cell phone's screen. It was a fifty-buck fine to talk while driving. He decided to risk it.

"Hello?"

"This is Broken Tooth. Did you get this thing nailed down?"

"I just left Night Train's villa. Night Train is on board but needs to talk to his teammates and convince them. We're going to talk later and finalize the deal."

"Night Train the boss. The others will go along, don't you think?"

"They should. There's been one change in plans. Night Train wants five hundred thousand in good faith money. I told him yes."

Broken Tooth cursed up a storm at this unexpected change in plans. Billy smiled into the cell phone. The fact that Broken Tooth was going to get cut out of the deal didn't mean that the Chinese gangster shouldn't pay for Night Train and his pals' signing bonuses. To Billy's way of thinking, this was only fair, considering the crap Broken Tooth was putting him through.

"You think I've got that kind of money lying around?" Broken Tooth yelled.

"You want me to call him, tell him the deal's off?" Billy said.

"I'll get money, but if you pull a stunt like this again, I'll put a bullet in your driver's head. You want that?"

"No."

"Then stop pulling shit with me."

Leon's life was on the line, and Billy needed to be careful. "Speaking of my driver, how's he holding up?"

"Your driver's got a big mouth. Real asshole."

"You didn't kill him, did you?"

"My bodyguards stuck his head in toilet and he nearly drowned. Guess he didn't know how to hold his breath. You want to talk to him? He sitting right here."

"Hey Billy, how's it going?" a weakened Leon said moments later.

"You don't sound good," Billy said, regretting the exchange with Broken Tooth.

"I've been better. You really think you can pull this thing off?"

"I'm sure going to try."

"Give me some odds."

"I'd say I've got a sixty-forty shot at making it happen."

"I can live with that."

Broken Tooth came back on the line. "I'll call you later to hear how things are going. Don't let me down, Cunningham."

"I'm going to make this happen. Just don't kill my driver," he said.

A bicycle cop appeared in his side mirror, pedaling fast. The sheriff's department maintained hundreds of hidden surveillance cameras on the Strip, the cops doing their best to keep order. He pulled his registration and proof of insurance out of the glove compartment.

"I'm about to get a ticket for talking on my cell phone. Talk to you later."

TWENTY

"Cut!"

Mags stopped in midsentence to stare at her director, a spoiled Hollywood brat named Hudson, Hud for short. Hud had a neatly trimmed goatee and an effeminate silver earring that she would have enjoyed ripping off his pink earlobe. They were on the twelfth take of a scene that a high school senior could have shot on a cell phone.

"What's wrong?" she asked.

"I don't know what you're feeling," Hud said.

"I'm feeling exhausted, that's what I'm feeling."

"I mean in the scene. You're a blank canvas. I need emotion, Mags."

She nodded tiredly. The scene called for her to walk across the floor of a busy casino while juggling two simultaneous calls on her cell phone. The first call was to her teenage daughter, with whom she was having a heated argument, the second to her meathead partner, who was constantly screwing up and the source of continual irritation. At the scene's end, she would spy a casino patron dropping a slug in a slot machine and arrest him.

The scene had seemed easy when she'd read the script; now, not so much. She didn't have another actor to play off and was struggling to stay in character.

"What are you feeling?" Hud asked.

"I don't have a clue. Why don't you give me a hint," she said.

"You've run out of patience with your bitchy daughter, whom you suspect of slipping out at night to go clubbing with her hot boyfriend, and you'd like to take your male chauvinist pig of a partner and close a door on his head. That sound about right?"

"Anger and frustration."

"There you go. Let's take it from the top."

Mags retreated to her starting point. A ponytailed grip stepped in front of her and held up a small board so it faced the camera. "*Night and Day*, take thirteen, walking through the casino," the grip announced.

"Action," Hud said.

She raised the cell phone to her face and started walking toward the camera. If the pilot bombed, she'd have to go back to hustling suckers. She'd just as soon paint houses, and she played back Hud's advice. Bitchy kid, asshole partner. That shouldn't be too hard.

"Now you listen to me," she said to her imaginary daughter. "I know what you're up to, and I want it to stop. You can't be going to clubs when you should be home studying. Hold on, I've got another call." Without breaking stride, she punched a button on her phone that allowed her to switch calls. To her imaginary partner she said, "Speak of the devil. Look, Jake, I'm sick of covering for you every time you go on a bender and miss work. Get your sorry ass over here." Ending the call, she punched the button and returned to her daughter. "You still there? Good. Now here's the deal. If I catch you skipping out again, you're grounded for six months."

She halted at a spot on the carpet with an *X* made of silver duct tape. The camera was a few feet away, doing a close-up. She put on her best pissed-off mother's face, then pretended to see a cheating patron putting a slug into a slot machine and said, "I need to run. I'll bring pizza home for dinner. Good-bye."

"Cut!" Arms extended, Hud came out of his chair. "Perfect—perfect! That's what I call acting. Mark my words, you're going to be a star."

"From your lips to God's ears," she said.

- - -

Filming a TV show was exhausting, and Mags went to her trailer and lay down on a cot. Amber was arriving tonight, and she wanted to be bright-eyed and bushy-tailed when her daughter stepped off the plane. A tapping on the door lifted her eyebrows.

"Come on in."

Rand entered wearing his best smile. The first time they'd met, Mags had fleeced Rand at poker. Instead of getting pissed, Rand had turned on the charm and offered her work. He was a phony, through and through, but he was *her* phony, so she put up with him.

"Hud said you were fantastic," Rand said.

"Doing the best I can. What's up?"

"We have a date with the gaming board. They're going to give us a tour of the surveillance control room of LINQ's casino."

"I'm beat. Why don't you go, let me get some rest?"

"No can do. You're playing a gaming agent in the show, and you need to see what these people actually do. Come on, it will be a good learning experience."

"But I can hardly keep my eyes open."

"In case you've forgotten, the gaming board is the key to our show's success. If they decide they don't like us, we'll have to switch locations." A plastic bag dangled in his hand, which he placed on the cot. "This was delivered by courier, courtesy of Special Agent Grimes. There was a note asking that I personally give it to you."

She sat up and had a look inside the bag. The breath caught in her throat.

"What is it?" her producer asked.

"A chip tray," she said.

"And what is a chip tray?"

Casinos gave chip trays to customers who purchased large amounts of chips, making it easier for the customer to carry around the chips, as opposed to stuffing them in their pockets.

The chip tray Grimes had couriered over had five tubes designed to hold twenty chips, a hundred chips in all. This was the standard size for every Vegas casino. The tray in her hands was altered. Each tube had been ground out with a router so it could accommodate an additional chip.

Mags had once lived in an apartment on the south end of town. Down the hall lived a Mexican girl named Louisa who worked as a cashier at Circus Circus. One night they'd gotten drunk on cheap wine, and Mags had persuaded Louisa to steal a chip tray and bring it home. The next night, Mags had gaffed the tray while explaining the scam to her new partner.

Louisa would keep the tray at her station in the cage. Mags would enter the casino and approach the cage when things were quiet, then pass $2,500 through the bars to Louisa. Louisa would exchange the money for a hundred green chips, which were worth twenty-five dollars apiece. But instead of putting twenty green chips into each tube, Louisa would put twenty-one.

Mags would visit the ladies' room with the tray, enter a stall, and deposit the five stolen chips into her purse. Then she'd enter the casino and play a slot machine. After an hour, she'd exchange the chips at the cage and leave $125 ahead.

The scam shouldn't have worked, yet it did. Every transaction inside the cage was videotaped and scrutinized. Only the dopes working surveillance thought a chip tray could hold only a hundred chips, so the scam flew right by them.

They'd pulled the scam twice a week for a year. Mags called it the Rent Scam, since the money went to covering their monthly rent. Every scam had a shelf life, and Mags had decided to retire the scam while they still were ahead.

Or so she'd thought.

If the gaffed tray was any indication, Louisa had found a partner and continued the scam until she got caught. That was how the gaffed tray had ended up in Grimes's possession.

But how had Frank tied the scam to her? Had Louisa grown a tail and ratted out Mags? That was the logical explanation, and since any videos of the theft from Circus Circus were long gone, Grimes had sent Mags the tray just to rattle her cage.

Frank was being a prick. Nothing new there.

A garbage pail sat in the corner of the trailer. The gaffed tray made a loud bang before falling inside. Mags checked her makeup in the vanity and went to the door.

"Are you going to explain?" Rand asked.

"There's nothing to explain," she said. "Let's go see what the inside of a surveillance room looks like, shall we?"

TWENTY-ONE

Back when the mob ran Vegas, lifeguard chairs could be found on casino floors, in which sat cigar-smoking gangsters who'd stared down at the tables, trying to catch cheats. After the corporations took over the town, these chairs were replaced with catwalks, letting security experts with binoculars watch the action through two-way mirrors in the ceiling.

Over time, cameras replaced catwalks. These cameras had pan-tilt-zoom lenses and were wired to the casino's surveillance room, where heavily caffeinated techs sat zombielike in front of monitors, hoping to nail a bad guy. These surveillance rooms were also above casinos, on floors with restricted access.

This arrangement had changed with modern casinos. Today's surveillance rooms were in basements and had special cooling systems so the equipment ran properly. They also had their own elevators, which eliminated any social contact with the casino's employees.

Special Agent Grimes awaited them in the lobby of LINQ. The knot in Grimes's necktie was undone, and his chin sported a dark shadow.

"Catch any bad guys?" Mags asked as they took the elevator down.

"Slow day so far. Like the present I sent over?" Grimes asked.

"What present? I didn't get any present."

"Let me guess. You've never heard of Louisa Cruz."

"Sorry. Name doesn't ring any bells."

Rand stared at the floor, pretending not to hear. The elevator landed and they walked down a hallway to a steel door with a security camera perched over it. Grimes hit a buzzer.

"Before we go inside, I need to remind you that it's against the law to take photos of the equipment. If I catch either of you doing that, I'll confiscate your cell phone. Got it?"

"Of course," Rand said.

"You're the boss," Mags added.

A short man wearing a turtleneck ushered them in. The room was dimly lit and designed like a bunker, and it took a moment for Mags's eyes to adjust. Twenty-eight monitors took up the main wall; in front of them sat a dozen techs at desks, using joysticks, keypads, and desktop screens to jump among feeds from the casino's many cameras.

At one desk sat a plump guy eating a burger in a fast-food wrapper. Frank slapped him on the shoulder. "This is Blake, one of LINQ's table games specialists. How's it going, Blake?"

"Living the dream," Blake replied without humor.

"Any bites?"

"Not yet, but the day's still young." With a flick of the joystick, Blake jumped from a craps table to a blackjack game with lightning speed. "I thought I saw your boy earlier, but it wasn't him. Is your offer still good?"

"Absolutely. Five hundred bucks if you nail him," Grimes said. "That goes for the other techs as well."

A glossy photograph was propped on Blake's desk. It was the same photo Frank had shown Mags of the Gypsies having lunch with the claimer. Frank had nailed two of the Gypsies already but let them slip through his fingers. Now he was offering a bounty to capture the third Gypsy in the photo—the one with the prominent Adam's apple, who would be easy for Blake or one of the other techs to spot if he entered LINQ's casino.

"You must really want to catch this guy," Rand said.

"That would be an understatement," Frank said. "The gaming board busted three hundred cheats last year, and all of them were small fries. The big ones almost always elude our net. But that's about to change."

Rand picked up the photo and stared at the faces in the group. "Who are they?"

"They're a family of thieves called the Gypsies who prey on the casinos. They specialize in well-orchestrated scams that have netted them millions of dollars."

"Millions? Wow."

"Wow is right. The older lady in the photo is a retired school principal and in cahoots with the Gypsies. She claimed a jackpot from a slot machine that the Gypsies rigged and split the winnings with them."

"I thought it was impossible to rig a slot machine."

"So did we. But the Gypsies figured out a way to open a machine and nullify the antitheft device while adding a special code that made the machine pay a jackpot if played a certain way. That's what makes the gaming board's work so challenging. Even when we're right on top of things, we're still a step behind."

"That's a good quote. Can we use it in the show?"

"No."

"Got it. Do you ever resort to unusual methods to catch cheats?"

Frank flashed a smile. "I'll have to take the fifth on that one."

"In the movies, the cheats get dragged to a back room and get the tar beaten out of them before they get turned over to the police," Rand said. "Does that really happen?"

Every damn day, Mags almost said.

"Not anymore," Frank said.

Blake leaped out of his chair like he'd been hit by a cattle prod. "Got him! Our boy just sat down at a hundred-dollar blackjack table."

"Put him on the wall," Frank said.

The twenty-eight wall monitors became filled with a live feed of the Gypsy with the pronounced Adam's apple. He was dressed casually, his face hidden by a pair of cheap shades and a baseball cap. The disguise had flown by the other techs; only Blake's trained eye had picked him up. Frank removed his wallet and slapped the bounty on Blake's desk.

"Treat your girlfriend to a nice dinner tonight," Frank said.

"I don't have a girlfriend," Blake replied.

- - -

Frank enjoyed busting cheats more than screwing. Mags knew this as fact, because Frank had once left their bed after getting a call about a cheat ripping off a casino.

Frank moved closer to the monitors with Rand glued to his side. Mags stayed by Blake's desk, wishing she'd never agreed to take this little tour. She'd said good-bye to the grifter's life and did not want to participate, even as a casual observer.

The Gypsy on the monitors didn't have a prayer. Frank would catch him in the act, video the crime from every conceivable angle, and bust him. Frank would also interrogate him and ask him to give up the rest of the members of his family. If the Gypsy didn't play ball, Frank would put him away for a long time.

The game was blackjack. On the monitor, the Gypsy was dealt a pair of aces. The Gypsy slid a second bet into the betting circle, indicating he wished to split the hand. Then a miraculous thing happened. The Gypsy's original bet of two black chips grew to three. The new bet also contained three black chips. Black chips were worth a hundred bucks. The Gypsy had added $200 to his bet without the dealer being the wiser.

"We need a close-up of that," Frank called over his shoulder.

"I'm all over it," Blake said.

"Did something just happen?" Rand asked, clueless.

"Our thief had an extra chip palmed in his hand, which he added to his original bet. Hustlers call it capping a bet."

"I didn't see anything," Rand marveled.

"He's pretty slick. We'll need to record him the next time he moves. That's the only way we'll be able to convince a jury that he was cheating."

"Are juries hard to convince?" Rand asked.

"In this town they are. Without rock-solid video evidence, a jury will not convict."

Frank went to Blake's desk and used a house phone to call the head of casino security. "The guy sitting at first base on table seven is capping his bets. Once we have enough evidence, I'll call you. Make sure you get his cell phone when you bust him."

Hanging up, Frank glanced at Mags. "Having fun?"

Mags thought she might get sick. The Gypsies were in Vegas running a scam with Billy, and there was every likelihood that Billy's number was logged on the guy's cell phone. That would put Billy in a bad light and allow Frank to ask a judge for permission to tap Billy's phones and put a tail on him. Eventually Billy would slip up, and Frank would nail him.

"Did you hear what I just said?"

Mags blinked awake. Billy had never used or abused her, and he would always occupy a special place in her heart, even if he was a devious little shit.

"Afraid not," she said.

"I asked you if you're having fun." Frank stepped closer, his eyes burning a hole into her soul like he knew something wasn't right.

"Time of my life," she said.

"Why do I think you're lying to me?"

"That's because everyone lies to you, Frank. You should be used to it by now."

Frank lifted his hand as if to slap her. He'd struck her several times when she was a snitch, then tried to make up for it with a shitty box of candy or flowers.

"Go ahead, try it," she said.

Frank growled under his breath and moved back to the monitors. Seeing her chance, Mags turned to Blake. "Where's the ladies' room? I need to powder my nose."

"It's behind the file cabinets." Blake lifted his bag of fries. "Want one?"

"No, thanks."

Mags found the restroom and went in. What she was about to do was illegal and could land her in hot water. She was risking everything, yet her heart said do it.

Her hand shook as she typed a text message to Billy on her cell phone.

TWENTY-TWO

The Stage Door was the ultimate dive bar. Three-buck beers, two-dollar shots, and reanimated road kill served as hot dogs were its big sellers. The marquee advertised the number of years remaining on the lease as a middle-finger salute to the casinos that surrounded it.

It was also a hangout for casino people, and it was not uncommon to find Billy at the bar, buying rounds while listening to dealers blow off steam. Dealers who hated their bosses or who had financial problems could often be recruited to rip off their employers.

Today, it was Cory and Morris who joined Billy at the water-stained bar. Cory played a video poker machine built into the bar. Without looking up, he said, "We found one of Broken Tooth's men."

Billy drank a Corona out of a frosted mug. He glanced over his shoulder to make sure no one was eavesdropping, then said, "I'm listening."

"I took your suggestion and did a Google search for the best authentic Chinese food in Vegas. A restaurant called Joyful House popped up. Five stars. The menu's in Chinese and serves shark fin soup and several dishes prepared with live fish. My gut told me this was the place, so Morris and I ate lunch there today."

Cory went silent. He was one card away from making a royal flush, which would pay out two grand. He drew the wrong card and punched the machine.

"Loser," Morris said.

"Shut up," Cory said.

"The suspense is killing me. What happened then?" Billy asked.

Cory picked up his drink and took a sip. "We sat near the entrance and ordered lunch. Around noon, one of Broken Tooth's goons came in and picked up two bags of food. The owner was working the cash register, and they talked in Chinese and were real chummy."

"So the owner knew him," Billy said.

"The goon had definitely been in before," Cory said.

"Did the goon make you? You said you were sitting by the entrance."

"Nope. We were wearing disguises," Cory said.

Cory and Morris had once done a job but failed to wear disguises. Billy had canned them over it, then taken them back, with the promise they'd never do it again.

"Nice to hear it," Billy said. "Did you follow him?"

"For about a mile. Then we stopped," Cory said.

"Why?" Billy asked.

"The goon was looking in his mirror as he drove," Cory explained. "If he made us, he could get out at a red light and shoot us. And our short, happy lives would be over."

Drive-by shootings were common in Vegas and rarely got solved. Cory's reasoning was sound, and Billy said, "We need to go back to Joyful House and set up surveillance. We'll use two cars to follow the goon and find out where Leon's being kept."

"I think we should go see Broken Tooth and do an exchange," Cory said. "We'll give him Travis, and in return he lets Leon go."

"That's a clever idea. Were you planning on kidnapping Travis?"

"That was the plan. It solves two problems at once. Leon would be let go, and Travis would get paid back for screwing us."

"Do you think Broken Tooth would shoot Travis?"

"Probably."

"Does that bother you?"

"No," they both said.

Billy's cell phone danced on the bar. Mags, of all people, had texted him. Their last meeting had ended in less than spectacular fashion, and he was still trying to get over it. Mags was the most screwed-up woman he'd ever known, yet he could not erase the notion that someday they were going to rob a casino together. He read her message.

Grimes going to bust one of the Gypsies

He texted her back. Where?

LINQ. Going down now. Good luck

Billy needed to call Victor and alert him that one of his family was in trouble. Cory had resumed playing video poker with Morris looking over his shoulder.

"I'll be right back," he said.

- - -

The Stage Door sat in an alleyway between Bally's and the Flamingo. He found a secluded spot beneath the monorail that ran between the hotels and made the call.

Kat answered her father's phone. "My father's taking a nap."

"One of your siblings is about to get busted by the gaming board," he said.

"What? Which one?"

"Whichever one is ripping off LINQ."

"Hold on, I'll go get my father."

"Hey Billy, what's going on?" Victor said, his voice thick with sleep.

"I just got tipped off that one of your kids is about to get busted at LINQ. Frank Grimes, the asshole who shot you in the leg, is running the operation."

"That must be my son Tommy. He called me earlier, said he was going to check out a new joint called LINQ. I'll call him right now and alert him."

"I'm on the Strip with two of my crew. I'm happy to help."

"I just might take you up on that. I'll call you back."

He ended the call. The sky was darkening, and the Flamingo's flashing sign looked like a Fourth of July display. He'd come to Vegas a decade ago thinking he'd last a year before the illusion wore thin. Only the opposite had happened, and his infatuation with the town had turned into a full-blown love affair. He craved action, and there was no other city in the world that had more action than right here. Victor called him back.

"I just spoke to Tommy. He didn't have a clue the gaming board was onto him. He's going to make a run for it but doesn't think he can get more than a few blocks. My kids can't get there in time. Can you help him out?"

"You bet. Tommy's tall, with a thick head of hair, right?"

"That's him. I really appreciate this, Billy."

"Don't thank me yet. What's Tommy's cell number?"

- - -

Billy sent Tommy Boswell a text, Pick you up on the Strip. Then he went inside to find Cory and Morris still at the bar. Morris had a Taser cupped in his hand and was giving the video poker machine a shock. The scam didn't work in casinos because of the cameras, but in a dive like this one, a Taser would produce free plays and even a false payout.

"Go get your car," Billy said. "We need to give Tommy Boswell a hand."

They followed Billy outside. Their black Infiniti SUV was parked in a handicap spot by the building. Cory had falsified medical documentation to obtain a handicapped placard under the belief that in a town this crowded there was nothing more valuable than free parking.

Billy started jogging toward the Strip. His plan was to head toward LINQ with his eye out for Tommy Boswell. Once he'd made visual contact, he'd wave Tommy toward the Infiniti, which would whisk him away to safety.

He suddenly stopped. A great plan, only he wasn't wearing a disguise. A street surveillance camera was going to pick up his face and connect him to Tommy Boswell.

He turned around and went back into the Stage Door. Up at the bar, a legless vet was chatting up a blind girl. The vet wore a Vietnam veteran tiger-stripe ball cap. Billy had bought the vet enough beers to feel comfortable interrupting the conversation.

"Twenty bucks for your cap," Billy said.

"Make it thirty, and it's yours," the vet said.

"Sold."

Money changed hands. Billy put on the cap and threw on his shades. Outside, the Infiniti idled by the curb. He trotted toward the Strip with the vehicle right behind him.

TWENTY-THREE

Reaching the Strip, Billy headed north, the Infiniti trailing behind him in the right lane. The sun had gone to bed and the all-night party was under way, with drunken tourists walking an imaginary tightrope down the sidewalk.

As Billy walked, he tried to see above heads in the crowd. When the Strip's hotels were booked solid, there were a quarter million people packed into the town. Right now, it felt like most of them were walking with him on the sidewalk.

This wasn't going to work. Tommy Boswell could be ten feet away, and he wasn't going to spot him. He decided to send Tommy a text.

Looking for you. Put your arm in the air.

Fifty feet ahead, a disembodied arm shot into the air. Not seeing who it belonged to, he climbed onto a machine that dispensed free flyers filled with ads for hookers. Tommy Boswell came into view, hustling down the sidewalk. Most cheats kept in shape by running, and Tommy had the long, effortless strides of someone who'd put in the miles.

A gang of determined gaming agents gave chase. Billy identified them by the bad haircuts they wore like badges of honor. Grimes was in front, yelling for Tommy to halt. When Tommy didn't oblige him, Grimes reached into his sports jacket for his sidearm. Gaming agents were allowed to shoot people who robbed the casinos, even if the thieves were unarmed. This was going to end badly. Jumping down, he pulled out his wallet and began throwing handfuls of cash into the air. "Free money! Who wants some free money?"

The crowd went ape. People screamed and grasped at the bills. Two tourists claimed a fifty at once. They ripped the bill in half and started fighting.

Tommy Boswell burst out of the crowd. "Hey, stranger."

"My friends are in the black Infiniti," Billy said. "Jump in the back and hit the floor."

"You coming?"

"Nope, I'm staying here. See you later."

Tommy ran between cars into the middle of the street, bent down, and did a duck walk to the Infiniti, where he opened the back door and jumped into the backseat. The door wasn't closed before Cory cut across two lanes of traffic, hung a left at the light, and vanished down a side street. Cory, once king of the fuckups, had pulled through like a champ.

Grimes and his posse were closing in. Billy flipped open the newspaper box and grabbed a handful of flyers. The cover read BUST YOUR NUT IN A CLASSY SLUT. Only in Vegas was that shit acceptable, and he walked with the crowd.

"Free newspaper. Who wants a free newspaper?"

At the block's end he stole a glance over his shoulder. The gaming agents were at the newspaper box, searching for their man. Grimes was on his cell phone and looked livid. Grimes was many things; stupid wasn't one of them. Thieves did not disappear without a trace, and Grimes knew the wool had been pulled over his eyes. But would he figure out that it was Maggie Flynn who'd betrayed him?

Yes, he realized, Grimes probably would.

- - -

Mags stood at the window in her suite in LINQ and stared down at the scene on the Strip. She'd watched a man run into the busy street and jump into a black SUV and the vehicle burn out. The guy could have been anyone; only her gut told her it was the same cheat she'd seen in LINQ's surveillance room ten minutes ago. Her text to Billy had saved the guy's neck.

She buried her face in her hands. She should have felt elated, yet all she wanted to do was slip into bed and pull the covers over her head. She wasn't a grifter anymore, she was an actress, and if she didn't start behaving like one, her new career would go off the rails faster than a runaway freight train.

She mixed herself a drink. Raising the glass to her lips, she heard a knock on her door. She stuck her eye to the peephole and spied Rand in the hallway.

"What's up?" she asked, letting him in.

"Can you believe we actually got to see a real live cheat ripping off a casino?" Rand said. "Amazing. Do you think the gaming board caught that guy?"

Mags parked herself on the couch and worked on her drink. "Who knows."

"Grimes said they were going to put the heavy on him. What does that mean?"

"If they got the chance, they'd knock the guy to the ground and pile up on him."

"Why would they do that?"

"Because it hurts."

Rand got a light beer from the bar. He did his best thinking when he had a prop in his hand. "That maneuver the guy was doing with his chips. What's it called again?"

"Capping. The cheat adds a chip to his bet if his hand's strong. The opposite is pinching. That's when the cheat steals a chip if the hand's a loser. The ultimate is the Savannah, when you switch the entire bet under the dealer's nose."

"How does that work?"

"The Savannah employs reverse psychology. The cheat bets two five-dollar chips with a five-thousand-dollar chip hidden on the bottom. If the cheat wins the bet, the house has to pay the cheat off. If the cheat loses the bet, he switches the bet for three five-dollar chips."

"Is that possible?"

"Yeah, with the right distraction."

"Wouldn't the dealer notice?"

"That's where the reverse psychology comes in. The dealer is trained to watch winning bets, not losers. The switch flies right by. It's a perfect move."

"I want to work that into the pilot."

"When?"

"First thing tomorrow."

"My daughter's flying in tonight. Can't this wait a few days?"

"It won't take thirty minutes. The Savannah. I love it. Get some sleep. You're looking a little rough around the edges."

"I didn't say yes," Mags reminded him.

Rand smiled like it was a done deal and left the suite. Mags hated when men played her. She poured herself a refill. There was another knock on her door. Through the peephole, she spied Billy in the hallway wearing a Vietnam vet cap. She pulled the door open without undoing the chain. "I don't want to see you anymore. Go away."

Billy's face caved. "Then why the text?"

"I did it for old time's sake. We're done, Billy. You have to accept that."

"But we could make a killing together."

"You're probably right. I just don't want to be a thief anymore."

"You sure don't act like it."

She tried to slam the door in Billy's face, but his foot kept it open.

"There's a reason I came," he said. "Grimes is going to figure out that you stuck a knife in his back. You need to be ready for him."

"I can handle Grimes. You need to leave, Billy. But before you do that, you need to promise me something. I want you to leave me alone. No more unexpected calls. I have enough drama in my life."

He looked hurt. Mags hated treating him this way but didn't see that she had any other choice.

"I'll leave you alone, but I want something in return," he said.

"Go ahead."

"The Gypsies have never been busted. How did Grimes make my friend this afternoon?"

"I thought you'd never ask. Stay right there." Mags got her purse and removed the photo of the Gypsies having breakfast with the claimer that she'd swiped off Blake's desk, which she passed through the door to him. "The woman with the white hair is a claimer who your friends used to steal a jackpot from Galaxy. Grimes made the connection and has distributed the photo to every surveillance department in town. The Gypsies are screwed. You can keep the photo."

He slipped the photo into his breast pocket. "What else does Grimes know?"

"Grimes knows that they're the Gypsies and that they've been ripping off joints for a long time. Grimes is trying to get his boss's job, and he thinks that busting them will be his ticket to the big time. He's determined to arrest your friends and put them away."

"We'll see about that."

"You think you can save them?"

"I'm sure going to try." He stepped away from the door and gave her a smile that would have melted most women's hearts. "Thanks for the save."

He was making the parting easy. Mags appreciated that, and she said a tender good-bye and shut the door. A bad feeling made her pull it open and stick her head into the hallway.

"Hey! What about our deal?"

Now at the elevators, he turned to look at her. "What deal?"

"You promised to leave me alone. I want to hear you say it, Billy."

The elevator doors parted. He got in without answering her.

"You dirty little shit!" she yelled after him.

TWENTY-FOUR

Billy stuffed the vet's cap into a wastebasket before coming out of LINQ and heading north on the Strip's crowded sidewalk. The party was in full swing, and the smells of booze and weed were as pungent as a cheap hooker's perfume. Weed was legal in Vegas, but it was a crime to do it inside a casino or in public, and that included having it in your bloodstream if a traffic cop pulled you over, but that didn't stop the stoners from lighting up whenever the mood suited them. He didn't have a problem with people getting stoned, unless they worked for him.

He came to the Venetian and glanced over his shoulder before going inside. He didn't think he was being followed, but he'd learned it never hurt to be careful. The Grand Canal Shoppes lined the Venetian's famed canals and sold everything from Salvatore Ferragamo to New York pretzels. The Rockhouse was a popular joint, with cute waitresses who got paid to dance whenever the music came on. Tommy Boswell, Cory, and Morris were sharing a plate of Dirty Jersey sliders in a corner booth. Billy took the empty spot next to Tommy and got hit on by a waitress in shorts and a bikini top.

"Hey, hey, the gang's all here," she said. "What's your pleasure, handsome?"

"You still have Big Dog on draft?" Billy asked.

"It's our biggest seller. Sixteen or twenty-two ounce?"

"Sixteen. And a glass of water."

The waitress left, and Tommy Boswell pushed the last slider Billy's way. The Boswells had ice cubes running through their veins, and you would never have known that Tommy had just escaped by the skin of his teeth from the law.

"Thanks for saving my neck," Tommy said.

Billy bit into the slider. Tommy had been made by the gaming board, which meant that some very good photographs of his smiling puss were being circulated to every law enforcement agent in town. Tommy was a wanted man and would remain that way for the rest of his life. For most cheats, being made was the kiss of death. The cheat could never enter a Vegas casino again without risk of arrest. This often led to the cheat getting a face-lift, or if that option wasn't acceptable, seeking another line of work. The waitress brought his beer, which he used to wash down his last bite. Then he took out the photo Mags had given him and showed it to Tommy.

"Recognize this?" Billy asked.

Tommy studied the photo. No smart cheat was going to discuss a prior job, knowing anything he said might come back to haunt him. That left Billy to fill in the blanks. "The lady with the white hair is a claimer your family used to steal a rigged jackpot. The claimer's behavior tipped off the gaming board, who secretly photographed Kat, Nico, and you having lunch with the claimer. The gaming board kept this photo in their database and waited for your family to show your faces again. Nico got made on Fremont Street, Kat got made at the Tropicana. Today it was your turn."

Tommy tried to slide the photo back to him. Billy stopped him.

"Keep it."

Tommy quizzed him with a glance.

"To show your father," Billy explained.

Tommy's face went blank. Tommy wasn't connecting the dots and seeing the big picture. In that regard, Victor's children and Billy's crew were light-years apart. Billy expected his crew to think on their feet and question him about aspects of their work. This was not the case with the Boswells, so Billy explained.

"Your family came to Vegas to do a job with my crew," he said. "The first night we visit a casino together, Nico gets made. Then it happens to Kat, now you. If you didn't have that photo, you might think that I had something to do with this."

"I'd never think that about you," Tommy said.

"Maybe not, but one of your siblings might," Billy said. "They'd think I ratted them out to the gaming board and set up your family. It happens. And then one day your family would find a way to pay me back."

The words were slow to sink in. When they did, Tommy's expression changed. He slipped the incriminating photo into the inner pocket of his sports jacket.

"You want me to have a sit-down with my father, show him the photo, and tell him the gaming board is on to us," Tommy said.

Billy nodded and sipped his beer. In the world of thieving, how you delivered bad news was often as important as the news itself.

"What then?" Tommy asked.

"Then I'll have to explain to your father how much trouble you're all in," Billy said.

- - -

Vegas had more public parking than any other city in the world, a gift from the saint that watched over motorized vehicles. Every casino had its own parking garage, and there were plenty more scattered along the Strip. Billy walked two blocks to Bally's parking garage and picked up his car, then caught up with Cory and Morris and followed them to the

Boswell's rented house. He stayed a safe distance behind, just to make sure Cory and Morris weren't being tailed.

A few blocks from the rented house, he got a call from Pepper.

"Is this the most beautiful hustler in Las Vegas I'm speaking to?" he answered.

"That's me," Pepper said.

"What does that make me, chopped liver?" Misty chimed in.

Pepper's cell phone was on speaker, and it was a party line.

"You should have told me we weren't alone," Billy said. "What's up?"

"Guess who called us earlier," Pepper said.

"Travis?"

"You're psychic. That rat bastard was in his car, asked if he could come over and discuss a business deal with us. I told him we were busy and hung up. Then I called the guard at the front gate to our club and told him not to let that fucking guy in if he showed."

"Did Travis say what his deal was?"

"Travis said he was going out on his own, and if we had any brains, we'd join him."

"Sounds like Travis is plotting a mutiny."

"He can walk the plank by himself," Pepper said.

"Travis also tried to get Gabe to defect," Misty added. "Gabe told Travis to go fuck himself and hung up on him."

The Boswells' place was up ahead. Billy needed to end the call but did not want to sound ungrateful. It would have been easier for Pepper and Misty to pretend that Travis had never contacted them. Instead, they'd reached out and leveled with him.

"Thank you for telling me this. I plan to deal with Travis once this job is done."

"You have my permission to shoot the rat bastard," Pepper said.

"Same here," Misty said.

"I'll let someone else do that. Later."

Cory parked in front of the house and killed his headlights. Billy drove past with one eye in his mirror, looking to see if they'd been followed. He'd taken every precaution to avoid a tail, but that didn't mean there wasn't one. At the next block, he did a U-turn, drove back, and parked in the driveway. He got out to find Tommy standing on the front lawn waiting for him.

"I texted my father and told him the score," Tommy said. "He's waiting inside the house with the rest of my family."

"Tell your father I'll be right in," Billy said.

"Will do." Tommy went up the path and disappeared inside the house.

The SUV was parked at the curb, its engine idling. Billy went to the passenger side and the window lowered. Cory and Morris looked at him from inside.

"Travis is at it again," he said. "He contacted Pepper, Misty, and Gabe and tried to recruit them to join his crew."

"Do I have your permission to shoot that asshole?" Cory said.

Cory had never shot anyone in his life, and Billy let the remark pass. "You both did good tonight. You made me proud. I'll call you tomorrow."

"Thanks, Billy," they both said.

- - -

Billy entered the rented house to find Tommy in the living room telling his family how the gaming board was on to them. Victor sat in a big leather chair, his children on couches or the floor. Tommy had given his father the photo taken with the claimer. Victor studied it before passing it around for his children to see. They'd been caught with their hands in the cookie jar, and the look on Victor's face bordered on disgust. His entire life, Victor had managed to avoid getting his picture taken and so had his kids. Like all good things, it had come to an end.

"Damn it," Victor said. "Okay, Billy, how bad off are we?"

He stood next to the fireplace with his arms crossed. "On a scale of one to ten, I'd call your situation a nine and a half. You need to pull up stakes and run."

"But the gaming board doesn't know my kids' names. You said the other night that we could put a disguise on Nico, and everything would be okay. Why can't we put disguises on Kat and Tommy and go ahead with our job?"

"The risk is too great," Billy said.

"Explain yourself, if you don't mind."

He stepped away from the fireplace. Victor had told him that the super con was his last hurrah. Once it was over, Victor intended to climb into his Cadillac and ride off into the sunset. He hated to be the one to tell Victor that the retirement party would have to wait, but he didn't see that he had any other choice. The gaming board had the Boswells in their crosshairs, and if they didn't hightail it out of town, their days of freedom would be over.

"You're right, the gaming board doesn't know your children's names," he said. "But chances are, they eventually will. Nico, Kat, and Tommy each visited a casino and were spied upon by casino surveillance. A pan-tilt-zoom camera can read the date off a dime. If Nico opened his wallet and exposed a credit card, the PTZ camera captured the name on the card. If Kat used her cell phone, the PTZ captured the number she called. The same for Tommy. If he used his cell phone or flashed the inside of his wallet, it got captured. That's enough information for the gaming board to track all of you down."

"No, it's not," Nico said. Nico was the heir apparent, and he knew how important this job was to his father. "I have a false identity I use for jobs, a guy named Andrew Allen. That's the name on my credit cards and my cell phone. Kat and Tommy also have false identities."

"Are these dead people?" Billy asked.

"Yup. We search the papers for obituaries of people who have died without any immediate family or survivors, and we steal their names and addresses and set up credit card accounts and cell phones in their names."

"How often do you rotate the names?"

"Every six months. If the gaming board does a trace, they'll turn up a dead end."

"No, they won't," Billy said. "The gaming board recently started using a software program called NORA. It stands for Non-Obvious Relationship Awareness, and it was developed by a data mining company that the government uses to track down terrorists. Let's say that the gaming board enters Andrew Allen into NORA. Even though it's a false identity, NORA can spit out every single person that Andrew Allen has made a phone call to or shared an address with. NORA connects the dots and will figure out who your family is."

Nico swallowed hard. "They can really do that?"

"Afraid so."

"Sounds like we're royally fucked."

"That's one way to put it."

"How soon should we leave?"

"Right now," Billy said.

TWENTY-FIVE

There were only so many ways to leave Vegas, and all of them were risky if the gaming board was hunting you.

The quickest escape was McCarran International Airport. But using the airport meant dealing with TSA, plus a small army of full-time cops and six dedicated FBI agents, all of whom communicated regularly with the gaming board.

The Greyhound bus terminal on South Main was another alternative, but there were plenty of cops there as well, looking for wanted thieves and criminals jumping bail.

The last route was by car. Most fleeing criminals took I-15 south into LA. Problem was, the cops had planted high-resolution surveillance cameras on light poles every few miles on I-15, and they used software programs to compare faces in the cars to those on wanted posters. Billy had also heard there were surveillance cameras hidden in cactus trees and billboards, although he'd never seen proof of this.

Three ways to escape, and none of them was foolproof.

At the end of the day, it was Victor's job to spirit his family safely out of Vegas. Victor chose the car escape, believing Kat, Nico, and Tommy would be safer at night on the highway. The Boswells had driven to Vegas in three separate vehicles, and Victor assigned three of his children to be drivers of the escape vehicles.

"I want you to leave five minutes apart," Victor said. "Kat, Nico, and Tommy, you need to stay hidden during the drive. Is that clear?"

"Should we lie on the floor of the backseat under a blanket?" Kat asked.

"That should do the trick," Victor said.

"No, it won't," Billy said. All heads turned to stare at him. "The surveillance cameras on I-15 have infrared lenses and can see into the back of cars. If the police spot something suspicious-looking in the car, that's cause to pull you over."

"Jesus. Then where should we hide?" Kat asked.

"I'd suggest drilling air holes in the trunk and hiding there. It's the safest way to go. Make sure your cars are filled with gas when you leave, so you can drive nonstop. Every gas station has hidden surveillance cameras, and the cops scrutinize every driver."

"You sound like you've done this before," Victor said.

Billy had helped cheats flee town many times. It was harder than people imagined, but with the right planning and attention to detail, it could be done. "It used to be easy to get out of town. Then the Crips gang out of East LA entered a casino with machine guns and robbed the cage. They escaped on the I-15 with their loot and were never caught. That's when the cops decided to install surveillance cameras on the highway."

"That settles it," Victor said. "Nico, Kat, and Tommy will hide in the trunks. We'll drill air holes and put pillows down to make everyone comfortable. Sound good?"

Victor's family agreed to the plan and went to make preparations. Victor stayed behind and spoke to Billy when it was just the two of them in the room.

"I owe you," Victor said.

"You don't owe me a thing," Billy said.

"Yes, I do. Any other cheat would have taken off once the gaming board showed their faces. You did the opposite. I owe you."

Billy decided not to argue with Victor over this. The cheat's code required Billy to help a fellow cheat in need with the understanding that one day, that cheat might help him out of a jam. What goes around comes around, as the old saying went.

"Let me ask you something," Victor said. "This asshole Grimes—why does he have it out for my family? What the hell did we do to him to deserve this?"

"Nothing that I know of," Billy said.

"Then why's he targeting us?"

"Because your family is his ticket to getting a promotion. Most gaming agents are drones. They punch a time clock and count the days to retirement. Grimes is a different breed of cat. He's a smart son of a bitch and can't understand why he doesn't get promoted."

"Why doesn't he?"

"I don't think he plays politics very well. In Vegas, it's all about juice. It's not what you know but who you know. Grimes is trying to get ahead on merit instead of kissing ass."

"Is that why he's after us?"

"You bet. If he can bust your family, he'll parade you in front of the newspapers and show everyone what a great job the gaming board does in policing the casinos. His superiors won't have any choice but to kick him upstairs."

"So this isn't about us."

"That's right. It's all about him."

- - -

Air holes were drilled in the trunks of the Boswells' three vehicles. Nico, Kat, and Tommy climbed into the trunks holding pillows to rest their heads upon. The cars departed at five-minute intervals, leaving Billy and Victor standing in the driveway beneath a waning moon.

"You going to fly out?" Billy asked.

"Have to. I can't sit for more than a couple of hours with my bum leg."

"I'll give you a lift to the airport."

"Much appreciated." Victor used his cell phone to book a ticket on a Southwest flight to Sacramento that left in a few hours, then went inside to pack. When he was done, Billy carried the suitcase outside and tossed it into the trunk of his car.

"Before we go, I need you to help me get rid of the blackjack table in the rec room," Victor said.

The lines at airport security were unpredictable. Billy didn't want Victor to miss his flight and said, "Plenty of people have blackjack tables. Can't you just leave it?"

"Afraid not. I told the owner that we were hardly going to use the place. It doesn't jibe with the story I told him. There's a fire ax hanging on the wall in the garage. Use that."

"It seems like a waste of a perfectly good table. I can hire someone to move it."

"Destroy it. No loose ends. You know the score."

"Whatever you say, Victor."

- - -

Billy chopped up the blackjack table while Victor sat in a chair in the rec room watching him. Victor wanted the table reduced to little pieces so that not even the garbage men would recognize what it had once been. It was harder work than Billy would have imagined.

"Is this small enough?" he asked, holding up the last piece of the table.

"A little smaller, if you don't mind. It still looks like a leg."

"Do you really think the garbage man's going to care?"

"You don't know who the garbage man is. Remember the mob boss Joe Bananas? The feds nailed him by going through his garbage and reading his mail. Stupid guinea didn't have enough common sense to shred his letters before he tossed them away."

Billy cut the remaining piece in half and showed it to Victor. "How about now?"

"Good enough."

In the garage were two wheeled plastic garbage cans. Billy brought them into the house and filled them with the remains of the table, then wheeled them outside and deposited them at the curb for the next pickup. He went to his car to find Victor sitting in the passenger seat.

"Did you figure out my super con?" Victor asked during the drive to the airport.

Billy said no. He'd examined the table while chopping it apart. It was ordinary, without any hidden crevices to hold a tiny camera that could pick off the dealer's hole card and relay the information to the cheat. The secret of Victor's ingenious scam was still safe.

"It's built into the equipment," Victor said.

Billy went over the double line. He righted the car before speaking. "You're kidding me. I looked at every square inch of that table."

"I noticed that. I discovered a flaw in the equipment that lets me rip the house off blind. It's happening at the factory, and the casinos don't know about it. Yet."

"You think they're going to spot it?"

"Eventually they will. Or another cheat will figure it out and rip them off. It has a limited shelf life. If it's not used soon, it will go away."

"You're saying the casino will replace the flawed piece of equipment, and your super con won't work anymore."

"Correct. Which leads me to my next question. We need a large crew to pull this off. My family is out of the picture. Do you have another team you can partner up with? I'd hate to see this fall by the wayside."

They had reached the airport with its confusing array of signs. Billy headed for the departure drop-off area while giving it some thought. He was on a first-name basis with the captains of several crews that made their living scamming the joints. There were cooler mobs that specialized in switching decks on unsuspecting dealers, past-posting crews that placed late bets at roulette, card-counting teams with hidden computers that bled the blackjack tables, and crews that manipulated the dice during craps for huge scores. Each crew was excellent at what it did and capable of pulling this off.

"I'd be happy to make some phone calls. What's our split?"

"You'll have to pay the other team half to get them to agree. You and I will split the other half. I know it's not what we agreed to, but it's still a huge score."

It *was* a huge score. And it was also better than nothing.

"I'm in," the young hustler said.

"Good. You can bring us our share, and I'll take you out to the best steakhouse in Sacramento."

Victor was paying him a compliment. He trusted Billy to deliver the money and not shortchange him and his family. That meant a lot to Billy. They shook hands, sealing the deal.

TWENTY-SIX

Cory and Morris went to Machine Guns Vegas to blow off some steam. There were many gun ranges in town, but only MGV offered military guns for rent. Just by plunking down a credit card, a customer could shoot a Barrett sniper rifle, a SPAS-12 dual-mode combat shotgun, or an M4 lightweight submachine gun used by SEAL Team Six.

They opted for the Three Gun Experience. For a hundred and ninety bucks, they got to shoot three weapons for forty-five minutes straight. Cory chose the AK-47, the M4, and the KRISS Super Vector, which looked right out of a sci-fi flick. Morris had his own preferences and chose the combat assault FN SCAR, the MP5 with a banana clip, and a fully automatic Uzi.

Together they shredded paper targets in the range. Cory preferred targets of flesh-eating zombies, while Morris liked killing terrorists. They were both steaming mad at Travis and made the targets pay for the big man's betrayal. It was bad enough that Leon was being held against his will because of Travis. Now Travis had attempted to get Pepper, Misty, and Gabe to jump ship. Travis was trying to destroy Billy's crew, the rat bastard.

Joining Billy's crew was the best thing that had ever happened to them. Not that long ago, they'd been selling worthless coupon booklets on the Strip. Billy had plucked them off the street and offered to teach them the art of the grift. They'd signed up, and the money had started to flow. They'd bought a new car, rented a house, and filled the fridge with all the delicious food they'd missed growing up. Their lives were heaven, and they were not about to let Travis jeopardize their good fortune.

Finished, they went to the Sand Dollar Lounge and downed shots of Cuervo with beer chasers while listening to the Moanin' Blacksnakes on the makeshift stage. Soon they were swimming in their chairs and feeling no pain.

"Want to get another round? My treat," Morris said.

Normally, Morris's paying for drinks was enough incentive for Cory to say yes.

"I'm toast," Cory said.

"You drunk?"

"As a skunk. How about you?"

"I'm on my way. How about shrimp tacos from the truck? I hear they're decent."

Cory grunted no. Shooting machine guns and quaffing beer usually lifted his spirits. Tonight was different, and his head was filled with bad thoughts. The band took a break, and the purple spotlights on stage went dark. Cory said, "What do you say we drive over to Henderson where Travis lives, hop the wall, and kill that son of a bitch."

"Are you serious?" Morris asked.

"Dead serious. Travis needs to be taken out of the picture."

"Don't you think Billy's already thought about this? Let him handle it."

"Billy's got enough on his plate. It's time we start pulling our own weight."

"I don't think that's a smart idea."

"You're a chicken. *Bock, bock, bock.*"

Cory became impulsive when he drank, and his threat to kill Travis was not an idle one.

Morris snatched the car keys off the table and rose from his chair.

"Let's get out of here," he said.

- - -

When Billy recruited people into his crew, he made them create identities for themselves in case they had the misfortune of getting arrested during a job and had to answer questions about their background and livelihoods to the police. These identities were natural extensions of who they were, making the details easy to recall.

Cory's and Morris's identities were of perpetual college students enrolled at UNLV. To make this look real, they paid tuition and took online courses and lived in a rented house two miles from the university's main campus, the neighborhood filled with students who never slept.

Morris drove down their block. Six bare-chested guys with long hair were playing a makeshift game of soccer in the middle of the street. A keg of beer was providing libations while flaming burgers cooked on an open grill.

"I want to kill that asshole Travis," Cory said.

"Stop talking like that, man. It's not healthy," Morris said.

"Some people need killing."

"He's twice your size. You wouldn't stand a chance."

"Muscle doesn't stop bullets."

Hearing Cory talk like this upset Morris. They had bounced around together in foster homes and watched each other's backs. Morris liked to think it was the reason why they weren't too damaged as adults. He pulled into their driveway and killed the headlights. They'd bought the house out of foreclosure and were still fixing it up. Cory crawled out and threw up in the bushes.

"You want to go to the ER, get your stomach pumped?"

Cory grunted in the negative. When the catharsis was over, he spoke. "The next time we go out, remind me not to drink tequila."

"You said that the last time you puked your guts out."

"This time, I mean it."

Morris unlocked the front door and went to deactivate the security system. To his surprise, it was already turned off. "Didn't you set this when we left?"

"I thought I did."

The house had a sprawling free-flow design with partial walls separating the rooms. In the center of the living room was a giant fish tank filled with exotics. Morris suffered from insomnia, and late at night when he couldn't sleep, he'd sit in front of the tank and watch the fish. The chair he used had a reclining feature, and he often dozed off in it.

Travis sat in that chair now, waiting for them.

- - -

"Hey guys, hope you don't mind, but I let myself in," the big man said. "Still had the key you gave me when you went on vacation and had me feed the fish."

A half-finished bottle of beer sat on the floor. Travis picked it up and took a swig. Cory started to walk toward their intruder. Morris grabbed his friend's arm and restrained him.

"You don't look too happy to see me," Travis said.

"You broke into our house," Cory seethed.

"I used a key. We need to talk."

"Get the hell out, right now."

Travis didn't budge. The tank's bright lights danced across his rugged features. Morris spied a bulge beneath Travis's shirt and guessed the big man was packing heat.

"I have a business proposition that's going to make you bookoo bucks," Travis said, as slick as a used-car salesman. "Sit down and take a load off your feet. You won't be disappointed by what I have to say."

"You're a fucking asshole," Cory spit at him.

"And a traitor," Morris chimed in.

"I won't deny it. But I'm not small-time anymore. And you both are. I found this little beauty on your kitchen table. What are we talking about, fifty years old?"

Travis removed a horse booster kit from the pocket of his shirt. The kit consisted of a miniature battery pack, a solenoid, and a radio receiver, the whole thing designed to be woven into a racehorse's tail. The cheat sat in the grandstands with a radio transmitter disguised as binoculars. During the race, the cheat would press a button that activated the solenoid and triggered a needle that jabbed the horse in the ass, making it run faster.

"It gets the money," Morris said defensively.

"It's bush league," Travis said. "You could drug the horse to run faster or shock it through the jockey's saddle. But stick it with a needle? You've got to be kidding me."

The horse booster was primitive, but sometimes primitive was okay. When the race was over, the jockey could tear the kit from the horse's tail and dispose of it. There was no telltale evidence, which couldn't be said for the other ways to fix the ponies.

Cory looked ready to jump their visitor. A capital idea, only Travis would draw his gun and shoot him. Morris dragged Cory over to the couch and made his best friend sit down beside him.

"Explain your deal," Morris said.

"Broken Tooth uses a network to place his bets for him," Travis said. "This network is in Asia and Europe, but no one in the good ole US of A. That's where you boys come in. You'll place his bets in the States and clean up. Broken Tooth had hoped to strike a deal with Billy, but it didn't work out."

"Why not? What did Billy do?" Morris asked.

"Broken Tooth thinks Billy's a snake. Billy wants five hundred grand in good-faith money to give to the Rebels' defensive players. Broken Tooth said it's too much. He thinks Billy's pulling a fast one."

"And you agreed with him," Cory blurted out.

Travis sucked his beer, his eyes never leaving Cory's face. "Broken Tooth wants to move on. I'm hoping you'll be smart enough to see what a great opportunity this is."

"Billy made you rich, and this is how you repay him?" Cory asked, the booze thickening his tongue. "What fucking rock did you crawl out from beneath?"

"Watch your mouth."

"What did Billy do to make you betray him? Did he say Karen was ugly? Or that your sleight of hand sucks? Come on, I want to know."

Travis's eyes flared, and he leaned forward in his chair. "You're going down the wrong road, Cory. Keep it up, and I'll make you eat those words."

"Answer the fucking question."

Travis touched the handle of his gun through the fabric of his shirt. "All right, I'll tell you what that asshole Billy did. He kept criticizing me, told me I needed to work on my dice and card switches, like I wasn't good enough. I got the money, didn't I?"

"You want to know the truth? Your technique sucks. If Pepper and Misty weren't distracting the pit bosses, we would have been caught by now, you stupid shit."

"Is that so?" Travis lifted his shirt, exposing his weapon. "Say it again, I dare you."

One of the advantages of learning to shoot at MGV was the staff. All ex-military vets from the wars in Afghanistan and Iraq, they'd drummed into Morris's head the importance of getting the draw on your opponent. Anyone could fire a gun and hit a target; the key to battle was getting off the first round. Reaching under the couch, Morris drew a Beretta M9 and took careful aim at their unwanted guest. The M9 had been the standard handgun across the military for twenty years and was absolutely lethal at close range.

Travis froze. His arms went into the air. "Morris. Please."

With his free hand, Morris picked up the remote off the couch and turned on the TV. The voices of two announcers broadcasting a basketball game filled the room, and he jacked up the volume.

Then Morris shot Travis dead.

TWENTY-SEVEN

Vegas never slept, and neither did its airport. Flights into McCarran arrived at all hours, with suckers pouring off the planes eager to blow their hard-earned cash.

Mags stood in the main terminal listening to the endless loop of promotional ads for the casinos play over the PA. It was worse than Chinese water torture, and if she could have found a live human being in the terminal, she would have bribed him to turn it off.

The big board flashed. Amber's flight had landed, and Mags nervously chewed her fingernails. Her baby had flown across the country to visit a mother she hardly knew. Maybe it was the start of a beautiful relationship, or maybe they'd end up at each other's throats. It really didn't matter. It was about to happen, and she'd never been more excited in her life.

Her trajectory was changing. She was starring in a TV show and getting paid to be an actress. *And* she didn't have the cops breathing down her neck. Life was good.

She got a text. I'm here!

Suddenly, she felt scared. Amber was twenty-one years old! Her daughter had slept with boys and knew how to survive in this cruel world. What the hell did Mags think she was going to tell Amber that her daughter didn't already know?

Nothing, that's what.

Mags hadn't been around for the important stuff. Her parents had raised Amber and molded her into the person she was today. Mags had sent checks and called on the important dates, but what good was that in the scheme of things?

Nothing, that's what.

The main terminal had a bank of slot machines. Mags sat down in a chair in front of one and buried her head in her hands. This was all wrong. She'd made a terrible mistake.

A hand touched her shoulder. "Mom?"

She slowly rose. The terminal was swarming with travelers wearing puffy jackets lined with down. Her baby stood before her dressed in a black leather jacket and a wool cap, and could have stepped out of the pages of a yuppie clothing catalog.

"You're taller than me." Mags gasped. "How did that happen?"

Amber kicked off her shoes and shrank two inches. "That better?"

Mags hugged her. "Much better."

- - -

Amber didn't have luggage, just a carry-on, so they went outside to the departure area as Mags sent a text to her driver. Thirty seconds later, a black stretch limo pulled up to the curb, and the uniformed driver jumped out and opened the passenger door.

"Welcome to Las Vegas, Ms. Flynn," the driver said to her daughter.

Amber looked at her mother before getting in. "This is so decadent."

"It gets better," Mags said.

They drank California champagne and ate caviar on crackers during the drive. It was Amber's first time in Sin City, and Mags had the driver take the long route. The town was jumping, and Amber lowered her window, her face bathed in blinding neon and all the false promises that it carried.

"What do you think?" Mags asked.

"All the amenities of modern society in a habitat unfit to grow a tomato," Amber replied.

"Whose line is that?"

"A really funny comic named Jason Love. Is it always this crazy?"

"This is nothing. Wait until the weekend rolls around."

At LINQ, Amber got the same royal treatment at the front desk, and she was presented with the keys to a suite on the same floor as Mags. They rode up on an elevator together still holding their champagne flutes and giggling like teenagers.

"Mom, I want you to be straight with me," her daughter said. "Are you really starring in your own TV show? Or is this just an elaborate put-on?"

"It's a pilot. And yes, I'm the star. Fingers crossed the network likes it."

"How could they not?"

Amber's suite was perfect, the lights turned low, music playing over the surround-sound system, a welcome basket of fruit and delectable chocolates on the night table. Amber got settled in and smothered a yawn. It had been a long day, and Mags kissed her daughter's cheek.

"Get some sleep. I'll order up breakfast in the morning. Then you can come to the set and watch us shoot a scene. Sound like fun?"

"Sure, Mom," her daughter said. "Whatever you want to do is okay with me."

- - -

Mags entered her suite to find a shooting script lying on the floor with a Post-it note from Rand. *The studio hired a script doctor to do a polish. Nothing major. See you in the a.m.*

She fixed herself a drink and thumbed through the script. The scenes that had yet to be shot were filled with changes and corrections, all of it in red pencil, just like her least favorite high school teachers used to do. Most of the changes were cosmetic, except for the scene where her crew rips off a Strip casino and Mags deposits the loot at the door of a women's health clinic that can't pay its bills. The script doctor had suggested having the scene happen during the day, so that Mags could interact with the clinic's owner. It would be more dramatic that way, the script doctor said.

She tossed the script to the floor. The show was called *Night and Day*. During the day, she was a gaming agent who busted crooks; at night, she was a thief who ripped off the joints. Having her rip off a casino during the day destroyed the whole premise of the show.

"Asshole," she said to no one but herself.

Someone was knocking on her door. Through the peephole, she spied Amber holding a bottle of wine and two glasses. She poured her drink down the sink before letting Amber in.

"I couldn't sleep," her daughter said.

Amber poured the wine, and they curled up on opposite ends of the couch and clinked glasses in a toast. Her daughter's eyes were filled with worry. Mags waited her out.

"I don't know how to say this, Mom, but you look terrible. Are you okay?"

"I'm fine," Mags said.

"Well, you don't look fine. You've lost weight and you have dark rings under your eyes. Are you sick? Don't lie to me about this, Mom."

Mags felt trapped. Amber had majored in criminology, and her line of questioning felt like a police interrogation without the bright lights. "Really, I'm fine. It's been a long day, and I'm running on fumes. I'm not lying to you."

"How much weight have you lost?"

"Fifteen pounds. You wouldn't believe how fat the camera makes you look."

"Are you taking speed to keep the weight off?"

"Whatever gave you that idea?"

"Your voice is too high-pitched. I studied substance abuse in school. They taught us how to recognize the different symptoms of drug abusers."

"And you think I'm abusing speed. How wonderful."

"Are you?"

"Does it really matter?"

"It does to me. You're the only mother I have, even if I hardly know you."

A horrible silence passed. Tears raced down Amber's cheeks. This was just as excruciating for her as it was for Mags. They both put their wineglasses on the coffee table. Then Amber crawled into her mother's arms, and they shared a good cry.

- - -

"Have you ever heard of a website called Silk Road?" Amber asked.

They had graduated to room-service nachos and cold beer. It was 2:00 a.m. and Mags was going to feel like crap tomorrow, but she didn't care. Something wonderful had passed between them, and Mags was going to hold onto it for as long as she could.

"That's the site that sold illegal stuff, like weapons and heroin."

"Right. Its creator's name was Ross Ulbricht, and he lived secretly in San Francisco. Here's the amazing part. The person who tracked Ulbricht down was a DEA agent named Gary Alford who works in Manhattan. Alford found Ulbricht without leaving his office."

"How'd he pull that off?"

"He used Google. Seriously."

Mags smiled through a mouthful of nachos. She hadn't eaten junk food since going on her diet, and she'd forgotten how truly great it tasted.

"For my class project, I had to track down a criminal using just Google, then write a paper about all the crimes the person had committed," Amber said.

"That sounds interesting. Which criminal did you pick?"

"You."

Mags choked on a nacho. She sucked down the rest of her beer, and the storm clouds passed. Amber's eyes had gone moist again.

"So you know about the cheating," Mags said.

"I figured it out when I was little," Amber said. "I always had new clothes and got great toys for Christmas even though Grandma and Grandpa were on Social Security. Then one day I got the mail, and it contained an envelope from you. I steamed it open and saw the money."

Back in her grifting days, Mags had carried a stamped envelope in her purse addressed to her parents. When the sucker was cleaned out, she'd stuff half the money into the envelope, find the nearest mailbox, and send it off.

"How much about me did you find?"

"A lot," Amber said. "You were busted more than a dozen times, but the charges never stuck. You must have had some good lawyers."

"How can you find that stuff if the charges didn't stick?"

"There's a website that has mug shots from every police precinct in the country. If you've been hauled in, they have your mug shot. They let you permanently un-publish a mug shot for a fee. It's blackmail, but I did it anyway."

"You made my arrests go away?"

"You bet. It was the least I could do."

"You're not mad at me for not being in your life?"

"I missed you, sure, but Grandma and Grandpa took great care of me. My other friends didn't have it so good. Their parents went through ugly divorces and they got hurt. Compared to them, my life was pretty stable. But I do have a question. Is that okay?"

"You mean about my busts?"

"Yeah. You were arrested in a casino in New Orleans for using a Taser while playing a slot machine. Your lawyer claimed a guy was stalking you, and the Taser was for protection, so the judge let you go. Were you cheating?"

"You bet. Every slot machine has a random-number-generator chip that is vulnerable to electric pulses. If you zap it in the right spot with a Taser, the machine will register a jackpot or let you play for free. I made a lot of money with it until the joints caught on."

"That's cool."

"Stealing isn't cool. Never has been, never will be. Don't think otherwise."

Amber's cheeks turned crimson. "But you made your living—"

"Yes, I did. It paid the bills, and that's the life I chose. But I knew it was wrong when I started doing it, and I don't want you doing it. Understand, young lady?"

"I've never stolen anything in my life."

"Ever shoplifted? Come on, be honest with me."

"Not once. Grandma would have killed me."

"Keep it that way."

"I will. Thanks for being so honest. It means a lot to me."

Her empty beer can did somersaults before landing in the wastebasket by the bar. Mags couldn't have repeated the shot if her life depended upon it. Amber's can followed, hit the wall, and miraculously landed in the wastebasket, the shot worthy of a highlight reel.

"It's way late. What do you say we get some sleep?" Mags suggested. "I have to be on the set at eight a.m. or the director will throw a temper tantrum."

"Is the director a jerk?"

"Everyone in the TV business is a jerk."

Mags walked her daughter to the door and gave her a hug. The toughest conversation in the world hadn't turned out to be so tough after all. All the bad things she'd done were in the past, and she hadn't felt this good in a long time.

"Good night, honey. Sweet dreams."

TWENTY-EIGHT

Wednesday, eleven days before the Super Bowl

A lot of cheats in Vegas also hustled on the links. It was a great way to stay in shape, work on your tan, and make a few bucks on the side.

Every golf hustle was different. Some cheats lied about their handicaps. Others resorted to having their caddies secretly move their opponent's balls to unfavorable lies. And there were cheats who coated their clubs with Vaseline to make the ball fly straighter. There were many scams like this, designed to give the cheat a few extra strokes during the course of a match.

Billy's scam used simple math to give him a mathematical edge over his opponents. There was no trickery involved, and as a result, he'd never had a sucker make a beef. The scam only worked at the Royal Links course, which was located ten miles east of the Strip. The course was designed to reflect the links-style play found on the British Isles. There was the Road Hole and Hell Bunker from St. Andrews and the infamous Postage Stamp from Royal Troon. Making par was a struggle for even the best golfer.

Billy was a member at Royal Links in good standing and friends with the golf pro. The pro had taught Billy how to hit his drives straight and true and how to sink a putt from ten feet out, every time. This was the key to Billy's scam—the ability to hit certain shots at certain times, every time. The pro would set Billy up to play with a wealthy guest looking for a friendly game. Most of these guests were strong players with lower handicaps than Billy. But that didn't mean Billy couldn't steal their money.

The scam always started the same way. Billy would play a few holes while making small talk. Where you from, what do you do, how many kids you got? It was his standard spiel and made the sucker think that Billy was a stand-up guy and not a person who'd resort to robbing him blind.

After three holes, Billy would ask the sucker if he liked to gamble. Every person who visited Vegas liked to gamble, being that there was nothing else to do in town except get drunk, eat, and see the shows. The sucker always said yes.

Billy would suggest two simple wagers. The first wager was to see who could drive the ball the longest without the ball leaving the fairway. The wager was for $500 per hole. If the sucker was wearing a nice shiny Rolex, the wager was a $1,000. The second wager was to see who took fewer strokes on the green. This wager also ranged between $500 and $1,000. During an average match, Billy would pocket between five and ten thousand bucks of the sucker's dough.

The secret to winning the drive was simple. The sucker drove the ball longer than Billy, but that wasn't an advantage on a links course, where sand dunes and narrow fairways resulted in balls not staying inbounds. Since the bet required the sucker to keep the ball on the fairway, the sucker's strength off the tee usually betrayed him.

Billy won this bet 70 percent of the time. To keep the sucker in the game, he'd sometimes deliberately blow a hole. Charity wasn't his strong suit, and he won the money back on the greens, where his putting excelled. His average for these wagers was also 70 percent.

Today's sucker worked in finance and was named Arnie. Every couple of minutes, Arnie's cell phone chirped like a sick bird. He'd say, "Hold on, I gotta take this," and play would stop so he could make another earth-shattering deal.

On the ninth hole, a golf cart pulled up with Morris driving and Cory in the passenger seat. Billy sometimes brought them to Royal Links to work on their games, and he guessed that they'd used Billy's name to get past the guards posted at the front gate.

Billy looked up from his putt. "What's up?"

"There was a problem last night," Cory said.

"What kind of problem are we talking about?"

"Travis came over to our place."

"It didn't end well," Morris added.

"What did you do, smack him in the head with a lead pipe?"

Morris dropped his voice. "Worse."

Morris was white as a ghost. So was Cory. Billy got his bag and put it in the back of their cart. Then he walked over to Arnie, who'd just wrapped up his call.

"I need to run. Let's do this again sometime," he said.

"You leaving?" Arnie asked.

"Business calls. You know how it is."

"But I'm way down. You need to let me win my money back."

To take your opponent's money before a match was over was considered bad action and would land Billy in hot water if the club found out. Suckers needed to believe they could win, even when they didn't have a snowball's chance in hell of coming out ahead. It was the hustle that kept Las Vegas going.

"We're square," Billy said.

Arnie's mouth dropped open. "You mean I don't have to pay you off?"

"That's right. Have a nice day."

- - -

The clubhouse looked like a sandblasted castle, the bar a stodgy British pub. It was quiet, and Billy chose a corner table away from the talkative bartender.

"The usual, Mr. Cunningham?" the bartender called.

"Yes, Nigel. The same for my guests."

"Coming right up."

Billy sat with Cory and Morris facing him. Neither had shaved, and they both wore yesterday's wrinkled clothes. They knew the importance of appearances, and this was totally out of character for both of them. Billy didn't need a crystal ball to figure out what had happened between them and Travis. It was written across both their faces.

Three pints of Newcastle brown ale were brought to the table. Billy clinked his glass against theirs in a toast. "Which one of you took Travis out of the picture?"

"How did you know?" Cory gasped.

"Educated guess. Was it you?"

"That distinction would go to me," Morris said. "He threatened Cory, and I shot him dead. Bastard wanted to start his own crew, if you can believe that."

"Any witnesses?"

Morris shook his head. He was normally the timid one. That had obviously changed. Morris was growing up, right before his eyes.

"What about your neighbors?" Billy asked.

"I turned the TV on full blast before I plugged him. It drowned out the shots."

"Is his body still in your house?"

"We wrapped him in plastic sheeting and backed the car up into the garage, then put him in the trunk," Cory said. "We rent an air-conditioned storage unit where we have a foot locker. We put the body in the locker along with bags of ice."

"So you iced him," Billy said.

The joke was lost on them. It was out of line to make fun of the dead, only the way Billy saw it, Travis's departure was a blessing and could not have come a moment too soon. Everyone got what was coming to him in this life, and Travis had gotten his.

"What did you do with his car?" Billy asked.

"We parked it in the garage at our house," Cory said. "We wanted to ditch it, but by the time we got back from the storage unit, it was light, and we didn't want anyone seeing us."

Up until this point they'd been batting a thousand. Keeping the car was a major foul ball, and Billy reminded himself that they were both still young. "The car is new and probably has a stolen vehicle recovery system. If Karen files a missing person's report with the cops, they'll turn on the system and find his car in your garage. You need to get rid of it."

"His wife is in Reno with her kids, visiting relatives," Morris said.

"Who told you that?"

Morris removed a sleek Samsung Galaxy cell phone from his pocket. "His phone did."

"That's his cell phone?" Billy said incredulously. "For the love of Christ, there are apps on the Internet that let you trace a cell phone just by number. Turn the fucking thing off."

Morris slid the phone across the table. "You need to read some stuff first."

"What stuff?"

"After I shot Travis, his phone let out a beep. Broken Tooth had texted him, wanting an update. So we texted him back."

"Please tell me you're kidding."

"What else were we going to do?" Morris said. "If we ignored the text, Broken Tooth would know something was wrong and kill Leon. We had to act, so we did."

"You realize that just about anyone can trace that phone."

"We know that. Come on, Billy, read it."

Billy hit the text icon on the cell phone's screen. A thread of messages between Broken Tooth and Travis appeared. Travis was big on the bullshit and had told Broken Tooth that Gabe, Pepper, and Misty were on board, when in fact the opposite was true. To complete the story, the final message in the thread claimed that Cory and Morris were ready to leave Billy's crew and run with Travis. This was the message that Cory and Morris had composed.

In disgust, Billy tossed the phone onto the table and shook his head.

"You guys are something else," he said. "You need to get rid of the car, the phone, and the body, and then you need to get the hell out of Vegas and lay low. And make sure you get the trunk of your car cleaned, just in case."

"What about the Gypsies' super con?" Morris asked. "You need us to pull it off. Let us hang around until the job's done, then we'll split."

It was all Billy could do not to explode. He reminded himself that Cory and Morris were invincible twenty-three-year-olds, and they had no concept of how miserable their lives would become if the police linked them to Travis's death.

"You'll leave once you finish cleaning up. Understood?"

"Are you firing us?"

"Call it a sabbatical. I don't want either one of you getting arrested."

"Where should we go?"

"Cancun's nice this time of year. You can stay at my condo."

Billy threw down money, and they walked out of the pub. No one said anything until they were in the parking lot.

"Are you going to try and save Leon?" Morris asked.

Billy nodded. He was expecting to meet up with Broken Tooth later and get the good-faith money to give Night Train and his pals. At this meeting, Billy would ask Broken Tooth to release his driver now, instead of after the big game. Billy had kept his end of the bargain and hoped Broken Tooth would cut him some slack.

His car was parked by the pub's entrance. Billy hit the unlock button on his key chain, then stopped. "Before you shot him, did you ask Travis what his beef was?"

"Yeah. Travis didn't like you critiquing his sleight of hand," Cory said.

"Pissed him off, huh?"

"In a major way."

Cheats who did sleight of hand were called mechanics. In Billy's experience, mechanics had inflated egos and high opinions of themselves. Every cheating move had a bad angle that could be detected by a powerful camera lens. Yet somehow Travis had forgotten this and let Billy's criticisms get under his skin. Talk about ruining a beautiful thing.

"Call me after you dump the body," he said.

TWENTY-NINE

Mags never knew what to expect when she came onto the set. It was always high drama, courtesy of Rand. He was obsessive about the show and always making changes. One morning, he'd handed Mags a brand-new scene, and she'd retreated to her trailer and spent an hour learning her lines. Another time, Rand ordered the director to reshoot the previous day's scenes because the lighting was off.

Every day it was something new.

This morning's surprise was a roulette wheel and table with a green felt layout. The pilot did not have any scenes with roulette, and Mags could only guess what Rand had up his sleeve. Hud stood off to the side with a cameraman. Their director was not happy with the change of scheduling, not that it mattered. Rand was the moneyman, and his word was law.

"Why, good morning, Mags," Rand said. "You look as stunning as usual."

Her reflection in the mirror this morning had looked anything but stunning. The show was eating her alive, and she put on her brave face. "Hello, Rand. I want you to meet my daughter, Amber. Amber, this is Rand Waters, our producer."

Rand's eyes fell upon Amber. "You look just like your mother, which is to say you're amazingly beautiful. Do you act? I'd love to fit you into the show."

"You've already corrupted one of us," Mags scolded him. "Leave my baby alone."

"Of course," Rand said. "We have a change in plans. The honchos at CBS are having a programming meeting tomorrow to discuss this fall's lineup, and I wanted them to see a clip of you doing the chip move you described to me. What's it called again?"

"The Savannah?"

"The Savannah. That has such a nice ring. Yes, that one."

"What about the scene that we're supposed to shoot?"

"It can wait. Now go get your makeup, and we'll get started."

"Wait a minute—where are my lines?"

"We're going to ad-lib it. Think of this like a visual postcard. You can say whatever you want, just be yourself and it will go great."

"What the hell is a visual postcard?"

"You know what I mean. Make it fun. The guys at CBS love this kind of stuff."

Rand went to talk to Hud. A hand dropped on Mags's wrist. It was the makeup lady. She was anxious to get started and make Mags look presentable to the camera.

"Are things always this chaotic?" Amber asked.

"This is nothing," Mags said.

- - -

Twenty minutes later, they shot Rand's visual postcard.

"Hello, my friends at CBS," Rand said to the camera. "It's with great pleasure that I introduce you to television's next sensation, the beautiful and talented Maggie Flynn."

The camera panned to show Mags behind the felt layout, flashing a smile.

"In *Night and Day*, Mags plays a Nevada gaming agent who catches cheats by day, then at night robs casinos being run by ruthless owners and donates the loot to charity," Rand said. "Think of it as Robin Hood takes on Sin City. To prepare for her role, Mags has taught herself scams being used to cheat the casinos. She'd like to share one with you now."

"Thank you, Rand, and hello everyone," Mags said, turning on the charm. "The scam I'm about to show you is called the Savannah and has cost Las Vegas's roulette tables millions of dollars. It may be the cleverest swindle ever invented."

She pointed at the cloth-covered betting area. "This is called the layout, and it's here that the swindle takes place. The roulette wheel has thirty-six numbers, a zero, and a double zero. There are two types of bets a player can make: inside bets and outside bets. Inside bets are wagers a player can make on a number coming up, and they have huge payouts. Outside bets offer smaller payouts but have better odds. A player can bet red or black, odd or even, high or low. These bets pay even money. The Savannah is done with an outside bet. Here's how it works. Rand is going to be our croupier. Ready when you are, my friend."

Rand edged up to the wheel. "Place your bets."

Mags removed three red chips from her purse. Red chips were worth five dollars apiece. She placed the three chips in an uneven stack on the red box on the layout.

"Let it rip," Mags said.

Rand spun the wheel and sent the tiny white ball spinning in the opposite direction. The ball came to rest on number sixteen, which was red. Mags clapped her hands.

"Look at that! I just won five thousand dollars!"

Rand acted puzzled. "But you only bet fifteen dollars."

"No, I didn't. See for yourself."

Rand spread the three chips on the red box. To his surprise, the bottom chip of the stack was a brown five-thousand-dollar chip. "How did that get there?"

"I put it there. You just didn't see it." Mags picked up the three chips and put them in a stack. "By pushing the top chip forward, the bottom chip is hidden from view."

"So it was always there, just out of sight."

"That's right. Now, I know what you're wondering. What happens if the little ball lands on a black number, and I lose the bet? That's where the Savannah happens. Roll the wheel again and I'll show you."

Rand resumed his croupier role. "Place your bets, please."

Mags again placed the three chips in an uneven stack on the red box. Rand spun the wheel and sent the little white ball in motion. This time, the ball landed on number thirty-three, which was black, a loser. Mags leaned forward and craned her neck to see. As she did, her hands briefly brushed her bet. So slight was her movement that it was nearly imperceptible.

"Damn!" she exclaimed. "I just lost fifteen dollars."

"No, you didn't," Rand said, completely in the dark. "You lost five grand."

"Afraid not. Have a look."

Rand spread the three chips in the red box. His face registered surprise. The bottom chip had magically turned red. "Where did the five-thousand-dollar chip go?"

"It's right here in my hot little hand."

Mags brought her left hand up to the camera and opened her fingers. Two red chips and one brown chip were palmed at the base of her fingers. Rand's mouth dropped open. So did the director's. And so did Amber's. She'd fooled them all.

"Every good scam has a clever angle that makes it work," she explained. "The Savannah is such a scam. Casino employees are trained to watch winning bets in roulette. As a result, they don't see the losing bet getting switched. It's the perfect swindle."

Rand let out a laugh, hamming it up. "And there you have it. The perfect con, delivered by the incredibly talented Maggie Flynn, star of *Night and Day*. We look forward to delivering a finished pilot to you in the next few weeks. Thanks for your time."

"That's a cut," Hud said. "Man, did that look sweet."

"Show me," Rand said.

Rand went around the table and stood with their director. Together they stared at the tiny screen on the back of the camera and watched Mags switch the stack of chips.

"Unreal," Hud said. "You hardly see her hands move."

"The guys at CBS are going to love this," Rand gushed.

Mags walked away from the table feeling queasy. She'd scammed plenty of casinos with the Savannah and never had a problem. Yet performing the move in front of a camera tied her stomach up in knots, and it made her wonder if she was cut out to be an actress.

"Mom, are you okay?" Amber asked.

"I'm fine. What did you think?"

"I think you're going to pass out if you don't sit down. You're all pale."

Amber found a chair, and Mags fell into it. She'd been running ragged for days, the tension building up inside her like a pressure cooker ready to explode. The show was riding on her shoulders, and the fear of failure had become too great. She couldn't handle it anymore.

"Stay put. I'm going to get you some water," Amber said.

Her daughter left. Mags tried to get her act together. The show was her chance to set a positive example for Amber. *Mom makes good* had a nicer ring than *Mom does time*.

Amber returned with a bottled water and a guest in tow. It was none other than Special Agent Grimes with a pair of nickel-plated handcuffs clipped to his belt.

Oh shit, Mags thought.

THIRTY

They moved the party to Mags's trailer. While Mags and Amber took chairs, Grimes positioned himself so he blocked the door. Frank wasn't like most gaming agents. The sole purpose of his life was to wage war against the town's cheats and hustlers, whom he despised. Mags had slept with him for eighteen months and still marveled at the darkness of his soul.

"I'm going to destroy you," was his opening line.

Mags lit up a menthol cigarette and blew a blue cloud in his face. "Really."

"Does your daughter know about your past?"

"What Amber does or doesn't know is none of your concern."

"My mom beat the casinos, and you weren't smart enough to catch her," Amber said.

Frank looked like he just might snap. Out of his pocket came the photo of the three members of the Gypsies having lunch with the claimer, which he waved in Mags's face. "I had these people in my cross-hairs. You tipped them off and they blew town, and my investigation went up in flames. You're going to pay for this, Maggie."

"I don't know what you're talking about, Frank, and that's the God's honest truth."

"Let me refresh your failing memory. While I was giving you and Rand a tour of LINQ's surveillance room, a tech named Blake made one of the Gypsies capping his bets at blackjack. You slipped into a restroom and either made a phone call or sent a text. A few minutes later, the Gypsy bolted and ran. We were right behind him, only his family had a getaway car, which the Gypsy hopped into. We got everything on tape, except the getaway car's license plate."

"What a shame," Mags said.

"Admit it, you tipped him off."

"I did no such thing."

"Of course you did! Why else would the Gypsy run? For the love of Christ, he left his chips on the table. He knew we were going to bust him because you told him."

"Where's your proof?" Amber interrupted.

"Who the hell is she, your fucking lawyer?" Frank snapped.

"Watch your mouth around my daughter."

"How touching. Maggie the doting mother. I can hear violins in the background."

"Up yours, Frank."

"Where's your proof?" Amber repeated.

"Right here." Frank flipped over the photo of the lunching Gypsies to reveal a phone number written on the back. "I distributed this photo to every tech on the Strip and told them I'd pay them a reward if they busted these guys. This particular photo was on Blake's desk at LINQ. We know that because Blake identified it for us. The phone number is a friend of his. You had a conversation with Blake, then asked him where the restroom was. When Blake wasn't looking, you swiped the photo off his desk and later passed it to the Gypsies."

"I did no such thing. I've never met these people in my life."

"Look, Maggie, the Gypsies run in a pack, and it occurred to me they might be renting a house. So I made Airbnb cough up the names of houses rented in the past few weeks, and I checked them out. The last one, on the north side, was empty. But we found the photo lying on the grass by the driveway. And since we can place you in the LINQ surveillance room the last time the photo was seen, we can connect you to them."

"No jury will buy that. Give me a break," Amber said.

"I'm not talking about a jury," Frank said. "If I convince a judge that your beloved mama is attempting to defraud the casinos, he'll let me turn her life upside down. I'll look at every cell phone call, every e-mail, every bank statement. No stone will be left unturned."

"You won't find anything," Amber said. "My mom doesn't do that stuff anymore."

"You might be right. Maybe we'll turn up nothing," Frank admitted. "But she'll still have to hire a lawyer. She won't be able to act in her precious TV show because she'll be too busy defending herself. We'll still win."

Mags rose from her chair. "No, you won't. I'll take a lie detector test and say that I've never met the Gypsies in my life. And your stupid investigation will end."

Frank slipped the photo into his jacket pocket and smiled. "Thanks for the heads-up. I'll make sure not to administer a lie detector test." Mags and Amber both started to protest, and he shut them down. "In case you forgot, my career is riding on this case. And that means more to me than all the tea in China. Get it, Maggie?"

"I don't know them, Frank. You have to believe me."

"I do believe you. But that doesn't mean I care."

"You dirty shit."

"Is that all you've got left in your sling? Pick up the phone and start calling your grifter friends. Find out where the Gypsies are. If you don't, I'll destroy you."

"This is blackmail."

"I won't argue with you there. Have a nice day."

Frank walked out of the trailer. Rand was standing behind the door and nearly got his nose broken. He had heard every damn word and looked fit to be tied.

Rand entered and shut the door. "How do we make this go away?"

Mags shook her head, defeated. "I have no idea."

"Will he take a bribe?"

"You want to give him money? We could all go to jail."

"We could have the carpenters working the shoot put new countertops in his kitchen. The wives always dig that."

"Jesus Christ, Rand. You've got to be kidding."

"What about appliances? All name brand. He can't say no."

"That's not going to work."

Rand was a Hollywood charmer. A knife could have been sticking out of his gut and he still would have managed to exude optimism. The smile slowly disappeared, revealing a deeply troubled man. "CBS has budgeted two million bucks for this pilot. If the shoot gets shut down, everyone will be fired, and my deal with CBS will fall apart. You need to fix this, baby."

"I don't know how to fix it," Mags said.

"You swiped that photo. You had to realize there would be consequences if you got caught."

Rand glanced across the trailer at Amber leaning against the fridge. His eyes stayed longer than they should have, then returned to Mags.

"I'm sure you and your daughter will think of something," he said.

THIRTY-ONE

Leaving Royal Links, Billy rolled down his window and let the desert air warm his skin. When he'd first landed in Vegas, he thought he'd walked into a pizza oven. Over time he'd gotten used to the intense heat and found himself looking forward to days when it broke a hundred degrees and the grass turned brown before his eyes.

He got a call as he pulled into Turnberry Towers. It was none other than Mags. Just yesterday she'd proclaimed that she never wanted to lay eyes on him again, and here she was, giving him an old-fashioned phone call. He answered with a cheerful, "Hey there."

"You stupid little bastard," she swore.

The valet approached. The valet liked his job too much, leading Billy to assume the residents' cars were being taken for unauthorized spins. He waved him away and parked in the building's shade. "I missed you, too."

"Fuck you, Billy. And the horse you rode in on."

"Are you going to explain what I did or just curse at me?"

"Frank Grimes just paid me a visit. Frank tracked down the Gypsies to a rented house on the north end of town. He went out there to arrest them, only your friends were gone. But they left behind a calling card in the grass next to the driveway."

"What kind of calling card?"

"Excuse me. *You* left a calling card in the grass by the driveway."

"I did?"

"Yes, you little turd. Remember the surveillance photo I gave you? Well, it must have fallen out of your pocket onto the grass."

He shut his eyes and took a deep breath. He'd given the photo to Tommy Boswell, who must have let the photo slip out of his pocket while he was climbing into the trunk of the getaway car. Even the best crooks screwed up and became complicit in their own demise. To make matters worse, the photo had landed in the hands of Frank Grimes, who prided himself on making cheats' lives miserable, one day at a time.

"Can the photo be traced back to you?" he asked.

"It sure can. You need to fix this, Cunningham. Right fucking now."

Mags was on tilt and running off at the mouth. He needed to look her in the eye and calm her down. Having her come to his penthouse was not a good idea, since she might say something out of line in front of the desk clerk or a resident and blow his cover. And then he'd have to go to the trouble of finding a new place to live.

Across the street, a brand-new joint called SLS shimmered like a mirage in the desert. He'd recently checked out the casino and found the pit bosses and dealers so green that they could have fallen off the backs of potato trucks. There were loads of dining options, ranging from super expensive to el cheapo, and he decided to meet Mags there.

"Meet me at Umami Burger at the SLS Hotel in half an hour. And don't be late." It was a crass thing for him to say. Mags had helped him, and in return he'd screwed up and put her in a bad light. But she still needed to be reminded who was in the driver's seat. Otherwise, she'd run all over him.

She started to royally curse him, and he ended the call.

- - -

Mags sat down at Billy's table at Umami. "Talk about treating a girl to a good time. This place is a toilet. At least you could have picked some place nice."

Umami was nothing to write home about. It had a split personality and billed itself as a burger joint, beer garden, and sports book. It did none of those things well. There was nothing to recommend it, except fifty big-screen TVs that made it impossible to eavesdrop. The gaming board had bugged bars all over town, and Billy chose his meeting places carefully.

"This is my daughter, Amber. Amber, meet Billy Cunningham."

Amber Flynn also pulled up a chair. She was a softer version of her mother, with short-cropped brown hair and a face that made you want to buy her a drink. She'd graduated college not long ago and had the self-assured air of a person who thought anything was possible.

"Nice to meet you," Billy said. "You guys want something to drink? Or a burger?"

"We didn't come here to eat," Mags said. "I'm going to get right to the point. Frank Grimes wants me to help him find the Gypsies. If I do that, he leaves me alone. If not, he's promised to turn my life upside down and destroy me."

"Is Grimes serious?"

"Dead serious. My producer knows."

"What does that mean?"

"It means that if I don't get Grimes off my back, *Night and Day* will be shut down, and I'll be out of work."

Billy glanced at Amber, then back at her mother. "How much does she know?"

"I don't keep secrets from Amber."

"You need to help my mother," Amber said, breaking her silence. "That asshole suit from the gaming board has it out for her."

"I'll do what I can," Billy said.

"That's not good enough." Amber sounded so much like her mother that it was scary. She put her elbows on the table and leaned in. "My mother helped out your friends, and you dropped a piece of evidence that's put my mother in a bad situation. I know you didn't do this intentionally, but you were still responsible, and you've got to own up to that."

Mags had told Billy that Amber had majored in criminology with a minor in psychology, making Billy think that Amber believed she might plumb the recesses of the criminal mind and learn what made people turn bad. In the meantime, she needed to be straightened out, so he said, "I didn't ask for your mother to give me that photograph. She didn't tell me that it could be traced back to her or that I needed to destroy it, which I would have been more than happy to do. So don't throw a guilt trip on me, okay? Shit happens, especially in our line of work."

That shut the kid up but fast. A waitress hit the table. Billy ordered three Sculpin IPAs before Mags or her daughter had a chance to read the menu. The waitress departed.

"I don't like IPAs," Mags said.

"Neither do I," her daughter echoed.

"It's an acquired taste." He paused to let that set in, then said, "Why does Grimes have it out for the Gypsies? There are other thieves he could chase who would land him a promotion."

"Frank said the Gypsies are special, that no one's ever caught them," Mags explained.

"He wants the recognition," Billy said.

Mother and daughter stared at him, not understanding.

"Grimes wants to be recognized by his superiors," he said. "It's what drives most people in law enforcement. They need a superior to tell them they're better than average."

"You're good," Amber said.

"Call it whatever you want," Mags said. "Grimes is hell-bent on nailing your friends to the wall. So what the hell are we going to do?"

Their beers came. Mags and her daughter sipped and winced. IPAs were a creation of the British army in their desire to bring beer to soldiers stationed in India during the 1800s. The beer's unusually strong hops were not for more sensitive palates or the faint of heart.

"We'll send Grimes in another direction," he said.

A spark of hope lit up Mags's face. Acting was draining the life out of her, and the bewitchingly beautiful creature who had seduced him into a life of crime was a shadow of her former self. It broke his heart, but he didn't see how he was going to get her back.

"How are you going to do that?" Mags asked.

The germ of an idea was forming in Billy's head. The Gypsies were a big fish, but there was an even bigger fish to be caught, one that would all but guarantee Grimes a promotion and get him the praise of his peers. He finished off his beer.

"Tell me," Mags insisted.

"I can't," he said.

"Why not?"

"Because I haven't entirely figured it out yet. But I will. You have to trust me on this. I'll get Grimes off your back, and you can go back to being a TV star."

"Is that a promise?"

"Yes, it's a promise."

Amber shot him a murderous look. "Well, aren't you Mr. Fucking Wonderful? 'You have to trust me on this.' Right. Like anyone is going to trust you. You don't have a plan at all. You're just bullshitting us."

"Amber, that's enough," Mags said.

"I don't care. He screwed up and needs to make things right."

Billy started to steam. He'd given Mags his word, and in this town that was better than a contract witnessed by a dozen high-priced lawyers.

Only Amber wasn't buying it, and he wondered if his hundred-dollar haircut or the crease in his trousers had turned her off.

"We'll probably never hear from you again, either," Amber added.

She had called him a snake. Billy didn't like it and decided to set Amber straight. "Your mother came to me because she knows I can fix this. How isn't important. Once I put my mind to something, I'll get it done."

"You're not that smart."

"You don't think I can do it?"

Amber shook her head; she had no faith in him at all.

"If I told you I was going to steal two grand from the casino, would you believe me?"

"Steal it how?"

"That's beside the point. Would you?"

"Sounds like bullshit to me."

"So you don't trust me when I say I'm going to do something."

"Not in the least," Amber said.

"Two grand in sixty minutes."

"Is he being serious?" Amber asked her mother.

Mags rose from the table. Her daughter had picked this fight, and Mags wasn't going to get in the middle of it. "I'll be outside in the car. Come out when you're done."

"But Mom . . ."

"Start timing me," Billy said.

- - -

Billy entered SLS's casino with Amber hot on his heels. Mags had spoken so highly of her daughter that he'd expected a polished young woman possessing loads of subtle charms. Amber was barely out of diapers and hardly knew the score.

The blackjack pit was hopping, the dealers smiling and friendly. He did a slow trawl of the tables, looking for a game that could be easily scammed. There were dozens of ways to cheat at blackjack that ranged from the obvious to the sublime. Billy had cut his teeth with these scams but over time had graduated to bigger things.

He zeroed in on a female dealer whose name tag said KENYA/CLEVELAND. Kenya was as pretty as a picture and all dolled up, her long fingernails perfectly manicured. No casino in town would have let Kenya deal blackjack, but SLS was brand new, and management didn't know better.

He turned to Amber. "Are you legal?"

"What is that supposed to mean?" Amber said.

"Are you twenty-one? Otherwise, you can't sit down at the table with me."

"Yes, I'm legal."

"They're going to want to see ID."

"I have a driver's license and my student ID."

"That should work. How much time do I have left?"

"Fifty-two minutes."

They took chairs at Kenya's table. Billy threw down $500 and Kenya turned it into chips. He placed a fifty-dollar bet for himself, another fifty for Amber.

"Is it okay if I coach my girlfriend?" he asked. "She's never played before."

"Coaching's allowed," Kenya replied. "Good luck."

Kenya dealt the round. Blackjack required that the dealer take the second card and slip it facedown beneath her first card, which stayed faceup. This facedown card was called the hole card. Its identity would be revealed only after the players had played their hands.

If Billy could determine the value of the dealer's hole card, he would possess an edge over the house that would allow him to win more than he lost. It was all about the odds, and this piece of information tilted the odds in his favor.

There were several ways to peek at a dealer's hole card. Each used a hidden device or an accomplice. Unless, of course, the dealer unwittingly gave away this information.

Dealers who gave away their hole cards were called flashers. Kenya was a flasher. As she slipped the second card beneath her first card, the nail on her manicured forefinger dug into the felt and caused the card to bow, briefly exposing its left corner. There wasn't enough time to read the card's value but plenty of time to determine if the card was a paint card or a number card. Paint cards had a lot of ink on their faces and were either a jack, queen, or king. Number cards were the rest of the cards in the deck.

On the first round, Kenya flashed paint. Ten in the hole. Kenya's face card was a five, giving her a total of fifteen. A stiff.

Billy had a fourteen and waved his hand over the cards, indicating that he would not take another card. Amber had a pair of tens.

"Should I stay?" Amber asked.

"Split them," Billy said.

Amber hesitated, then split her tens and doubled her bet. Kenya dealt a five on the first ten, a six on the second. Both hands were stiffs. Amber groaned.

"It's not over," Billy said.

Kenya flipped over her hole card, revealing a jack. Kenya dealt herself a third card and busted. She gave a practiced smile and paid off her customers.

"I just won a hundred bucks," Amber said under her breath.

"You sound surprised," Billy said.

"Do it again."

Kenya was as easy to read as an open book. Billy took his sweet time and slowly built up his winnings. Had he won too quickly, it would have alerted a pit boss or a sharp tech in the surveillance room that something fishy was going on at Kenya's table.

Amber said little, content to watch the scene play itself out. She was like a sponge, and little seemed to escape her attention. Glancing at her watch, she said, "Time's almost up."

Billy visually counted their chips. They were ahead $2,200. Rising from his chair, he graciously tossed Kenya a two-hundred-dollar tip.

"Thanks for the good time," he said.

- - -

Casinos were designed for their patrons to lose track of time, and the blinding afternoon sunshine caught Billy by surprise as he walked out of SLS.

"I think I figured out your little scam," Amber said. "It was based upon our dealer's long fingernails. She kept scraping the felt, and you spied her hole card."

Amber was sharp, but he wasn't about to tell her that.

"What if I told you that you were wrong?" he said instead.

Her face crashed. "Then how did you do it?"

"Doesn't matter. What matters is, if I tell you I'm going to win two grand, I'll win two grand. And if I tell you that I'll deal with a slimy gaming agent giving your mother a hard time, I'll take care of him."

"Can you really fix my mother's problem?"

"Stop questioning me, will you?"

She briefly stared at the ground. "I'm sorry I underestimated you."

"Don't do it again."

"I won't."

"Your mother loves you more than anything in the world. You know that, don't you?"

"Yeah, I know that."

"She'd do anything for you, she loves you that much."

"I figured that out."

"Glad to hear it." He took out his winnings and shoved the money into her hands. "Now, go show your mother a good time."

"The money's mine?"

"Yes. There's plenty more where that came from."

She hesitated. The good angel sitting on her shoulder said, *Give the money back, it's stolen.* But the bad angel perched on the other shoulder said, *Take the fucking dough and have a party, this is Vegas, kiddo.* The bad angel won, and she shoved the money into her pocket.

"What's the deal between you and my mom?" she asked.

He wasn't going there, and he started walking backward.

"You're in love with her. I can see it in your face."

"It was nice meeting you," he said.

"You're the devil, aren't you?"

The words stung more than he would have liked.

"I'm whatever you want me to be," he said.

THIRTY-TWO

Getting rid of Travis was proving trickier than Cory and Morris had anticipated. They'd stowed his body in their rented storage unit at night when no one was around. Now, in broad daylight, the facility was swarming with people, and they couldn't move him without being seen. Certain criminal acts you could talk your way out of. Unloading a corpse wasn't one of them.

Cory sat behind the wheel of the SUV. He'd placed a call to Billy and was waiting for a call back. Billy was the champ at fixing messes and would know how to dispose of Travis. Before coming to Vegas, Billy had worked for a gangster, and he knew all sorts of valuable stuff.

While he waited, Cory watched horse racing from Santa Anita on his cell phone using an app called BetAmerica. His account with BetAmerica also let him place wagers. He also had accounts with sites with catchy names like Twin Spires and Horse Races Now.

The horses exploded out of the gate and galloped around the track. A ringer named Sally Boy pulled ahead and never looked back. It won at odds of ten-to-one. Cory had bet $500 on Sally Boy, which put him ahead five grand. He'd also bet $500 on a nag, which finished dead last. The racing sites monitored their customers' action and would become suspicious if a customer won too much, too often. By purposely betting on a losing nag in the same race as a ringer, he was avoiding any unnecessary scrutiny.

Morris climbed in and took the passenger seat. Morris hadn't slept and looked like death warmed over. The shock of having shot Travis was slow to wear off.

"Any word from Billy?" Morris asked.

"Not yet." They fell silent. The car's interior was suffocating. Morris held his hands in his lap. His fingers were trembling as if he had palsy. Cory had read that when a cop was forced to shoot and kill a suspect, the cop was put on leave for several weeks. Cory had thought this was an administrative thing but now realized otherwise. The cop needed to heal.

"So where are we going to hide out?" Morris asked.

"Billy suggested we head down to Mexico."

"Refresh my memory. What's in Mexico?"

"Billy owns a beachfront condo in Cancun that he hustled off a rich sucker with the newspaper scam. We'll hang there and drink piña coladas and look at pretty girls."

"Sounds good. What's the newspaper scam?"

"I never told you about this? It's beautiful."

"Lay it on me. I could use some cheering up."

"It's done at a hotel pool. The cheat and the sucker play high-stakes gin rummy. At the next table sits the cheat's partner smoking a cigar and reading the newspaper with a slit in it. The partner peeks through the slit at the sucker's cards and signals their value by coughing."

"The sucker doesn't notice?"

"Guys who smoke cigars cough a lot. It flies right by the sucker."

"We should try it in Cancun. Who's going to feed the fish while we're gone?"

Cory started to say, "Travis," but stopped the word from leaving his mouth.

"You think Gabe will do it?" Morris asked.

"The way Gabe feels about me these days, he'll probably poison them."

"You really in love with his daughter?"

"It's starting to feel that way. I'll find out when I'm in Cancun, see how long it lasts when we're apart. Absence makes the heart grow fonder. Yeah, right."

Morris suddenly punched the dashboard and yelped in pain.

"Why did you do that?" Cory asked.

"I never should have shot Travis. I should have just let him shoot his mouth off and he would have left. Killing him proved nothing."

"Travis had it coming. If I'd gotten my hands on the gun, I would have shot him. That asshole was destined to die in our house, so stop flogging yourself."

More silence. They both were craving a joint. Getting high was how they calmed themselves down. But they'd sworn off the dope, and neither wanted to be the first to bend.

"What are we going to do in Mexico besides get sexually transmitted diseases?"

"A couple of weeks ago, Travis told me about a project he was working on for Billy," Cory said. "I'm going to ask Billy if we can take it over. It will give us something to do."

"What kind of project?"

"Travis called it the Same Key project. It's based upon the principle that companies will cut corners by putting out duplicates under the belief that no one will know. Ford did it years ago when they only put out four keys for their station wagons. Word eventually got out, and Ford got in trouble, but it still goes on."

"In the casino business, too?"

"Especially in the casino business. Back in the old days, each slot machine needed a key to open it. Several manufacturers cut corners by having a skeleton key that could open all their machines. It worked great, until a gang of cheats made a copy and went around rigging jackpots. The casinos lost a bundle."

"But that can't happen now," Morris said. "Can it?"

"Billy thinks it can. There are more than a hundred thousand slot machines in Vegas and another fifty thousand video poker machines. By law, each machine is required to have its own source code embedded in the EPROM chip that keeps the game from getting corrupted. Billy thinks there are machines out there that share the same codes."

"These machines would be made by the same company."

"Correct. It would save them a fortune by sharing codes. The machines would be vulnerable, but they're banking on the belief that no one will realize what they've done."

"Like Ford."

"Exactly. Just like Ford."

Morris was feeling more like himself and sucked on his swollen knuckle. "So how are we going to figure this out while we're sitting on the beach in Mexico?"

"That's the fun part. The companies that manufacture the games are publicly held. We look at their quarterly reports and see if any have been reporting unusually high profits. If one is making more money than the others, they're probably cutting corners and sharing codes."

"Stock reports," Morris said.

"You don't believe me."

"It sounds far-fetched."

"Travis said this was the way Lumber Liquidators got caught."

"Those were the guys who put embalming fluid in the flooring."

"Right again. A hedge-fund manager analyzed their stock report and didn't understand why profits were so high. He investigated and found they were putting bad chemicals in their products. Stop sucking your hand. It makes you look like a baby."

"What happens if we find a company that's making more money than the others?"

"Billy will buy two of their machines and have Gabe pull out their EPROM chips and see if the codes match. If they do, it's off to the races, my friend."

It all sounded fine and dandy, but it didn't explain how they were going to dispose of Travis without being spotted and going to prison. They were in a heap of trouble if Billy didn't come to their rescue.

Cory's cell phone chirped. "It's Billy," he said.

Morris tried to eavesdrop, and Cory pushed him away. The call was a short one. Cory hung up and started the car.

"Lock the unit," Cory said. "Billy's come up with a plan."

THIRTY-THREE

Gabe's home in Silverado Lakes was the crew's unofficial meeting place. The neighborhood was sleepy, and the nearby pizza joint delivered.

After his wife split, Gabe had chosen to redecorate with expensive grown-up toys. An elaborate train set filled the living room; a slate pool table was in the den; and Ping-Pong, foosball, and pinball were in the family room. It was the perfect man cave, and his crew usually enjoyed a few games before getting down to business.

Not today. They sat at the kitchen table, as still as an oil painting. It was weird without Travis. The big man was the life of the party, and his loss left a void. Wanting to lift the mood, Billy said, "Show us the gaffed coin you created for the Super Bowl coin flip."

Gabe produced a gold coin from his shirt pocket. The size of a silver dollar, it had the Vince Lombardi Trophy on one side, the participating teams' helmets on the other. Gabe explained how the coin's extra thickness had allowed him to insert a capsule of mercury and a microtransmitter in its center. On Gabe's iPhone was a special app with two buttons. The red for tails, the green for heads. Pepper was given the honors and flipped the coin into the air.

"Heads," Billy said.

Gabe pressed the green button. The coin hit the table showing heads. "I've tested it a thousand times. The micro-transmitter shifts the mercury to the opposite side, producing the desired result. It never fails."

"How far away can Cory and Morris be with your iPhone to make it work?"

"Three hundred feet max. If they sit in the first few rows of the stadium, no problem."

"Call a scalper and buy two front-row seats on the fifty-yard line," Billy said to Cory. "You and Morris are going to the Super Bowl next Sunday."

"Not Mexico?" Cory asked.

"No. I came up with a way to dispose of Travis's body that will leave you and Morris in the clear."

"Cool," Cory said.

The words cast a pall over the others. Billy studied their faces before speaking again. "Travis was a dumb bastard, but that doesn't change the fact that we all liked him. If you have something you'd like to get off your chest, do it now."

"I just don't understand why Travis broke bad on us," Misty said. "We were his friends. His situation was different having a wife and kids, and we went out of our way for him."

"I know you did," Billy said.

"And we covered for him," Pepper added. "Remember that time at Harrah's when Travis threw the dice down the table, and the palmed pair hidden in his hand fell on his chips? I pulled my titties out of my blouse and swung them in the employees' faces to give Travis a distraction so he could clean up. I don't pull my titties out for just anybody, you know."

"You saved his ass," Billy said.

"Damn straight I did. So why did Travis turn on us? I know Travis told Cory it was because you criticized him, but hell, we all criticized him. That wasn't the real reason Travis screwed us. It had to be something else."

Billy didn't see the point in kicking a dead horse. Travis should have been happy with his deal. The big man had run with Billy the longest, had made the most money, lived in a nice house, had two new cars, and took his family on great vacations. But Travis had a dark side that the others hadn't seen. He had frequented hookers and picked fights in bars with strangers. And the big man had stolen from every casino he had worked for. Nothing had ever been good enough for him. Travis had been destined to blow himself up; it was simply a matter of when.

"Some dogs just like to roll in shit," Billy said.

His crew nodded agreement. Vegas was filled with self-destructive people. The catch was that none of them had recognized this flaw in Travis.

Billy was glad to have that out of the way, and he got down to the business at hand.

"I've got a plan to get rid of the body, save Leon, and also put the screws to that little rat bastard Broken Tooth," he said. "Call it killing three birds with one stone. It will work a little differently than our casino heists. Cory and Morris will pair up, as will Pepper and Misty, while Gabe will run solo. I'm not going to share your roles with the others, in case one of us gets busted by the gaming board."

"The gaming board is involved in your plan?" Cory asked.

"That's correct."

"But I thought you were on their Most Wanted list."

"I am. But that doesn't mean I can't get them to help us. I have something the gaming board wants, and they should be willing to work with me."

"Why are you keeping us in the dark?" Gabe asked.

"It's for your own protection. If you don't know what the others are doing, you can't give up the information if you get hauled in."

"Got it," Gabe said.

"Didn't I see this in a movie once?" Misty asked.

"*Reservoir Dogs*," Pepper said. "Will we have aliases like Mr. Pink and Mr. Brown?"

"Not this time," he said. "I want each of you to pack a suitcase. Once Leon is out of danger, you'll need to hightail it out of town. Cory and Morris will head to Phoenix to get ready for the Super Bowl scam. Gabe, I suggest you go with them in case your trick coin malfunctions before the game and needs fixing. Pepper and Misty, you can go wherever your hearts desire."

"We can stay with my girlfriend in LA," Pepper said.

"That works. There's one more thing. I live by the cheater's code, and I expect you to as well. People think it's funny that criminals would follow a code, but it's what keeps the profession alive. You've got to have rules, even if you're in the business of breaking the law.

"One of the most important rules is that a cheat should never put another cheat in a compromising situation. If a cheat gets caught, he should never rat out his partners. And a cheat should never intentionally screw up another cheat's score. Those two things are forbidden. In the old days, you'd get a bullet in your head for breaking these rules."

He paused to let the words sink in, then continued. "I should have killed Travis the moment I figured out he'd betrayed us. Travis put all of us in harm's way, not just Leon. But I loved the big guy, so I held back. That was my mistake, and I'm sorry." He looked at Morris. "And I owe you an apology."

"You do?" Morris asked.

"I owe you an apology because I didn't do my job. If I'd handled this differently, you wouldn't have had to shoot Travis. That was my responsibility, and I'm sorry, man."

"Thanks, Billy. That means a lot to me."

"You're welcome. Now, let's go rescue Leon and set things right."

THIRTY-FOUR

"Frank, you know how badly I want you to get my job," Bill "Trixie" Tricaricco, director of field agents for the Nevada Gaming Control Board, said. "You've paid your dues, my friend. But I can't just hand it to you like a baton at a relay race. You have to earn it."

Grimes went stiff in his chair. What the hell had Trixie just said? Grimes had arrested more casino cheats than any of his peers. If the report card was graded based upon number of busts, then Grimes got nothing but straight As. And then there was the matter of Trixie and Grimes having murdered a contract killer named Wilmer Haney and his despicable son and burning the Haneys' house down to hide the crime. Didn't that count for something?

"But I've earned it," Grimes protested a little too loudly.

"But what have you done for us lately?" Trixie said. "I know that sounds trite, but it's the truth, Frank, and you haven't had a bust in a while. That's not like you."

"I thought I was a shoo-in. You said so yourself."

"I did. But that was before Little Miss Debbie Do Good stole your thunder. That young lady is a force to be reckoned with."

"Debbie's only been here three years. I've put in ten."

"The boys upstairs like her. She's made some busts, and she's got great legs."

Special Agent Debbie Goodman had a horseshoe stuck up her ass. Do Good had made several solid busts, the most recent a Strip casino laundering cash using an intricate series of wire transfers. The Strip casino had paid a huge fine, and Debbie's stock had risen in the department. This was the first time Grimes had heard she was vying for Trixie's job, and it galled him.

"When will your replacement be announced?" Grimes asked.

"A few days before I retire," Trixie said.

"Which is when?"

"I'm blowing out of here in two weeks. I'm still waiting for the paperwork to get processed. Folks in Carson City don't know the meaning of fast."

"So I still have time," Grimes said.

"For what?"

"To bust the Gypsies and get your job."

"I thought you told me the Gypsies slipped town and left a cold trail."

"I haven't given up yet."

"You've got a lead on them?"

"Yes. And I plan to work it until I find them."

"That's the spirit, Frank."

Trixie unscrewed a bottled water and took a long swallow. There was an ugly rumor swirling around that Trixie would soon be in the employ of Pearl Gaming, which owned four casinos in town. There was nothing wrong with Trixie entering the private sector; government employees did it every day. The problem was with Pearl. A month did not go by when one of their casinos wasn't getting fined for running games that did not pay out the advertised rate of return. Pearl's management didn't care, and they simply paid the fines and continued to break the law. Only the threat of the gaming board revoking Pearl's gambling license would change things, but the gaming board hadn't yanked a casino's license in forty years.

Hearing a knock on the door, Trixie barked, and a timid secretary stuck her head in. "There's a man on the phone who needs to speak to Frank."

"Take his number, and Frank will call him back," Trixie said.

"I tried, and he refused to give it to me. He said it's urgent."

"Maybe that's your lead on the Gypsies," Trixie said.

Grimes's cheeks burned. Trixie, his boss and friend, was telling him to leave. The shelves behind Trixie's desk were bare, the mementos boxed away. Trixie already had one foot out the door, his days of dealing with field agents a thing of the past.

"I'll catch up with you later," Grimes said.

"You do that, Frank. And good luck."

He was going to need it.

- - -

Grimes parked his burly frame into the chair in his cramped cubicle. He had a number of snitches on his payroll, and it wasn't uncommon for one to call needing money to bail his sorry ass out of jail. Grimes yanked the phone out of its receiver and said, "This is Special Agent Grimes. To whom do I have the pleasure of speaking?"

"This is Billy Cunningham," the voice on the other end said.

Grimes gripped the receiver so hard it made his hand throb. If any single cheat had hurt his reputation and stunted his chance for a promotion, it was Cunningham, and it was all he could do not to curse him out. "You just pulled me out of a meeting. This better be good."

"I need your help," Cunningham said.

"That's the funniest thing I've ever heard. You calling me for help. Ha-ha."

"There's something in it for you."

"I'm hanging up the phone. Have a nice day."

"There's a Chinese gangster in town trying to fix the Super Bowl. His name's Broken Tooth, and I can help you nail his ass."

"His name's Broken Tooth? Get real."

"Guy's got his own page on Wikipedia. Check him out if you don't believe me." Grimes decided to do just that. On his cluttered desk sat an ancient PC. He got on the Internet and with Google's help was soon reading a page devoted to a notorious Chinese criminal named Wan Kuok-koi, aka Broken Tooth. According to the article, the guy was a public menace and had fixed hundreds of sporting events around the world. As a result of his gangster lifestyle, a meat cleaver had mangled one of his arms.

"You still there?" Cunningham asked.

"I'm here," Grimes said. "So how does this guy plan to fix the Super Bowl?"

"Broken Tooth approached me to talk to players for the Rebels who spend their off hours at a private villa at Caesars. The plan is for the players to fix certain plays, which will cause several proposition bets to fall his way. Broken Tooth needs the money to finish building a beachfront resort he owns in China so he can live happily ever after."

"Did you approach the players?"

"I sure did."

"I should arrest you right now."

"I didn't have a choice. Broken Tooth's goons kidnapped my limo driver and are holding him hostage."

"You're saying this Chinese guy blackmailed you."

"That's right. Now are you interested, or should I call the FBI?"

Fixing the Super Bowl. The words floated through Grimes's brain like a banner being pulled by a prop plane. Sporting events were being fixed every single day, and the Vegas sports books took a beating because of it. But because these fixes took place outside of Nevada, the gaming board was powerless to stop them. It occurred to Grimes that this would be a first.

Movement caught his eye. Trixie's office had a glass wall, and he spied Debbie Do Good standing in front of Trixie's desk, working her charms. He came out of his chair.

"I'm interested. Where are you?"

"I'm at a joint called Herbs and Rye."

"Never heard of it. You'd better give me directions."

"Head west on Sahara and make a U-turn after crossing Valley View. Look for the dark, plain building next to the ARCO gas station and use the red door. I'll be waiting for you."

"Yes, you will," Grimes said.

- - -

There were so many gin joints in Vegas that Grimes had given up trying to keep track of them. In the good old days, the bars had served whiskey, wine, and beer. Today, the bars had wine cellars, fifty craft beers on tap, and exotic cocktails that took five minutes to prepare.

Grimes came through the front door of Herbs and Rye and stopped to let his eyes adjust. The place had a handful of customers, all tourists. Grimes could tell they were tourists because they were getting drunk in the middle of the day. Cunningham sat at the end of the bar, eating a plate of calamari. He waved to Grimes like an old friend.

Grimes gritted his teeth and headed down the bar. Not that long ago, he'd taken a contract out on Cunningham's life, a plan that had blown up in his face. And now here he was, about to get in bed with the little bastard. He didn't care. He wanted that corner office.

He sat on a stool next to Cunningham and ordered a beer. He wasn't supposed to drink on the job, but if he ordered a nonalcoholic drink in a bar, everyone would know he was a cop.

Cunningham pushed the calamari his way. "Have some. It will make you feel better."

"Who said I wasn't feeling well?"

"It's written all over your face. You look like crap."

"What's all this shit it's mixed with?"

"Banana peppers, prosciutto, and cherry pepper aioli. It's really tasty."

Grimes stuck a piece into his mouth and chewed. It was the best calamari he'd ever tasted, but he wasn't going to tell Cunningham that.

"Start from the beginning, and don't leave anything out," Grimes said.

"Two nights ago, Broken Tooth paid me a visit down on Fremont Street. He's got this plan to fix the Super Bowl by bribing the defensive line of the Rebels. Problem was, I wasn't interested."

"Really? Sounds right up your alley."

"I don't like sports betting. Too many things can go wrong. Broken Tooth got pissed when I said no, so he kidnapped my limo driver, Leon, and is holding him ransom."

"You have a driver?"

"Part-time. Broken Tooth had his goons kidnap Leon and is holding him until I get this done."

"Is Leon a member of your crew?"

"I've told you, I don't have a crew."

"Right. Does Leon drive the getaway car when you do your jobs?"

"I don't know what you're talking about."

Grimes finished the calamari. So far everything Cunningham had said rang true, but he wasn't going to make a decision just yet. Wiping his mouth with a paper napkin, he said, "Which Rebel players did you talk to?"

"I met with Night Train McClain and his buddies on defense. Night Train wasn't interested and told me to take a hike. That's why I called you. If I tell Broken Tooth the bad news, he'll have one of his henchmen put a bullet in Leon's skull."

"You haven't told Broken Tooth."

"Nope."

Grimes sipped his beer in thought. He'd been trying to run down Cunningham for ten years and had come up short. Like a grand master at chess, Cunningham was always several moves ahead of his opponents, a master at anticipating what his adversaries were about to try.

"What's your plan?"

"Broken Tooth wants to give Night Train and his pals upfront money as a show of good faith. I was going to tell Broken Tooth that the fix was in and pick up the money."

"How much we talking about?"

"Five hundred grand."

This was sounding better all the time. "And that's where the gaming board comes in."

"Correct. I'll wear a wire when I go see Broken Tooth. I'll get him to talk about the fix, and you can record it. Then I'll get the five hundred grand from him and hand it over to you. That should be enough to arrest his sorry ass, don't you think?"

It was more than enough. Broken Tooth would go down hard, and Grimes would get the credit. If that didn't get him kicked upstairs, nothing would.

"When is this meeting with Broken Tooth taking place?"

"I'm waiting for him to call me. Hopefully this afternoon."

Grimes winced. He needed time to set this up properly. "Can you stall him?"

"I can try."

They finished their drinks. Cunningham's cell phone on the bar began to vibrate. The young hustler raised the cell phone to his face and answered the call.

"Hello?"

Grimes's hearing was better than a dog's. The caller was Chinese and had a voice as pleasing as fingernails scraping a chalkboard. Grimes heard the words *Super Bowl* come out of the caller's mouth and knew that everything Cunningham had said was true. Flashbulbs exploded, and for a moment he could hardly think straight. This was the moment he'd been waiting for, and he didn't care if a little scumbag hustler was responsible for it.

"Tell him yes," Grimes whispered.

"What time?" Cunningham said into the phone. "Six o'clock tonight?"

Grimes looked at his watch. It was three thirty. Two and a half hours was hardly enough time to set up a proper sting, but it would have to do.

"Tell him you'll be there," Grimes whispered.

"That works for me," Cunningham said into the phone. "Where?"

Cunningham motioned for something to write with. Grimes pulled a pen from the pocket of his sports coat, and Cunningham wrote down an address on a cocktail napkin.

"I'll be there." Cunningham hung up.

Grimes paid for the drinks and food. It was his way of telling Cunningham that the past was behind them. Cunningham seemed to appreciate the gesture and stuck out his hand.

"This feels like the beginning of a beautiful friendship," the young hustler said.

It was all Grimes could do not to wring Cunningham's neck. He hated Cunningham with all his heart and soul, but that was meaningless right now. Grimes needed help. And when you were drowning, you couldn't be too choosy about who threw you a life preserver.

Grimes briskly shook the young hustler's hand.

THIRTY-FIVE

Wearing a wire just wasn't what it used to be.

Back in the good old days, a plant would go to a meeting wired up, get a crook to make an incriminating statement, and record it so the DA could use it against the crook in court.

This was easier said than done. Wearing a wire was cumbersome and consisted of a miniature tape recorder attached to the informant's waist, with wires secured to a microphone that was taped to the informant's chest. It was a bulky setup that required the informant to wear a long-sleeve shirt and a sports jacket to hide the apparatus. If a wire slipped free and made itself visible, or if the crook patted the informant down and discovered the deception, the plant was forced to jump through a window to avoid retaliation.

Not anymore. Today, wires were digital. An informant no longer needed to have a tape recorder attached to his body. Instead, he wore miniaturized recording equipment hidden in the button of his jacket, the point of a pen, a cuff link, or the edge of a tie clip. He could be patted down by a crook and not get caught. Thanks to the technological revolution, snitching had gotten a whole lot easier.

Billy sat in a room of the Nevada Gaming Control Board's headquarters getting outfitted with a wire. Never in his life had he expected to be doing this. The gaming board was the cat and he was the mouse, and the mouse never willingly entered the cat's lair. But he was desperate to save Leon and help Maggie, and sometimes desperation was the mother of invention.

"Hold still," Grimes said.

Grimes had decided to put the wire in a button on Billy's silk shirt. Grimes had chosen the top button because it would be closest to Broken Tooth's mouth when the Chinese gangster started talking and incriminated himself in the fixing of the Super Bowl. Because English was a second language to Broken Tooth, it would be important for Billy to stand close and get Broken Tooth to speak clearly so the recording equipment in the gaming board van would be able to record what Broken Tooth was saying. Otherwise, they were wasting their time.

Billy looked down at the button Grimes was attaching to his shirt. The shirt was made by Versace and had a busy blue-and-gold Baroque print with front-button closure and a hidden placket. He'd paid $600 for the shirt, and it was one of his favorites. The button hiding the wire was a different shade of beige than the shirt's other buttons but was hidden by the placket.

"The button's the wrong color," Billy said.

"It's close enough. Besides, he's not going to see it," Grimes said.

"He'll see the button if my shirt parts open."

"What are the chances of that happening?"

"Fifty-fifty. Either the shirt opens up, or it doesn't. Can you get another button? Just to be on the safe side?"

"This is the only one I've got. Look, he's not going to see it. Just go in there, get him talking, and once he implicates himself, we'll break down the door and bust him and his goons. Your driver will walk away unharmed."

"My driver's name is Leon," Billy said.

"So?"

"I care about Leon. That's why I came to you. I want to save him from getting shot. Are we clear about this?"

"Sure. No reason to lose your cool."

"I just wanted to make sure we were on the same page."

The special agent nodded like they were on the same page. Only that was a lie. Grimes didn't give a rat's ass if Leon walked away with his skin; Grimes's only concern was having his ugly puss splashed across the front page of the newspaper and getting his long-overdue promotion.

Grimes took a step back to admire his handiwork. The button was heavier than the other buttons and created a crease in Billy's fancy shirt. Billy could see the crease but hoped no one else would.

Grimes moved to a desk on the other side of the room. Picking up a pair of headphones, he fitted them on his head. "Start talking in your normal voice."

Billy started talking in a normal voice. Grimes shut his eyes and listened. Then he nodded and removed the earphones. "Clear as a bell. How good is Broken Tooth's English?"

"It's chipped," he said.

"Meaning what? That he sounds like the illegal taking your order at a Chinese restaurant?"

"It's a little better than that."

"We need to be able to understand what Broken Tooth's saying, otherwise the case will get thrown out of court. You'll need to stand right next to him and get him to talk in a clear, concise manner. Otherwise, this won't work."

"He's holding Leon against his will. Doesn't that count for something?"

"The fact that Broken Tooth kidnapped your driver doesn't mean he's trying to fix the Super Bowl. Broken Tooth can tell the judge that your driver borrowed money from him and refused to pay it back. I've had that happen in kidnapping cases before. Does your driver have a record?"

"Yeah, Leon's got a record."

"The judge will take that into account. Look, Cunningham, I've played the game long enough to know what the rules are. Your job is to get Broken Tooth to discuss how he plans to fix the Super Bowl and that he's giving you money to bribe the players. That information has to come through on the recording, otherwise this won't fly."

"Got it." He fingered the button on his shirt. "What's the range on this thing?"

"More than a quarter mile."

"Does that take into account that Broken Tooth is inside a building, and that the transmission will have to go through walls?"

"Can't you get Broken Tooth outside?"

"That's a bad idea."

"Why?"

"Broken Tooth's a pro. He knows about wires. If we go outside, he'll want to take a drive, and your transmission will be lost."

"Then what's your plan?"

"Broken Tooth will be contacting me soon. I'll go pick up the money and make sure Leon's okay. I'll engage Broken Tooth in conversation and get him to drop his guard. I'll steer the conversation to the fix and get Broken Tooth to implicate himself. Once that's done, you and your posse can come to the rescue. That work for you?"

"Good enough. You going to be carrying?"

"Look at the clothes I'm wearing. A gun would stick out. No, I'm not carrying."

"I just wanted to be sure."

Billy glanced down at the crease in his shirt. He followed the maxim that the people he did business with were just as smart as he was. If he thought the button looked funny, Broken Tooth would think it as well. And if that happened, Broken Tooth would go berserk and have his goons tear Billy's arms out of their sockets and beat him to death with them.

"Sure you can't do anything about this button?"

"Tuck your shirt into your pants and tighten your belt. That will hide it."

Billy gave his suggestion a try. The crease went away. It was as good as he could hope for. Grimes said, "I've got some people you need to meet."

The special agent picked up his headphones and transmission equipment and walked out of the room. Billy followed him, looking down to see if the crease reappeared. It didn't, and he forced himself to put it out of his mind.

- - -

Grimes escorted Billy to the building's subterranean level where the weaponry was stored. Four gaming agents awaited them. The agents—two white, one Latino, one black—were lean and mean, all of them clean shaven with cropped hair and no visible tattoos. They looked like grown-up choirboys.

Introductions were made. Billy acknowledged each agent with a curt nod. The agents were not his friends and never would be. Billy had stolen so much money from the casinos that the gaming board had taken to plastering Billy's face in every surveillance room while accusing him of more thefts than any human being was capable of committing. They were desperate to bring him down, and the irony of their working together was not lost on him.

Grimes explained how the bust would go down. Grimes and the agents would be in an unmarked van and would tail Billy to the meeting. The agents would wait outside on the street in the van, electronically eavesdropping on Billy's conversation with Broken Tooth. Once Broken Tooth had handed over the money to bribe the Rebel players, the agents would show their faces and make the bust.

"Any questions, ask them now," Grimes said.

There were no questions. With Grimes in the lead, the agents crossed the hall to a room where the heavy weapons were stored. A clerk working the counter assigned each agent a sawed-off shotgun along with a bulky bulletproof vest and a ballistic helmet. It occurred to Billy that he would be the only participant in this little drama who would not be armed or have a way of defending himself if things went south. He was trusting Grimes with his safety, and he hoped it wasn't a mistake.

The gaming agents fitted on their body armor and loaded their weapons. Grimes watched them as they did this, then got dressed and loaded up.

"Let's roll," Grimes said.

They took an elevator to the main floor and piled out. Beads of sweat did a slow death march down Billy's face. Grimes questioned him with a lifted eyebrow. Billy didn't want to admit his fear and said, "Why the sawed-off shotguns?"

"They work better in close quarters," Grimes explained.

THIRTY-SIX

The gaming board parking lot faced the intersection of North Las Vegas Boulevard and East Washington Avenue. Miles away from the glitz and glitter of the Strip, the most action you were going to find here was a tumbling sagebrush or a blue hair trudging back to his apartment carrying a sagging bag of groceries.

Billy sat in his car with the AC blowing on his face. Across the lot, Grimes and his posse stood next to an unmarked white van, going over last-minute details on how they planned to bust Broken Tooth and his gun-toting goons. Despite its Wild West culture, Vegas had strict gun laws, and agents of the law did not take kindly to criminals who used firearms while committing crimes. Often, these criminals got shot and killed for their trouble.

Billy's cell phone lay on his leg. Using one hand, he texted different members of his crew to make sure they were ready to help bring their buddy Leon home.

You got the counterfeit money? he texted Gabe.

Yessir. In two suitcases, like you said, Gabe wrote back.

Billy had to tell Gabe something only once for it to get done right. Next up were Cory and Morris, the two members of his crew he was most worried about. They were both stressed out over Travis's shooting and didn't need the added worry of dumping his body.

Did you put T in your car? Billy texted.

Yeah. Wrenched our backs dragging him, Cory replied.

Anyone see you?

No. Put a screen in front of the unit like u said. Worked great

This will be over soon. You guys okay?

Cory didn't respond. There was no doubt in Billy's mind that he and Morris were both hurting. A few weeks from now, after this debacle had played itself out and they were home free, the three of them would get together for a long weekend and party up a storm. It was one way to start the healing process and get Cory and Morris back on track. Bad shit happened in their line of work; how a person dealt with it defined their careers and their lives.

His final text was to Pepper and Misty. The girls had a special role in the little charade they were about to pull, one that required them to get face-to-face with Grimes and distract him. Grimes was many things, but a rube was not one of them. If Grimes suspected that Pepper and Misty were trying to trick him, he'd haul them both in.

You ladies ready?

Primed and willing. When do we go on? Pepper texted back.

Soon

Billy looked up. Grimes was marching toward him with a snarling look on his already ugly puss. The cell phone was balanced on his leg, and he flipped it so the screen was facing down and dropped it on the passenger seat. He rested both hands on the steering wheel.

Grimes stuck his head into the driver's open window. "What are you doing?"

"Enjoying the beautiful outdoors," he said.

"Don't be a smart-ass. I saw you looking in your lap. Admiring your junk?"

"It's worth admiring, or so I'm told."

"Very funny. Did Broken Tooth contact you?"

"Not yet."

Grimes breathed his foul breath on Billy's face. Every cop he'd encountered, from the streets of Providence to the fancy casinos of Vegas, spouted noxious breath that could not be quelled by Tic Tacs or vigorous mouthwash. Billy had decided that it was a by-product of the job. Dealing with lowlifes and miscreants created a bile-producing creature in the stomach that simply could not be quelled.

"Then who are you texting? Your crew?" Grimes asked.

"I wasn't texting and I don't have a crew."

"You'd better not be messing with me."

Truth ran both ways. Right now, Billy wasn't feeling any, and he exploded. "How do I know you're not messing with *me*? How do I know that you won't shoot Broken Tooth and then turn your gun on me? Or have one of your men do it?"

"Don't think I haven't considered it," Grimes said, playing tough.

"But you won't?"

"No sir."

"Like I should trust you? Right."

"Nothing's going to happen to you, Billy, and on that you have my word. I need you to stand up in front of a judge and tell him the story you told me. Otherwise, I don't have a case."

"You're not going to waste me."

"Wouldn't dream of it."

It was just like Mags had said. Grimes was determined to get that promotion, even if it meant getting in bed with his worst enemy, which happened to be Billy.

"But don't think that changes things between us," Grimes said. "If I catch you doing anything funny before this bust goes down, I'll drag you out of that fancy sports car and kick your ass until your nose bleeds. Am I making myself clear?"

"Loud and clear."

Billy's cell phone vibrated on the passenger seat. "This is Billy," he answered.

"This is Broken Tooth," the caller said. "I've got the five hundred grand. You ready?"

"I'm ready."

"Good. You know Joyful House restaurant on Spring Mountain Road?"

It was the same restaurant where Cory and Morris had spotted Broken Tooth's henchman picking up take-out food. "I've heard of it," he said.

"Be in the parking lot in thirty minutes. Don't be late."

"We're going to do the exchange in the parking lot? We could get robbed."

"Don't be stupid. My men will meet you, bring you here. Then we'll do exchange."

"Got it. I'm leaving right now."

There was silence on the line. Billy went rigid in his seat. He'd screwed up. The previous two times he'd spoken with Broken Tooth, he'd demanded that Broken Tooth put Leon on the line to confirm that his driver was still alive. Billy hadn't done that this time, and he felt certain that Broken Tooth had picked up on the discrepancy.

"But first I want to speak with my driver," he added.

"Your driver is taking a nap," Broken Tooth said.

"Wake him up. If I don't talk to my driver, our deal is off."

"Don't argue with me!"

"Do it, or I'll hang up on you."

Broken Tooth dropped the phone on a table, the sound like an explosion in Billy's ear. He glanced at Grimes. The special agent was not happy with this development and started to voice his displeasure. Billy silenced him with a finger to the lips. Leon came on the line.

"Hello?" His driver's speech was slurred.

"Hey, Leon, it's me, Billy. You don't sound so hot. You okay?"

"They beat the shit out of me."

"What did you do this time?"

"They like to watch Chinese TV on their smartphones. Some stupid variety show. There was a girl singing off-key, so I asked them to turn the volume down."

"How bad did they beat you up?"

"Can't see out of my left eye, and my ribs are busted. I think my nose is broken, too."

"I'm going to get you out of there, man. That's a promise."

"You better hurry up, because I can't take much more of this."

Broken Tooth came back on the line. "You satisfied?"

"Why did you have to hurt him?"

"Your driver's got a big mouth. Lucky to be alive. Joyful House on Spring Mountain Road. Be there in thirty or my men will kill your driver."

"Don't do that."

The call ended. Billy dropped the phone into his lap and used his hands to massage his face. It hurt him to hear Leon sounding so bad. Grimes touched Billy's sleeve.

"If it makes you feel better, I can have an ambulance waiting nearby."

He stared into the special agent's face. There was a tinge of compassion beneath the ugly that hadn't been there before. Like the criminals they chased, cops' souls were often scorched beyond repair or healing. Grimes had fallen far, but he hadn't fallen all the way.

"That would be great," he said.

Grimes made a phone call to arrange for an ambulance to be at the ready. Ending the call, he hustled over to where his posse was gathered. The gaming agents piled into the van and followed Billy out of the parking lot.

As Billy drove to Joyful House, he used one hand to send his crew a group text telling them the rescue was on. Hitting "Send," he realized his hand was shaking. He'd never been more scared in his life, and he tossed his phone on the passenger seat and stared at the road.

THIRTY-SEVEN

Joyful House was the anchor tenant of the Spring Oaks Plaza Shopping Center and advertised itself as one of the country's top fifty Chinese restaurants. Vegas did not believe in zoning, and the center also housed a discount furniture store, a gun shop, and a massage parlor.

Dinnertime and the parking lot was nearly full. Billy took a space away from the restaurant's entrance, by the street, while the gaming board's van parked in front of the gun store with Grimes at the wheel. The plaza was a hub of activity, and the van blended in nicely.

Billy's crew arrived in three vehicles and parked across the street in front of a store called Psychic Castles, which sold lucky charms and crystals. Cory and Morris drove their Infiniti SUV, Gabe his old diesel Mercedes, the girls a sexy red BMW that Pepper had recently bought.

Everyone ready? he texted.

His crew responded with a chorus of thumbs-up emojis. A minute later, Broken Tooth's henchmen pulled into the lot in their rental, parked in a handicapped spot by the restaurant's front door, and got out. Their knuckles sported flesh-covered Band-Aids, which Billy guessed were a result of the bashing they'd given poor Leon.

One of the bodyguards wore a man bun. He called for Billy to stay put and entered the restaurant with his partner. Billy's cell phone rang, and he grabbed it off the passenger seat.

"What do you want?" he answered.

"Are those Broken Tooth's men?" Grimes asked.

"No, they're the Boy Scouts."

"Never hurts to double check. Say something into the button on your shirt. I need to check the transmission again."

"You've got to be kidding me."

"Just do it."

Billy dipped his chin and spoke into the button. "This is a test of the emergency idiot system. This is only a test."

"You're not funny," Grimes snapped.

"Got to run. Remember, if you shoot me, your case goes south."

"Don't tempt me, Cunningham."

He ended the call and took a deep breath to calm his nerves. The henchmen emerged with two shopping bags of takeout. Billy got out of his car and walked toward them.

"Ready when you are," he said.

"Not yet." Man Bun pointed at the roof of the rental. "Hands there."

Billy slapped his hands on the roof. Man Bun patted him down, then stuck his hand underneath Billy's shirt and ran his hand over the young hustler's chest, searching for a wire. Satisfied, Man Bun jerked open the rental's passenger door.

"Get in."

Billy got in, and the bodyguards sandwiched him into the front seat like a human sardine. The rental pulled out of the lot heading west on Spring Mountain Road and was soon doing eighty miles an hour. Billy wasn't wearing a seat belt and hugged the dashboard, fearful of being hurled through the windshield if they made a sudden stop.

"Slow down!"

Man Bun let out a brutal laugh. A mile later they slowed to sixty miles per hour, and the rental took a left on Lindell Street on two wheels. A mile after that, the daredevil move was repeated, this time on West Flamingo, followed by a quick right on El Camino and into the driveway of a one-story house with shuttered windows and zero landscaping, the rental's wheels screaming as the brakes were finally used. Billy spotted a mailbox hugging the sidewalk: number 4021.

The garage door went up, and the rental entered. Billy stole a look in the mirror. The van with the gaming agents was nowhere to be seen. You're screwed, he thought. The garage door came down, bringing darkness. The car doors were opened, and the car's interior light came on. The henchmen got out. Billy followed, and the bags of takeout were shoved into his arms.

"Here, mule," Man Bun said.

"I hope you got enough for everyone," he said.

Man Bun opened an interior door that led into the house. They entered single file and passed through a small kitchen into the living room. The Chinese food smelled absolutely delicious, and Billy promised himself he'd try Joyful House if he got out of this alive.

Mismatched furniture and no wall coverings gave the living room a nightmarish feel. Blinds covered the windows, the main light coming from the flat-screen TV, on which a game show was playing. Broken Tooth sat cross-legged on the carpeted floor, watching his prize cricket do battle with a smaller, less skillful opponent. If Billy had gotten a thousand crooks together and asked how many owned a champion fighting cricket, only one hand would go up, and it would belong to this crazy loon. His gut told him to make a run for it while he still had a chance, only there was still the matter of poor Leon, who sat bound in a chair in the corner. His driver looked worse than advertised, his eyes slits, his nose caked with blackened blood.

"Look what the cat dragged in," Leon whispered.

"Hold tight, my man," Billy said.

The contest over, Broken Tooth scooped the smaller cricket off the floor, bit its head off, and spit it away, all the while giving his guest a suspicious stare.

"Tell me how the meeting with the football players went," the Chinese gangster said.

"Like a charm," he replied, speaking clearly so the wire hidden in his shirt would pick up every word. "Like I told you over the phone, I cheated Night Train and his buddies at cards. When Night Train tried to pay me off, I gave him his money back. That got his attention."

"Very smart. He in your debt now," Broken Tooth said.

"That's right. He owes me. That's when I broached the subject of his fixing next Sunday's Super Bowl. I offered to give him and his friends five hundred grand in good faith. My gut tells me he's on board: all I have to do is deliver the money. You got the cash?"

Broken Tooth's eyes went wide. Scooping his prize cricket off the floor, he leaped to his feet and wagged a crooked finger in his guest's face. "Why you say 'next Sunday'? Everyone know when Super Bowl is! Why you just say that?"

Billy froze. He'd said "next Sunday" to avoid Broken Tooth getting an acquittal based on a technicality. Broken Tooth, as clever as a shit-house rat, had picked up on it.

"It's just an expression of speech, that's all," he said.

"Bullshit. You're wearing a fucking wire!"

"No, I'm not. Your man patted me down at the restaurant parking lot."

"That doesn't mean shit. You could have a wire stuck up your asshole."

"Stop being so paranoid. I'm clean."

"You're not clean! Take off your clothes right now!"

A man had to know his limitations. For Billy, it was letting a stranger investigate his anal cavity. The game was over; now it was time for the cavalry to make their entrance and save the day. Of course, the gaming board might not have pinpointed which house Billy was holed up in. That was easily fixed, and Billy snatched the prize cricket out of Broken Tooth's hands and held the struggling insect between its front legs like a chicken wishbone. The cricket was stronger than he'd anticipated and nearly wiggled free.

"He's a tough little sucker. Did you really pay twenty grand for him?" he asked.

"Give him to me, or my men will kill you," Broken Tooth seethed.

"Only if you say please."

"Don't mess with me, Cunningham!"

He planned to hold the cricket hostage until the front door came down. "The address where you can find me is 4021 El Camino," he said into the middle button of his shirt.

"What did you just say?" Broken Tooth said.

"Repeat. 4021 El Camino. Hurry up. It's getting hairy in here."

"He's wearing a wire! Take him out!" Broken Tooth said.

The henchmen sat at the dining room table partaking of the takeout delicacies. Jumping up, they drew guns and moved toward their guest. They meant business, and Billy mimed pulling the cricket apart. Broken Tooth screamed like a mother seeing her infant tortured.

"Better not shoot," Billy said.

"You are going to die," Broken Tooth said.

"Everyone has to go sometime."

The game was over. Broken Tooth chopped the air like he was breaking a board. Man Bun aimed at Billy's temple. The cricket dropped from his hands to the floor.

"Do it," Broken Tooth said.

Man Bun closed one eye and steadied his arm. Billy's life flashed before his eyes. The past ten years had been one long joyride, and his only regret was never ripping off a joint with Mags by his side. A splintering sound shattered the air as a battering ram took down the front door. Moments later, the gaming agents rushed into the living room brandishing their shotguns.

Billy dove headfirst to the floor as the first shot was fired.

THIRTY-EIGHT

Billy hated guns for the simple reason that they were rarely accurate, even at close range. Ninety percent of the time, the wrong thing got hit.

Lying on the floor, he watched the fusillade of bullets hit everything but their intended targets. In a movie, it would have been funny, but not so in real life, where a ricochet could have taken out him or Leon. Grimes finally settled things and got close enough not to miss. The house shook as the henchmen's bodies hit the floor. It was all Billy could do not to yell, "Timber."

The gaming agents relieved the henchmen of their weapons before checking for pulses. Grimes came over to where Billy lay, saw he wasn't harmed, and said, "We got lost. Thanks for giving us the address. Which one is Broken Tooth?"

There were only two bodies lying on the floor. Broken Tooth had taken a powder and made a run for it. Billy said, "He must have bolted. Check the back bedrooms."

Grimes barked an order, and the posse charged down a hallway into the rear of the house. Broken Tooth had short legs and smoked like a chimney; he wouldn't get very far. Billy hoped the gaming agents shot him in the back when they caught up with him.

Billy pulled himself off the floor and went to check on Leon. His driver's eyelids were shut. Billy's heart skipped a beat, fearing the worst. "Leon, my man. Talk to me."

Leon cracked an eye. "They done shooting?"

"The rodeo is over."

"Thank you, Jesus."

Billy undid the ropes, and Leon ran his hands across his body for bullet wounds. "I'm good. Who are these guys with the shotguns?"

"Gaming board."

His driver's voice dropped. "I thought the gaming board was after you."

"Not today." Billy stole a glance over his shoulder. Grimes was kneeling beside the bodyguards checking for signs of life and paying Billy and Leon scant attention. Grimes had dropped his guard and had no clue that he was about to be played.

Billy pulled out his cell phone and texted his crew.

You're on

"Who you talking to?" Leon whispered.

Billy silenced him with a finger to the lips. He was still wired up, and he tore the button off his shirt and tossed it away before edging up to Grimes. The special agent was closing the dead henchmen's eyelids with his fingertips.

"My driver's going to be okay," Billy said.

"Glad to hear it. These assholes weren't so lucky," Grimes said.

"Karma's a bitch. My driver wants something to drink. Okay if I use the kitchen?"

"Be my guest."

"You want me to get you something?"

"No thanks."

Billy had a look around the living room. The good-faith money for Night Train and his teammates was somewhere in the house. The trick would be to find it without Grimes noticing. Grimes took out his cell phone and called the on-call ambulance to give them the address. It was all the distraction Billy needed, and he entered the adjacent dining room. Two bulging leather satchels sat on the dining room table. He parted the mouth of each. Stacks of newly printed C-notes stared back at him.

Bingo.

He carried the bags into the kitchen. Opening the interior door to the garage, he pressed the automatic garage door opener above the light switch. The garage door lifted, and he went outside with the money. His crew's three vehicles were parked by the curb, and the driver's window of each vehicle came down. His crew looked at him expectantly.

"Leon says hello," he told them.

Smiles all around. His crew had never looked happier.

Gabe got out and did the exchange with Billy at the curb. Gabe's two leather bags didn't look anything like Billy's bags, but since Grimes hadn't seen the bags, it didn't matter.

Billy went over to Cory and Morris's SUV. "You boys ready?"

"As ready as we're ever going to be," Cory said. "Can we back up into the driveway?"

"Don't see why not."

Next stop was Pepper's red BMW, where he stuck his head into the driver's window.

"You're up. Get ready to turn some heads," he said.

Pepper and Misty had dolled themselves up to look like high-priced call girls. Prostitution was illegal in Las Vegas, but you never would have known it scrolling through the thousands of escorts and boy toys advertising their services on the Internet.

Billy walked back into the house and put the new bags on the dining room table. The bags contained half a million dollars of counterfeit money another hustler had paid Billy off with on a shared job. The other hustler had disappeared into the wind, leaving Billy high and dry. Billy had decided to keep the phony money, believing it would one day come in handy.

He grabbed a bottled water from the fridge and returned to the living room. Grimes's men had caught Broken Tooth and dragged him back in through the rear door of the house. The Chinese gangster had suffered bruises and cuts and lost the fake cap on his signature front tooth. In his hands was his prize cricket in its carrying cage.

He handed Leon the bottled water. Whispering, he said, "We're going to have visitors. When they come in, start moaning like you're hurt."

"Sure, boss," his driver whispered back.

The doorbell chimed. Grimes said, "That must be the ambulance," and told the Latino gaming agent to answer it. The Latino agent went to the broken front door. It was still on its hinges, and he gently opened it. Pepper and Misty stood outside, wearing miniskirts and halter tops and showing plenty of skin. They brushed past the Latino agent and entered the foyer.

Leon started moaning. Grimes hurried over to him.

"What's wrong?" Grimes asked.

"I'm hurting all over," Leon said.

"Lie on your back on the floor."

Leon got on the floor and kept up the dying-man routine. Grimes looked genuinely concerned. Leon was a major witness to Grimes's case and was worthless dead.

Misty and Pepper chatted up the Latino gaming agent. The front door was still open, and Misty shut it with her heel. The gaming agents were effectively tied up. Grimes had to deal with Leon, the Latino agent was busy with Pepper and Misty, and the remaining three agents were babysitting Broken Tooth, leaving Cory and Morris free to move Travis into the trunk of the rental parked in the garage without anyone being the wiser.

"You didn't call our service asking for two girls?" Pepper asked.

"No, ma'am," the Latino agent said.

Pepper acted put out. "Then who did?"

"Maybe you have the wrong address," he said.

"Ah, come on. You sure one of you boys didn't call?" Misty said playfully.

"Ma'am, we're with the enforcement division of the Nevada Gaming Board," the agent said, becoming irritated. "You're going to have to leave."

Grimes caught the drift of the conversation and lifted his head. "Carlos, tell those whores to hit the road, or I'll run them in."

Pepper and Misty left in a huff. The Latino agent shut the door and returned to the living room. "Maybe one of them called the girls," he said, indicating the stiffs.

"They're not much use to them now," Grimes said. "Make yourself useful and search the place." To Billy he said, "Does your driver feel good enough to give us a statement?"

Leon had returned to his chair and was sipping the bottled water Billy had brought from the kitchen. Billy said, "Are you up for that?"

"I think I can manage," Leon said.

"I'm talking about going down to the police station and being questioned for an hour or more," Grimes said, just to be sure Leon understood. "It's important that we get your statement while the events of what happened are still fresh in your mind."

"I'm your man," Leon said.

"Perfect." Grimes spoke to Billy. "You, too."

"I'd be more than happy to give you a statement," Billy said.

Grimes acted like he'd just won the lottery. The local media always made a fuss when the gaming board busted a notorious cheat trying to rip off the town. Grimes was about to be turned into king for a day; if the gaming board didn't promote him, one of the casinos would lure him away to run security. The future was looking bright for Frankie boy. Moments later, the Latino gaming agent appeared in the living room.

"Hey, Frank, I just found a dead guy in the garage," he said.

"Jesus Christ. I'm coming."

Grimes left the room. Leon lowered his water bottle and gave Billy a hard look.

"Is that who I think it is?" his driver whispered.

"I don't know who you think it is," Billy whispered back.

"Travis. I heard him talking to Broken Tooth on the phone."

"So you know."

"Yeah. He betrayed us. Good riddance," his driver whispered.

"Cunningham, get the hell over here!"

Grimes filled the living room doorway, his face livid. Billy swallowed hard and obeyed. He followed Grimes through the kitchen into the garage and immediately saw the problem. The garage door was raised. It had been closed when the gaming agents had raided the house. Grimes had spotted the discrepancy and knew that he'd been set up.

The trunk of the rental was open. Travis's rigid body lay inside. Grimes grabbed Billy by the collar and pulled the young hustler down so his face was next to the dead man's.

"Who is this guy? And don't tell me you don't know him."

"So help me God, I've never seen him in my life," Billy said.

THIRTY-NINE

No job ever went perfectly. Cues were missed and lines were flubbed. It was part of the thieving business, and Billy was not going to hold a grudge against Cory and Morris for not shutting the garage door in Broken Tooth's rented house. Cory and Morris's assignment had been to stuff Travis in the trunk of the rental and flee the scene, which they'd done. He hadn't told them to shut the garage door, so the blame rested squarely on his shoulders.

"You sure you don't know this guy?" Grimes asked suspiciously.

"No sir," he said.

"Why does my gut tell me that you're lying?"

"Maybe your lunch isn't agreeing with you."

"You're not funny."

Grimes pulled Travis's wallet from the dead man's back pocket and extracted his ID. Grimes then made a call on his cell phone and ran a background check. Travis had a clean record, and there was nothing that tied him to Billy or to cheating casinos. Grimes ended the call with a scowl on his face. "Stiff's name is Travis Simpson. Worked as a blackjack dealer for the casinos, doesn't have a criminal record. How do you know this guy?"

"I don't know him," Billy said.

"I think you're lying. In fact, I'm sure of it. While we were inside the house, those two hookers blocked the front door while your crew put Simpson's body in the rental. You want me to believe Broken Tooth murdered this guy, but I'm thinking that isn't the case."

"I don't have a crew."

"My mistake, so sorry. So who shot this poor bastard? Was it you?"

"I didn't shoot anybody. I don't even own a gun."

"If I searched your place, I wouldn't find a weapon?"

"No sir."

"Then a member of your crew shot him. Is that the story?"

"I don't have a crew. Maybe I should call my lawyer."

"That's totally up to you."

"Let me rephrase that. Do you want me to call my lawyer? Because if I do, I won't give you a statement, and your case will go right down the shitter."

Grimes snarled like a junkyard dog. "What did you just say?"

"Get the potatoes out of your ears. If you're going to pin a murder rap on me, I'll stop helping you. If I do that, then all you have is a recording of Broken Tooth talking about fixing the Super Bowl and no witnesses to back it up. A smart lawyer will get your case tossed."

Billy had the special agent over a barrel. Without Billy's statement and later testimony, the case against Broken Tooth could not move forward and would eventually be thrown out. Only this was not the way Billy wanted things to go. If the case blew up, Grimes would resume harassing Mags and ruin her career, and Broken Tooth would be set free and more than likely come after Billy. He decided to shift tactics and play nice.

"Can I make a suggestion?" he asked.

"I'm listening."

"Before you decide to accuse me of murder, why don't you check the dead guy's cell phone? Maybe he was working with Broken Tooth and they talked to each other."

"Even if they were talking, it doesn't explain the open garage door."

"Who knows how the damn thing got open? It's irrelevant."

"You are one sneaky son of a bitch, you know that?"

"Check his phone. That's all I'm asking you to do."

He was giving Grimes an out. Connect Travis to Broken Tooth and forget the rest. Grimes decided to run with it. The special agent tugged Travis's cell phone from the dead man's pants pocket, powered it up, and searched the phone bank.

"Well, look at that," Grimes said.

"You found something."

"Sure did. There's a number in the recent calls that he called nine times in the past three days. And text messages to that number talking about a fix."

"A sports fix?"

"Yeah."

"The Super Bowl?"

"It sure reads that way."

"My driver was kidnapped Sunday night. Are there any text messages or calls before then?"

"There are. So what?"

"The guy in the trunk was talking to Broken Tooth before I got involved. He and Broken Tooth had a disagreement, and this poor guy got whacked."

"Is that the story you want me to believe?"

"Come up with a better one."

"I still don't know who this number belongs to."

"Call it and find out."

"You're just filled with good ideas, aren't you?"

"Just trying to help."

Grimes called the repeated number on Travis's cell phone. As the call went through, Grimes entered the house through the kitchen with

Billy on his heels. The unmistakable sound of a ringing cell phone pierced the air, and Grimes followed it into the living room, where Broken Tooth's sleek black cell phone lay on the couch. It was invisible, save for its flashing screen. The special agent picked it up and stared at it.

"Is it a match?" Billy asked.

In police work, there were always loose ends and unanswered questions. Except when the situation was a setup. Grimes knew this and so did Billy. But that didn't change things. Grimes had enough evidence to put Broken Tooth away for the rest of his life.

Broken Tooth sat miserably in a chair, looking defeated. Without his henchmen to do his bidding, Broken Tooth was a shell, lacking the power to threaten or coerce. His prized cricket sat on the floor in its carrying cage, beating its wings together the way crickets did.

"You're under arrest for the murder of Travis Simpson," Grimes told him.

Broken Tooth stared at the special agent for what seemed like an eternity.

"Lying bastard. I didn't kill anyone," Broken Tooth said.

"Watch your mouth. You killed Travis Simpson and put his body in the trunk of your rental. Or your men did. Really doesn't matter, because you're in charge."

"Dirty fucking cop! This is setup," Broken Tooth said.

Grimes had a short fuse. He moved to smack Broken Tooth in the kisser, then had a change of heart and kicked the carrying cage that lay on the floor. The door popped open, and the cricket hopped out and began scurrying across the floor, moving as fast as its six legs would carry it. Grimes put his size twelve directly over the helpless insect. The cricket froze, a goner.

"Don't," Broken Tooth begged.

Grimes ground the insect into the carpet, grinning perversely.

FORTY

The gaming agents split up. While the posse transported Broken Tooth to the jail in old downtown in the van, Grimes climbed into the back of the ambulance and took Leon to the ER at Summerlin Hospital Medical Center to get checked out with Billy accompanying them.

The staff at Summerlin wasted no time going to work on Leon. Leon's nose was broken, and he had four cracked ribs that made breathing difficult. His heart rate was also elevated, and the doctor in charge suggested that Leon stay the night.

"I want to sleep in my own bed," Leon said. "I haven't seen it in a while."

The doctor prescribed medication that would help Leon sleep and wished him a speedy recovery. Leon climbed into a wheelchair, and Billy wheeled him out of the ER. Grimes had not left Leon's side and seemed genuinely pleased that Leon was going to be okay.

"Are you still up to giving a statement tonight?" Grimes asked. "We really need to hear your side of things while it's still fresh in your mind."

"I can do that," Leon said. "Can we stop and get some food? I'm starving."

"Not a problem. What's your pleasure?" Grimes asked.

"Anything but Chinese."

A cruiser picked them up and took them to the jail, stopping at a BK on the way. Leon hadn't lost his appetite, and his order set Grimes back twenty bucks. Grimes didn't seem to care; the gold ring was in his grasp, and he was not going to let it out of his sight.

When Las Vegas was originally built, the founding fathers had deliberately not built a jail, preferring to use the decrepit police station in old downtown to process criminals. This way, tourists visiting the Strip were not exposed to the town's underbelly, the offenders shoved into police cruisers and whisked away from the neon playground.

The jail was a toilet. Tiny cells, bad food, über-mean cops. Leon gave his statement in a second-floor interrogation room while Billy sat on a stiff wooden bench in the hall. It felt strange to be here not wearing handcuffs.

Billy was up next. Grimes focused on Broken Tooth approaching Billy to fix the Super Bowl and how Leon ended up being kidnapped when Billy refused to play along. Grimes was building his case, and he kept his questions straightforward and simple. As they neared the end of the questioning, one of the gaming agents from the posse entered the interrogation room and whispered in Grimes's ear. Grimes shut off the tape recorder sitting on the table.

"You and your driver need to wait downstairs," Grimes said.

Billy hated being in the jail. He'd been brought here many times for questioning. Even though the charges had never stuck, every employee of the jail knew who he was.

"For how long?" he asked.

"Until I come and get you," Grimes said.

"Something wrong?"

"Who said something was wrong?"

"Just a hunch. You'd make a lousy poker player."

"Be a good boy and go downstairs and wait with your driver. I won't be long."

Billy decided not to push his luck. He found Leon fast asleep on the bench in the hall. He gently shook his driver awake, and they took an elevator downstairs to wait in the lobby. Leon was strong enough to walk and managed a brave smile.

The lobby was filled with the worst miscreants that Sin City had to offer. People who got arrested tended to be losers, and their families and immediate friends were bigger losers. Billy and Leon parked themselves on two plastic chairs in a corner.

"Who took out Travis?" his driver whispered.

"Morris," Billy whispered back.

"Man, that's a surprise. Didn't think he had the balls."

"Me neither."

"I saw Grimes holding Travis's phone. What if he finds our phone numbers on it?"

"Not going to happen."

"You scrubbed them?"

Billy nodded. Cory had gone through Travis's phone and erased all ties to Billy and the crew, including contact info, phone calls, and text messages. The only person who could be tied to Travis through his cell phone was Broken Tooth. It was a nice, tidy package, done up in pretty wrapping paper and tied with a bow. Billy hoped Grimes appreciated the effort.

Twenty minutes later, Grimes came downstairs and motioned for them to follow him outside. Standing on the curb, Grimes glanced in both directions before speaking. "I've been told to keep a lid on this. How good are you two gents at keeping your yaps shut?"

Billy laughed under his breath. So that was why Grimes had gotten pulled out of the interrogation room. His superiors had caught wind of the bust and were afraid of the ensuing negative publicity. When it came to keeping secrets, the city of Las Vegas had no equal.

"For how long?" Billy asked.

"Until the Super Bowl's over," Grimes replied. "My boss spoke to the head of league security with the NFL and told him of Broken Tooth's plans. My boss said that no players were involved, but do you think that mattered? No sir. It didn't matter one bit."

"The head of league security told you to put a lid on it, and you agreed?" Billy said skeptically.

"Hardly. The head of league security called the commissioner of the NFL, the commissioner called the mayor, the mayor called my boss, and my boss ordered me to put the kibosh on this until the game's over. You know what they say. Shit flows downhill."

"So you're not charging Broken Tooth with fixing the big game," Billy said.

"That will come later," Grimes said. "Right now, Broken Tooth is charged with killing Travis Simpson. We have enough evidence to make that charge stick. When the Super Bowl's over, we'll add the other charge of conspiracy to fix a sporting event. Until that happens, you boys need to keep quiet as church mice. You can't breathe a word of this to your friends or anyone else. That goes for your crew. Think you're up to the challenge?"

"Sure," Leon said.

"I don't have a crew," Billy said.

"Then why do you need a limo driver for your jobs?" Grimes snorted.

Billy didn't have an answer for that one. Grimes gave them a parting snarl and went back inside. Billy took out his wallet and handed Leon some money. "Do me a favor and take a cab home. I need to talk to Grimes in private."

Leon stuffed the money into his pocket. "When I first went to work for you, I thought you were a prick, didn't care about nobody but yourself. Thanks for proving me wrong."

Leon walked down to the corner of the street. There was usually a yellow cab trolling the area around the jail looking for an easy fare. Billy went back inside and spotted Grimes punching an access code into a door reserved for law enforcement.

"Hold on," he said.

The special agent turned to face him. "What do you want?"

"Five minutes of your time."

"I'm busy."

"You changed the terms of our deal."

"As I just explained to you, I didn't have a choice."

"I brought this deal to you, remember? I held up my end of the bargain and delivered Broken Tooth, and now you're changing the terms."

"It was out of my hands," Grimes said, his mouth growing tight.

"You change the deal, I want something in return, or I won't play ball with you."

"You can't bolt now."

"Try me."

Back outside they went. Leon was gone, and the air pulsed with the blare of a distant police siren. Grimes was at his best when he was calling the shots. That wasn't the case now, and the special agent squirmed beneath the glare of the harsh streetlight.

"Spit it out, before I choke it out of you," Grimes said.

Billy crossed his arms in front of his chest, savoring the moment. When he felt Grimes had had enough torture, he told the special agent what he wanted.

FORTY-ONE

The evening had started innocently enough. Amber had wanted to check out the shops on the promenade tucked on a narrow strip of real estate between the Flamingo Hotel and the LINQ. Seeing a chance to do some mother/daughter bonding, Mags had agreed.

The promenade was nothing to write home about. Overpriced sunglasses, brightly colored sneakers made in China, and a shop that turned cell phone photos into priceless memories to last a lifetime. The stores were mostly empty and would be gone in a few months.

The excursion was starting to feel strained. Mags had spent so little time with Amber during her daughter's upbringing that it was difficult to have a casual conversation about even the most mundane topics. Mags didn't know her daughter's likes, dislikes, dreams, or the things that made her happy. It was a big blank canvas.

When all else fails, get something to eat. Mags offered to buy dinner, and Amber said okay. The promenade featured a host of restaurants that served everything from barbecue to sushi. Mags had heard good things about a Mexican joint called Chayo, so they went there.

Chayo had a hopping bar that served fifty brands of tequila and a mechanical bull in the center of the room. Bull rides cost a few bucks and lasted a minute, if the rider could stay on. Some businessmen were betting one another who could stay on the bull the longest.

The hostess seated them next to the action, then a waitress took their order. Corn cakes stuffed with grilled chicken and two margaritas. The drinks came before the food. They banged them back and got settled in. Mags ordered another round.

"That blond guy's got Velcro on his butt," Amber said. "He hasn't fallen off once."

"He's a ringer," Mags said.

Their food came, sizzling hot. Mags blew on a corn cake before taking a bite. It was still too hot, and she sucked down a mouthful of her drink to put out the fire.

"How do you eat so much and manage to stay so thin?" Amber asked.

"Nerves," Mags said.

"You're not forcing yourself to throw up, are you?"

Mags shook her head and kept eating. She'd stepped on the scale in her suite this morning and done a double take. She was a pound below her high school weight, and it had nothing to do with her diet, which consisted primarily of room-service food. Being an actress was eating a hole in her, not that Rand or anyone else on the set seemed to care. She looked great on camera, and that was all that mattered when shooting a TV show.

"If that guy's a ringer, what's he doing?" Amber asked.

"He's working a scam with the bartender," Mags explained. "Each guy has a shot of tequila before he gets on the bull. The bartender is pouring out of a different bottle for his partner. I'm guessing it's colored water. The blond guy acts drunk, but he isn't. He's also really good on the bull. Probably comes in after hours and practices. He's a hustler."

"Is there any game in this town that isn't rigged?"

"Hell no. How do you think they pay for those chandeliers and fancy carpets?"

"That's funny, Mom. Do you miss it?"

"You mean the grifting?" Mags wiped her mouth with a napkin. "It was a huge rush. After I took down a sucker, I'd be on cloud nine. And it never got old."

"Then why did you quit?"

"Because of guys like Frank Grimes trying to throw me in jail, that's why."

Amber fell mute. Talk about killing a buzz. Mags waved at the waitress. A fresh round of drinks appeared as if by magic.

"You don't like talking about this stuff, do you?" Amber asked.

"It's the past, honey. I walked away from it."

"Do you have any regrets?"

Mags turned in her chair so she faced the mechanical bull. The blond guy wasn't giving the suckers a chance. Winning too much, too often, had killed many a scam. If Blondie was smart, he'd fall off and lose a few times. That was the best way to keep suckers in the game.

Amber held a pair of dice beneath her mother's nose. They looked familiar, and Mags rolled them in her palm. One was normal, while the other only had fives and sixes printed on it.

"Where'd you find these?"

"In a drawer in your bedroom. Grandma said they were the reason you left Providence."

"What else did she tell you?"

"Grandma said you were afraid of going to jail and my getting stuck in a foster home, so you turned my custody over to them and left. She said you did it to protect me."

"She's right."

"Will you tell me the story behind the dice?"

"If I do, can we end this conversation?"

"Sure, Mom."

"The scam's called the Tat. I pulled it during happy hour in bars. I'd sit at the bar and wait for some suckers to come in after work. They'd always want to buy me a drink. That's when I'd signal the bartender to start the play."

"The bartender was involved?"

"You bet. It made the play look legit. A paper cup with a die sat by the register. The bartender would offer to roll the sucker for the drink. The bartender would shake the die inside the cup, then look at the number facing up. He did this three times and added up his total. Then it was the sucker's turn. If the sucker's total was higher, his drink was free. If it was lower, he paid double."

"When the game was over, I asked to play. The suckers always said yes. At first, it was for drinks. Then we'd graduate to money. Five bucks a game, then ten, then twenty. I'd lose a few rounds and wait until the bets got big. Then I went for the kill."

Mags rolled the dice on the table and smiled at the memory.

"You haven't explained how the scam works," her daughter said.

"It's simple. The mis-spotted die was hidden in my pocket. When I wanted to rip off the sucker, I switched it for the regular die and rolled nothing but fives and sixes. The sucker didn't notice because only the top side of the die can be seen inside the cup. I'd switch the normal die back into play to clean up. The gaffed die went into my pocket with the winnings."

"What if the sucker also rolled fives and sixes? You might lose."

"Not likely. The odds of rolling a five or six are two in six. Multiply that by three, and the odds grow to one in twenty-seven. I'll take those odds all day long."

Amber returned the dice to her purse. The mystery had been explained, and the look on her daughter's face bothered Mags. "I want you to promise me you'll never try this."

"Mom, I already told you—"

"Everybody's honest when they can afford to be. One day when you're down on your luck, you might decide to try the Tat. Promise me that you won't."

"Don't you trust me?"

"Yes, I trust you. But that doesn't mean you can't be tempted."

"All right, Mom. I promise I won't try the Tat. Ever."

They shook pinkies on it, and things were good again. The sound of a cell phone broke the spell. Amber pulled hers out and stared at the face.

"Must be yours, Mom."

Mags took out her iPhone. It was Billy, and she let the call go into voice mail. A minute later, he called her again. "Not now," she answered. "I'll call you later."

"Your problem's all fixed," Billy said.

She nearly dropped the phone. "You saw Grimes?"

"You could say we spent the afternoon together."

"He's going to leave me alone?"

"Grimes gave me his word he'll stop hassling you. If he ever bothers you again, give me a call, and I'll straighten him out."

"You blackmailed him, didn't you?"

"Yes, I did. Are we square?"

"Yeah, Billy, we're square."

"Now go be a TV star."

"I'll do that, Billy. Thank you."

She said good-bye and put away her iPhone. The sneaky little shit had pulled through and done right by her. There weren't many cheats she could say that about. Hell, there weren't that many *people* she could say that about.

"Mom, why are you crying? What did he say?"

"Billy fixed my problem. The gaming board is off my ass."

"Wow—that was fast."

Fairy tales did come true, even in a world like hers. Mags flagged down the waitress.

"Get us another round," she said. "We're celebrating."

FORTY-TWO

Billy sat at the dining room table in his condo, sipping a bourbon. The five hundred grand they'd stolen from Broken Tooth sat in a towering pile at the table's center. Some heists were sweeter than others, and this one had a special taste all its own.

The gaming board would eventually learn that the money in their possession was bogus. A bank would give them the bad news, or a gaming agent would steal some of the money and attempt to spend it. And then all hell would break loose.

Billy didn't care. As far as the gaming board was concerned, Billy had never touched the money and could not be blamed for the fact that it was counterfeit.

Billy's crew had blown out of town. Cory and Morris had flown to Cancun and were staying in Billy's beachfront condo, Gabe had gone to San Diego to spend time with his ex and his two daughters, while Misty and Pepper were LA-bound for some R&R. Billy had told them to enjoy their time off and that he'd contact them when it was safe for them to return home.

He drained his glass. He needed to go see Night Train and break the bad news that the NFL knew that he'd been approached to fix the

Super Bowl. The NFL would put so much heat on the game that Billy didn't think Night Train would want to risk fixing a single play.

He poured himself a fresh bourbon. The fix had just gone down the toilet, and so had Victor's super con. On the plus side, Leon was still breathing, and Mags could pursue her acting career without interference. It hadn't worked out all bad.

He took his drink onto the balcony. The Strip's blinking neon called to him like a gang of childhood friends wanting him to come out and play. Not tonight. The gunshot blasts from the shootout were still ringing in his ears, and he needed to sleep them off.

Inside the condo, his cell phone rang. His crew was supposed to call only in case of an emergency. He went inside and retrieved his cell phone from the table. It was Victor.

"I was going to give you a call," he said. "Grimes found the rented house and just missed busting your family. I got him off your scent, but I can't promise you much more."

"How did you get him off our scent?" Victor asked.

"It's a long story. Did your kids make it back to Sacramento okay?"

"Everyone got home in one piece, thanks to you."

"Anytime, Victor."

"I want to ask you a question, Billy, and you need to be up front with me. Nico wants to hit Vegas next week and pull the super con. He thinks that we can wear disguises and get away with it. I don't think that's wise. Vegas is your town. What do you think?"

Billy hesitated. Nico was Victor's favorite son, so he crafted his response carefully. "I think that would be unwise. Your family isn't off the gaming board's radar. Grimes will create profiles of Nico, Kat, and Tommy and share them with the town's casinos. I hate to tell you, Victor, but your family needs to stay away from Vegas for a while."

"Nico thinks disguises will work. Not so?"

"You can't hide who you are. You left enough information at your rented house for the gaming board to find you. They picked through garbage cans to see what kind of food your family likes to eat. And they'll contact the cable company and find out which programs and movies you watched during your stay."

"There's a record of that?"

"Yes. The smart box on every TV records the shows that are watched."

"What good does that do them?"

"It's all about information. Let's say your family returns to Vegas and stays at Aria. Nico goes into the casino, and the facial recognition program built into the eye-in-the-sky spots him. Nico's in disguise, so the casino can't be entirely sure it's him, so they follow him.

"Nico goes to a restaurant and orders a burger. The casino checks the profile and sees that your family likes McDonald's hamburgers based upon what they found in your garbage. Then Nico goes to his room and watches TV. The casino compares the programs to those watched at the rented house. Maybe Nico likes rugby on ESPN, and there's a record of that from the house. Those are three matches, so the casino contacts the gaming board and relays their suspicions. The gaming board will put Nico under surveillance, which is the kiss of death."

"I didn't know the gaming board was that sophisticated," Victor said.

"Afraid so. And they're getting better every day."

"Can we ever come back?"

"Give it a year. Pick a busy holiday weekend and stay in a hotel off the Strip. You'll fly under the radar. It's all about picking your spots. It's how I've lasted so long."

He had done enough talking. He'd warned Victor that his family was in danger, and that was all he was required to do. The bourbon burned going down.

"Are you still interested in working our super con?" Victor asked.

"Afraid not. My crew's no longer available. You're going to have to put it on hiatus."

"Can't. The secret won't be good for much longer."

"Are you going to tell me what it is?" Billy asked.

"I'm surprised you haven't figured it out. The cards in the game are marked with luminous paint."

"But there's equipment at the table that sees the marks."

"That's the flaw. The equipment doesn't work."

"Is this true at all the casinos in Vegas?"

"No, just the MGM Grand properties. MGM hired a company in the Philippines to make their blackjack tables, and the company screwed up. The people running MGM will figure it out eventually. We have to move fast."

"What are you suggesting?"

"You must know another crew you can trust. Bring them on board and scam the MGM properties this weekend. You'll make a killing."

He put his glass on the table and gave it some thought. He might be able to recruit a crew on short notice, but there was always the chance that once they knew how the super con worked, they'd cut him out of the action and keep the money for themselves.

He needed a crew he could trust. A group of seasoned grifters who could waltz into a casino, start playing blackjack for big stakes, and not draw heat. Thieves with larceny in their hearts who'd do what he told them.

His eyes locked on the towering pile of greenbacks on the table. The Super Bowl fix was off, but what if he made Night Train another offer, one that could make the famous football player and his buddies lots of money? Would they do it?

He didn't see why not. Night Train and his boys were practiced in the art of stealing and would be as effective scamming a casino as they were cheating at poker. Best of all, the casinos thought they were dumb jocks and wouldn't mind losing money to them, believing they'd eventually win it all back.

He smiled into the phone. "Now that you mention it, maybe I can find another crew."

"Who do you have in mind?"

"Some professional athletes. They're built in with the casinos and are staying at Caesars."

"How big are their credit lines?"

The bigger the credit line a sucker had, the more money the sucker could wager. And if the sucker was cheating, the casino's losses could be staggering. Night Train and his pals were regulars in the casinos, and Billy had to think their credit lines were substantial.

"Big enough," he said.

"All the better," Victor said. "For the super con to work, the cards need to be painted. Are any of your new crew painters?"

Painting the backs of playing cards was an art honed from years of practice. Billy didn't think Night Train had ever put anything on the back of a card except an accidentally spilled beer.

"No, afraid they're not," he replied.

"How about yourself?" Victor asked.

"I've done it a couple of times and didn't get caught."

"You feel comfortable painting all the high cards in a single-deck game? You'll need to do this in multiple casinos for the super con to work."

He swallowed hard. "That's a lot of cards to paint, Victor."

"Yes, it is. Kat and Nico do the painting for my crew, and they were going to split up the duties between them when we pulled this off. It's a lot of work, but the payoff's huge."

Victor had thrown him a curveball. Victor had never mentioned that painting was involved in the scam because he planned to have Kat and Nico handle it. But with Victor's family out of the picture, the job of painting the cards now rested on Billy's shoulders.

A bad thought flashed through his mind. Maggie Flynn was a painter, and a damn good one at that. She had a unique technique that let her paint five cards at a time before having to return to her purse to apply the special substance to her fingertips. A single-deck game at multiple casinos would be a day in the park for Miss Maggie.

Mags was perfect for the job. But would she do it? His gut told him no. She was done with the life, but that didn't mean he wasn't going to ask her. There was too much money at stake for him *not* to ask her. The worst thing she could do was throw another glass at him.

"I know somebody," he said. "Her name's Maggie Flynn."

"She any good?" Victor asked.

"They don't come any better than Mags. Now, tell me about this flawed piece of equipment at the MGM properties. It's killing me not knowing."

FORTY-THREE

Thursday, ten days before the Super Bowl

Early morning was Billy's least favorite time of day. Beneath the breaking sunlight's harsh glare, there was no magic in Sin City, the casinos' garish facades showing every crack and paint chip. Pulling into Caesars, he grabbed the two bags of money he'd stolen from Broken Tooth off the passenger seat and got out.

"Would you like a bellman to help you with your luggage?" the valet asked.

"I can manage," he said.

He walked unescorted to the football players' villa. Choo-Choo greeted him at the front door. "You again. What's in the bags?"

"Money. Lots and lots of money," he said.

"Well, come on in."

Choo-Choo led him into the dining room. Room service had delivered a spread of food befitting an Arab prince sneaking away for an illicit weekend. Bagels, lox, caviar, cream cheese, champagne, bacon, eggs, and sweet-smelling sausage. Night Train sat at the head of a long table with Sammy, Clete, and Assassin beside him.

"Help yourself," Night Train said.

"I already ate." He cleared a spot and put the bags on the table before taking a chair. He'd constructed a story that he needed to sell to Night Train and his teammates. The story had just enough truth in it for them to believe him and become partners in the super con. "I hit a snag with the Super Bowl scam. My partner got busted and is cooling his heels down at the Clark County jail. He's going to be out of commission for a while."

Night Train chewed on a piece of bagel. "What did he get busted for?"

"Seems he murdered a guy."

"That's heavy. Can he be tied to us?"

"No, you're in the clear."

"Then why kill the scam? We're still willing to fix the plays. You can place the bets yourself, and we'll split the winnings. That's a hell of a lot better deal for you. You'll make more money with your partner gone."

"My partner is known for fixing sporting events. The only sporting event on the horizon is the Super Bowl. The gaming board isn't stupid, if you know what I mean."

"You're saying there's going to be extra scrutiny on the game," Night Train said.

"That's right. If something suspicious happens, it will draw heat."

"Not necessarily," Night Train said. "Every player steps on that field with butterflies in his stomach. I know, because I've been there. Balls get fumbled; players screw up. No one's going to cry foul if we fix a few plays. You rig the coin toss, and we'll do the rest."

"You sure about this?"

"Positive. We'll make a killing."

It couldn't have gone better if Billy had scripted it. Cory, Morris, and Gabe would need to go to Phoenix to rig the coin toss, but that was easily done. Not wanting to appear too anxious, he let a moment pass, then took his next shot. "I have another business proposition for you. Tomorrow, I want you to help me burn several MGM casinos with a super con. It won't require any rehearsal or lines to memorize. It's a piece of cake."

"Sounds interesting," Night Train said. "What's our take?"

"Half, just like the Super Bowl fix."

"Which is what? Say fifty grand, and I'll toss you on your ass."

The message was clear. Night Train and his buddies would not rob for chump change. If you're going to sin, sin boldly, or so the sentiment among the thieving class went.

"It all depends upon the size of your credit line with MGM. I'm assuming you guys have large ones," he said.

"My credit line with MGM is two million bucks," Night Train said.

"Same here," Choo-Choo said.

"One point five million," Sammy said.

"Me, too," Assassin said.

Clete's credit line was the same. Billy couldn't have asked for a better crew to pull off Victor's super con. Night Train and company were built in with MGM. None of the MGM casinos would get suspicious if they gambled for high stakes, since they'd done so before.

"You want us to put up our own money? Is that the deal?" Night Train asked.

Billy's cheeks burned. "You think I'm trying to hustle you?"

"It crossed my mind."

"No, you don't have to put up your own money. You'll use the good-faith money I was going to give you to fix the game." He turned the bags upside down, and the money he'd stolen from Broken Tooth poured onto the table.

Night Train looked confused. "I'm good with that. But why did you ask about our credit lines?"

"Your credit line is your identity inside a casino," he explained. "The pit boss pulls it up on his computer, sees that you're a high roller, and won't get nervous when you place big bets."

A smart cheat never admitted he didn't understand something. The remark put Night Train in a new light and made Billy wonder if the famous football player was just a dumb jock with a portfolio of bankrupt business ventures. It was how most pro athletes ended up.

"With our credit lines, how much can we steal?" Night Train asked.

"Multiply your credit line by two," Billy said. "That much. Maybe a little more. Then the casino cuts you off. There's only so much bleeding they'll take."

"Our combined credit line is eight and a half million bucks. You're saying we can steal twice that much with this super con, and we get to keep half?"

"That's right."

Night Train glanced at his teammates. A silent agreement was reached, just like that.

"Count us in," Night Train said.

No one ever said yes that quickly to a heist. There were always fine points to be ironed out and agreed upon. His suspicion that Night Train might be broke now included his pals. That was why they'd jumped at the chance to make a quick hit on fixing the Super Bowl, and it was why they were talking to him now. They needed the dough.

He'd found the perfect partners. Thieves by nature with nothing in their wallets. If the super con went according to plan, who knew what the future might hold?

"I think this calls for a toast," he said.

"Have to be quick. We're due at practice in two hours," Night Train said.

"I'll make them light," he said.

- - -

The villa had an entertainment room with a full bar. Billy offered to fix the drinks and pulled an expensive bottle of champagne out of the fridge along with a carton of OJ.

"How do mimosas sound?" he asked.

The football players chorused their approval. They'd parked themselves in front of a flat-screen TV to watch a video of the Louisville

Volunteers, their opponents next Sunday. The video ran in slow motion and was filled with white arrows and lines drawn by an invisible hand.

"Godfrey looks stiff in the pocket, doesn't he?" Choo-Choo said.

"Sure does. He's got no lateral movement," Sammy said.

"What's wrong with him?" Billy asked, serving their drinks.

"Herniated disc. Got injured in the divisional round against Indianapolis," Night Train explained. "They're going to dope him up for the big game and hope he doesn't say anything stupid when a mic gets shoved in his face."

The five men erupted into laughter. Neil Godfrey was the Volunteers' star quarterback and quickly becoming a household name. A fresh-faced kid out of the University of Georgia, he'd set all sorts of passing records during his rookie season last year and become a media darling. It was hard to turn on the TV and not see Godfrey hawking some brand-name product.

"I didn't see Godfrey listed on the Volunteers' injury report," Billy said.

"The league doesn't want it out. They want to keep the point spread tight," Night Train said.

"Who's Louisville's backup quarterback?" Sammy asked.

"Sycamore. The Jets cut him, and the Volunteers picked him up," Night Train said.

"Is he any good?"

"Sycamore's way good. But he gets tight under pressure and starts throwing picks. He's been released by every team he's played for."

The video of Godfrey continued to run. Night Train held up his empty glass. "Hey, barkeep, how about another round? Make it super light so I don't fall down during practice."

"You got it." He collected the empty glass and went behind the bar. Louisville wasn't going to fare very well next Sunday with an ailing quarterback, all but ensuring a Rebels win. Night Train and his teammates had won the Super Bowl before, and they were about to win it again. They were going to end their careers on top, and then ride off into the sunset.

He fixed the drink. The OJ was done, and he tossed the empty carton away. Lying in the trash was a stack of official-looking documents with the NFL's logo stamped on the top of each page. Their being in the garbage didn't seem right, and he pulled them out to have a look.

They were contracts. The first was for Night Train to host the NFL pregame show on NBC, and it included working the playoffs and next year's Super Bowl. It was a sweet deal, and would let Night Train's star continue to shine after his playing days were over.

The next contract was for Choo-Choo to work as a color commentator for the NFL Network. It had lots of perks, including first-class travel to all the games and a generous food and wardrobe allotment. The other contracts were for Clete, Sammy, and Assassin to work as talking heads for ESPN and Fox Sports One. The terms were also lucrative.

He returned the contracts to the trash. Just a few days ago, the NFL's commissioner had met with the football players on the villa's balcony. He had to believe the commissioner had flown to Vegas to discuss the jobs described in these contracts. Why they'd ended up in the garbage was a mystery, and he supposed the football players were holding out for more money.

He served Night Train. The video of Neil Godfrey was still running. Night Train sipped his drink and said, "The things you just heard about Godfrey are top secret. Understood?"

"Loud and clear," he said.

"When do we get to see this super con?"

"Don't you have to go to practice?" he asked.

"We've got time." Night Train made the screen go dark with the remote. "Me and my boys want to see what we're getting ourselves into."

"Understood. Step right this way," he said.

- - -

Billy decided to use the antique card table in the corner of the entertainment room for the demonstration. The football players pulled up chairs while he remained standing. "MGM owns twelve casinos on the Strip. Tomorrow morning, I'm going to rig a blackjack game in five of those casinos. I will then contact you and tell you which casinos are your targets."

"Why not tell us now?" Night Train asked.

"Because I don't know which ones they are."

"You've lost me, man."

"MGM's blackjack tables have been compromised by a faulty piece of equipment that makes it impossible for the pit boss to detect marked cards. I plan to secretly mark cards in five MGM casinos. I need to visit the different MGM properties to determine which are the best targets. Then I'll contact you and give you the names of which casinos will be taken down."

"Don't the casinos change their cards every few hours?" Night Train asked.

"They used to, but it was costing too much money," he said. "Now they change cards once a day, early in the morning. It's an easy schedule to work around."

"Mark them how?" Night Train asked.

"I'm going to use luminous paint to mark the tens, jacks, queens, kings, and aces."

"Don't you need special glasses to read that stuff?"

"Tinted sunglasses do the trick," he said.

"But a pit boss can read luminous marks," Night Train said. "That's why a pit boss will come up beside the dealer and watch the game. They have a special way of reading the backs of the cards. I saw it on the Discovery Channel. Or was it bullshit?"

"It was real," he said. "Like I said, the equipment at MGM properties is flawed and won't allow the pit boss to read the marks. We're home free."

"If this scam takes place at five casinos, how are you going to be in five places at once?" Night Train asked.

"The scams will be staggered over the course of the day," he explained. "I'll hop between casinos and work with each of you."

He paused to let everything sink in. Satisfied that his partners were on the same page, he continued. "Each of you will scam a different MGM casino. Before you show up, you're going to call the VIP host and announce your arrival. By doing that, you're guaranteed star treatment when you walk through the front doors. Got it?"

"That shouldn't be too hard," Night Train said.

"When you visit your assigned casino, be sure you wear your Super Bowl rings and lots of bling. Remember, you're pretending to be BPs."

"BP? Like the oil company?" Choo-Choo asked.

"BP stands for Big Player. Also known as a sucker."

Choo-Choo scowled, as did the others. They'd been pissing away their money for years without understanding the arrangement, so he explained. "There are three kinds of players in a casino. Advantage players, who have an edge over the house. Think card counter. Then there are cheats that rob the joints, like me. Everyone else is a sucker. There are no winners."

"No winners?" Choo-Choo said.

"No sir. If you won all the time, they'd ban you."

The football players nodded. So far everything he'd said had made sense. Now came the tricky part.

"Blackjack games have different betting limits," he said. "Low-limit tables have minimum bets of five dollars and maximum bets of five hundred dollars. High-limit tables have minimum bets of a hundred dollars and a maximum of ten thousand dollars. The games I'm going to rig will be low limit. Know why? Because surveillance hardly watches low-limit games."

"How do you make money in a low-limit game?" Night Train asked. "Even if you're cheating, you can't win that much."

"You're going to ask the pit boss to raise the limits at your tables. But first you play for a little while and lose. That's when you ask the pit boss to raise the table limit so you can bet more. When the pit boss asks you how much, you say, 'Ten grand a hand.'"

"Will he go along with that?"

"Of course he'll go along with it. It's what suckers do when they get behind. At that point, you should have drawn a good crowd. I'll be in the crowd, wearing my tinted sunglasses. That's when we start scamming."

Night Train wasn't far behind and said, "You're going to read the dealer's cards and signal us how to play our hands. Is that the deal?"

"Correct. I play your hands for you, and we clean up."

Night Train flashed his famous smile. His teammates also looked happy. If the boss was good with the scam, then so were the troops.

"Remember," he said. "You're pretending to be suckers. That means talking to the crowd and flirting with the girls. In other words, don't get serious when you start winning."

"Just keep acting like dumb shits, is what you're saying," Night Train said.

"I can do that," Choo-Choo said.

"No problem," Sammy chimed in.

Clete and Assassin grunted that it wouldn't be hard to act like dumb shits.

"Last thing," he said. "When you reach a million bucks in winnings, you ask the pit boss to raise the table limit to fifty grand a hand. The pit boss will say yes, in the hopes you'll lose everything back that you've won." He paused. "Are we good?"

"I think we're real good," Night Train said. "Aren't we, boys?"

His teammates bobbed their heads in unison. Loyal to the point of being blind, they would have jumped into a vat of boiling oil if Night Train had asked them to.

It was time to explain the signals. Signals let a crew secretly communicate inside a casino. For the super con, Billy planned to employ a sky signal. A sky signal was visible to the crew but invisible to the surveillance cameras, which filmed straight down from the ceiling.

The sky signal used a common beer bottle, held at chest height. If the bottle was in the left hand, with the right hand below but not touching it, this meant take a card.

If the bottle was held with the right hand, with the left hand below, this meant to stand pat. The difference in these two actions was plainly visible to a player at the table but couldn't be seen—or filmed—by the eye-in-the-sky.

Left hand holding the bottle, take a card. Right hand holding the bottle, stand pat.

The third signal was called the chin. If Billy dipped his chin, it meant start the play. This was also invisible to the eye-in-the-sky.

He ran through the signals a dozen times, just to make sure the football players got it right. In conclusion, he said, "If I take a drink of my beer, it means we're done. Any questions?"

There were none.

"Now get to practice before you're late," he said. "The prop bets can't be fixed if you guys are benched at the start of the game."

"You got it, boss," Night Train said.

And with that, the football players burst out laughing.

FORTY-FOUR

Mags came to the set filled with confidence, the burden of Grimes's threat to destroy her career a thing of the past. The world was her oyster, and she couldn't wait to nail today's scene and deliver the kind of performance the CBS honchos needed to green-light *Night and Day*.

To her surprise, the set was deserted. No cameramen, no crew, no snippy director with a bad attitude, and, worst of all, no Rand. The shoot had been cancelled, the equipment packed up, and no one had bothered to tell her.

"Somebody should have called you. I mean, you are the star," Amber said.

"This is Hollywood, honey. They call you when they feel like it."

She checked her cell phone. There were no messages, leading her to wonder if Rand was sick in his room. On a hunch, she called the hotel's main line and asked for him.

"I'm sorry, but there's no one registered in the hotel under that name," the operator said.

"He's staying in your damn hotel. Check again," she said.

The operator's fingers danced on a keyboard. "Here he is. Rand Waters. According to my computer, he checked out late yesterday. Is there someone else you'd care to speak with?"

She was shaking with rage and hung up. Rand had run out on her like a cheap one-night stand. No message, no note slipped under her door, nothing. She marched off the set and into the hotel with her daughter on her heels.

"Where are you going?" Amber asked.

"To the bar to talk to my cameraman, Sean Mulroney. Sean will know what's going on."

True to form, Sean was perched on a stool in LINQ's bar getting plowed. Despite the early hour, Sean's nose was deep purple, his eyes bloodshot. Mags took the adjacent stool while Amber sat down next to her mother. Sean nodded drunkenly.

"Sean, this is my daughter, Amber," Mags said. "Amber, meet Sean Mulroney, the best cameraman in Hollywood."

"My mom's told me all about you," Amber said.

"Whatever she told you was a lie. Either of you ladies want a drink? It's on me."

"We're good," Mags said. "What's going on, Sean? Where's the crew?"

"They were sacked." To the bartender he said, "Another round, my good man."

Mags's face nearly hit the bar. "When? By whom?" It was the wrong thing to say, and she grabbed Sean by the wrist. "Did you get canned as well?"

Sean did not reply until he had a fresh beer in one hand, a shot in the other. "I will answer your questions in the order in which they were received. The firing took place at eight a.m. this morning on the set. The executioner was none other than the evil Rand Waters, who spoke to us from LA using Skype on a laptop computer that sat on a chair. Rand gave no explanation but simply stated that our services were no longer required. And yes, I also got the boot, which led me here to my present endeavor."

Her show was over. Mags knew that soulless sharks ran Hollywood, but she had convinced herself that she'd come out on top. Stupid her.

Sean laid a gentle hand on her wrist. "Don't tell me you didn't know."

"No, not a word."

"Rand's a bastard. If it's any solace, I thought you did a fine job."

She kissed his cheek. "Thank you for saying that. You take care."

"May our paths cross again."

Mags left the bar beneath a dark cloud. For the last few months, *Night and Day* had consumed her life. With acting classes, rehearsals, and coming to Vegas to shoot the pilot, she hadn't contemplated her future if the show got cancelled. Reality had just dumped a hundred pounds of steaming shit on her head, and it was all she could do not to scream.

"What are you going to do?" her daughter asked.

"Maybe I'll take a vacation, go back east. Like a roommate for a few months?"

"You can always stay with me, Mom."

Mags went to her trailer to grab her belongings. Stepping inside, she found Billy sipping a bottled water. Billy had warned her this might happen, and it was all she could do not to slap him.

"Go away, Billy. Leave us alone."

"We need to talk. I have a proposition for you," he said.

"Not interested." The trailer had a built-in dresser. Mags pulled open the drawers and removed her things, which she handed to her daughter while trying to ignore him.

"How come the set's so quiet?" he asked.

"The show is on permanent hiatus."

"I'm sorry to hear that. Maybe this will cheer you up. I'm doing a job and I need your help. Think of it as a last score for old time's sake."

"I told you, I'm done with grifting."

"You haven't heard the terms. I'll pay you half a million bucks to paint cards."

A plastic hairbrush bounced on the floor. Mags picked it up and tossed it to Amber. Her checking account had all of nine hundred bucks in it. Without the money from the show, she had no source of income and no immediate opportunities for work. She was flat broke and might end up living out of her car if her luck didn't improve. No doubt about it, she needed a savior, but not this one. She'd promised herself she was going to stop thieving, and it was a promise she intended to keep, no matter how harsh the outcome might be.

"Not interested," she said.

"It will be like stealing candy from a baby," he said, unwilling to quit. "You're going to paint cards in low-limit blackjack games, which are hardly watched by surveillance. The scam won't take place until after you're gone. You'll be out of the line of fire."

"My face is known to every casino in town."

"You'll be in disguise. They'll never spot you."

When opposing forces collide, bad things occurred. The urge to smack Billy in the face was growing stronger, and she turned to her daughter. "Let's get some breakfast."

Amber looked upset with her. Did her daughter want her to take the job? They left the trailer without saying good-bye and headed across the empty set. She heard the trailer door being shut behind them.

"Go away. I mean it," she said.

"How can you run away from half a million bucks? Just answer me that," he said.

"I don't have to explain my decision to you."

"Remember the day we met in Providence? You told me that you dreamed of coming to Vegas and joining a crew. You said the crews made the big money. I'm giving you the chance to fulfill that dream. Do one more job and walk away. You won't regret it."

Why wouldn't he listen? She had made a clean break and kissed her past good-bye. No one had an issue with that except Billy. He was preventing her from escaping the black impulses that had consumed her for so long, and it made her want to hurt him. Reaching LINQ's front entrance, she spun around. When he smiled, she slapped him.

"Last time. Leave me alone," she said.

He brought his hand to his lips and came away with blood. It seemed to startle him, and he retreated a few steps. "Whatever you want, Maggie. But will you answer one question for me?"

"Will you leave if I do?"

"Yes."

"Fire away."

"If you were so intent on running away from being a thief, why did you agree to play a cheat in a TV show? How is that different from before?"

She swallowed hard. "Just . . . leave."

"The answer is, it isn't. You're a thief and always will be. It's in your blood. Think about it."

"Go, damn it!"

"Nice meeting you," he said to Amber before walking away.

FORTY-FIVE

Pulling into the valet area of Turnberry, Billy spent a moment behind the wheel in thought. He had less than twenty-four hours to find a painter if the super con with the football players was going to succeed. That was hardly enough time with a casino scam.

Rushing a job was never smart, but he didn't have any other choice. After this weekend, the football players were off to Phoenix for Super Bowl week, and his window of opportunity would be lost.

He scrolled through the names of local cheats in his cell phone's directory. Painters were in short supply these days. The good ones were traveling the country fleecing the Native American casinos where the security was second-rate. He stopped on the name Casey Duvall. They'd worked together a decade ago running with a crew led by an old-timer named Crunchy. One night on a dare, Casey had painted all the high cards in a blackjack game at Bellagio using Vaseline, the jar conveniently tucked between his legs with the lid unscrewed. Casey had brass balls and would be perfect for this job. He called his old friend and heard him answer.

"Casey, this is Billy Cunningham. How you been, man?"

"Billy C, as I live and breathe, it's good to hear your voice. What's shaking?"

"I've got some business to discuss. You free tomorrow?"

"For you, man, of course."

A rapping on the side glass made Billy jump. He turned his head to stare at the ugliest of sights. It was Grimes, and the special agent looked fit to be tied.

"I've got company. Let me call you later."

"You know where to find me," Casey said.

He ended the call and lowered the passenger window. "Hey. What's up?"

"Let's go for a ride," Grimes said.

"Is something wrong?"

"There sure is."

Maseratis were designed for people of smaller stature. Grimes climbed into the passenger seat and tried to put his seat back. When it didn't budge, he let out a curse.

"Who designed this fucking car, a bunch of circus midgets?"

"Any place in particular you want to go?"

"Just drive around."

The Las Vegas Country Club was Turnberry's immediate neighbor. Billy did a slow loop around the emerald green eighteen-hole golf course wondering what he'd done to warrant a visit from Grimes. The special agent popped gum into his mouth and chewed vigorously.

"I have a problem that needs fixing. Broken Tooth hired a fancy lawyer out of LA named Max Stein. Stein was originally part of O. J. Simpson's dream team, only he broke his ankle skiing and had to sit out the trial. Stein appeared in court today and told the judge that neither Broken Tooth nor his henchmen killed Travis Simpson, and that the body in the trunk of the rental was a frame-up. The judge ordered that we do a forensic test on the two handguns we found in the house. Guess what? Neither handgun killed Travis Simpson."

"That's a problem," Billy said.

"Yes, it is. So here's what I need. One of your friends shot Travis. Call him and find out where he ditched the weapon. I'll go get it, and we'll switch it for one of the guns we found at the house. Then we'll run another ballistics test and get a match."

"You didn't share the first test with the judge."

"That happens tomorrow. When it does, the test will be positive. Now make the call."

They came to a red light. Billy braked and turned in his seat. "How do I know that you're not wearing a wire and that this whole thing isn't a setup to frame me?"

Grimes blew a bubble in the young hustler's face that burst with a loud *snap*. "You think I'd incriminate myself and throw my career down the drain by what I just said? Wise up. I need the murder weapon, and I need it right now. Make the call before I get pissed."

"What if my friend threw the gun over the Hoover Dam, and it can't be retrieved?" he said. "What are you going to do then?"

"Your friend buried the gun in a deserted lot. I know that because I was a homicide dick for five years, and that's what most killers do. The deserted lot is within a radius of two miles of where your friend lives, and it's about three feet down in the ground."

"Can I pull over?"

"Be my guest."

Sunrise Hospital and Medical Center was another Turnberry neighbor. He parked in the lot and called Morris's cell phone. Morris picked up on the first ring.

"Hey Billy, what's up?"

"I need you to tell me where you ditched the piece," Billy said.

Morris made a gagging sound into the phone. "What are you talking about?"

"Where's the gun? Just tell me, and then hang up the phone."

The line went still. Billy shut his eyes, praying that Morris wasn't one of those small percentage of shooters who'd buried his gun in some exotic place.

"There's an empty lot down the street from our house," Morris said, breaking the silence. "Cory and I buried the gun there and filled the hole with empty beer cans. That was Cory's idea, in case somebody with a metal detector found the spot and decided to dig."

"Any landmarks?"

"Not that I can think of. We covered the spot with garbage to hide it."

"Where in the lot?"

"Dead center. You going to tell me what's going on?"

"Later. Keep the faith."

- - -

He had no trouble finding the empty lot where Morris and Cory had buried the murder weapon. Parking at the curb, he popped the trunk and got out with Grimes. He grabbed the tire iron from beneath the spare tire and tossed it to the special agent. Grimes tossed it right back.

"You want me to dig it up?"

"Yeah. I want to see you sweat," Grimes said.

He found a collection of trash in the center of the yard and took a picture on his cell phone, which he texted to Morris with a note. Is this the spot? Morris texted him right back and said it was. He kicked away the trash, then used the tire iron to break away the dirt, which was packed down hard. As it became soft, he switched to using his hands and pawed away like a dog.

"This had better be the right spot," Grimes said.

The sun was brutal and perspiration poured off his brow. It occurred to him that if this wasn't where the gun was buried, they had a serious problem that he couldn't fix.

"Does the judge know that Broken Tooth tried to fix the Super Bowl?" he asked.

"Not yet," Grimes said, working his gum.

"Why don't you tell him and get the ball rolling?"

"Can't. We have our orders, and I'm not going to break them. Do you know how much money the Super Bowl generates for this town? More than a hundred million bucks is wagered at the sports books alone. Nothing is going to be said about the fix until the game's over. Can't you work any faster? I'm getting hot."

- - -

He was soon drenched. The hole was three feet deep, so where the hell was the gun?

"Looks like we've got company. Stay here."

Pinning a silver badge to his lapel, Grimes marched over to a white-haired man walking his dog who was coming toward them. They engaged in conversation, and Billy caught enough to realize that the man was part of a citizen's watch group assigned to keep the neighborhood safe. A pesky bastard, exactly the kind of guy Grimes didn't want snooping around.

His fingers touched the curved handle of a firearm. He cleaned away the dirt and watched the gun's barrel take shape at the bottom of the hole. He stole a furtive glance at the man with the dog before pulling the buried weapon from its hiding place. The gun tucked safely beneath his shirt, he hustled over to his car and hopped in. The weight of the world had lifted from his shoulders. Grimes took the passenger seat, and Billy cleaned his fingerprints off the gun, then passed him the weapon.

"Beautiful," Grimes said.

FORTY-SIX

Returning home, Billy killed the engine and waited for Grimes to speak. He knew of cheats in town who had unique relationships with the gaming board, but he'd never expected to join their ranks. He disliked people who enforced the law for the simple reason that many of them would have become criminals had they possessed the smarts and the cunning. Not able to make the mark, they'd lowered themselves to catching the very people they aspired to be.

"This is a nice place you live in," Grimes said. "What's the security like?"

"First-rate. Why?"

"I want you to stay here until the conspiracy charges against Broken Tooth are filed. Don't go out unless it's absolutely necessary."

"You think Broken Tooth will go after me?"

"I wouldn't put it past him. If you sense trouble, call me right away."

They exchanged cell numbers. Billy would have to get the number changed when this was over, otherwise Grimes would use it to track him inside the casinos later on. Even though they were now joined at the hip, they were not, and never would be, friends.

"This doesn't change things between us," Grimes said, as if reading his thoughts. "The next time I catch you and your crew scamming a casino, I'll bust you."

"I wouldn't expect anything less," Billy said.

"Did it ever occur to you that if you went legit, how successful you'd be? Your file says you went to MIT on a scholarship. Take those brains and apply yourself to running a real business. You might surprise yourself."

Billy couldn't help but laugh.

"You think I'm being funny?" Grimes said, growing angry. "You're going to end up rotting in prison. You'll regret not listening to me."

Grimes was steaming. But he didn't get out of the car and storm off. It made Billy wonder if the special agent was telling Billy a hidden truth about himself. Grimes was a smart son of a bitch, and Billy wondered if Grimes secretly regretted not venturing out on his own, instead of seeking the safety of law enforcement work and the benefits that came with it.

"When I was growing up, I read a book called *Little Man*. You know it?"

Grimes stared at him out of the corner of his eye. "No."

"It was about the life of the gangster Meyer Lansky. Lansky was the moneyman for the mob, had to be one of the smartest guys who ever lived. He could sit in the stands watching a baseball game and calculate the different players' batting averages each time they came up to the plate. He was carrying all that information around in his head, along with the figures for all the rackets the mob ran. He was a genius."

"That's impressive. What's your point?"

"When Lansky got older he tried to go legit. He moved to Florida and ran a restaurant and a string of dry cleaners and other businesses with his brother Jake. They all failed, and Lansky lost his shirt. Success has nothing to do with how smart you are. It's about luck."

"Is that why you keep stealing?" Grimes asked. "Because you're afraid of failing in the real world? The fact is, Billy, you never tried the real world, so there's no way you'd know."

Billy turned to face his adversary. "You want to know why I steal? I steal because it's a blast. Every time I rip off a casino, it feels better than having sex. I'm also damn good at it. The day it turns into a job, I'll quit."

"You've got it all figured out, haven't you?"

"I know what makes me happy. Do you?"

Grimes snorted contemptuously. That was enough of an answer in itself. Billy said, "Let me know if there's anything else I can do to help your investigation."

"Fuck you."

"Let's part friends, shall we?"

Grimes got out, rifled the valet stand for his keys, then entered the parking garage in search of his car. He was like an active volcano, the bad stuff bubbling just below the surface. Billy hoped like hell Grimes got his promotion; it might keep the special agent out of his hair.

His cell phone vibrated. It was Casey, calling him back.

"Sorry about that. Are you up for some fun and games?" Billy said.

"I'm in my car, heading to LA," Casey said.

"Trouble?"

"Afraid so. I've been running a chip cup scam at one of the Venetian's craps tables. This afternoon, the dealer flipped the cup over and exposed it to the eye-in-the-sky. They arrested him."

"Think he'll turn on you?"

"My gut says he won't. But just in case he does, I'm going to be far away from Vegas. I've booked a one-way ticket to Hawaii out of LAX tomorrow morning."

No simpler cheating device had stolen more money from the casinos than the chip cup. It was a tin shell designed to look like a stack of low denomination chips, its purpose to secretly steal high-value chips inside its shell. The dealer did the stealing, then sold the chip cup stuffed with chips to his partner sitting at the table.

A great scam, except for one minor problem. The chip cup was on the table in plain view. If a suspicious pit boss picked it up, Katy bar the door. Or in Casey's situation, the clumsy dealer fumbled and turned the cup over, exposing its false construction. Either scenario would lead to immediate arrest and a lengthy stay in the gray-bar motel.

"Sure I can't talk you into coming back?" Billy said.

"Christ, Billy, I'd like nothing better than to run with you again. We had a blast back in the day. You were the champ when it came to thieving."

"I'll make it worth your while."

"Don't tempt me, man. I need to leave town and let the dust settle."

"I'll give you half a million bucks."

"Oh man. I wish I could say yes, I really do."

"What's holding you back?"

"I did time a few years back. Worst experience of my life. I won't go back."

Nevada had an unwritten policy when it came to dealing with cheats. The courts sent them to the state's most notorious penal institutions, where cheats lived in tiny cells without air conditioning, ate food unfit for a dog, and tried to survive among rival gangs trying to kill each other. Billy couldn't blame Casey for not wanting to go back.

"I understand. I hope it works out for you," he said.

"Good luck with your scam," Casey said.

"I'm probably going to do the painting myself. Any tips you can share?"

"Sure. The person most likely to catch you painting is the dealer. Make sure you sit at a crowded table. The more distraction, the less chance you'll get caught."

"I'll remember that."

"Keep your thumb still when you paint. If your thumb starts flapping, you're cooked."

"Got it. Thanks, man."

Soon Billy was in his penthouse apartment fixing himself a cup of coffee. When it came to thieving, necessity was the mother of invention. If he couldn't hire a painter, he'd do the job himself. From the hall closet he removed a video camera and tripod stand, which he set up at the dining room table. Then he got several decks of cards and a small round tin of luminous paint from his study.

He hit the record button on the video camera and took a chair at the table. Picking up one of the decks, he dealt himself a blackjack hand, then opened the can and covered his thumb and forefinger with the invisible substance.

He practiced painting the backs of the two cards. A light brush of the fingertips was all that was necessary. If done right, the move was barely perceptible. If done wrong, the move would wake the dead, and he'd get hauled off to jail.

He went through an entire deck, then stopped and programmed the video camera into the TV in the living room so he could critique himself. The video came on, his hands filling the screen. He watched himself and nearly choked. His technique was amateurish and would be easily spotted by a sharp dealer.

He returned to the dining room and started over. Casey had said not to flap his thumb. That was easier said than done. He went through two more decks of cards, watched the tape, and still caught himself in the act every single time.

He got more cards from his study and started over. He was determined to get the move down right, the conversation with Grimes fresh in his mind. Thieving was his life; the day he quit would be the day they put him in the ground.

FORTY-SEVEN

Friday, nine days before the Super Bowl

Mags and Amber cabbed it to McCarran the next morning. Inside the terminal, blaring commercials for musical revues and magic shows playing at the Strip casinos ran endlessly on large screens. Listening to them for too long could lead to insanity, even death.

Mags stood in the check-in line with her daughter. They'd hardly spoken during the ride, and now Amber was not making eye contact. How long would it be before they saw each other again? A year? Two? Maybe never? She tried not to cry, but it was hard. Twenty-four hours ago, her life had been filled with the stuff that dreams were made of. With the suddenness of a lightning strike, it had turned into a disaster movie. Hardship and failure had defined most of her existence, and she could deal with it. What she couldn't deal with was having Amber experience the failure with her. That part was tearing Mags's heart out.

It was their turn. Amber handed her driver's license to a ticket agent with a zombie personality. The agent typed her info into a computer and said, "Sorry, your flight's been delayed. The scheduled departure is now eleven a.m. Next, please."

Amber's shoulders sagged. She was ready to go home and put her mother's mess of a life behind her. "That sucks. Where's a good place to get some breakfast?"

"There are a variety of restaurants at your gate," the ticket agent said.

"My mom can't get out to the gate without a ticket. What about the main terminal?"

"Try the Starbucks in the Esplanade. Next, please."

The Starbucks was like a visit to happy town. Five employees manned the counter, flying high on caffeine and the corporate desire to please. Mags was starving and ordered two double-smoked bacon, cheddar, and egg sandwiches and a fruit bowl to go with their coffees.

"Looks like you got your appetite back," her daughter said.

Mags took a monster bite out of her sandwich. "It never went away."

"You deliberately starved yourself? No wonder you look so unhealthy."

"It was Rand's suggestion. He said the cameras make actors look fat. I was sick a lot, come to think of it."

"You're borderline anorexic and you're also a nervous wreck."

"And your point is?"

The sandwich was soon reduced to greasy remains. It had been months since Mags had eaten a meal without counting the calories, and she went to the counter and ordered a chocolate chip muffin that had caught her eye and returned to the table munching on it.

"Mom, I want to ask you a personal question. Please don't get mad."

Mags groaned inside. The visit was nearly over, and Amber was going to lower the boom and ask Mags why she hadn't been around to see her daughter grow up. There was an answer, but it wasn't pretty. Being a thief and having a kid didn't go together, so Mags had dumped Amber on her folks, split town, and never looked back. Sure, she'd sent money and the occasional gift, but that was only to assuage her own guilt. It was only later that she'd regretted the decision not to raise her child, but by then Amber was grown up.

"Sure, honey."

"Did you quit being a thief and decide to become an actress for me?"

The question caught her by surprise. "Whatever gave you that idea?"

"Because you sent me an airline ticket and asked me to come out here. You sounded so damn proud over the phone when you told me your pilot had been picked up by CBS. You didn't call Grandma or Grandpa with the news; you called me. You wanted to impress me."

She took a deep breath. Amber had her dead to rights.

"Maybe I did. Is that wrong?"

"I think it is. It changed you, and not in a good way."

"What are you saying? That you liked me the way I was before?"

"Your being a grifter doesn't bother me. If you're clever enough to take their money, go ahead. I'm cool with it. What I'm not cool with is you thinking you shamed yourself, and that you need to turn yourself into an overnight success to impress me. I don't like that at all."

"You think it's okay I rob casinos?"

"It doesn't bother me."

Mags was more than a little surprised. Most people accepted that casino games were rigged in the house's favor, just like carnival games were rigged. The small percentage of people who felt otherwise had been victimized by a casino and held a grudge.

Amber had grown up in Providence, which was a short drive to the Native American casinos in Connecticut—Mohegan Sun and Foxwoods. Had Amber gambled at one of these joints and gotten cleaned out? Or had she worked for them as a dealer or cocktail waitress and been screwed over? Either scenario was plausible, and Mags decided to tread cautiously.

"Why do you hate the casinos?" she asked.

"During high school I used to hang out at my friend Brie Hartman's house. On Sundays, Brie's grandmother Rose would come over and cook these amazing meals. I got invited over a lot. It was always a great time.

"One day, Rose got sick with pneumonia and went into the hospital. She died a few days later. I went to the funeral with Brie and her family. It was really sad.

"After the funeral, Brie told me that Rose had willed her house in Connecticut to Brie's mom, and that her mom planned to sell it and use the money to put Brie and her sisters through college. The Hartmans didn't have much, so Brie was really excited.

"Brie's mom got a good offer. They went to close and discovered the Mohegan Sun Casino had a lien on the property. Rose owed them all this money. Every Sunday during her drive home, Rose would stop at the casino and play the high-stakes slot machines. The poor woman was an addict. Do you think the casino had the decency to cut her off? Hell no. When she died, she owed them three hundred and ten thousand dollars.

"The house went for two hundred and ninety thousand. The Hartmans had to sell Rose's car and her belongings at a yard sale to pay the debt. Brie's mom didn't end up getting a penny from her mother's estate. The casino got it all."

"They snapped her," Mags said.

"Is that what they call it? Well, it broke the family in half. The Hartmans hired a lawyer to see if it was legal, and sure enough, it was. The casinos have an agreement with every state that lets them prosecute people with debt. Even dead people. When I found out that you cheated the casinos, it made me so happy. I know that sounds weird, but it did. You're aces in my book, Mom. And so's your friend Billy. He's cool, too."

"You told me Billy was a snake," Mags said.

"That was before he saved you from the gaming board."

How strange was that? Amber didn't have a problem with Mags's criminal past, but she did have a problem with her mother being an actress. Mags had misjudged the situation completely, but at least it had worked out in the end.

It was getting late, and she bought Amber a bag of chocolate chip cookies for the trip before they went in search of her daughter's terminal.

FORTY-EIGHT

Billy sat on the balcony of his condo, soaking up the morning sunshine. He normally slept in, but today was different. Today he was going to paint cards at blackjack tables at five MGM casinos and, if things went according to plan, live happily ever after.

Going inside, he removed the video camera from its tripod and connected it to the TV. Soon he was watching yesterday's practice sessions. His painting skills were nothing to write home about, and his thumb still slightly fluttered whenever it touched the back of a playing card.

You go to battle with the army that you have. He couldn't improve his chops, but he could disguise himself so no one would notice him. Casino employees were trained to watch high rollers because they had the money. As a result, these same employees often ignored players with limited bankrolls who rolled in off the street. These players were seen as a nuisance who contributed little to the casino's bottom line.

It was an exploitable flaw. He went to his bedroom and entered the walk-in closet. On one wall were the expensive threads he wore at the clubs. Gucci, Versace, all brand names. On the other wall, the ragged clothes for the disguises he wore robbing the joints. Levi Strauss, Gap, and the crap they sold at Kohl's. The question was, what role would he play this time?

He decided to be a ranch hand. Nevada was home to several large cattle ranches, and it wasn't uncommon for a ranch hand to drive his dusty pickup into town for a wild weekend. He grabbed a pair of loose-fitting jeans and a denim shirt off the rack.

On the shelf above the rack was his collection of caps. These included baseball caps, caps from conventions that had come to town, and wacky caps sold at tourist shops. Caps were important when creating a disguise. The rim hid the cheat's face from the eye-in-the-sky, and it also allowed the cheat to establish an identity.

He chose an NRA camouflage cap that he'd bought off a farm boy down on Fremont Street. The cap had "outdoors" written all over it. He got dressed and appraised himself in the mirror. He liked what he saw, except his face. His skin was too smooth to be a ranch hand, his teeth too straight. From a drawer he grabbed a bridge and stuck it into his mouth. The bridge gave him a wicked overbite and distorted his face to the point of being unrecognizable.

He again consulted the mirror. Better but not perfect. Ranch hands lived outdoors and had bronze-colored skin. His skin was a pleasant tan and might get spotted by a sharp pit boss if he wasn't careful.

In the bathroom, he pulled a can of fake spray tan off the shelf and applied it to his neck, face, and the back of his hands. Before his eyes, his skin changed color and took on a darkish hue. He returned to the bedroom and had a look.

"Yee-haw," he said to the mirror.

His final stop was the wall safe. He removed two five-thousand-dollar stacks, which he slipped into his pants pockets. Before he started painting cards, he needed to lose. By losing, he'd further establish himself as a sucker and draw no heat.

Time to leave. At the front door, he realized he'd forgotten the tin of luminous paint. He asked himself if he was really cut out for this job. Painting was an art, and he was a mere apprentice. He was putting himself at risk.

But the reward was worth it. Seventeen million bucks for a single day's work. It didn't matter that the money would be split with the football players and with Victor. It was still a huge score, and he didn't walk away from huge scores.

The tin of luminous paint in his pocket, he took the elevator downstairs. Walking outside to the valet stand, he took out the bridge and removed his camo cap. The valet did a double take anyway, the clothes not in character for the tenant who occupied a penthouse suite.

"Sorry, Mr. Cunningham. The clothes sort of threw me," the valet said.

"I'm slumming it today," he explained.

"You buy a tanning bed?"

"Got a little too much sun on the golf course. You know how it is."

"Tell me about it. I'm out in the sun all day. I'll bring your car right up."

The valet hustled away. Billy retreated to the shade and put his disguise back on. Then he worked on his new identity. He decided to call himself Ty Lubbick because it sounded like a cowboy name. Having just gotten paid, Ty had driven to Vegas looking for a good time.

"Name's Ty, Ty Lubbick. Nice to meet you," he said, working on his drawl.

A red Corolla nudged the curb. The vehicle looked familiar but not the train wreck who climbed out. A blonde wearing hideous purple fingernail polish and too much makeup chewing on a wad of bubble gum. She threw him a disapproving glance.

"You can't be the valet." Her accent was back east and harsh.

"No, ma'am," he said. "If you're in a rush, you can leave your keys with the front desk manager. His name's Jo-Jo, and he's an honorable fellow."

"You don't say. Don't I know you?"

"I don't believe I've had the pleasure."

"What's your name?"

"Ty Lubbick."

"I've seen you before, Ty, haven't I?"

"I wouldn't know. I work on a ranch roping cattle."

"You don't say. A real live cowboy."

Trying to smile while wearing a bridge was difficult, but he did it anyway. The blonde was still trying to place him, and he refused to wilt beneath her stare. Finally, she gave up.

"Thanks for the help," she said.

"Yes, ma'am," he said.

She went inside. Her dress was of simple design and hung straight to the ground. The type of dress an overweight woman might wear, only the blonde didn't look overweight. He glanced into the Corolla and spied a pack of Kools stuck in the cup holder.

"For the love of Christ," he swore.

He went inside to find her standing at the front desk. Jo-Jo was on the phone and hadn't gotten to her yet. He took the dangling set of car keys from her hand.

"Didn't expect to see you again," he said quietly.

Her head snapped. "Billy? As I live and breathe. I had no idea."

"What are you doing here?"

"I changed my mind. I want in. I know it sounds crazy. Please don't blow your top."

"Let's take this outside, shall we?"

His car idled at the curb, the valet standing by the driver's door. Billy tossed him the keys to Mags's car. "Do me a favor, and park my friend's car for me."

"Sure, Mr. Cunningham. You guys going to a costume party?"

Billy didn't want the valet telling the other tenants about this. The building was filled with old people who had nothing better to do than gossip and spread rumors. Pulling a hundred off the stack in his pocket, he stuffed the bill into the valet's shirt pocket.

"Put a lid on it."

"Of course, Mr. Cunningham. My lips are sealed."

- - -

Leaving Turnberry, Billy took Paradise to East Sahara. Instead of heading west to the Strip, he chose the opposite direction and pushed the accelerator to the floor.

"You're going in the wrong direction. Slow down," Mags said.

"Don't tell me how to drive," he said. "I'm going to ask you some questions, and if I don't like the answers I get, I'm going to toss you out of the car while it's still moving."

Mags started to argue, then thought better of it.

"Fire away," she said.

"What the hell is going on? I made you the deal of a lifetime yesterday, and you slapped me in the face. Now you show up on my doorstep wanting in. Did something happen in the last couple of hours I should know about? And don't you dare bullshit me."

"My daughter talked me into it."

His foot involuntarily came off the gas, and the car slowed. "Your kid told you to?"

"In so many words, yes."

"Why? Is she hard up for cash and plans to hit you up?"

"It was nothing like that. Amber realized I took the TV gig to impress her. Seems she was already impressed with her old lady. My baby's got a hard-on for the casinos. I got her on a plane, went home, put on my Molly Maid disguise, and drove over. If that doesn't work for you, I'll get out at the next block. No hard feelings."

It sounded crazy enough to be true. "Does your kid cheat?"

"No. But she's been tempted. She carries around a gaffed die that I used back in Providence to scam businessmen at the bars."

"Are you cool with that?"

"That's none of your fucking business."

"Normally, I'd agree with you. It isn't any of my fucking business. Only you want to do a job with me, and I need to know where your head is at. Now answer the question."

"No, I'm not cool with it. I made Amber promise me that she'd never resort to thieving, and she gave me her word."

"Are things good between the two of you?"

"Yeah. It was a good trip, even if my show did get cancelled."

"You're not bitter about that?"

"Sure I'm bitter. But I'll get over it. Life marches on."

He'd heard enough. Mags had a thick skin; it was one of the reasons she'd lasted for as long as she had. At the next intersection, he did a U-turn and reversed course, causing the Strip's gaudy skyline to appear in the windshield. Mags managed a smile.

"Are you really going to give me half a million bucks for this job?" she asked.

"Have I ever lied to you before?"

"No, but there's always a first time."

Mags didn't fully trust him. Billy couldn't say he blamed her. Running out on her after sharing a bed had to be one of the stupidest things he'd ever done.

"You'll get every penny. You have my word," he said.

"There you go," she said.

FORTY-NINE

If there was any person inside a casino who Billy feared, it was the pit boss.

Pit bosses ran the blackjack games and were trained to watch dealers and players for any suspicious behavior. If cheating was suspected, a pit boss would pick up a house phone, call security, and have the offending party hauled away.

There were more than five hundred pit bosses employed in Las Vegas. One hundred of these were seasoned pros who could smell a hustle a mile away. The rest didn't know jack and had gotten their jobs because they had juice within the casino.

Billy maintained a database of pit bosses, which included the pit boss's name, his casino, a description of his physical appearance and hair color, and whether or not he was a problem. The information was kept on Billy's phone, giving him easy access.

The first MGM property he and Mags visited was the Luxor. The most outrageous joint on the Strip, the Luxor was designed like an Egyptian pyramid and had a three-hundred-thousand-watt beam spitting out of the top along with an ersatz Sphinx guarding the front entrance.

"I'll wait for you in the bar," Mags said.

He took a stroll through the blackjack pit. He counted four single-deck games where a dealing shoe was not in use. One of these games would soon have its cards marked with luminous paint. A flashy female pit boss with red hair stood in the pit's center, supervising the action. He pulled her up on his database. Her name was Lexie Lowman, and she was new.

He found Mags at a table in the bar. "Pit boss is green. This shouldn't be too hard."

"You going to run interference for me?" she asked.

"That was the plan." Taking a stack of hundreds from his pocket, he slipped them to her beneath the table. "Here's your play money. There are four tables with handheld games in the pit. Pick any one. I'll join you in a few minutes."

"Got it. That bridge in your mouth is hideous."

"I was just going to say the same thing about your disguise."

"Thanks. By the way, did you bring the paint?"

Taking the tin of luminous paint from his other pocket, he also passed it beneath the table. Mags slipped the tin into her purse and rose from the table.

"It's great to finally be running together," he said.

She flashed a smile. Beneath the hideous makeup and sloppy wig, she was still a beauty, her smoldering green eyes an invitation for the best kind of trouble. Slinging her purse over her shoulder, she sauntered out of the bar and entered the blackjack pit.

It didn't take Mags long to pick her spot. Like a shark smelling blood in the water, she sat down at a table with a break-in dealer, which was a dealer in training who worked a low-limit game during slow times, and threw three hundred-dollar bills onto the felt. The dealer made the exchange and pushed two stacks of chips toward her.

Billy left the bar a few minutes later and approached Mags's table. The seats had filled up, leaving only one empty chair. He grabbed it.

"Name's Ty Lubbick," he announced. "Nice to meet you all."

The other players at the table grunted hello. Casinos were fun places at night. But in the morning, they were deadly, the atmosphere as lively as a supermarket checkout line.

"Is this a lucky table?" he asked, keeping up the banter.

"It hasn't been so far," one of the players grumbled.

"Maybe we can change that."

He tossed $200 onto the felt, and the dealer turned it into chips. The dealer said, "Place your bets," and each player placed chips into the betting circle.

The dealer clumsily sailed cards around the table, hitting drinks and stacks of cards. Sailing cards was an art that this dealer had yet to master, and he mumbled an apology.

Billy looked across the table at his partner. Mags lit up a cigarette and returned the pack to her purse. Her fingers found the tin of luminous paint, unscrewed the lid, and applied a tiny amount to all five fingertips. Every painter had a unique style. For Maggie, it was the ability to load up for five applications at once.

As Mags checked her hand, her first and second fingers did the dirty work and painted the backs of the cards. The movement was light-years ahead of what he'd been practicing in his condo, her movements so polished they were nearly invisible.

The dealer coughed violently. Most dealers hated players who smoked but couldn't voice a complaint without fear of losing their jobs. The consummate pro, Mags knew better than to have the dealer pissed off at her.

"Should I put this out?" she asked.

"That's okay," the dealer said.

"No, it's not. You're allergic. I'll get rid of it."

Mags crushed the butt into the metal ashtray built into the table. Billy loved it. Mags had turned the dealer into a friend, always a smart play when scamming a game. Mags could not paint all the high cards without some help. On the next round, Billy pointed at the words printed in gold on the felt layout. "Excuse me, but what does it mean, 'Dealer stands on soft seventeen'?"

The dealer explained the rule. When the dealer received an ace and a six, it was considered a "soft" total of seventeen, and he was required to stand pat and not take another card.

"Got it," Billy said.

While this conversation took place, Mags painted two more cards.

And so it went. For the next half hour, Mags painted cards while Billy kept the dealer distracted. It went without a hitch and reminded him of that day in Providence when Mags had recruited him into helping her sell fake cashmere sweaters to a bunch of hard hats working a construction job. That event was a turning point, and it led to his becoming a grifter.

Mags had made it seem easy to separate suckers from their money. In reality, hustling was hard work, dangerous as well. Except with Mags, for whom stealing was absolute child's play. Leaving Luxor, they rode an otherwise empty tram to their next target, the MGM Grand.

"You haven't lost your touch," he said.

"Old habits die hard," she said.

"How many cards in the deck did you paint?"

"All the high ones. I counted."

The admission blew him away. Because the game was single deck, Mags had memorized each card she'd painted and kept the information stored in her head.

"I'm not just another pretty face, you know," she added.

FIFTY

The pit boss at the MGM Grand was a rookie, and Billy and Mags found a single-deck blackjack game and went to work. The hotel was hosting a convention, and there was plenty of action inside the casino. As a result, Billy had to distract the dealer only a handful of times.

"Give me some ten-dollar chips," he said, throwing money on the felt.

"I'm afraid I can't do that," the dealer said politely.

"Why not?"

"The casino doesn't have ten-dollar chips," the dealer explained.

"That's crazy. Every casino has ten-dollar chips. What's wrong with this place?"

The dealer acted confused. No casino in the world had chips with a denomination of ten dollars. But that hadn't stopped cheats from posing this question to dim-witted dealers and momentarily distracting them while their partners did the dirty work.

Painting the deck at the MGM went without a hitch. Thirty minutes later, they walked out the front door and down the sidewalk to the intersection of Tropicana and the Strip. Their next stop was the Mandalay Bay, another MGM property. It was two blocks away, and they decided to hike it.

"I want you to explain something to me," Mags said. "The casinos have equipment that detects luminous paint on the backs of cards. How do you plan to get around that?"

"The equipment at the MGM properties is flawed," he said.

"It's flawed at all their casinos?"

"Yup. The parent company switched suppliers, and the new company screwed up."

"No wonder you want to jump on it. What happens when MGM finds out the equipment isn't working properly?"

"We'll be long gone by then."

"You said that you were using football players as takeoff men. Be careful. I worked a scam in Atlantic City with two guys who played baseball for the Yankees and they were a nightmare. Never again."

"Why—did they try to hit on you?"

"Guys hit on me all the time. I don't have an issue with that. The problem is with dumb jocks. Most of them are spoiled rotten brats who never grew up. You tell them to do one thing, and they say yes, then do another thing entirely. I later checked out the baseball players and learned they'd been in trouble their whole lives but were never held accountable. They were a total liability."

"The football players have been working a poker scam. They're part-time grifters."

"Doesn't matter. They're still jocks, and used to having things their own way. Mark my words, one of them will go sideways on you. It's their nature."

The street entrance to Mandalay Bay resembled a temple and was designed to make visitors feel like royalty. Once inside, Mags headed straight for the Eyecandy Lounge while Billy wanted to check out the blackjack pit. The pit boss was another rookie. Beautiful.

He entered the lounge to find Mags watching a couple practice their moves on the dance floor. "Pit boss isn't going to be a problem," he said.

“Then let’s do it.”

Mags started to stand. Billy placed a gentle hand on her sleeve and she sat back down. “Would you reconsider joining my crew? Your chops are incredible. Run with me, and you’ll never get caught again. That’s a promise you can take to the bank.”

“I thought you already had a mechanic. What’s his name? Travis?”

“Travis is out of the picture. I need to find a replacement.”

“Is that what I am, a replacement? Not interested, thanks the same.”

“I’ll make you a partner. You’ll get half.”

“Jesus, Billy, what’s come over you?”

“We were made to work together. I know it, and so do you.”

Normally, he would have never had this conversation while on a job. But he’d decided it was now or never. If Mags didn’t join now, she’d leave town and he’d never see her again, and he didn’t think he could live with that. He wanted another chance to make things right and see what might happen. And he was willing to split the money just to give it a shot.

She rose from the table. “The only thing I know right now is that I need a nice long vacation when this is over. You’re going to have to wait for your answer.”

“Take all the time you need,” he said.

“I will.”

And with that, she entered the casino.

FIFTY-ONE

The last two stops on the victory tour were the Mirage and Aria. As with the three previous stops, the pit bosses were new to their jobs, and Mags painted the high cards at single-deck games in each casino without drawing any heat.

They drove back to Billy's place so Mags could pick up her car from the valet. Mags sensed that Billy wanted an answer, only she wasn't prepared to make a commitment just yet. She needed to let her head clear before she jumped back into a life of thievery.

Billy parked in front of the empty valet stand.

"Does the valet have another business on the side he's running?" she asked.

"Everybody in this place has another business on the side," he said.

"When am I going to see my money?"

"How about tomorrow night? I can drop by and deliver it, take you out to dinner."

And work her over some more.

"Call me first," she said.

- - -

Mags drove to LINQ. She needed to collect her things from her suite and check out of the hotel. It was going to be tough leaving the life of a TV actress behind, but she could handle it. She'd walked arm in arm with bad luck and trouble for most of her life and had gotten used to the special brand of misery they created.

She checked out at the front desk and said good-bye to the receptionist. Going outside, she pulled her wheeled suitcase to the curb where the valet had parked her car. Rand, her betrayer, stood a few yards away, chatting on his cell phone. Every man she'd ever known had done a number on her at one time or another; it seemed to be part of the male genetic makeup. But Rand was the ultimate destroyer of dreams, and she got right in his face.

"Hey, asshole."

"Hold on a second," Rand said to whoever he was talking to. "There you are. What's with the crazy getup? You look like a street person."

Mags snatched the cell phone out of his hand and gave it a heave. It landed on the concrete with a sickening crash, its face going dark. Rand yelped like he'd been kicked.

"That was the head of CBS I was talking to!"

"You crummy shit, I should cut your balls off!"

"What's come over you? You're acting like a demon."

"How do you expect me to act? You cancel the show and run out, and don't even have the courtesy to tell me? You are the most two-faced bastard I've ever met."

"Who said the show was cancelled?"

"It's not?"

"Hell no!" He paused to make sure she wasn't going to attack him, then said, "We have a date with destiny, Mags. You and me."

"What the hell's that supposed to mean?"

"Not here. I'll tell you in a nicer setting, where we can celebrate."

"Celebrate what?"

"You're going to be a star, my friend. And I'm going to be able to tell people that I was there when it happened."

- - -

Guy Fieri's Vegas Kitchen & Bar had a respectable lunch crowd. Rand got them seated at a booth next to the window and ordered the signature Tattooed Mojitos and a plate of sliders.

"Why did you run out on me?" she said, in no mood for games.

"I got a call from the head honchos at CBS two days ago, telling me to jump on a plane and get back to LA on the double," he said. "I figured they were going to drop the ax and cancel the show. It's not the first time it's happened to me."

"You could have told me that before."

"Wait, it gets better."

The drinks came, and he clinked his glass against hers and took a mighty sip. "Boy, that tastes good. Where was I? Oh right, in LA with the boys at CBS. I walk into a huge meeting room, and there are six of them huddled around a desk like a bunch of squirrels. They rush me, and I think, what's going on? Are you going to leave your drink? It's really tasty."

"Cut to the chase," she said.

"You don't look happy. What's wrong?"

She nearly stuck a fork into his face, just to see if he'd bleed. "Everything's wrong. Now tell me what the hell's going on before I mutilate you."

"That's funny. Okay, so the boys at CBS are shaking my hand and making nice. It's a real love-in. And one of them says, 'She's amazing, Rand. We watched the tape of her doing the Savannah move and were blown away. Where did you find her?' I told them that I met you playing poker and that you cleaned me out. That sealed the deal."

"What deal? What are you talking about?"

"You sure you don't want your drink?"

Mags pushed her untouched glass across the table. Rand lifted it to his lips and took a healthy gulp. "Boy, that tastes good."

"If you don't tell me what's going on, I'm going to poke your eye out."

"I was just getting to that part. It seems the boys at CBS weren't sold on *Night and Day*. The plot was a little too esoteric for them, if you can believe that. They were planning to run the pilot next summer to see if anyone watched it. That all changed when they saw you doing the Savannah move. You rocked their world, Mags."

"I did?"

"Yes! Strong female characters are driving broadcast TV, and you're as strong as they come. They've cleared a slot in next fall's lineup for the show. Tuesday night, nine to ten p.m. It doesn't get any better than that. You're going to be a major star, Maggie."

"If the show's still on, why did you fire the crew?"

"Not my call. The boys at CBS want a seasoned crew, so they instructed me to let everyone go, including that idiot director and screenwriter. They're bringing on a whole new gang with tons of experience. We're starting from scratch."

"Is that normal?"

"In Hollywood it is."

Her head was spinning. Instead of pinching herself, she took her drink back and saw the glass was empty. Rand signaled the waiter for another round.

"They liked me?"

"They *loved* you."

"You'd better not be pulling a fast one."

"Come on, you know me better than that."

"Why didn't you call me? Or send me a text? Why the radio silence?"

"I wanted to tell you in person and see the look on your face. Texts are too impersonal, don't you think?"

Mags said nothing. She wanted to believe him, only his words weren't ringing true. Her cell phone beeped in her purse, and she pulled it out. Amber had sent a text, saying she'd gotten home safe and what a great time she'd had. The message nearly made her cry.

"You thought I'd left you high and dry?" Rand said. "Never in a thousand years would I do that to you. That day you fleeced me at poker, I knew you were special. That's why I worked so hard to sell you to CBS. It's the one network that appreciates talent."

The next round came. Mags took a healthy gulp of her drink. The alcohol hit her stomach like a hand grenade and made her nostrils burn.

"They ordered twelve one-hour episodes," he said. "You'll be paid fifty thousand per episode, which works out to a cool six hundred grand. Not bad for a newbie actress."

It all sounded great, but it still didn't change the fact that Rand had run out on her. What if the honchos at CBS had told Rand that Mags had zero talent? Would the smooth-talking prick have bothered to fly back to Vegas to break the bad news? She didn't think so. Instead, he would have left her high and dry, gone onto his next project, and wiped her from his memory. She pulled off her wig and tossed it on the table.

"Tell them I want more money," she said.

"What? You can't be serious."

"I'm dead serious. Tell them I want seventy grand an episode."

"Maggie, please, that's not how the business works."

"Do it anyway. You can use my cell phone."

She gave him her cell phone and Rand made the call.

"You're way out of line, you know that?" he said as the call went through.

"What else is new?" she said.

FIFTY-TWO

Like a play, cheating a casino had three distinct acts. The beginning, the middle, and the end.

In the first act, the cheat sat down at a game and pretended to be a sucker. Since 99 percent of players in a casino were suckers, this was relatively easy and required little more than the cheat yucking it up and having a good time.

In the second act, the cheat turned the tables on the casino and began to win. This was when the play became complicated. The cheat needed to stay in character and give the casino the false impression that his winnings would be returned in short order.

In the final act, the cheat walked away with the casino's dough. In many ways, this was the hardest act of all, for it was totally out of character for anyone who gambled to quit while ahead. Gamblers lived for lucky streaks, and a winning gambler rarely quit.

Night Train and his buddies knew these things. They'd been cheating at poker for years, and a poker scam was structured the same as a casino scam, with three distinct acts. This was why Billy believed the football players would pull through with the super con.

After parting with Mags, Billy took the elevator to his condo and donned a new disguise. This time, he opted for jeans, a lime green polo shirt, a navy blazer with mother-of-pearl buttons, and cowboy boots that made him three inches taller. Cotton balls were shoved into both sides of his mouth to widen his face. To further trick the cameras, he treated his hair with a product called Caboki. Derived from a plant, Caboki instantly bonded to his existing hair and erased any visible spots in his scalp. His hair looked like a lion's mane.

He applied gel and spiked it. The face in the mirror didn't look anything like the guy who'd just helped Maggie Flynn paint cards in five MGM casinos.

In his dresser were a dozen pairs of shades, ranging from cheap to expensive. He chose a pair of Ray-Ban Predators. Dark sunglasses were needed to read luminous marks, the darker the better. Some cheats preferred shaded contact lenses, but Billy had found that they impaired his vision.

He got a call from Night Train. Yesterday at the villa, he'd instructed Night Train to stop communicating via phone calls until the super con was over. It had obviously escaped Night Train's memory.

"We finished practice early. Coaches had us in full pads in this heat. Guys were passing out," Night Train said. "I was just calling to see if the blackjack scam was all set."

"It is indeed," Billy said. "Do yourself a favor and don't call me anymore. If we get caught, the police will confiscate our cell phones and look at our calls. If they see we've been talking, we're screwed. We'll communicate by text message from now on. When we're done, you erase the texts, and the evidence disappears."

"That's smart. You know all the angles, don't you?"

"It's all in the details. Hang up, and I'll send you the schedule."

The call ended. Billy sent a text to Night Train with the names of the five MGM properties they were going to rob, along with the times Night Train and his teammates needed to arrive at the casinos.

Luxor 4:00 p.m.
MGM 6:30 p.m.
MB 9:00 p.m.
Mirage 11:30 p.m.
Aria 2:00 a.m.

Night Train sent him a reply. Got it. Will you be in disguise?

Smart question. Billy took a selfie and sent it to Night Train. This is what I look like. I'll be standing by the blackjack game that we're going to scam.

Who you want at each casino? Night Train replied.

Your call

He waited a minute to see if Night Train needed any more clarification. Mags telling him about the baseball players screwing up her play in Atlantic City had planted a seed of doubt in his mind, and that was never a good thing.

All good? he texted back.

Another minute passed.

Yeah, we're good, Night Train finally replied.

Where did you go?
Had to take another call

He started to steam. He had half a mind to walk away and not look back. Only millions of dollars were waiting to be stolen from Luxor, Mandalay Bay, MGM Grand, the Mirage, and Aria, and he was willing to work with dumb jocks to make it happen.

No problem, he texted back.

- - -

Luxor was their first target. At 3:40, Billy parked in the two-story garage behind the hotel and strolled down a covered walkway to the rear entrance. Taking an escalator to the casino, he got a beer at the bar and headed over to the blackjack pit. The casino was quiet, and he took a chair at a slot machine across from the rigged blackjack game and slapped on his Ray-Bans. It was like having X-ray vision, and he knew exactly what the dealer was holding.

At four o'clock, one of the football players would appear and start playing blackjack. It would take roughly ninety minutes to steal the desired amount. Once the money was won, he'd head down the street to the MGM for the six-thirty start, steal their money, walk to Mandalay Bay, scam them, then retrieve his car and hit the Mirage, then drive to Aria. By early tomorrow morning, they would have seventeen million bucks of casino money. It got him excited just thinking about it.

By 4:10, none of the football players had arrived.

What's going on? he texted Night Train.

Sammy's on his way, Night Train replied.

What's the holdup?

A commotion lifted his head. Sammy had arrived with all the bluster of a professional wrestler entering the ring and was stopping to sign autographs. Billy got out of his chair and took his position next to the blackjack game with the painted cards.

Sammy spotted him and sauntered over. His legs were wobbly, and he grabbed the back of a chair to steady himself. Right then Billy realized the problem. Sammy was drunker than a sailor on a navy payday. Sit down before you fall down, he thought.

"Hey!" Sammy said.

A small mob of people had gathered around the table, and the remark could have been directed at anyone. Billy played stupid and sipped his beer.

"This table?" Sammy asked.

Billy nearly ran. But that would have drawn suspicion, and right now, no one else in the casino knew the game was rigged. He decided to use that to his advantage and salvage the situation. "Sit down and enjoy yourself," he replied.

The crowd laughed. A sloppy grin creased Sammy's face.

"I think I will," the big Samoan said.

- - -

At first, the scam went like clockwork. Sammy lost every hand by making boneheaded decisions, just like Billy had instructed him to do the day before. Then came the critical part when Sammy asked the pit boss to raise the table limit. Billy gave him the chin.

"Got it," Sammy said.

Again, the remark caused no problems. Sammy asked the dealer to summon the pit boss. A man wearing a tailored suit came to the table and introduced himself as the pit boss.

"I'm losing my ass. Can you raise the limits?" Sammy asked.

Each shift was judged by the amount of money it made. Sammy was about to put the shift ahead, or so the pit boss mistakenly thought. "How about a minimum thousand-dollar bet, maximum twenty thousand," the pit boss suggested.

The crowd oohed and aahed. This was big time.

"Works for me," Sammy replied.

The table had a small LED display with the table limit displayed in red digital numbers. The pit boss punched the buttons and changed the limits to $1,000–$20,000.

"Good luck," the pit boss said.

Sammy made a twenty-thousand-dollar bet and the dealer dealt the round. Using his glasses, Billy read the dealer's cards and saw a weak hand. With the beer bottle, he signaled Sammy to take a card. Sammy said, "Hit me," and was dealt a ten, giving him a total of nineteen. Billy gave the signal to stand pat. Sammy said, "I'm good."

The dealer showed his hand, a seventeen, a loser. The crowd cheered.

Within twenty minutes, Sammy had half a million dollars of the house's money. The crowd was now five deep, with people straining to see. A cute cocktail waitress appeared and placed a hand on Sammy's shoulder.

"Can I interest you in a drink?" she asked.

"Gimme a rum and Coke," Sammy said.

Billy smelled a rat. The rap against the Luxor was the sparse number of cocktail waitresses, and his gut told him the cute cocktail waitress had been sent over by the pit boss. Soon she would return with a drink made with 150-proof rum and light on the Coke, aka a mickey. And before you knew it, it would be lights out for the big Samoan. It was one way to stop a winning streak, and the casinos did it constantly.

It was decision time. End the play or keep stealing until the final curtain went down. Greedy bastard that he was, he decided to keep stealing.

The cute cocktail waitress returned holding Sammy's beverage on a tray. Billy considered tripping her but couldn't get close enough.

The glass was huge and contained a lot of booze. The pit boss wasn't taking chances. The bloodshed had to be stopped, one way or another.

Sammy sucked the beverage down like a runner on a hot summer day. A magical look spread across his broad face. Billy stepped back, knowing what was about to happen.

"Place your bets," the dealer said.

As Sammy reached for chips, he froze, his eyelids flickering like a dying light bulb before closing. Pitching forward, his body hit the table and he slid to the floor. A Good Samaritan rushed to his aid and attempted to revive him.

Billy wanted to help but feared the drunk football player would slip up and alert the pit boss they were in cahoots. That left him no other choice but to bolt. Heading for the exit, he spotted the pit boss standing off to the side, nodding approvingly.

FIFTY-THREE

Billy texted Night Train as he hurried down the sidewalk toward the MGM Grand.

Sammy passed out at the Luxor. How could you let him get that drunk?

Wow. You leave him there? Night Train texted back.

Wow was not the right response. Was Night Train also three sheets to the wind? Night Train and his buddies were like a pack of stray dogs; if one of them got in trouble, they all got in trouble, and Billy couldn't imagine Sammy getting soused without his pals doing the same. He started to cross when a bus's horn sent him scurrying back to the sidewalk.

What the hell else could I do? he texted back.

He win much?

Half a million bucks

Sounds like your scam works

Had Night Train sent Sammy to test the waters? It was a low-rent move but not a total surprise. The light turned red. He texted his reply as he crossed. The play is off

That got Night Train's attention.

No, man, we're good. Choo-Choo heading for MGM Grand now, Night Train replied.

He better not be drunk, he wrote back.

- - -

Choo-Choo wasn't drunk when he entered the MGM Grand with a pair of hookers draped on his arms, but he was flying high on coke, the evidence caked on his nostrils. Seeing Billy, Choo-Choo took a chair at the targeted blackjack table, while the hookers remained standing. The hookers had trouble written all over them. One blonde, one redhead, wearing leather miniskirts and stilettos. It occurred to Billy that these ladies hadn't happened along. They'd been partying at Caesars with the football players and, like a pair of wolves, had attached themselves to Choo-Choo and planned to roll him once the right opportunity presented itself.

The dealer was a jovial guy with a handlebar mustache. "Place your bets."

Choo-Choo lost the first hand and the ones that followed. Soon half his stake was gone. Billy gave the signal for Choo-Choo to ask the pit boss to raise the table limit.

"These little bets don't interest me. Can you raise them?" Choo-Choo asked.

The pit boss wore designer threads and a silk tie. The average pit boss took down seventy-five K a year but dressed like a *Fortune* 500 CEO. It came with the territory.

The pit boss took the bait and raised the table limit. Choo-Choo placed a big bet and the hand was dealt. Choo-Choo's hand was a seventeen. Billy read the luminous paint on the dealer's hole card and knew that the dealer had nineteen. Conventional play said that Choo-Choo should stand on his hand. Only that would have resulted in Choo-Choo losing and further depleting his stack. Billy signaled Choo-Choo to take a card.

"Hit me," Choo-Choo said.

"But you have seventeen. Basic strategy calls for you to stand on seventeen," the dealer said helpfully.

"I always lose on seventeen. Gimme a card."

The dealer dealt a three, giving Choo-Choo a total of twenty. The dealer turned over his hand and acted surprised. The other players at the table congratulated Choo-Choo.

"That's what I'm talking about," Choo-Choo said.

Billy and Choo-Choo quickly stole a million bucks. Then a bad thing happened. Choo-Choo's hands began to tremble, and he knocked over his towering stacks of chips.

"Sir, are you all right?" the dealer asked.

It was a legitimate question, seeing that the football player looked ready to pass out. Choo-Choo took a deep breath and tried to collect himself.

"Would you like me to call the house doctor?" the dealer asked.

"No need for that. Where's the head?" he asked.

The dealer pointed to the restrooms, which were located a few steps from the blackjack pit. Choo-Choo rose and addressed the hookers. "Mia, Roxanne, you guard my chips. Don't let nobody touch them."

Asking a pair of hookers to guard your chips was an invitation for disaster. Choo-Choo left the table and disappeared into the men's room. Mia, the blonde, sat on the corner of Choo-Choo's chair, while Roxanne, the redhead, sat on the opposite corner.

The dealer glared at them, knowing trouble when he saw it.

A minute passed. The dealer dealt cards to the other players while keeping an eye on Mia and Roxanne. Billy decided it was time to see if Choo-Choo was still among the living.

The MGM's men's room was known to cheats for its shoeshine stand. Miguel, the stand's proprietor, sold information he overheard while shining shoes. Billy had done business with Miguel before and was on a first-name basis with the Cuban immigrant.

"Hey, Miguel, how's life treating you?" he asked.

"Every day is better than the next. Do I know you?"

"Billy Cunningham."

"Didn't recognize you, Mr. C. How you been?"

"Can't complain. Which stall is the football player in?"

"Third from the end. Your friend's in rough shape."

He banged on the stall door with his open palm. "You doing okay in there?"

The stall door cracked open. In Choo-Choo's massive hand was a tiny spoon with a lump of white powder. "Just getting a little pick-me-up. I'm running on fumes."

"How long have you been partying?"

"Since we got back from practice. I wouldn't call it a party. The NFL stuck a knife in our backs, so we decided to tie one on." Choo-Choo dug out a hit and sent it up his nostril.

"What do you mean, they stuck a knife in your backs? What did they do?"

"Night Train didn't tell you what happened?"

"Afraid not."

"Well shut my mouth. Let's pretend this conversation never took place."

Choo-Choo pocketed the drug paraphernalia and came out of the stall. He had a real spring in his step and his body language was back to being positive. Billy said, "You need to clean yourself up," and

Choo-Choo joined him at the sinks. "We're up to one million in winnings. I'm going to end the play when it reaches two and a half million."

"I thought we stopped at two million," Choo-Choo said.

"Sammy came up short at Luxor. We need to make up the difference."

"Got it."

Choo-Choo left the restroom first. Billy spotted Miguel on his shoeshine chair, reading the sports section. He stuffed several bills in Miguel's shirt pocket.

"Mum's the word."

"You got it, Mr. C," Miguel said.

- - -

The average Strip casino had several million dollars in chips distributed among its table games, and it was management's job to keep track of this inventory and protect the games where the chips resided. Chips were no different from cold, hard cash. A chip could be cashed in at any time, or it could be taken to another casino and cashed in. They were easy to carry and never lost their value. Money made the world go 'round, but in Las Vegas, chips talked the loudest.

Chaos described the situation Billy found upon returning to the rigged blackjack game. A small army of security guards ringed the table and was warning patrons to stay back. Chips lay scattered beneath the table, and the dealer was busily picking them up. Mia and Roxanne lay facedown on the floor, their blouses torn. Each had a burly security guard pinning them down. Billy came up behind Choo-Choo and gave him a nudge.

"What's going on here?" Choo-Choo said under his breath.

"Looks like your friends tried to steal your chips, so the casino put the heavy on them," Billy whispered back. "I'd suggest you disassociate yourself from them when the cops come."

"I'll tell the cops I met them at the bar. What about the money I won?"

"The dealer will hold your chips for you. Once the dust settles, cash out and leave."

"I really messed up bringing them here, didn't I?"

Billy pulled him away from the table and the security cameras' watchful eyes. The top of Billy's head barely reached Choo-Choo's chin, but he didn't let that temper what he was about to say. "What's wrong with you guys? I give you a chance to make a huge score, and you get messed up and call some sleazy hookers? I thought you were smart. I was wrong."

"It's not like that," Choo-Choo said. "The NFL fucked us. We had to blow off steam."

"You should have done it on somebody else's dime."

Choo-Choo acted ashamed, not that Billy cared. The damage was done, and all the apologies in the world were not going to fix things. He left the casino without saying good-bye.

FIFTY-FOUR

The MGM Grand had an elevated pedestrian walkway that connected it to New York New York on the other side of the Strip. Billy hiked across it and was soon sitting at a bar inside the casino, drinking a beer and trying to calm down.

As a rule, he avoided alcohol during a heist, but this was an exception. The football players were behaving like a bunch of crazy college kids, and it was a miracle that security at the Luxor and the MGM Grand hadn't discovered they were being scammed and busted them.

While he drank, he surfed the Internet on his cell phone. Choo-Choo's comment about the NFL double-crossing them had come out of left field. The Rebels' defense was famous, and he didn't understand what the NFL could do that would be seen as a betrayal.

On a hunch, he went to ESPN's site and scrolled through the headlines. Stories about the upcoming Super Bowl were in abundance, with both teams getting plenty of ink. The Vegas bookmakers had the Rebels as underdogs but only by a field goal. That would change before the game when money betting on the Rebels rolled in.

A story posted the day before caught his eye. *"Is this the final curtain call for the Rebels' vaunted defense?"* Was this the story that had gotten

Choo-Choo so ticked off? He clicked on it and had a look. It had been written by a staff writer for ESPN who quoted anonymous sources claiming that Night Train and his pals were planning to announce their retirements after the Super Bowl. The writer made it sound like it was a done deal, and went on to talk about their long and storied careers and how they were shoo-ins to be inducted into the Pro Football Hall of Fame when they became eligible.

He exited the article and thought about what it said. So what if Night Train and his pals were planning to retire? If the NFL had leaked the story, what was the harm? It didn't hurt anyone. Maybe the problem was the article's timing. Maybe the football players didn't like the NFL stealing their thunder to get a nice story. It was their careers, after all.

At the end of the day, he didn't think it really mattered. Night Train and his teammates' careers were coming to a close, and they needed to get used to no longer being in the limelight.

His cell phone vibrated in his hand. Caller unknown. He answered it.

"It's me," Night Train said.

"I told you no phone calls," he exploded.

"I'm calling from the lobby of the hotel, so there's no worry."

"No worry? Did Sammy tell you about his little stunt at the Luxor? He was so drunk he passed out at the table. If that didn't take the prize, Choo-Choo showed up at the MGM Grand high on coke with two hookers who tried to roll him. Your friends are insane."

"Look on the bright side. Sammy and Choo-Choo won a million and a half bucks, and there are still three casinos left to be ripped off. You can't quit now, man."

Every commotion inside a casino drew scrutiny, especially when large sums of money were lost. There was no doubt that security at Luxor and the MGM Grand were reviewing the surveillance tapes of Sammy's and Choo-Choo's huge wins to see if cheating was involved. Billy wanted to believe the scam was disguised well enough to pass muster. But there was always a chance that a sharp security person would smell a con, and things would quickly go south.

"Yes, I can," he said.

"We won't let you down again, and that's a promise," Night Train said.

Billy wanted to believe that Night Train's word meant something. But he didn't feel that way about Night Train's teammates. If Billy were going to scam another casino today, it would be with the man he was talking to on the phone, and no one else.

"I'll keep going, but there's going to be a change in plans," he said. "We're going to hit one more casino, just you and me. Your friends are no longer part of the equation."

"Don't trust them, huh?"

"About as far as I can kick them."

"I can live with that. Which casino do you want to hit?"

"The Mirage. It has more high rollers than any joint in town. The casino won't be as nervous if you beat them out of a huge score, because they'll win it back from another player."

"How huge?"

"Ten million bucks."

"You want me to steal ten million? That's a big number."

"We need to make up lost ground. Are you in or out?"

"I'm in. What time does this party start?"

He glanced at his watch and saw it was almost eight. He needed time to retrieve his car from Luxor's parking garage and drive to the Mirage. The trip was only a few miles, but on Friday night, that might take an hour or more.

"Nine thirty, and don't be late."

"I'll be there with bells on my feet," Night Train said.

He ended the call, hoping he wasn't making a mistake. The bartender asked if he wanted another beer. It was time to switch drugs, and he ordered coffee instead.

FIFTY-FIVE

When the Mirage opened its doors in 1989, everyone had laughed. It had cost more than six hundred million bucks to build and had huge overhead. In a city built upon unlimited buffets and nickel slot machines, a joint with real gold dust in its windows would surely fail.

The opposite had happened. High rollers had fallen in love with the ambiance and five-star amenities, and the casino quickly became one of the most profitable in the world.

Nearly thirty years later, serious gamblers were still in love with the Mirage and regularly gambled away millions of dollars in its Polynesian-themed casino. It was high-roller heaven, and Night Train's high-stakes play was going to fit right in.

At nine thirty, Night Train appeared in the casino wearing a white silk shirt and black linen pants, his platinum Rolex shining as if radioactive. He cleaned up well and looked like a player.

Night Train stopped to have his picture taken with an adoring fan. His smile lit up the room, and it was easy to see why he'd done so well pitching products on TV.

Next stop was the blackjack table, where Billy stood with his beer bottle. Night Train took a chair and said hello to the three middle-aged drunks at the table. The drunks had sunburns, and Billy guessed they'd spent the afternoon at Bare, the hotel's topless pool bar.

"My name's Mel," the closest drunk said. Mel was a poster boy for the evils of alcohol abuse, his nose a bouquet of broken blood vessels. "I think you're the greatest goddamn football player who's ever lived. I followed you during your college days all the way up through the pros. You're the best defensive player ever. Isn't he, guys?"

Mel's buddies chorused agreement. Mel pulled out his cell phone and a group photo was taken. "Who's gonna win the Super Bowl?" Mel asked.

Part of being a celebrity was dealing with blowhards who pretended to be your friend but who wanted nothing more than to get a selfie taken so they could share it with their friends.

"The best team will win," Night Train replied.

Night Train threw his wad on the table, which the dealer turned into chips. Night Train lost his first hand. Mel and his buddies lost their hands as well.

"It's none of my business, but shouldn't you be home resting?" Mel asked.

Night Train gave Mel a simmering look. Mel looked pleased with himself, believing that because he was in a public place with his buddies, no harm could possibly come to him.

"This is how I like to relax," Night Train said.

It was a great answer, and Mel nodded appreciatively. Night Train kept losing and eventually asked the pit boss to raise the table limit. The pit boss agreed, and Night Train pushed twenty grand in chips into the betting circle. The cards were dealt. Night Train's cards totaled seventeen. Seventeen was a weak hand, and the dealer was showing a nine. Billy had read the luminous mark on the dealer's down card during the deal. It was a ten, giving the dealer a total of nineteen. If Night Train didn't take another card, he would lose the hand and be way down.

Billy signaled with his beer bottle for Night Train to take a card. Night Train had been around the block and knew that he needed to take the card without making it look suspicious.

"What do you think?" Night Train asked the drunks.

Mel had lapsed into silence, nursing his buzz. To be asked advice by a celebrity was a moment to be savored, and he sat up straight in his chair.

"The way your luck's been running, I think you should take a card," Mel said.

"Dealer's been beating me pretty bad, hasn't she?" Night Train said.

"Your luck's about to change," Mel said.

"You think so?"

"Yeah, man, you're due. Isn't he, guys?"

Mel's buddies agreed that Night Train's luck was indeed about to change.

"Hit me," Night Train said.

The dealer dealt Night Train a seven, giving him a total of twenty-one. Mel threw both his arms into the air the way a ref did to indicate a touchdown had been scored.

"You da man!" Mel exclaimed.

Night Train won the hand and began to beat the house silly. Soon he was betting fifty thousand a hand and raking in the chips. Asking Mel for advice was a smart ploy and took the heat off the play, and Night Train kept right on doing it. The few times that Mel didn't give him the proper answer, Night Train said, "I don't think so," and won the hand on his own.

Soon Night Train's winnings exceeded a million dollars. The pit boss hadn't started to sweat, convinced it was nothing more than a lucky streak. Night Train started to play two hands at a time and, within another twenty minutes, reached the two-million mark.

A cocktail waitress appeared with a tray of shots. She served the four men at the table.

"These are on me," Mel said.

Night Train took the shot, happy to play along. The four men clinked glasses and knocked back their drinks. Mel didn't need any more liquor in him, his face so red that he appeared ready to explode. Mel dropped his voice to a conspiratorial whisper.

"Is it true you're going to retire?"

The words hit a nerve. Night Train scowled and put down his shot glass. "That's just a rumor. Don't go spreading that shit around."

"But I heard it on ESPN," Mel said.

"Don't believe everything you hear on ESPN."

"You're saying ESPN made it up? You know what they say, where there's smoke, there's usually fire. Did ESPN find out you were retiring and decide to spill the beans? Come on, you can tell us the truth."

Mel and his buddies leaned in like a gang of schoolyard chums. It was all good fun, or so they thought. Night Train's expression turned to menace. "Drop it. Right now."

"Whoa," Mel said, feigning surprise. "Don't get scary on us, big guy."

"You're talking about my personal life. Let it go."

"No need to threaten. We're just interested, that's all."

"I answered your question. Now shut up."

Mel acted hurt and let the alcohol get a hold of his tongue. "What happened? Did your body quit on you? Happens to the best of them, pal."

The dealer dealt the round. Night Train was boiling and stared at his cards.

"Winners never quit, and quitters never win," Mel said.

"I won't ask you again," Night Train said.

Mel said it again, and his buddies started laughing. Night Train's left fist shot out. *Pop, pop, pop,* it went, smacking Mel and his buddies on the jaw. Not a full punch, just a jab, but delivered with such accuracy and lightning speed that it sent each man sprawling to the floor.

"Police! Somebody call the police!" Mel screamed, holding his face.

Billy started backing up. He should have listened to his gut and called off the play after the bad scenes at the Luxor and the MGM Grand. But greed had gotten the best of him.

Leaving the pit, he began to jog. Because Night Train had assaulted three patrons, Mirage's security was required to review the game's surveillance tapes. They would look at the events leading up to the altercation, and they'd also scrutinize Night Train's play. They would see that Night Train had deviated from basic strategy several times, yet come out on the winning end. They would realize they'd been cheated, even if they didn't know how.

Night Train's life was about to be turned upside down.

The Mirage's self-parking garage was on the north side of the hotel. Billy tossed his sunglasses over the wall and was starting to get into his car when two uniformed security guards caught up with him. They had their batons out and meant business.

"Put your arms up," a security guard ordered him.

Billy raised his arms and was patted down. "What did I do?"

A smack in the back of the head had him seeing stars.

"Shut up and start walking," the security guard said.

FIFTY-SIX

Being a celebrity had its privileges.

In casino parlance, to backroom a person meant to place an undesirable patron in a small, windowless room while the casino's security decided the next steps to be taken.

The Mirage had two such rooms. Mel and his two buddies were put in one, while Billy and Night Train were placed in the other. To dissuade Night Train and Billy from talking, a muscle-bound security guard named Clyde occupied the room as well.

Casino security was on the low end of the food chain. Not able to pass the entrance exam to become a cop, they toiled in the casinos, earning lousy pay and getting zero respect. As a result, most security guards had bad attitudes. Clyde was an exception and seemed to like his work. He was also a die-hard football fan and would have washed Night Train's feet if asked. They talked football for a few minutes before Night Train requested a cold bottle of water.

"I can do that," Clyde said. "How about your friend?"

"You want something?" Night Train asked.

Billy declined. Clyde walked out of the room, leaving them alone.

"Room bugged?" Night Train whispered.

"Uh-huh. You're going to need a good lawyer," Billy whispered back.

"I don't need a lawyer."

"Yes you do. If they decide to arrest us, don't talk to the cops."

Night Train laughed under his breath. He was so full of himself that he actually believed he could punch out three guys in a casino and not get charged. Maybe in his hometown he could get away with assault, but it wasn't going to fly in Vegas. The casinos were the city's lifeblood, and patrons who broke laws inside them were punished for their transgressions.

"Cops won't arrest me. Not part of the script," Night Train said.

"What are you talking about? What script?"

"The script that calls for a happy ending as the baton is passed and everybody walks away a winner. That script."

"I don't know what you're talking about."

"You're not as smart as you think you are."

"I get reminded of that every day. What script? Come on, man, tell me."

The door opened, and Clyde entered holding a bottled water.

"Bet you a hundred bucks nothing happens to me," Night Train said.

"You're on," Billy said.

- - -

The minutes morphed into hours. Clyde ran out of memorable sporting events to talk about and lapsed into silence. The rattle of the air conditioner blowing through the clogged ceiling vent soon became torturous. The walkie-talkie clipped to Clyde's belt came to life.

Clyde took the call and hung up. "Judgment day, gentlemen. Let's go."

Soon they were riding in a service elevator to the third floor of the casino. The doors parted, and they marched down a hallway lined with the offices of company executives. Night Train smoothed down his hair as he walked.

"See. No cops," Night Train said.

"Let me guess. Cops aren't part of the script," Billy said.

"You catch on fast."

A pair of polished double doors awaited them. They entered a conference room with an oval table surrounded by leather chairs. A gang of suits stood by the windows, framed by the blinking neon skyline.

"It's been an honor. Good luck next Sunday," Clyde said before departing.

Billy counted four suits. None wore badges or the trademark cheap haircuts that defined the town's gaming agents.

"Hey Cutler, fancy seeing you here," Night Train said.

One of the suits came forward. Tall and broad-shouldered with a receding hairline, he had the harried expression of a man at the end of his wits. "Excuse my French, but you are one stupid son of a bitch."

"What did I do?" Night Train asked innocently.

"You cheated the Mirage along with your friend here," the suit said.

"Me? Cheat? Stop talking nonsense."

"I'd suggest you sit down. Both of you."

Billy and Night Train seated themselves at one end of the table. Night Train poured two cups of water using the pitcher and pair of glasses sitting on the table. "This is Scott Cutler, head of the NFL's League Security. Me and Scottie go back a ways," he told Billy.

"Nice to meet you," Billy said to Cutler.

"Both of you, shut up," Cutler said. "These three gentlemen standing behind me run the Mirage's surveillance department. They told me that you and your friend rigged a blackjack game and stole two million dollars. I'm going to let Louis Falanga, the head of Mirage's surveillance, explain exactly what you did."

Falanga stepped away from the window and cleared his throat. His ghostly pale skin bespoke a man who spent daylight hours in front of a video monitor in a windowless room.

"We reviewed your play frame by frame," Falanga said. "It was highly suspicious, to say the least. You seemed to know what the dealer was holding, so we examined the cards. The backs of all the high cards were marked with luminous paint."

"How did that happen?" Night Train asked.

"Shut up and let him talk," Cutler said.

"We couldn't understand how the pit boss supervising the game didn't spot the marks," Falanga said. "The discard tray built into the table is made of red plastic and designed to let the pit boss stare through its back wall and detect luminous paint. Only the tray wasn't working properly. Nor are any of the other discard trays in the casino. We think the manufacturer screwed up and added a dye to the plastic that destroyed its ability to spot luminous marks."

The cat was out of the bag. Mirage's surveillance team had doped out the super con and would alert the other MGM properties to check the discard trays at their tables. By tomorrow, the faulty discard trays would be replaced by trays made to spot luminous paint.

"What does this have to do with me?" Night Train asked.

"Every high card at your table was marked," Falanga replied. "Your accomplice stood nearby wearing sunglasses, which allowed him to read the marks on the dealer's cards. Your accomplice then signaled you how to bet, which you did, and won. Cheaters call this scam the anchor, because it always gets the money. Except today. Today it blew up in your faces."

Falanga was gloating. He'd get a bonus for this bust, not that he deserved it. The Mirage would never have discovered they were being swindled if Night Train hadn't blown his cool and punched out the drunks. But Falanga would take the glory anyway. "Your teammates pulled the same scam at the Luxor and MGM Grand earlier today,"

Falanga said. "The cards in those games were marked with luminous paint as well."

"I didn't mark any cards or rig any discard trays," Night Train said.

"That's a clever choice of words," Falanga said. "Maybe you didn't, but your friends did. We have surveillance videos of two players, a man and a woman, who paid a visit to the Luxor, MGM Grand, the Mirage, and Aria earlier today. The man distracted the dealer while the woman expertly marked the backs of cards with luminous paint."

"What does that have to do with me?" Night Train said.

"Everything," Falanga said. "The man who came earlier in the day is the same man sitting beside you. We turned the videos over to the gaming board so they could make a definitive match."

Night Train gave Billy a hard stare. "This guy marked the cards?"

"Correct. He helped the woman mark the cards, then returned a few hours later and read the marks while you and your teammates cleaned up," Falanga said.

"You sure it's him?"

"Ninety-nine percent sure."

"Same clothes, same hair, same everything?"

"No, he changed outfits and hairstyles. But we're sure it's him. Your friend has a long history cheating the town's casinos. The gaming board is reviewing the surveillance tapes right now and will soon give us the go-ahead to prosecute him."

"That's all news to me."

Falanga acted flustered. He'd said plenty but accomplished little. Cutler took over. "The NFL wants this situation to go away," Cutler said. "Your teammates stole one million five hundred thousand dollars from the Luxor and MGM Grand. If they give the money back, the Luxor and MGM Grand won't press charges."

"I can't speak for those guys," Night Train said.

"Then the three of you will go to jail."

Cutler had drawn a line in the sand. Night Train scratched his chin, as if deep in thought. "When you put it that way, maybe I can talk them into it."

"Is that a yes?"

"Yeah, it's a yes."

Billy could not believe his ears. The NFL had cut a deal with MGM's management to save Night Train and his pals from the ugly publicity that an arrest would bring. The MGM got nothing for playing nice, unless there was a piece of the puzzle that he wasn't seeing.

"What about the gentleman next to me?" Night Train asked.

"We'll let the gaming board deal with him."

"You have to cut him loose, too."

Cutler's jaw went hard. "I don't think so."

The room grew quiet, with neither side budging. The cheater's code required Night Train to do whatever necessary to help his partner out of a jam, even if it meant putting his own neck on the chopping block. But it occurred to Billy that if Night Train and his teammates did get arrested for their involvement with the super con, they wouldn't be able to pull off the Super Bowl fix next Sunday, and he'd be out two major scores instead of just one.

He kicked Night Train under the table. "Save yourself," he whispered.

Night Train gave him a look. Billy returned the look and gave him the chin.

"You sure?" Night Train whispered.

Billy nodded. He'd dealt with the gaming board before and always came out on top.

"You win," Night Train said to Cutler. "I'll talk to my guys and tell them to return the money. And for the record, this gentleman next to me is completely innocent."

The deal had been struck. Night Train rose from his chair and went to the double doors with Cutler on his heels.

"Hello."

Grimes filled the doorway, his silver badge pinned to his lapel. Gaming agents only wore their badges when they were about to make an arrest.

"Who are you?" Night Train asked.

"Special Agent Frank Grimes with the gaming board. I should be arresting you, along with your teammates. Count your blessings and get out of here before I change my mind."

"Yes, sir."

Night Train shot a parting glance at Billy before departing. The NFL's reputation had been saved. America's favorite pastime would survive another Sunday.

Grimes closed the doors and came around the table, bumping Billy's chair as he did.

Shit, Billy thought.

FIFTY-SEVEN

The Nevada Gaming Control Board was nobody's friend. Over the course of a year, it busted just as many casinos for not paying taxes and money laundering as it did cheats for stealing. Nobody in Vegas liked the gaming board, and that included Falanga and his cohorts. Grimes came around the table to where Mirage's surveillance team stood. No one shook hands.

"Hello, Special Agent Grimes," Falanga said, striking a formal tone. "I was just explaining to our suspect how you were reviewing the surveillance tapes and would link him to the card-marking scam at the MGM's casinos."

"That was stupid," Grimes said.

"Is there something wrong?" Falanga said, taken aback.

"Our suspect is a known cheat. The less he is told about our investigation, the better."

"Sorry," Falanga said.

Grimes turned his attention to Billy. The special agent's face was filled with hostility born from a decade of fruitless investigations and botched stakeouts. Ten years of wasted effort was enough to bring out the worst in a man, and Grimes looked bent on revenge.

"This little prick has ripped off every casino in town," Grimes said. "You name the game, he's scammed it. Our file on him is as thick as a high school yearbook. We've gotten close to nailing his sorry ass plenty of times but always come up short. He's a goddamn plague."

Grimes put his hands on the table and let a moment pass. His stare was unrelenting.

"Which is why I'm sorry to tell you he's not the guy who helped the bag lady mark the cards in your casinos," Grimes said.

Falanga's jaw flapped open. "He's not?"

"No sir. I reviewed the surveillance tapes myself, frame by frame. It's not him."

Falanga angrily balled his hands into fists. "But he has to be involved. He was standing behind the table wearing sunglasses each time our casinos got ripped off by one of the football players. He was reading the marks and signaling his partners."

"Have you been in your poker room lately? Everyone wears sunglasses," Grimes said. "The fact that this little rat was in your casinos wearing shades doesn't prove a damn thing. And without proof, I can't arrest him."

"You're letting him go?"

"I don't have a choice."

The air trapped in Billy's lungs slowly escaped. Grimes's story was total bullshit. The gaming board's file included Billy's weight, height, how he walked, shape of his ears, and other salient physical features. Grimes could have matched Billy to the ranch hand seen on the surveillance videos with Mags but had chosen not to, knowing that if Billy got busted, his case against Broken Tooth would get flushed down the toilet, along with his promotion.

Billy rose from his chair. "Can I go?"

"Sit down. We're not done with you," Falanga barked.

"Yes we are," Grimes said.

"But he cheated us!" Falanga said.

"You can't prove that," Grimes said. "If you detain him any longer, he'll have grounds to sue you for false imprisonment."

If there were a group of people that hated Billy more than the gaming board, it was the town's surveillance directors. Their efforts to nail Billy had left them with nothing but egg on their faces.

"Get out of here, before I throw you out," Falanga said, reduced to threats.

- - -

An elevator took Billy to the main level. His feet sprouted tiny wings as he walked the concrete sidewalk to the parking garage where his car awaited. He'd once read that getting married and having a kid was the strongest bond two people could share. He didn't think that was true. The strongest bond two people could share was committing a crime together. When two people broke the law, they shared a singular experience that was theirs and theirs alone. It was a bond stronger than love or blood, and it would never fade. He and Grimes now shared such a bond, and he could only imagine where it would take them.

The Strip was a mob scene, the traffic bumper-to-bumper. It was that way most of the time, yet Billy didn't care. He drove the Strip whenever he had time to kill, the garish billboards and outrageous people lining the sidewalks making him feel more alive than any place he'd ever been. There was nothing pretty about it, nor did it hold any subtle charms. It was all about the action, and the Strip had more of it than the rest of the cities in the world combined. He got a call from Grimes, his partner in crime.

"Hey boss," he said by way of greeting.

"You are the definition of a problem," Grimes said.

"I'll take that as a compliment."

"Go home and pack yourself a suitcase. You're taking a trip."

"I am?"

"The FBI tipped us off that a hired killer from Hong Kong illegally entered the country last night through LAX and is heading to Vegas. There's a contract out on your life."

"Broken Tooth?"

"That would be a logical guess. He doesn't want you testifying against him. I'll pick you up in front of your place in forty-five minutes."

"Exactly where am I going?"

"That's up to you."

"Should I be scared?"

"I would be."

He wasn't afraid of dying, just not today. He departed the Strip at the next intersection and took the back roads home with one eye on his mirror.

- - -

He was waiting by the curb in front of his building with a packed suitcase when Grimes pulled up in a Jeep Cherokee with tinted windows. The desert sun was brutal on paint jobs, and the hood was flaking away in large chips. Maybe when Grimes got his promotion he'd lose this piece of junk and get himself a sexy new ride.

Grimes refused to make eye contact as he drove. "You owe me."

"No kidding," he said.

"I mean that. We need to come to an understanding."

"What's that?"

"You told me the Rebels' defense said no to fixing the Super Bowl. Then these same players try to rip off the casinos with you in charge. That tells me you've corrupted them. I don't know what your arrangement with them is, and I don't care. Just keep your nose clean until we bring the case against Broken Tooth and don't scam any casinos. Because, so help me God, if you get busted, I'll fuck you."

There were poker rooms and casinos in every state in the union. If his trip took him to a place where one of these fine establishments existed, and he saw an opportunity to make some money, he wasn't about to turn his back and walk away.

"Fuck me how?" he asked.

"I'll put the screws to Maggie. You wouldn't want that happening, would you?"

"Mags has nothing to do with this," he said.

"Bullshit. I have more videos of her cheating than I do of my kids growing up. I compared them to the video of the bag lady marking the cards. Same technique. It's her."

Billy stared at the white lines in the highway. He liked to think he could weasel his way out of just about any jam. But Mags was not so lucky in that regard, and another encounter with the gaming board would do her in. A plane roared overhead as they neared the airport.

"I won't scam any casinos until this is over," he said.

"Glad to hear it. Pick a terminal, and I'll drop you off," Grimes said.

He chose Terminal A. Maybe he'd go somewhere warm where there were golf courses so he could hustle some old geezers for pocket change.

"Do you know what this hired assassin looks like?"

Grimes pulled up a photo on his cell phone that showed a thick-faced Chinese male with a unibrow and a snarl as mean as a junkyard dog. He texted it to Billy as he drove.

"Send it to your crew. Just in case," the special agent said.

"I told you—"

"I know, I know, you don't have a crew. Do it anyway. This hit man is a member of a secret society based in Hong Kong called the Chinese Assassins Corps. They've been murdering people for more than a hundred years and are real pros."

"Thanks for the warning."

The Jeep's front tire kissed the curb. Billy had a thought and said, "Why did MGM decide not to press charges against the football players? They caught them red-handed."

"MGM got a call that told them to let them go."

"A call from whom?"

"You don't know?"

"No, should I?"

Grimes gave him a smug look. "You're not as smart as you think you are."

Grimes was the second person to tell him that. Billy hated to be kept in the dark and decided to press the special agent for an answer. A TSA officer's whistle cut him short.

"Get out before this asshole tickets me," Grimes said.

He opened the passenger door and put a foot on the curb. Hoping to bring Grimes's guard down, he waited a beat before turning around. "Night Train knew he wasn't going to jail. He even bet me a hundred bucks. How could he know that?"

"You'll figure it out someday," Grimes said. "Have a nice trip."

FIFTY-EIGHT

Saturday, eight days before the Super Bowl

Billy went to Scottsdale to work on his golf game and decided to stay at the Phoenician. The luxury property sat on two hundred and fifty manicured acres and had security guards roaming the grounds. Broken Tooth's hired killer would have a hard time locating him here.

Saturday morning found him playing in a foursome on the resort's championship course. His playing partners were ophthalmologists attending a convention who boasted how they were able to write off their stays if they attended a single one-hour-long seminar. Everybody had an angle they were working; for the eye doctors, it was ripping off Uncle Sam.

The golf over, he retired to his residence and ordered room service. Soon he was eating a club sandwich and watching ESPN's *SportsCenter*. Next Sunday's Super Bowl was the hot topic, and nearly every story was devoted to a player profile or an analysis of how the teams stacked up.

If the pundits were to be believed, the Rebels were in trouble. A video of Sammy passed out at Luxor had surfaced along with a story about the defense's wild partying. This news had created a negative spin, and the bookies had made the Rebels a ten-point underdog.

Finished, he pushed aside his plate. There were no stories about Night Train punching the drunks or cheating the Mirage. It was like it had never happened. Then the announcer said a story about Night Train was coming after the commercial break. Here we go, he thought.

The commercial ended and the story began. In a somber tone, the announcer stated that Night Train had suffered an injury and was doubtful for the Super Bowl. A video played of Night Train in practice wearing a bulky knee brace. It switched to a female sportscaster interviewing the famous football player on the sidelines.

"I'm here with Night Train McClain, captain of the Rebels' defense," the female sportscaster said. "Night Train, can you tell us what's wrong with your knee?"

"I hyperextended it in the first round of the playoffs, and it flared up a few days ago," Night Train said.

"How does it affect your play?"

"My lateral movement's not a hundred percent."

Billy was stunned. He'd been around Night Train plenty and hadn't seen evidence of any physical problems. The guy was in incredible shape.

"Do you think you'll be ready for the game?" the sportscaster asked.

"I'll have to see how my knee feels," Night Train replied.

"Do you want to play?"

"Of course I want to play. But I'm not going to play injured. That will only hurt my team's chances, and I'm not going to do that."

"That sounds like a no."

Night Train shook his head, as if to say, *It's out of my hands.*

"The game won't be the same without you," the sportscaster said.

"I have to do what's best for my team," Night Train said.

The interview ended. He killed the picture and leaned back in his chair. Without Night Train in the game, the Rebels' defense would likely sputter and give up a lot of points, and they'd probably lose. Worse, there would be no one making sure that the defense fixed the prop plays. All his hard work had gone up in flames, and there wasn't a damn thing he could do about it.

He sent a text to Cory, Morris, and Gabe, and shared the bad news.

The room's minibar had vodka and Bloody Mary mix, and he fixed himself a drink. He normally didn't drink this early but needed to kill the pain of losing such a huge score. It would be a long time before a scam like this came along again.

He drank the beer while staring at the blank TV. Night Train's decision not to play didn't make sense. Even if his knee was hurting, he could still start the game and set up the fixed plays before hobbling off the field. Night Train was a hustler, and hustlers didn't walk away from scores that put money in their pockets.

So why was Night Train taking a powder this time? There had to be a real good reason, and he found himself thinking back to his conversation with a coked-up Choo-Choo in the john at the MGM Grand. Choo-Choo had said that the NFL had stuck a knife in their backs, and when Billy hadn't understood, Choo-Choo had told Billy to forget the conversation had ever happened.

Stuck a knife in their backs how? This was Night Train's and his teammates' last game in the pros, and they were prepared to knock an injured Neil Godfrey out of the game and all but ensure a Rebels win. It was a storybook ending to five storied careers, so how could the NFL possibly screw them?

He spent a while thinking about it. The Bloody Mary was feeling like a bad idea, and he made himself a cup of coffee with the Keurig machine and let the caffeine do its thing. As the last drop touched his lips, the answer became as apparent as the nose on his face. Night Train and his pals had been breaking the rules for years, and the NFL had been letting them get away with it. Now the NFL was calling in their chits, and had told Night Train and his teammates that it was time to let the new kid on the block have the glory, and to go soft on Godfrey. To make this easier to digest, the NFL commissioner had flown to Vegas and offered Night Train and his pals lucrative jobs as sportscasters. When they'd balked, the NFL had turned ugly and blackmailed them.

That was the reason behind Night Train's knee injury. Night Train didn't want to end his career by besmirching himself, so he'd decided to sit on the bench and not participate.

It didn't need to end like this. Night Train needed to be shown there was another way out, and Billy was willing to be the one to do it. But before he flew back to Vegas, there was the matter of the hired Chinese assassin looking to take him out. He called Grimes and left a message on the special agent's voice mail. An hour later, Grimes rang him back.

"Your ears must be burning. We got him."

"The Chinese assassin hired to kill me?"

"Yes, sir. Eight o'clock this morning. He was stopped at a traffic light at the corner of Sahara and the Strip. He tried to pull a piece and the police shot the bastard dead. You should have seen the arsenal stowed in the trunk. Two assault rifles, two handguns, and a sniper rifle. You wouldn't have stood a chance if he'd found you."

"You sure it was the right guy?"

"He had your photograph in his wallet. And a scorpion tattoo beneath his shirt collar. That's his society's secret symbol. We got the whole thing on cruiser cam. I'll text it to you."

"Is it safe for me to come back?"

"It's safe. Remember, you've got to keep your nose clean."

"You got it."

Grimes sent him a text with an embedded video of the shootout. Billy watched as two Metro LVPD cops approached a car parked at the intersection with the Chinese assassin at the wheel. Like a scene out of the Wild West, everyone drew their guns, and the assassin lost.

He normally didn't get his jollies watching people get shot to death, but the Chinese assassin had been gunning for him, so he watched it again. It was safe for him to go out in public, and he picked up the house phone and called guest services.

"How may I help you, Mr. Cunningham?" a cheery receptionist answered.

"I need a cab to the airport," he said.

FIFTY-NINE

He took a puddle jumper to Vegas and grabbed a cab to Caesars. The Rebels' practices ended by midafternoon, and he was hoping that Night Train was back at his villa. Billy called his cell phone and got patched into voice mail.

"This is Billy. You and I need to talk. Call me."

The minutes slipped by without a call back. The times he and Night Train had been together, the famous football player's cell phone was always within arm's reach. Night Train had gotten his message but was avoiding him. Billy called him again.

"There's nothing wrong with your fucking knee. If you don't call me, I'm going to call the sportswriter on the local paper and tell him I saw you doing cartwheels. Call me."

Night Train called him back in a panic. "You in jail?"

"Hell no. I beat that rap," he said. "What's this crap on the news about you not playing in the Super Bowl?"

"My knee's acting up. It's an old injury."

"What about our deal? I've got a lot riding on this."

"I'm sorry, man, but I can't risk my health. You know how it is."

"No, I don't. I want to talk to you face-to-face. We had a deal."

"Sorry, man, but our deal's off," Night Train said.

"I don't think so."

"You can't make me do something I don't want to do."

"That's where you're wrong. Choo-Choo told me the NFL was screwing you guys. It took me a while to figure out what he meant. This is your last game. How could the NFL possibly screw you at this point in your careers? But then it hit me what they wanted. I know what it is, and if you don't meet with me, I'll tell my friends at the gaming board what's going on."

"You can't do that."

"Try me."

"I thought you were my friend."

"I am your friend. I brought you two deals worth millions of dollars. You and your teammates blew the first deal, and now you're going to sit out the game and blow the second deal. You're the one who's not being a friend."

"You don't understand the situation."

"On the contrary, I understand everything, which is why we need to talk. This is about your legacy, man. You can't take a dive for these fuckers."

The line went quiet. He had Night Train dead to rights, and they both knew it.

"Give me an hour. I just got back from practice, and I need to take a shower," Night Train said. "There's a cigar bar in Caesars called the Montecristo. I'll meet you there."

"One hour it is."

- - -

Caesars was jumping. The entrance resembled a parking lot, and he watched the cab's meter run while waiting to be dropped off. Soon he was in the main lobby. While guests waited on line to register, there was a bust going down, courtesy of the gaming board. The busted cheat wore silver bracelets and stared dejectedly at the floor. The gaming agents were so focused on their suspect that they didn't see Billy come in.

He circled around them. The busted cheat's wardrobe screamed Russian. Run-down Nikes, a threadbare sports jacket, and a sheared haircut more befitting a war refugee. The casinos knew about the Russian gangs and had trained their surveillance teams to be on the lookout. Their scam was called whacking. A Russian cheat would stand next to a particular make of slot machine and record the machine's play on a cell phone. The machine had a flawed random number generator chip that spit out predictable sequences every few hours. The Russian left and went to a motel, where the information was sent to a foreign server that calculated when the machine would pay a jackpot. Upon returning, the Russian would play the same machine and eventually win.

A great scam, unless you happened to get caught. Nevada had a law that forbade using an electronic device to beat its games, including cell phones. Cheats who got busted using devices went down hard.

"Coming through," a voice said.

A uniformed bellman pushing a luggage cart bore down on him. His name tag said KENNETH/SAN DIEGO. As Billy moved to let him pass, the bellman stopped and drew a pocket-size Beretta from his pants. He jammed the barrel into Billy's rib cage.

"Start walking toward the elevators," the bellman said.

Billy's eyes darted around the lobby. He counted five gaming agents, only they were too preoccupied with their bust to notice that something bad was going down.

"Let me guess. Your name isn't Kenneth, and you're not from San Diego," he said.

"Hong Kong. Keep walking. I'll shoot you right here if I have to," the bellman said.

"With all this heat?"

"I'll be gone before they know it."

The elevators were at the far end of the lobby. He began walking, praying that an opportunity would present itself to alert the gaming agents. The bellman hung close to his side.

"You don't look Chinese," he said.

"Plastic surgery. It took three operations."

"Your English is good, too. No accent."

"Rosetta Stone."

"I'll double your fee if you let me go."

The gun's barrel was suddenly in his ass. It made him jump a little. They came to the bank of elevators, and the bellman summoned a car. Billy stole a glance at the mirrors that lined the wall. None of the gaming agents had followed them. Was this the end? It sure felt like it.

"How did you know I'd be here?" he asked.

"Broken Tooth said you'd come back to Caesars to talk to the football players, iron out the details. Broken Tooth is smart that way," the bellman said.

"How long you been waiting?"

"Two days."

"And the hotel didn't notice?"

The bellman laughed under his breath. "I took a job. They're shorthanded, so I agreed to work double shifts. It was only a matter of time before you came in, and I spotted you."

"You got lucky, admit it."

"Luck had nothing to do with it."

An elevator car landed and its doors parted. The car was empty and they boarded. He spun around and watched the bellman slip the gun into his pocket, then draw a gilded knife with a pearl handle from a sheath hidden by his vest. The tip of the knife was dripping a substance the color of gold, and he guessed it was some kind of exotic poison. Elevators had surveillance cameras, only no one in the casino ever watched them. The doors began to close.

"Any final requests?" the bellman asked.

"Just don't make me suffer," he said.

SIXTY

A man's foot stopped the elevator doors from closing all the way.

"Drop the knife and put your arms in the air," a voice said.

The doors opened, and Grimes entered the car aiming his gun. The bellman was no fool and let the knife slip from his fingers before lifting his arms over his head. Billy spied a colorful scorpion tattoo beneath his starched shirt collar.

"You know this guy?" Grimes asked.

"Believe it or not, he's Chinese and an assassin," Billy said. "I guess the first one was a decoy. Be careful, he's got a gun in his pants pocket and the knife is filled with poison."

"Thanks for the warning. Okay, friend, step out of the car, real slow."

The bellman stepped out of the car, and Grimes stuck his hand in the bellman's pocket and relieved him of his weapon. He had the bellman put his hands behind his back so he could cuff him. Then he read the bellman his rights, which he recited from memory. It was all Billy could do not to give the special agent a hug, but he didn't think the gesture would be appreciated.

"How did you spot us?" he asked.

"I've developed a sixth sense whenever you're in a casino," Grimes said. "The hairs on the back of my neck go straight up. Lucky for you, huh?"

"I'll say. I could have been ripping off the joint."

"Get the hell out of here," Grimes said.

- - -

The Montecristo Cigar Bar was designed for private conversation. A hostess escorted Billy to a private room called the Vault, where Night Train sat on a leather couch puffing on a cigar and watching a wall of TVs. The room was otherwise empty, and Billy pulled up a chair.

"Cigars are bad for your health," he said.

"Haven't you heard? This is my last game. Might as well start enjoying myself." Night Train picked up a box from the table and offered his guest one. Billy accepted and lit up.

"Tasty. What are they?"

"They're called PGs. They're from the Dominican Republic."

He blew a smoke ring and watched it rise to the ceiling. "It took me a while to put the pieces together. Sometime after the playoffs, the NFL asked you to take it easy on Neil Godfrey, who's playing injured. That would let your opponent win, because Godfrey can pick you apart if he has the time. You didn't like it and started hanging out at Caesars to blow off steam."

Night Train puffed on his cigar and said nothing.

"The NFL commissioner flew in to Vegas and had a meeting at your villa. The commish offered you sports-casting jobs if you agreed to throw the game, only you said no dice."

"Who told you about the sports-casting jobs?"

"I found the contracts in the garbage in your villa. You thought the whole thing was settled, but then the NFL did something to you and your teammates that wasn't right. It made you so angry that you threw a party at Caesars with hookers and blow and plenty of booze. Normally, you'd never do something that reckless before the Super Bowl, but this situation was different. The NFL fucked you, and you were mad as hell about it."

"You don't miss much," Night Train said.

"Like I said, it took me a while to piece it together. But I'm still missing the important part. I don't know what the NFL did that made you guys blow up. What do they have, photographs of you robbing a bank?"

"Worse. They kept files on us dating back to our rookie years, stuff so old that we'd forgotten about it. If we don't do as they want, the stuff gets leaked to the press."

"Must be bad."

"It is. When we entered the league, the NFL let us think we could do whatever we pleased, that there were no consequences. But they were writing everything down in case they needed to use it as leverage someday."

They smoked their cigars and watched the college basketball games playing on the TVs. Night Train had gotten away with crap his whole life, not realizing there were strings attached. Everyone needed to have principles, even thieves. Somehow, Night Train had lost sight of that.

"You ever play sports?" Night Train asked.

"I was in the math club," he said.

"I played football the whole time I was growing up. Pop Warner, junior high, high school, college. I loved every game. Then I got drafted. My first year in the NFL was a real wake-up call. The amateurs were about winning and losing. Not the pros. It was all about TV ratings."

"You're saying the pros are fixed?"

"The games are scripted. Not all of them, but enough to drive ratings."

"Do the owners know this?"

"Hah. It was their idea."

"You've lost me. Why would the owners do that?"

"Because they have a revenue share with the TV networks that broadcast the games. CBS, NBC, ESPN, the NFL Network, they split the money they make with the owners. The amount is supposed to be a secret, except the Green Bay Packers released it in a financial report. Each team's owner gets a quarter billion dollars a year just from the networks."

He was starting to see the picture and nodded.

"Like I said, it's supposed to be a secret," Night Train said. "TV ratings drive revenue for the owners, so it's in their best interest to broadcast games that generate big ratings."

"How many games are you talking about?"

"It's different every year. The season starts, and the teams play for a few weeks, and the NFL looks at the ratings. Maybe Buffalo has an explosive running back who's breaking all sorts of records. Or the Dolphins' quarterback is on fire. The NFL looks for good story lines, and those are the teams that get the help. Happens every year."

"What kind of help?"

"A ref calls back a crucial play during a tight game. Or a placekicker is told to miss an extra point. I played a game where the other team's defense had microphones hidden in their helmets that picked up our offense's plays. The referees could hear static coming out of the helmets but ignored it."

"Did you ever do that?"

Night Train gave him a look. "I've shaved points a few times. But I've never gone into the tank."

"You've never deliberately lost a game."

"Never."

"But why would the NFL do this? The Super Bowl is the most watched sporting event in the world. People are going to tune in regardless. They don't need to fix it."

"That's not how the NFL sees it. Neil Godfrey is a rising star. Time to pass the torch and make him a superstar. It will be good for ratings next season."

"Is that what the commissioner told you?"

"In so many words. When we said no, the NFL manufactured broadcasting jobs for us. When we said no to that, the front office leaked a story to ESPN saying we were retiring."

"Weren't you?"

"It was up in the air. Our contracts were up, but there were plenty of teams that would sign us. Once the NFL leaked the story, the decision was out of our hands. No team will sign a player who's thinking about spending Sundays mowing the lawn. Our careers were done."

"But you still said no."

"Yes, we did. That's when the NFL told us they had files with every bad thing we'd ever done. If we didn't play along, they'd release stuff to the media and screw us over. It made me feel so shitty that I put a brace on my knee so I could sit out the game and not be a part of it."

It was as ugly as it got, and they stopped talking for a while.

"What's Godfrey's deal?" Billy asked. "Is he a phony?"

"Hell no. Neil Godfrey's legit. He's the next big superstar. That's why the owners want him to shine this Sunday."

"Can the Rebels' defense stop Godfrey if you're not playing?"

"Probably not."

"So you're still throwing the game even if you sit out."

The words were slow to sink in. When they did, Night Train shifted uncomfortably on the couch. He had allowed a group of filthy-rich owners to compromise his principles so they could line their pockets with gold, and it was tearing him up.

"Makes you feel like a slave, doesn't it?" he said.

"Watch it," Night Train warned.

"You were a slave the day you signed your first contract; you just didn't know it."

"Shut up, or I'll rip your fucking head off."

"What would your old man say if he knew?"

"Leave my daddy out of this, or I'll hurt you. I mean that."

"What are you getting in return for selling out? A crummy broadcasting job? Does that come with another script with your lines spelled out for you? You're at the end of your career. Be your own man, and walk away on your own terms. Make your old man proud."

"Didn't you hear me?"

"Do it for him. You won't regret it."

Night Train backhanded him in the mouth. It was like having a door slammed in his face, and Billy tumbled out of his chair. His head banged against the floor and he momentarily blacked out. When he came to, the couch beside him was empty.

He left the cigar bar rubbing his chin. The people he cared about were ending conversations by smacking him in the face. He was only being honest with them, which maybe was the problem. The truth hurt, so they took their pain out on him.

But had he broken through? Would Night Train see reason and not sit the game out? He didn't know Night Train well enough to hazard a guess.

He walked through the lobby of Caesars. The promenade of shops was lined with windows overlooking the hotel swimming pool, and he spotted the figure of a man sprinting across the grass, his legs pumping furiously. It was Night Train, and he was running like a man possessed.

SIXTY-ONE

Thursday, three days before the Super Bowl

He went into seclusion in his condo at Turnberry. Each morning before hitting the exercise room, he tuned in to ESPN to hear the latest scuttle about the Super Bowl. The Rebels defense's wild times at Caesars continued to be a hot topic. Every day, a new tantalizing piece of information emerged, with stories about all-night parties, illegal drugs, and high-priced call girls. The Rebels were now a twelve-point underdog, and the announcers were spending more time discussing this year's star-studded halftime show than the game itself.

He was lacing up his sneakers when there was a news flash from the Rebels' practice facility. A breathless female sportscaster filled the screen. Next to her stood his old pal Night Train. Night Train had his uniform on, and his brow was beaded in sweat.

"I'm here with Night Train McClain, captain of the Rebels' defense," the sportscaster said. "Night Train, I'm told you have some news to share with our viewers."

"We took the brace off last night and tested my knee. It's still a little tender, but I should be good to go," Night Train said.

"That's fantastic. Will you be starting on Sunday?"

"I told Coach I was ready, so yeah, I'm starting."

"Any truth behind the rumors that this will be your last game?"

"I'm not thinking that far ahead."

"Your team is a heavy underdog with the odds makers. How do you feel about that?"

"We're going to give it our best shot and see what happens."

"Good luck on Sunday."

Every interview Night Train gave to the media ended with him flashing his famous smile. But not this time. Today, he was all business, and he gave the camera a cold shoulder before walking away. He acted like a man with something to prove.

Billy killed the picture with the remote. It was all he could do not to start dancing. He used the landline to call downstairs to the exercise room and speak to Bridgette, his personal trainer. "Hey, Bridgette, it's Billy. I'm afraid I have to cancel this morning's session," he said.

"Would you like to reschedule for tomorrow?" Bridgette asked.

"I'll let you know."

Going outside onto the balcony, he found a shady spot and waited fifteen minutes before placing a call to Night Train on his cell phone and getting sent to voice mail. "I saw you on ESPN. Glad you're feeling better. Let me know if our deal's back on." A minute later, he got an answer in the form of a text. Can't talk. Deal's on. Sorry I smacked you.

The deal was on. It made every bad thing that had happened in the past two weeks seem worthwhile. His next call was to Cory and Morris. They'd gone to Cancun to work on their tans and had e-mailed him photographs of the bikini-clad women they'd met on the beach.

"Hey, Billy, long time no talk," Cory answered. "How's it going?"

"Great. You guys still hanging in Mexico?"

"We are. It's boring. You've seen one perfect body, you've seen them all."

"Did you scalp those fifty-yard-line tickets for the Super Bowl?"

"We're trying to. We put them on Craigslist."

"Don't sell them. Get on the next plane to Phoenix. The fix is on."

"It's on? That's awesome."

"One more question. Is your web still good?" A web was a network of gamblers spread around the country who placed bets on fixed sporting events. By using a web, a cheat could place large sums on an event and spread the pain around without drawing heat to himself.

"They're good," Cory said. "Do you want them to bet on the prop bets we discussed?"

"Yes. We've got a new bet to add. The Rebels to win."

Cory howled disapprovingly. "Have you watched TV recently? The Rebels' defense is like something out of *Animal House*. They're going to get wiped off the field."

"No they're not."

"You know something I don't?"

"Yes I do."

"This is huge. How much do you want to bet on them?"

"The farm," he said.

- - -

His next call was to Victor Boswell. Victor ran a bowling alley in Sacramento that acted as a front for the family's illegal activities. It was here that Billy found Victor working the front desk, the thunder of crashing pins filling the background.

"How's it going, Billy? Did things work out with the super con?"

"Afraid not. We got caught."

"Let me put you on hold. Kat, take over for me." Victor came back on the line a few moments later. "You got caught? Are you calling me from jail?"

"I managed to wiggle my way out of it. I'll tell you the bloody details over a drink someday. I wanted to pass along a hot tip. You should bet on the Rebels this weekend."

Victor whistled into the phone. "Can they make the spread?"

"Screw the spread. The Rebels are going to win the game."

"You're sure about this?"

"I've never been more sure about anything in my life."

"I'm looking at the Vegas odds on my computer," Victor said. "The Rebels are a huge underdog. The Vegas bookmakers have been right in picking the winner for fifteen of the last sixteen Super Bowls. They're not dummies, Billy."

"I didn't say the bookmakers were dummies. They just don't know the deal for this particular game. If you don't want in, just say so, and I'll call someone else. No hard feelings."

"Of course I want in. I just want to make sure this is on the level. What do you want us to cover? I know plenty of bookies in Northern California we can hit, and I can send my kids to Reno and Lake Tahoe and have them place wagers with the sports books there."

"That works. I've got Vegas covered, and my guys have a web that will cover the bookies in the rest of the country. We're going to make a killing, Victor."

"I would say so. Let me jump on this. Thanks for thinking of me."

"Anytime, my friend."

- - -

His last call was to Grimes. He would have liked to be in Phoenix this weekend to make sure nothing went wrong with the rigged coin toss, but there was a chance that his face might show up on a camera during the game, and that would look bad, considering he was going to testify in front of a judge about the game being fixed. The smart call would be to stay home, and he decided to rent a suite at a fancy Strip hotel and party with the members of his crew not at the game, so they could dine on great food and drink the best booze. But before he made preparations, he needed to be sure no more men with scorpion tattoos were looking for him.

A receptionist answered Grimes's line. The special agent was in a meeting and could not be disturbed. Billy told her it was urgent. Grimes called him back within seconds.

"Lay it on me," Grimes said.

"Is it safe for me to leave my condo?"

"It's safe. We interrogated the bellman and got him to confess. The first hit man was a decoy, just like you thought. The bellman was the real assassin. I took the precaution of putting Broken Tooth in solitary so he can't make any more phone calls and hire another killer."

"You're my hero."

"Up yours, Cunningham."

Billy tried to end the call but Grimes stopped him.

"Before you step foot outside of your building, I want you to promise me that you'll keep your nose clean until Broken Tooth is charged with trying to fix the game," the special agent said.

"I already told you I would," he said.

"I want to hear you say it again."

"I promise to stay out of trouble until Broken Tooth is charged."

"Why are the hairs standing up on the back of my neck?"

"Maybe it was something you ate," he said.

SIXTY-TWO

Sunday, the Super Bowl

If you weren't living on the edge, you were taking up too much space.

By Sunday morning, the Rebels were fourteen-point underdogs. No one who followed football believed they had a chance to win. Billy got on the horn and persuaded a loan shark he knew to lend him half a million bucks, which he wagered on the Rebels with a local sports book.

Then he went to work on planning his Super Bowl party. The Flat Suites at the M Resort were his favorite accommodations in town, the views from the top-floor suites spanning more than 270 degrees. Securing one at this late date set him back thirty grand.

He checked in early Sunday afternoon. First job was to inspect the bar that came with the suite. He'd called in his order, and he wanted to make sure the hotel had gotten it right. There was a bottle of aged Glenlivet with Leon's name on it. Pepper and Misty drank Porn Star cocktails made from Blue Curacao and Sour Puss raspberry liqueur, and the bar had enough to keep them happy. In the fridge was a six-pack of award-winning craft beers that he was looking forward to sampling. A short while later, room service delivered a tray of shrimp cocktail, lobster tails, and appetizers with exotic names. He sampled every item, wanting nothing but the best.

Misty and Pepper were the first to arrive. They'd driven five hours from LA and were exhausted. The food and drinks quickly brought them around. When they were finished, he explained the deal. "We're rooting for the Rebels. If they win, you win."

"How much do we win?" Misty asked.

He told them the number. It was the same amount they would have made with Victor's super con. Misty let out a whistle. Pepper also approved.

"What if they lose?" Pepper asked.

"Then we go on food stamps," he said.

Leon showed up not long after the girls. Billy's driver looked like a new man. His broken ribs had healed, and he'd gotten his busted nose straightened.

Billy fixed everyone drinks, and they clinked glasses in a toast. A few minutes later, he received a text from Cory and Morris that included a selfie taken at University of Phoenix Stadium where the big game was being held. The accompanying message said they were in their seats on the fifty-yard line, ready to try out Gabe's latest creation.

A minute later, Gabe texted him. Gabe had gone with Cory and Morris that morning to meet with the head referee and give him his final payment for switching in the gaffed coin. Gabe had decided to see the game and had bought a scalped ticket, so he was also in the stadium.

Everything was set. The game officially started at 3:18 Pacific Standard Time. At three o'clock, they hunkered down in front of the suite's flat-screen TV and suffered through the tail end of the pregame show and a slew of really awful commercials.

"You sure this is a sure thing?" Leon asked.

"I've never been more sure of anything in my life," Billy said.

"That's strong," his driver said.

The teams came onto the field and were introduced to the roars of the eighty thousand rabid fans packed into the stadium. Representatives from both teams met in the middle of the field for the coin toss. The head referee explained that it was the Rebels' turn to call heads or tails this year. Night Train did the honors for his team.

"Heads," Night Train said.

The head ref said, "Rebels call heads," and flipped the coin high into the air. Billy held his breath. Gabe had claimed the gaffed coin was foolproof, but that was in practice. What if the transmitter in Cory's cell phone died and the coin came up tails? Or the TV equipment on the field interfered with Cory's cell phone's transmission? Stranger things had happened, and it felt like an eternity before the coin hit the ground.

"Heads it is," the head referee announced. "The Rebels have won the coin toss. Would you like to receive or kick?"

"Kick," Night Train said.

"The Rebels have elected to kick. Good luck, everyone."

The air trapped in Billy's lungs escaped. While the players exchanged handshakes and wished one another good luck, the head referee slipped the gaffed coin into his pants pocket and switched it with a regular coin, which he'd later give to a celebrity attending the game, as was a Super Bowl tradition. All their bases had been covered.

True to Night Train's word, the opening kickoff sailed out of the Volunteers' end zone, and the game began with the ball on the Louisville twenty-five-yard line. On the very first play, Choo-Choo grabbed the Volunteer center's face mask and committed the game's initial penalty. On the next play, Sammy took a spill and did not get up, bringing the Rebels' medical team to rush onto the field so they could help him to the sidelines. The game had just started, and Night Train and his boys had fixed three prop bets—the coin toss, the game's first penalty, and the game's first injury. The fourth fixed prop bet would be an accumulation of penalties by the Rebels' defense and would not be completed until the end of the game.

So far, so good. These bets paid even money and would turn a nice profit. But the real payoff would be if the Rebels won the game. Billy had wagered every cent he had on this happening. In hindsight, it had to be the craziest thing he'd ever done. If the Rebels lost, he'd be flat broke and owe money all over town.

He realized he didn't care. It was all about the action. Without it, life was hardly worth living. The Rebels got possession and drove the ball down the field to the Volunteers' twenty-yard line, where the defense stiffened. The field goal team came out, and the kicker put the ball through the uprights. Rebels up by three.

His crew cheered.

On the Volunteers' next drive, Neil Godfrey threw three perfect passes and scored the game's first touchdown. No wonder the NFL was banking on him to be their next golden boy. He was a gifted athlete with plenty of poise.

Rebels down by four.

The teams alternated scoreless possessions. With three minutes left in the half, Godfrey dropped back, surveyed the field, and cocked his arm. From out of nowhere, Night Train blew past the coverage and ran Godfrey over.

Billy leaped out of his chair. "That's what I'm talking about!"

Night Train stood over Godfrey, gloating. A referee flagged him for unsportsmanlike conduct. The Rebels now had four penalties, the Volunteers only one. The final prop bet was looking good.

Godfrey was injured and did not get up. A motorized cart came onto the field and loaded him up. As the star quarterback was taken away, he waved weakly to the crowd.

The half ended with the Rebels still down four. Pepper knelt beside Billy's chair.

"We're losing," she said.

"It gets better," he said.

- - -

The halftime show was a bunch of country and western stars who would have been happier breaking beer bottles over one another's heads than sharing the same stage. It mercifully ended, and a trailer promoting a new fall show came on. Maggie Flynn's ravishing face filled the screen, her hair bouncing seductively on her shoulders. CBS's newest hit show, *Night and Day*, would debut on Tuesday nights in September. Don't miss it.

He'd been trying to reach Mags for days. There was still the matter of the half a million bucks he owed her. Texts and voice messages had produced no response. Now he knew why. Her ship had righted itself and she'd jumped on board, and he realized their paths would probably never cross again. He told himself that he'd get over her, but that was a lie. You never got over a woman like Maggie Flynn.

The second half began. The Rebels took the kickoff and scored a touchdown on a long drive. Rebels up by three.

Volunteers' ball. Sycamore, their backup quarterback, fumbled the snap on the first play. The Rebels took over, but the Volunteers' defense held, so they settled for a field goal.

Rebels up by six.

"Is Godfrey going to come back and play?" Pepper asked.

"He's got a bad back. He's probably at the hospital, getting X-rayed," Billy said.

"You knew he was hurt, didn't you?"

"Whatever gave you that idea?"

The Rebels scored another field goal and a touchdown, and the third quarter ended with them up by sixteen. Night Train was having a career-defining performance. Batting down passes, blowing by the defense, pressuring Sycamore, throwing running backs to the ground—it was the stuff of highlight reels. Of the twenty-two players on the field, Night Train was the one everybody was watching.

The fourth quarter was a defensive battle, with neither team scoring. With three minutes left in the game, the Volunteers finally reached the end zone and executed a successful two-point conversion, then went for an onside kick, got the ball back, and kicked a long field goal. The Rebels' lead had been whittled to five points with a minute and a half on the clock.

The Rebels got the ball after the ensuing unsuccessful onside kick but fumbled on their first play from scrimmage. The Volunteers took over with no time-outs left. Sycamore completed a short sideline pass at midfield. Clock stopped. There were sixty seconds left in the game. If the Volunteers scored another touchdown, the Rebels would fall short, and Billy would lose every penny to his name.

Pepper covered her eyes. "I can't watch this."

Billy started to sweat. He had taken a gamble on another man's ability to rise above the forces trying to suppress him. The odds were in his favor, but that didn't mean he was going to win. Sycamore completed two quick passes—one up the middle, another to the sideline. Thirty seconds left. The Volunteers were on the Rebels' ten-yard line. A field goal wasn't good enough; only a touchdown would secure the win.

Volunteers in the shotgun. The ball was snapped and the wide receivers sprinted toward the end zone. Sycamore tossed the ball, his intended target a receiver in the corner of the end zone. Night Train blew past the coverage and leaped into the air, his fingertips nipping the football as it left Sycamore's hand, causing it to gyrate straight up in the air.

The crowd jumped to their feet. So did Billy. When it came to athletics, there was no such thing as luck. This was especially true for professional sports. It was all about hard work and being in the right place at the right time.

This was Night Train's place and his time. The football landed in Night Train's outstretched hands, and he cradled it like a baby and sprinted to the opposite end zone.

Game over.

Outside the suite, a glorious display of fireworks lit up the sky. Leon started yelling like he'd won the lottery, and the girls started dancing. Billy pulled up the calculator app on his cell phone and did the math. All totaled, he'd just won twenty million bucks on the prop bets and the Rebels' win. With half going to Night Train and his teammates and another three million for his crew, he'd clear seven million. It was a monster score, and he should have felt on top of the world, but the realization that he'd never see Mags again was haunting him. He'd won the game but lost the prize.

He dropped into his chair. He couldn't ever remember feeling this bad after pulling a heist. The money was worthless without someone to share it with. His crew decided to take the party downstairs to the M's bar. Pepper stopped in the doorway. "You going to join us?"

"Not tonight," he said.

"Why so down in the mouth? We won."

"I'm just worn out. It's been a long couple of weeks. I'll catch up with you later."

Pepper started to say something but decided not to and left. He continued to watch the TV. The scene on the field was bedlam. A small stage was wheeled out, and the Rebels were presented with the Lombardi Championship Trophy while brightly colored confetti filled the air. After the ceremony was over, a reporter cornered Night Train and stuck a microphone in his face.

"Congratulations. You've just been named the game's most valuable player," the reporter said. "How do you feel about that?"

"It's a real honor." Night Train paused. "I'd like to dedicate this game to my father. He sacrificed a lot for me. This one's for you, Pop."

"What are you going to do next?" the reporter asked.

That was a good question. Night Train's playing days were over, and the NFL would surely take the broadcasting job off the table. Every professional athlete had to walk away from the game they loved, and few knew where that journey would take them. But Night Train got to depart with the gift of knowing that he'd played his last game the right way, without resorting to compromising himself or the sport that he loved. Night Train flashed his famous smile.

"That's easy. I'm going to Las Vegas."

- - -

He killed the picture with the remote. Had this been a movie, he would have walked off with the beautiful girl on his arm and lived happily ever after. Instead, he was going home alone.

"I want my money," a female voice said.

His head snapped. Mags had materialized in the doorway wearing a leather skirt and red blouse. She'd cut her hair short and dyed it blonde and wore a pair of owlish glasses. The new look was different enough to beat the surveillance cameras, and he wondered why she'd done it.

He rose from his chair and approached her. It was a mirage, or maybe his mind was playing tricks on him. He placed his hand on her arm, just to see if she was real.

"How did you find me?" he asked.

"You once said the M was your favorite place to watch sporting events. I convinced the guy at the front desk I was your girlfriend, and he gave me a room key."

"That was clever. What's with the new look?"

"I've decided to quit show business and go back to stealing."

"But I just saw a trailer for your show."

"It's a secret. Filming starts Monday morning. I want that prick Rand to come to the set and not find me there. Let him twist in the wind for a while."

"Rand really hurt you, huh?"

"He most certainly did. Not as bad as you hurt me but damn close. The difference was, you said you were sorry and tried to make things right. That fucker never apologized. Rand doesn't care what happens to me, and he never will."

"Are you sure that's what you want?"

"I've never been more sure in my life. Now where's my money from the super con?"

"It blew up in our faces. The good news is, I just made seven million bucks off the Super Bowl, which you can help me spend. Sound like a plan?"

"Seven million? And to think I met you selling newspapers on the corner in Providence." She put her arms around his neck and kissed him. "What did you do, fix the game?"

"It's a long story."

Her heel caught the door, shutting it. Her eyes were on fire, and her hand started to undo the buttons on his shirt.

"Those are usually the best kind," she said.

ACKNOWLEDGMENTS

Most writers are fortunate to have a good editor in their corner. For this book, I had three editors helping me, the brilliant Jacque Ben-Zekry, the always patient Liz Pearsons, and the incomparable Kevin Smith. I would also like to thank my wife, Laura, whose enthusiasm has never waned. Brian Touhy, whose writing on sport fixing opened my eyes to an area of cheating that I knew little about. And to the crew of cheaters I met in Las Vegas who agreed to let me tell their story.

ABOUT THE AUTHOR

Photo © 2007 Robert Allen Sergeant

James Swain is the national bestselling author of *Take Down*, *Bad Action*, and the Tony Valentine Series. His books have been translated into a dozen languages and have been selected as Mysteries of the Year by *Publishers Weekly* and *Kirkus Reviews*. Swain has received a Florida Book Award for fiction, and in 2006 he was awarded France's prestigious Prix Calibre .38 for Best American Crime Writing. When he isn't writing novels and screenplays, he enjoys researching gambling scams and cons, a subject on which he's considered an expert.